YESTERDAY

A Novel of Reincarnation

by

Samyann

Yesterday

Yesterday

Yesterday

To my BFF

Yesterday

CHAPTER 1

"**W**ho needs a shrink when you have a cat?"

Amanda Parker sipped Merlot, gazing at the Navy Pier Ferris wheel from the window of her apartment. "What can you say when somebody asks, 'How did that make you feel?'" She turned to the attentive gaze of her angora cat, still and black as a shadow. "That's easy. I felt like tap dancing. And then I fired him. Oprah, my dear, you and I are officially finished with therapy."

The cat's green eyes blinked in mild interest.

"Sure, I know the five stages of grief." Amanda ticked them off on her fingers. "Denial, anger, bargaining, depression, and acceptance." She walked to the sink with her empty glass. "Yeah, well, they skipped one: resignation." She glanced back at the cat. "Resignation to one's fate."

Oprah stretched out a long, furry leg and commenced her meticulous grooming.

Amanda looked out the window again. A tall ship leaned into the ever-present wind on Lake Michigan, pleasure boats and dinner cruises dotting the harbor. Tiny lights twinkled in the sky above the wheel. *I'm making progress. My heart no longer aches at the sight of a plane.*

She padded toward the bedroom, Oprah at her heels. Amanda wasn't depressed, or at least she didn't think so. But there was no acceptance.

Instead, she was resigned to the aftermath.

* * * *

Amanda stepped from the State and Lake train station, squinting in the morning sunlight. Tiny calcite fragments sparkled in the sidewalk. She hitched the strap of her bag onto her shoulder and wrinkled her nose at the pungent smell of diesel exhaust. A bus belched a hot, moist gust that whirled her skirt as it trundled past.

A homeless man, dressed in rags and reeking of old beer, barred her path. A headless doll hung by a string from a shopping cart piled high with black trash bags. Broken, brown teeth showed through a ragged beard shot with white. He thrust a wrinkled yellow paper with a lopsided cross and REPENT! printed in block letters. Rheumy eyes peered urgently into hers, and in a guttural whisper he croaked, "End of the world, Sister. Do you know the Lord?" Amanda recoiled and sidled around the man, grateful for the aroma of fresh bread as she strode past the open door of a bakery.

Her pace slowed as she admired two mounted policemen. Sun glinted on polished buckles and stirrups. The Chicago Police Department uniforms were spotless, and the officers' boots gleamed.

What is it about a man on a horse that makes him extraordinary? She smirked. *Well, for one thing, it's incredibly sexy. Horse and man as one.*

Dark sable coats shone, long black tails swished, the hollow clatter of hooves clashed and melded with horns and a crossing guard's whistle. One of the policemen raised his hand to a little girl waving at him from the back seat of a yellow cab. The animals were oblivious to traffic.

Hoof to pavement, hoof to cobblestone. Hooves on wood.

An elevated train rattled overhead and its brakes emitted an ear-splitting shriek. Amanda froze. Time stretched into surreal slow motion.

The dull silver train rocked on the tracks above. The rail on the outside of the curve bowed outward and separated from the roadbed. The first car inched ponderously into space like an enormous caterpillar reaching at air. It spit orange and white sparks, gnawed at wooden ties and steel rails. Rivets popped. Girders groaned. Cement columns burst, spewed dust, and dropped exploding chunks. Metal ripped metal.

Amanda's pulse surged with the deafening crescendo. One of the policemen leaned back and struggled to control his mount. The horse tossed its huge head to break free of restraint. Cement crashed at the animal's feet and it reared, flailing hooves reaching high, eyes bulging. The man slid from his saddle and fell heavily into a clutter of wreckage. A panicked whinny pierced the pandemonium, an agonized scream of terror as the horse galloped down Lake Street with the other officer in pursuit.

He's not moving! The man's immediate danger catapulted her to a run. *Can I pull him out of the way?* She raced to him, seized the collar of his jacket, then leaned back and heaved. She glanced up again and dragged his limp form through a litter of rubble, out of the path of the falling train. *How's this possible? He's twice my size.*

Amanda screamed with the blasting crash of the train through the second story of a building across the street. Backing toward the sidewalk, her heels struck the curb and she fell to the concrete. Amanda slammed her head on the pavement and cried out in pain. With strength still welling from unknown depths, she leaned forward, reached under his shoulders, and hauled the man's body closer.

The policeman coughed and lifted his head. Debris rained down around them. He twisted around and took her in his arms, tumbling them across the sidewalk away from the chaotic street. They came to rest against the granite threshold of a storefront. He lay on top of her, shielding her from falling stonework.

The rear of the car piercing the building teetered, then thundered to the street, shattering the pavement where the policeman had fallen moments before. The officer tightened his grip and the earth trembled against her back. Shards of glass burst from a large window, glittering like diamonds in the bright sunlight. Amanda raised an arm across her face and a searing pain tore through her.

A thick pall of dust engulfed them, and her eyes stung with the acrid stench of burning creosote and hot steel.

For a long moment they lay still in the doorway of an antique shop, their arms around each other, legs tangled in an awkward embrace. Amanda's pounding pulse danced with the hammer of his heart against hers.

* * * *

Chest heaving, Officer Mark Callahan lifted his head. Sweeping back long chestnut hair from her forehead, he met startling blue eyes welling with tears.

I know her.

He desperately searched her face. *How?*

The young woman's arm slipped from around him and her chin quivered. Heart racing, Mark touched his palm to her cheek, and whispered, "Don't cry...you're safe now...you're safe." The girl's rigid tension melted into the limpness of a rag doll as her eyes closed.

An old man in a white apron banged on the glass of the shop door and tried to push it open against them.

Mark held his hand out, stopping the door. "Wait!" He shifted his weight to his knees and ran his eyes down the woman's small frame and back up to her face.

She's hurt. Christ, she's hurt.

Blood flowed from a horrid gash over her right eye; her left arm was at an odd angle. And she was out cold. An awning crashed against a window next to them, dropping a load of debris to the sidewalk. Mark held out an arm to protect the girl and tossed a broken brick away from her shoulder. *I've got to move her.* Slipping his arms under her knees and

11

behind her back, he inched her away from the door.

The shopkeeper pushed the door open and waved them inside. He nodded toward Mark's squawking radio. "You call for help on that, ja?"

"Yeah, where—"

"Put her down over here." The man pulled a dust cloth from the pocket of his apron and waved his arm toward a green horsehair sofa.

Mark laid the girl down and unclipped the handset from his shirtfront. "Get something under her legs, okay? Careful of that arm. What's your name?"

"Ed, Ed Morgen. I see everything. She bleeds pretty bad." Ed put the cloth on the young woman's forehead and pressed his hand against it. "This is some girl."

"Yeah, she is." Mark spoke into his radio, dropping to one knee. He laid his hand on hers, frowned at the girl, and shook his head. *Where in hell do I know you from?*

She was ghostly pale, and he placed two fingers on her neck to check her pulse. A dazed businessman leaned against the shop window and stared at his bloodied pants leg as people around him ran and stumbled. Mark rose and walked toward the door as he said over his shoulder, "There's all sorts of ambulances on the way, and they know she's here. Her pulse is strong, but keep an eye on her and don't let up on that compress."

* * * *

Amanda's head pounded and her arm throbbed as consciousness returned. *Sirens. How could there be this many sirens in the whole world?*

She tried to move the cloth from her face enough to open her eyes.

A hand gripped her wrist. "No, we must keep pressure on this." The man lifted the rag to inspect the wound, placed it back on her forehead. "You still bleed a lot."

Amanda's blurry vision cleared. She pushed back a corner of the compress and looked up into a kind face peering at her with concern. A wispy halo of white hair circled his balding head, half-moon spectacles on the tip of his nose.

Closing her eyes, she whispered, "Where am I?"

"Lexington Antique Shop. An ambulance comes soon. You're going to be okay. He called for help, that policeman."

"Who are you?"

"Ed Morgen. This is my shop. You rest until they come."

A tall grandfather clock came into focus, standing against the wall to Ed's left. The distant cacophony of sirens faded to a murmur. The wood of the case glowed, dark and intricately carved. Her eyes were drawn to the pendulum's rhythmic movement and her vision clouded.

As blackness enveloped her, Amanda drifted into a distant tick…tick…tick…tick…

Yesterday

CHAPTER 2

Blistering pain…a woman's scream, her own. Amanda bit her lip to keep from screaming again. The round face of a large black woman swam into focus. Amanda recognized the dark blue uniform of a fire department paramedic. Tears welled. "Please…oh, Jesus…you're hurting me."

The woman continued to wrap something around her arm and smiled. "Hey, blue eyes, glad you're back. I know it hurts, baby, but you're gonna be fine. What'd you do, girl, try to stop that damn train all by yourself?"

Two men lifted her to an ambulance stretcher and Amanda cried out, "No! Don't…my arm…please."

The medic rested a hand on Amanda's shoulder and spoke in a soothing voice. "You just relax now, honey, and take some deep breaths."

She tried to obey, gasping through choked tears. Darkness returned, and Amanda floated off to dreamless sleep.

* * * *

When she opened her eyes again, the paramedic had become a matronly nurse with short blond hair wearing pink scrubs, and the chaotic street was now a quiet hospital room.

The woman's face broke into a friendly grin.

15

"Hello, there. You've been going in and out on us for a while, but I think you're back for good now. I'm your nurse tonight; my name is Diane. You took a pretty good whack on the noggin, but the CAT scan's normal and you got off with a dozen stitches and a headache. You did manage to break your left forearm...I hope you like the cast; they come in colors these days. Looks like the folks in the ER decided to try to match those blue eyes. You'll be fine."

Amanda laid her hand across the cast on her arm and closed her eyes. *The drugs...the train...a horse. A clock?* "My cat..." She was surprised by the dry, scratchy sound of her voice.

"That'd be Oprah, right?"

Amanda nodded.

"All taken care of. Mary Axelrod. She just left, but she wanted to be sure we told you that Oprah is with her, so you have nothing to think about but getting better."

"How'd Mary know?"

"You're a pretty famous young lady, Amanda Parker. You're all over the news. And that policeman? Must have been here for hours, sitting in that chair right over there. The hospital won't be letting any of those reporters around you, so don't you worry."

Reporters? It was a private room with one bed, but it wasn't intensive care. There were lots of flowers. "Where...what hospital?"

The nurse turned to leave the room. Over her shoulder she said, "Northwestern. We'll take good care of you."

Beeping heart monitors, rattling dinner carts, muffled voices, and mild sedation melted into a twilight sleep. Amanda awoke to the sound of a quiet rustle. She turned her head, opened her eyes. A large bouquet of pink roses lay on the bed. Her gaze traveled up to a rugged face marked with concern. *That policeman.*

"Hello, Miss Parker."

The man was broad-shouldered, with curly black hair, and tiny laugh-lines at the corners of dark brown eyes. Amanda glanced at the bandage around his hand and then back to his face. "You okay?"

"Just a scratch. It's nothing."

"Find your horse?"

He smiled. A warm baritone with a faint Irish brogue said, "I did. I call him Boomerang, but he had no intention of coming back, I'm thinkin'. If it hadn't been for my partner, my noble steed would have run all the way back to the stables." He frowned as he took in the gauze above her eyebrow. "You shouldn't have done what you did, Miss."

Amanda's voice was just above a whisper, groggy. "Thanks for the flowers." *What makes me think I knew him before the accident? Must be the wonderful stuff they're pumping into me.* "You can go. You don't have to—"

"I'm not leaving, not yet. Not before you listen to what I have to say." He pulled a chair up to the side of her bed and sat down.

She turned to face him. "What's your name?"

"Mark my word, it's a fine one."

17

"Don't make me laugh."

He tipped his head with elaborate politeness. "Mark Patrick Callahan, at your service."

Amanda closed her eyes again, a rueful smile on her face. "Well, ain't that a nice Irish name for one of Chicago's finest." She turned toward him and sighed deeply. "What is it you have to say, Mark Patrick Callahan?"

He hesitated, visibly moved. "I owe you my life. Thank you, Miss Parker."

Amanda liked his deep voice. She closed her eyes and whispered, "Amanda."

Her breathing became steady and deep as the sedative did its job. He stood, gently lifted the blanket over her hand, and left the room.

* * * *

Mark swiveled his chair side-to-side, tapped his fingers on the armrests, and stared at his computer screen. Despite his familiarity with the CPD database, he had found only basic information about the beautiful young woman who had saved his life. Amanda Parker was a local girl, twenty-six years old, single, with no criminal record. Her driver's license and voter registration were both current. *Nothing here. Damn. What the hell is it about her?*

He leaned forward and typed her name into the Google search engine. *Well cripe! That helps a lot. Goddamned media didn't wait long.* He clicked on the first link, the Chicago Sun Times. "Local Woman Saves Cop". Mark scanned the story, and several others. All were basically the same. The third search page showed a link having something to do with an art gallery.

"Got lucky on that one, bud. Coulda killed a bunch." His partner, Pete Mahoney, leaned against the desk and scratched the side of his chin. "You are one lucky bastard, Callahan."

Mark raised his eyebrows, waiting for the inevitable punch line.

"That'd been me, I'd 'a been tryin' to figure out how to slip it to her while we were rollin' around on that sidewalk."

Mark grimaced at the remark and turned off his monitor. "Come on, you moron. Let's take the ponies for a ride."

They walked toward the stable as Pete said, "I'm just sayin'."

"Yeah, I heard you. It's just that it's supposed to be the other way around."

"Didn't think of that. She should be screwin' me instead, right?"

Mark shook his head. He couldn't help but chuckle at the wide smile and freckled face of his redheaded partner. Pete was a ringer for Alfred E. Newman on the cover of Mad Magazine. "Idiot. The cop's supposed to save the civilian's life, remember? Mahoney, you're one perverted jerk."

"You see me as I see myself." Pete nodded. "Fortunately, my current squeeze would agree. You gonna go visit that chick again?"

"There's something about her...I don't know." Mark ran his hand down Boomerang's sleek flank.

"I just can't put my finger on it."

"You done any diggin'?"

Throwing a blanket across the shiny sorrel back, Mark said, "Yeah. Nothing. A regular Mother Teresa, as far as I can tell."

"Now that would be one hell of a waste. You didn't answer the question: Are ya gonna go see her again?" Pete grunted, cinching the girth of his saddle.

"I sure as hell don't plan on saying something stupid like 'Don't I know you?' It's not like I've ever seen her before." Mark fastened a bridle buckle. "It's more just kind of a feeling. Doesn't make a damned bit of sense."

"Making sense is not your strong suit. If she's a complete stranger, you ain't never met."

Mark rested a hand on the rump of his horse. "Yeah, I know, and therein lies the mystery." Glancing up at Pete, Mark patted Boomerang's neck. "Ready for the preflight?"

They walked around both animals and checked girths, bits, reins, and saddles. Running his hand down a foreleg and examining a shoe, Pete said, "All systems go. Mount up, Officer Friendly."

* * * *

Mark consulted his watch as the elevator door opened. Twenty minutes until visiting hours were over. He walked down the hospital corridor as two men approached in animated conversation.

The shorter of the two loosened his tie as he said,

"She only put in one day and Plethora is all over the news. We couldn't buy this kind of publicity."

As they continued past him, Mark heard the response. "If we wanted it. Did you see all those flowers? Even some from the mayor's office. Alex, the damn cable networks are onto this story. It's virtually world-wide publicity."

The other voice faded as they walked away, "With any other…"

Mark turned as they moved down the hall. *Only a day? Wonder what Plethora does…something to check out.*

He tapped on the open door and walked into Amanda's room. The orange and red of sunset streamed through an open window. She turned toward him with a questioning look that quickly changed to a smile. "Well, if it isn't the lovely and talented Officer Callahan."

Mark pulled a chair close to the side of her bed, and leaned toward her, resting his forearms on his knees. "Your humble servant. The last word you said to me was 'Amanda,' so you'd better call me Mark." He glanced at her cast and back to her face. *God, those eyes are blue.* "How are you feeling?"

"As my godmother would say, good enough to walk a barbed wire fence with a wildcat under each arm." Her eyes narrowed as she said in a conspiratorial tone, "Ready to get out of here. You're a cop, go pull some strings."

"Sounds like you're feelin' pretty good." He leaned back in his chair and smiled. "No pull with this bunch, I'm afraid. In the ER, I can swing a cup

21

of their infamous hospital coffee, but that's about the extent of my influence." Amanda's hair had been washed since she was admitted, and it framed her face on the pillow like a lustrous fan. An antique silver locket on a delicate chain rested in the hollow of her throat. It was heart-shaped, deeply carved, and the sun caught a tiny glint of blue as she turned toward him. He pulled a pen from his breast pocket and started to write on her cast. "Lucky I carry a felt-tip."

"Keep it clean," Amanda smiled.

"Cell number. We're going to dinner." He slipped the pen back in his pocket. "I gotta go; my partner's downstairs. They told me you could leave tomorrow morning. You have a ride home?"

She frowned at the numbers on her cast. "Pretty sure of yourself, aren't you officer?"

Mark winked. "Your call." He rose from his seat to leave the room. "Either you dial that number, or someone with handcuffs will find you."

CHAPTER 3

Mary Axelrod hovered over Amanda, tucking the granny afghan around her and pushing a mug of hot chamomile tea into her hand. Her cottony hair pulled into a loose bun, Mary's angular frame was clad in casual clothes that suited her: green plaid shirt over forest green tee, brown slacks, and well-worn moccasins covered in turquoise beads. She settled into an overstuffed sofa immediately opposite her goddaughter and peered over rectangular wire-rimmed glasses, only her head reflecting the gentle tremor of palsy, more obvious in her gravelly voice. "Okay, now that you're finally home—"

Taking a sip of tea, Amanda gave no response. She stretched her slender legs and crossed her ankles on the coffee table as she waited for the eruption.

Mary had a frown on her wrinkled face, gray eyes intense, her lips an angry pucker. "What in the goddamned hell were you thinking, child?"

Amanda laughed.

The frown deepened, and the quaver in Mary's voice was a touch more noticeable. "Not funny. You scared the hell out of your brother and me. You could have gotten yourself killed, young lady."

"I didn't, and I'm fine."

Mary's lips flattened to a straight line.

23

"But if you make me laugh like that again, you're going to bring my headache back in spades."

"What'd the doctors at Northwestern say?"

"That I'll be good as new."

"And?"

"And this will be on for six weeks." Amanda knocked the fiberglass on her arm.

"What about that?" Mary tapped wrinkled fingers on her own forehead.

"No scar; stitches out in ten days." Amanda raised her brows. "Are you about done?"

"Anything else?"

"Nope."

Mary's face softened and she leaned forward. "Okay, now to something really important." With an impish smile she said, "Tell me about that handsome policeman you nearly killed yourself over. His face has been on every newscast."

Amanda shrugged. "I don't know anything about him." She traced the phone number on her cast with a finger. "Just some guy. I don't know him."

"You think he's single?"

"Quit trying to be a matchmaker." She sipped her tea. "It doesn't suit you."

Mary leaned back on the sofa. "You're right. But you do have to admit that he's one fine specimen. Don't think I'd mind a tumble with him myself, given the opportunity."

Amanda snickered at the image. "You're doing it again."

"Laughter never hurt anybody, dear. It's nice to see you laughing again. How'd you manage to avoid all those snooping reporters?"

"Well, the hospital was great; they let me use a staff entrance. Tom's car was right there." Amanda sighed, setting her mug on the coffee table. "Tomorrow will be another story, though. Seems they know where I work. Plethora's torn about how or even whether to use this…event. I hope they don't, but I'm not really sure what it's all going to mean. I can't think of how it would be of any value to such a strait-laced outfit." She grimaced. "I can't exactly be incognito with a sling on one arm and stitches in my forehead, but I'm not worried. I'm probably old news by now, anyhow."

"Dream on, kiddo." Mary rolled her eyes. "What you did was above and beyond in anybody's book. You saved the life of a Chicago policeman. I really don't know if I would have had the nerve."

"I do, and you would have."

"I'd like to think so. Probably would have lost it, and shit my pants to boot."

"Mary! You certainly wouldn't have just stood there and watched a man die."

"Hopefully we'll never know."

After a few seconds of silence Amanda said, "I gave my therapist his walking papers."

Eyes steady on Amanda, Mary stuck out her lower lip, waiting.

"All I ever got from that old poop was a series of thoughtful nods and stupid questions." Amanda squirmed in her chair. "I have much better luck with the cat." She smiled slyly over her mug. "At least Oprah's more understandable because she licks her butt if she doesn't agree."

As Amanda intended, Mary laughed. "Okay, you win. I didn't think you'd stick it out with conventional therapy for very long anyway."

"You know I'm more comfortable talking to you. I'm fine and it's been months since Joe died. With this new job, I'll be plenty busy."

"You know I won't shrink my friends. So you're no longer a friend."

"Fair enough."

They both smiled at the absurdity. Mary was Amanda's godmother. She was also an extremely successful psychologist with a select clientele acquired only by referral. She saw whom she wanted and never hesitated to be blunt and forthright in her assessments. Her office was her home, her hours whatever she said they were.

As their mother's older sister, Mary had taken Amanda and her brothers in following the deaths of their parents. Unmarried by choice, Mary had not even been aware of the chasm of need in her own life until the sudden arrival of the children. Even now that Amanda and Tom were young adults with lives of their own, they continued to be the center of her world. Tom, his wife and kids, and Amanda were Mary's family. The love was deep and mutual.

Amanda spoke to the phone number penned on her cast. "When I was waiting in that store for the ambulance, there was this old grandfather clock." She scanned the room, paused at nothing, and stared at a billowing red spinnaker on the lake. "I can't put it into words. It's a beautiful thing, very old. The movement of the pendulum, the ticking...I don't know. It was sort of hypnotic. I have no idea why, but I felt drawn to reach out to it, for it...something." She turned to Mary. "That's pretty silly, isn't it?"

"Not really. You were hit on the head and you like clocks. Where is it?"

"At an antique store, near the office."

"So go check it out again. If you like it, buy it. Early Christmas present. You can cram it in here." Mary looked around the room. "Somewhere."

"Thanks for keeping an eye on Oprah." Hearing her name, the cat jumped to Amanda's lap, demanding attention. She scratched absently between furry ears. "It's a new job, and I've already missed too much work."

"You're not planning to go in tomorrow, are you?"

"Yep. I'm fine, and they've been great, but I need to get back there." Seeing Mary begin to percolate, Amanda quickly continued, "I'm sitting at a desk, and if I need to, I'll leave early."

The older woman's tart glare over her glasses made Amanda suppress another smile. Mary grumbled, "Your dinner will be ready and waiting for you on my kitchen table at six."

"I don't know what I would do without you."

Mary pushed herself up and moved toward the door. "I do. You'd have nobody to nag you. See you tomorrow night." She stuck her head back around the door. "And go look at that clock."

Oprah nudged her head under Amanda's hand,

her purr rumbling like an idling Harley. Absently stroking the lush, silky fur, Amanda sipped aromatic tea. The enormity of the event poured forth a wave of exhausted realization. *I saved his life. He would have died. Why was I there, at that time, in that place? Where did that strength come from? Mary's right. I could have been killed. What's the big deal about this whole thing? I sure don't feel like a hero.*

She continued to stroke the cat as her eyes roamed the room. Chinese Buddha of jade, Indian porcelain doll, Persian rug on a wall, figurines from the Vatican, Hummels from Germany, an Irish Beleek vase. Memories of sights and smells and textures, all from countries beyond the imagination of most, treasures meant to help her forget. The furniture was an eccentric hodgepodge, but she cared little so long as it didn't fall apart.

Though the gleaming hardwood floors of the ancient brownstone creaked with age, she could barely hear Mary moving around overhead. The wind outside might be strong enough to pull up trees, but it would barely rattle a window in the peaceful quiet of her apartment.

* * * *

Morning sun streamed through the window in the bathroom and Amanda glanced up at the oval mirror. Dark brunette hair created a striking contrast with her pale skin. A long, graceful neck complemented high cheekbones and the almond eyes of a distant Cree ancestor. *Too long, like a damn giraffe. Altogether an ordinary and unimpressive face.* The tiny scar in the center of her chin was the only evidence of a tomboy childhood. A melancholy smile formed as she thought of Mary's philosophy of life: *'Trees grow tall for the sake of the view. Falling is a small price to pay if you see something interesting on the way up.'*

She ran her fingers over the numbers written on her cast and her mind drifted to thoughts of Joe. *I don't want this. I don't want to care about someone again, ever.*

With effort, she used her good arm and the fingers of her left to turn a black and white paisley scarf into a makeshift decorative band across the wound on her forehead, the scarf ends falling down the side of her face. Swirling a long black cape around her shoulders, concealing the sling, she peered critically at her reflection, and then shrugged. *I look like a 1960s flower child.* Brilliant blue eyes glinted back approval.

* * * *

It was a bright, cool morning, and a refreshing breeze brushed Amanda's face as she walked up the subway stairs and headed toward her office. She neared the building and a young man with a television camera on his shoulder walked toward her. A blinking red dot from his camera was aimed like the eye of a sniper rifle at her face. Next to him strolled a young woman in a dark burgundy suit, a cutesy walk bouncing more than her improbably blonde hair. Amanda sighed. *It would appear that my studied attempt at camouflage was a waste of energy.*

"Good morning, Amanda. Can we take just a few minutes of your time?" Without waiting for a reply the reporter continued, "What was it like on that terrible day? Did you intend to save Officer Callahan's life?"

Amanda stopped and gazed evenly at the young woman for a moment. She glanced at the camera lens, and back at the reporter. "Please don't ask me any more questions. I don't have anything to say." Amanda continued down the sidewalk.

The reporter followed. She gave Amanda a practiced smile, and pressed. "Can you tell us how you felt? Were you afraid?"

Amanda stopped walking and raised a gloved hand to the camera. She gave the cameraman a friendly smile. "Can you please turn that off?"

He lowered the camera, shrugging to the reporter.

Amanda nodded to him. "Thank you." She looked the reporter up and down, settling on her inquisitive brown eyes. "What's your name?"

The woman turned from the cameraman to Amanda. "Pamela Allen, Channel 8 News."

Resuming a quick step toward the revolving door, Amanda said, "If you would like to call the Plethora offices and arrange an interview, Pamela, they may schedule a press conference or something. I suggest you think long and hard about what happened that day. People died. If you ambush me again, you'll succeed only in getting me angry. I'm sure you don't want your boss or the people of Chicago or the competitors of Channel 8 to know you can only ask stupid questions."

Amanda pushed at the revolving door and glanced over her shoulder. The reporter and cameraman were huddled in conversation.

She punched the number twelve in the elevator. *How in the world can a train accident prove of any value to Plethora? They appraise valuable antiques and publish a magazine.*

The office was a bright loft. Rust colored brick walls were decorated with large framed antique-related magazine covers and a well-used dartboard. The room was divided into cubicles with chin-high tweed covered partitions affording some privacy. Given the activities of the previous few days, Amanda was pleasantly surprised by the quiet surroundings. Sitting at her desk, she could hear a few one-sided telephone conversations and the hum of a copy machine nearby. She spent a couple of hours working her way through an accumulation of email, and was almost finished when her phone buzzed.

"Amanda Parker."

"Hey, this is Alex. Can you come down to the conference room?"

"On my way." Amanda rested her hand on the phone. *Well, here it comes. They're probably going to fire me. Plethora doesn't want the publicity this accident is creating. This place is pretty discrete, an exclusive house.*

Stopping outside the conference room doors,

Amanda ran her hand across the scarf, hoping it looked fashionable in addition to concealing. She pushed through the door and was greeted with a patter of applause from her coworkers. Amanda touched her throat as they stood.

Alex Bennington walked toward her with a grin, his casual demeanor a sharp contrast to his dark suit, cufflinks, and red power tie. "Congratulations, Amanda." He laughed and guided her to a seat. "You look like you've stopped breathing. Don't do that, please."

Blushing with embarrassment, she smiled at the faces around the conference table. Relief flooded through her. "Thanks, everyone."

Alex took a seat. "What you did was extraordinary, and it goes without saying that we are all honored to be associated with someone of such amazing courage." He scanned the gathering and returned his eyes to Amanda. "Afraid you're just going to have to suffer through some water-cooler admiration for a while." He smoothed his tie. "That said, we're not exactly sure what to do with this...*situation* regarding the media." Alex tapped his pen on the polished walnut surface and continued, "One thing we're united on is that whatever we do will be your decision. We'd just like to present the company opinion."

Amanda stayed silent.

"First, the media are demanding a press conference, and how we handle this needs to be decided now. The press conference is tentatively scheduled for three." He looked across the table.

"Grace, I'm tossing the ball to you here."

Prior to the incident, Amanda had only put in one full day at Plethora, so she didn't know the attractive, gray-haired woman. *Must be Alex's assistant or secretary.*

Grace straightened a stack of papers in front of her and said, "Sure. Here are the options: One, we respectfully bow out of media requests, and let the story die. Two, we move down the path of greatest exposure and accept any and all comers. There have been several, including *Today, Good Morning America, Late Night*, afternoon talk shows and on." She smiled broadly at Amanda. "One of Plethora's employees has valiantly saved the life of a Chicago policeman; these television shows all want her as a guest." She took off her glasses. "It's all or nothing."

Alex turned to Amanda. "Do you have any thoughts on this?"

She glanced at the eyes around the table focused on her and felt her arm itch with perspiration. *I do, but is it what they want to hear?* "Well, yes. I... That sort of sensationalism couldn't reflect well on the image of quiet discretion our clientele have come to expect from Plethora."

Alex smiled and dropped his hand on the table. "I wholeheartedly agree. Your astute understanding of the...*shyness*, for lack of a better word, of our client base, is the reason we wanted you on our team. We'll cancel that press conference and make a generic statement of our collective admiration." Alex stood and surveyed the group. "I think that

33

says it all, so let's get back to work."

With her new job secure, and the questions regarding unwanted publicity for Plethora decided, the tension that stiffened Amanda's neck eased.

* * * *

Thrilled the day was over and the media at bay, Amanda walked out of the office and toward the antique store. Apparently things had heated up elsewhere in the world or the city, deflecting attention from her. *It's finally over.*

A tall perfume atomizer with a graceful taper of mossy green glass was in the display window of the antique shop. The bottle was original, the silver of the bullet-shaped top dull with age. *Definitely a DeVilbiss, pre-1920.* Peering further into the shop, she saw a tiny lamp with a domed shade dripping ruby-colored beads, a white porcelain washbasin and matching ewer, and the oddly intriguing antique clock.

Musty and mystifying attic smells drifted from old furniture and clothes as Amanda entered the antique shop. Two men were shaking hands by the counter, one the old man she vividly remembered as Ed Morgen, the shop owner.

The other was Mark Patrick Callahan.

CHAPTER 4

Amanda's startled expression vanished, replaced with a bewildered stare. Mark Callahan's uniform this evening was a black tuxedo, creating an image far from her initial perception of him. At a glance, she could tell the tux wasn't rented because the fit was too exact. Perfectly tied bowtie, matching studs and cufflinks. A blue fob glinted on the heavy gold Albert chain draped across his vest. *Dashing.*

The tinkle of a bell over the doorway announced Amanda's entrance, drawing Mark's attention to her. He scanned her head to toe, met her eyes, and smiled. Amanda's face flooded with warmth and her heart jumped.

Mark walked toward her and placed a hand on her upper arm. With the smoky baritone she remembered, his brogue barely noticeable, he said, "Amanda. It's nice to see you." He glanced over his shoulder at Ed and back to her. "Wish I had time to buy you a drink or something. I'm on my way to Holy Name Cathedral."

Pulling her eyes from the clock, she said, "That's fine, I'll be a while, anyway." His eyes followed hers as she glanced at it again.

Ed's face wrinkled a grin. "Here you are, officer." He passed a small black plastic bag to Mark. "These will do nicely."

Mark shook his hand again. "Thanks, Ed." He

guided Amanda in the direction of the clock, his hand resting on her lower back as he spoke over his shoulder. "I'll drop in again next week and have another cup of that coffee of yours."

When Amanda and Mark neared the clock, she backed away. *I suppose I should say something about the tuxedo. It's only polite and he does look extraordinary.* Unexpectedly caught by his handsome face and masculine, yet gentle manner, she glanced over his suit. His youthful, weathered complexion contrasted strikingly with the snowy white of his dress shirt. "You...I've never seen you dressed." Amanda's eyes sparkled and she smiled. "Up, I mean."

Mark laughed. His eyes held hers, the laughter friendly and contagious.

"You know what I mean. You look great. Getting married or something?"

"Best man, and thanks. You should smile more. It's nice."

His gaze dropped to the locket on her neck. Meeting her eyes again, he shrugged. "I confess to being a last minute shopper." He awkwardly raised the sack. "Gift for the groom." Mark looked around the store. "This is on my beat, so thought I'd stop in on my way to the church. What brings you back here?"

"This."

They stepped to the clock together. The face was made of ivory, inlaid with elegant Roman numerals and mellowed with age. Intricate gold filigree around and throughout the face drew the viewer's eyes to a colorfully painted moon-phase dial of dark blues and greens. They listened to the determined tick, conveying centuries of mystery and a stoic witnessing of many lives. Carved faces of forest animals peeked around the gentle curves of trees framing a deeply etched glass door. The hood of the tall cabinet swept softly from each corner toward a flame spiral in the center.

The grandfather clock started to chime and Amanda met Mark's eyes. The sound was soft, but compelling. Low in pitch and a million miles away, it conveyed a haunting, magical authority.

Amanda whispered, "St. Michael's chimes."

Mark reached for her hand, pressing it to the case. She felt the reverberating breath of each tone…and every beat of his pulse. The chime was followed with a deeper, and equally distant, authoritative gong in sequence with the pendulum, six resonant tones. The unexpected intimacy of their touch mingled with the life and warmth of the old clock.

Breaking his stare, Amanda raised her gaze to the ivory face again as she said, "It's almost as if it can speak."

"In a way, it can."

Mark still held her hand against the clock, and Amanda was surprised that it wasn't awkward. She withdrew her hand as he dropped his own into a trouser pocket. *What is it? His eyes, that crooked smile? There really is something about him.*

Decision was reflected in his brief nod. "Dinner. Tomorrow evening. 8:00."

It wasn't a request, but it wasn't a demand either. A statement. Amanda surprised herself with her own smile. "7:30."

"Would you prefer a quiet place or—"

"Yes."

"Me, too. I know just the place, casual but classy." He nodded at the clock. "Six. I'm due at Holy Name by six-thirty at the latest." He shrugged. "I have the ring in my pocket. I guess I better get over there."

Absorbing the clock's detail, Mark scanned the towering spiral at the peak and down the trunk to the pendulum swinging steadily behind the glass door. Etched deer stood in each corner of a narrow beveled window. Proud, brave, and curious, they gazed alertly into the eyes of the viewer. His gaze settled on the carved face of a squirrel, an acorn in its paws. "You have elegant taste. This is beautiful." He surprised her with his next statement, "Belgian, late 18th century, right?"

Ed Morgen walked toward them. "An imposing thing, ja?"

Mark held up his hand and smiled at Ed, then spoke to Amanda. "If I get in this discussion, I'll be late. The bride will do something painful to the groom and worse to me." Backing toward the door he tipped his head toward her. "I'll see you tomorrow, 7:30." Waving the bag to Ed he said, "Thanks again." Mark turned and left the store. The bell over the door danced as he raised a hand and jogged toward a taxi.

He knows 18th century art. This might be an

interesting dinner, but that's all its going to be, dinner. Still acts pretty sure of himself. She turned her attention to Ed. "Yes, the clock *is* wonderful. My name is—"

"Oh, my! I know who you are! You are *the* Amanda Parker." His eye wrinkled to a wink. "You make me famous, too."

Amanda smiled in return and extended her hand. "Should I call you Ed?"

"You remembered?"

Laughing as they shook hands, she said, "Of course. Can you tell me about this clock?"

"What I know is not so much. It has many secrets, I think. You would maybe like some coffee?"

She glanced at the clock and back to him. "That's very kind, but no. I'm fine. What do you know?"

Ed rubbed his chin with long, pale fingers and studied the dial.

The old man's silence forced her to look toward him in anticipation. His face reflected thought, and he finally nodded. "I find this at an auction on Elm Street, a home filled with many, many old things. As soon as I see it, I know I must have it."

She raised a hand to touch the wood of the cabinet. "An estate auction?"

"The woman who owned this clock before was very old and lived in that house for a long time before she died." Ed shrugged as he continued, "In the back is carved 'Wellington 1873', but this piece is much older than that. At first, I am not sure I want to sell it. But I can't say no to you." He nodded

39

several times, eyes roaming the detail of the clock. "Mark is a good man, and you save his life. If you want it, we can talk about the price."

Ed turned meeting Amanda's gaze.

"Why wasn't it for sale, Ed?"

He looked back at the clock for a long time. "I'm not sure I can say." Pausing, he added, "Maybe I like it some. But it's yours."

* * * *

Touching up her lipstick, Amanda wondered if she should attempt to cover the scar on her forehead. Mark had said the restaurant was casual. She chuckled at the thought of the bargaining involved when she bought the clock. Ed Morgen was a master at the art of selling antiques. He also managed to make the entire process enjoyable, and Amanda would have spent considerably more than she did. The clock was in remarkable condition, and Mark was right: it was indeed 18th century. She was surprised that she was looking forward to this date with him. A decision about the scar was made for her as the gate buzzed. She looked at her brow critically and decided it was fine.

Amanda opened the door to see Mark leaning against the doorjamb, swinging a pair of handcuffs on his index finger, a mischievous smile on his face.

"I told you that you would either call, or a cop with handcuffs would find you."

She smiled in return. "You can't fit those things around this cast, so I wasn't worried."

He looked down at the sling. "Damn, I didn't think of that."

Amanda giggled at his frown. *This is going to be a nice evening.*

"Come on in. Oprah, meet Mark. Mark, this is Oprah, my roommate. Something to drink?"

Oprah rubbed around Mark's ankles, meowing a noisy welcome to the new visitor.

"Whatever you're having," Mark replied. With an exaggerated bow to the cat he said, "A pleasure to meet you, Oprah." She jumped to a chair, sniffed the knuckles of fingers presented to her, rubbed her cheek against them, and dropped to the floor.

Amanda nodded once at the cat and presented Mark a dazzling smile. "She approves. Scotch or bourbon okay? You don't have to drink red wine."

"Scotch. But a very short one because we have reservations and I'm driving. Actually, the restaurant is only about six blocks from here, if you care for a long stroll. We need to leave now if we're going to make it in time."

"Paper cups legal, officer? A walk sounds great."

He laughed. "I'm not on duty, and you're my kinda girl. Scotch and a splash."

* * * *

Amanda noticed that they were walking in step, even though he was several inches taller, and glanced at him as she asked, "So tell me, how'd you gravitate to becoming a police officer?"

Mark dropped his eyes and shrugged. "Gramps

was a cop; Pop was a cop; I'm a cop." He smiled at her profile. "It wasn't in the plan, but it's what some may call the Chicago way."

She laughed. "You have me curious. What *was* the plan?"

"It's complicated…originally med school." He placed a hand under her elbow as they crossed State Street. "Two years at Trinity College in Dublin on a scholarship from the diocese, directing my efforts toward a degree in psychiatry. But, as John Lennon said, 'Life is what happens while you are busy making other plans.' College roommate was the groom yesterday." The laugh lines at the corners of his eyes deepened with a smile.

"How'd it go?"

"The bride glowed as expected. Very traditional affair."

"I'm still curious. Why didn't you stay in med school?"

"That wall in Grant Park for Chicago cops killed in the line of duty has Pop's name on it. Two kid sisters at home, so I had no choice but to help out financially. Pop's friends had friends who knew friends who had friends, and ba da boom…I'm graduating from the academy."

"Sorry about your father."

"He was a detective, so he knew the risks. So did Mom."

"Doesn't sound complicated to me. You did what you had to do. You like it? Being a cop, I mean?"

Mark gave her a side-glance. "Yes, I do, very much. I turned my lemons into lemonade a long time ago. Compared to the grueling demands of the medical profession, being a cop has its advantages. Not quite as glamorous, but still fulfilling, at least to me."

He abruptly stopped walking and turned to face her. He finished his scotch in a long swallow, dropped the empty cup into hers and took them both. "I think it's my turn to ask a question."

She presented him a wry smile. "Okay, shoot."

"I have three. Where did you get those beautiful eyes and why do I think I know you?"

Amanda was unsure of how to answer, but her smile widened. "Suspense might make the evening more interesting, so I choose to answer neither of those. What's the third question?"

"It's not a question. You're going to marry me."

She laughed. "Excuse me?"

"What were your words? 'Doesn't sound complicated to me?' We're obviously destined for each other, so we might as well get the details out of the way."

Handsome as hell, but as arrogant they come. "A proposal on the first date? I must have missed something. Remind me again later."

"Count on it."

She raised her brows, "Since that's the case, I might as well start nagging you now. Do you mind telling me where we're going?"

He reached for her arm and guided her back into step with him as he chuckled. "You're a touch sassy in addition to being beautiful. I'll play. The restaurant's called Fra Diavolo. It's in the old Starks mansion on Pine Street, goes back to before the Great Chicago Fire. Nice wine list and an excellent Italian menu. For me, the big attraction isn't so much the food as the place itself, an elegant old building with incredible woodwork. I'm probably speaking out of turn and should ask you if you've ever been there."

Seems he's as charming as he is arrogant. "No, and it sounds intriguing."

* * * *

Amanda smoothed the damask napkin in her lap as her eyes adjusted to dim, recessed lights. All tables were set for two or four, a fire burned in the corner fireplace, and soft classical music seemed to come from nowhere. Dark woodwork surrounded them and contrasted with white linen. From the hall opposite them, a broad, curving staircase swept upward to the floor above. "I agree this is extraordinary. Are all the rooms this cozy?"

The waiter placed a vodka martini in front of Amanda. Mark took a sip from his scotch and water, leaned back in his chair, and smiled at her. "They're all small like this one. No more than four or five tables. Love the intimacy. I do know it used to be the home of a Great Lakes ship's captain. Built in around 1850. Wife died, he sailed away, never came back." Amanda lifted her martini glass as he added, "Typical tragic 1800s story. Wound up in the hands of a couple of spinsters or something."

As they sipped their drinks, she studied the

marble fireplace mantle. "Do you plan on finishing med school?" Amanda turned to his silence.

Mark's hands folded around the glass in front of him and he responded with a gleam in his eye. "Do you always ask so many questions without answering any?"

Amanda sipped her drink. "To answer yours, I inherited my eyes from my mother, and I have no idea."

"They are dazzling eyes, indeed."

Her face warmed. She wasn't sure how the conversation had turned so personal. *I'm not getting involved with this guy, with anyone.*

"Did I say something?"

"No. No, you didn't."

Their waiter returned to the table and Mark ordered more drinks by nodding toward her glass and raising his own.

He sipped his scotch. "So why the frown?"

Amanda circled the rim of her martini with a polished nail. "Okay, *The Reader's Digest* version. Up until this point, my life has been a series of disasters, and it's my intent to create no more." She glanced up to see that he was listening intently.

"Go on. That statement alone is too short, even for *Readers Digest.*"

She cleared her throat. "When I was very young, my parents died in an car wreck. I was old enough to understand what had happened, and old enough to miss them terribly." She continued to run a finger around the glass. "A few years later, my older brother was killed in a boating accident. The damned fool and his college buddies had too much to drink and shouldn't have been out on the lake to begin with, but...anyway. I was twelve."

The waiter placed two fresh cocktails on the table. "Are you ready to order, or would you like more time?"

Mark touched her hand. "I'll order for us both, if that's okay with you." He spoke briefly to the waiter, who nodded and left the table.

She took in the comfortable exchange. *Dinner sounds light and elegant.*

"Sorry for the interruption. What was your brother's name?"

"Connor. I think the hardest part was talking about him with my younger brother, Tom."

Mark nodded. "Losing a big brother would be tough for a guy. Where's Tom now?"

For the first time in the conversation Amanda's face lit up. "Here, in Evanston. He's happily married with three brats I take great pleasure in spoiling."

Their wine arrived and Mark nodded his approval. The waiter filled their glasses, placed the bottle on the center of the table, and offered them another cocktail or appetizer.

Mark raised his brows at Amanda, "Care for anything?"

"No, this is fine."

The waiter inclined his head and backed away.

"Seems like you've had your share of troubles."

He's comfortable in his own skin. Sure of himself.
"Like I said, my life has been a series of disasters."

"It's a wonder you've maintained your sanity. I

don't know that I could."

"Whether I have or not is a subject open to debate."

Mark shook his head in response, staring into his drink.

Should I say more? Why not? "Seven months ago, my fiancé died in a plane crash. His name was Joe. Since then, up until I started the job with Plethora, I've been traveling the world. Just trying to stay one step ahead of the next catastrophe, I guess. Are you ready for the last one?"

The Irish in his voice was more pronounced. "You've got to be putting me on. There's more?"

She sipped her martini and slid a napkin to him holding the olive from her drink. He absently accepted. "Only one, and it's comical compared to the others." *This should send him packing.* "An affair with a married man." She shrugged, "Stupid, I know."

Amanda's eyes met his as he touched his glass to hers. His gentle baritone seemed to evoke an ancient Celtic breeze. "*Go maire sibh bhur saol nua.*"

She hesitantly touched her glass to his.

He winked at her quizzical expression. "May you enjoy your new life."

Yesterday

CHAPTER 5

Amanda stretched herself awake and rolled onto her back at the song of St. Michael's chimes. She counted the sonorous tolling of the hour...*five, six, seven*...and slipped a finger under her cast. The itch was maddening, bringing her fully awake. *Bless whoever the hell's taking this damn thing off today.*

Late that afternoon, she returned from the hospital liberated, the insufferable cast gone.

She took her time in the shower, grateful to scrub some life back into her skin. *Hope he doesn't take this invitation to dinner wrong, but he's been so persistent. I'm not leading him on, am I? No. I've been nice, nothing more, polite. He can't be misinterpreting this.* She stood with both hands against the tile on either side of the spray and let the hot water relax and warm her throughout. *I can't let myself get into anybody, especially him. He looks at me like he knows everything about me and yet is baffled by knowing nothing at all. Now, there's a convoluted thought. Damn, there's just something about him.*

The telephone's quiet ring interrupted Amanda's thoughts. She stepped from the shower, wrapped herself in a bath sheet, and cinched it above her breasts. She started to towel her hair dry as a deep voice, Mark's voice, emanated from the answering machine in the living room. Her pulse leaped as she lowered the towel and stared at her reflection.

"I'll be about thirty minutes late. Hope that's okay. See you then." Click, dial tone, silence.

She brushed her teeth and ran fingers through damp hair. Reveling in being able to tie a sneaker lace without the encumbrance of a cast, Amanda heard a key in the door. She walked toward the living room as Mary entered with a laugh. "Amanda, look."

Oprah sat like a statue no more than a foot from the grandfather clock, her long tail curled around her like a protective fluffy boa sheltering her paws. Only her black head moved back and forth in perfect time with the pendulum.

"She does that all the time. I think she's found a new friend and is sure it wants to come out and play. She feels sorry for it, all alone in there."

Mary and Amanda headed for the kitchen. "Now that is imaginative thinking, dear. A black cat feels sorry for the pendulum of an antique grandfather's clock. Sounds like a lovely Edgar Allan Poe plot, wonderful! Wonderful! What are we having for dinner?"

"It seems Mark likes corned beef, boiled. A bit pedestrian, but what can I say? I've never made it before, so you're in charge. I got all the ingredients from an Internet recipe."

"Pedestrian it may be, my dear. But made right, boiled corned beef is a collation fit for the gods. It is a delicious, traditional, Irish meal. The Internet is occasionally very wise." She rolled her eyes and growled, "But rarely a match for an old Swedish psychotherapist."

Mary made herself at home and moved efficiently through cupboards and drawers seeking the tools she required. A peeler and knives followed colanders and pans. Potatoes, onions, cabbage, and carrots were pulled from the fridge. Mary tied a frilly apron around her waist and soon the tiny, immaculate kitchen was in the complete disarray of her busy activity.

Watching with amusement, Amanda knew this was her godmother's equivalent of seventh heaven. Mary was running the show, bustling, and firmly in charge.

"I'm thrilled that you've invited Mark for dinner. It's about time. You need to move on with your life, and he's a nice young man from everything you've said."

"He's nice, but it's only a good-friends relationship."

"He's not gay, I'll assume." Mary peered over her glasses. "It's not like you have 'balls for breakfast' tattooed on your forehead or anything."

Amanda laughed. "In your inimitable fashion, you get directly to the point. We're simply friends. Period. Quit pushing that agenda."

"What's for dessert?"

Amanda sat at the table. "Sherbet parfait pie, in the freezer." She glanced up to see Mary's hands shaking from her mild palsy. "Do you want me to peel or something?"

Mary's hands paused, still as stone. She gripped the paring knife preparing to pierce an onion. She looked over her glasses at Amanda again, the quiver having moved from hands to head. "No, dear." She resumed working on the onion. "I can hear the gears grinding in your brain from here. What are you thinking about?"

The lovely old clock, visible from Amanda's seat, had completely captivated Oprah. She touched the glass door with her paw. "Nothing, I guess."

"Sure, and the Pope never had a wet dream."

Her gaze moved back to Mary and she chuckled. "Irreverent old fart, aren't you?"

Taking her time to respond, she placed the onion on the cutting board. "Irreverent, occasionally. Old, hardly. Fart?" She shrugged. "I suppose. Talk, smarty."

Amanda smiled and stared into her coffee. "The clock. I know I've seen it before. Not one like it, but that specific clock. It's the sound of the chimes, the looks of the moon dial, the animals in the carving. But that's not possible."

"Maybe that isn't so strange."

Amanda tipped her head and frowned. "What do you mean?"

Sliding the cutting board along the table, Mary sat down opposite her. "Maybe you actually have seen it before, that's all." She shrugged one shoulder as she peeled the brown paper skin from the onion. "At an antique show, an estate sale, whatever, dear."

"No. That doesn't work. According to the man I bought it from—a really sweet old guy, by the way—it's been in an old woman's home for years, longer than I've been alive."

Mary began to work on another onion. "I can surely see why you'd find that mysterious."

"There's more." Amanda stood and went to the coffee pot, poured another cup and returned to the table. She set the cup down and began to pace. "I feel compelled to look at it. It's funny, but I'm just drawn to it, especially when it chimes. I find myself standing in front of it, touching it, listening, and suddenly feeling sad. Sometimes I'm not sure how I came to be standing in front of it. When I hold my hand to the case, I…"

Amanda tossed her hands and plopped in a chair.

"Well, dear. I'm sure if you think about it enough, a light bulb will burn brightly in your brain and remind you that you did see it before, and exactly where."

"No. I haven't." Amanda shook her head. "I know I haven't." She dropped her palm to the table. "But I have, damn it."

They pondered possibilities, each from a personal perspective. Their eyes met at the sound of the clock's melodic chimes and held as the deep gong announced seven o'clock. The buzzer of the front door interrupted their thoughts.

* * * *

When Amanda opened the door, Mark presented her with a bottle of Merlot and a sheepish smile. "Sorry I'm late."

"Bushmills for you?"

"You are singing my tune." He tipped his head to

the cat. "Nice to see you again, Oprah." She rubbed her sleek frame around his legs and returned to her vigil in front of the clock. "It smells great in here, makes my stomach growl."

With a wide smile, Mary tossed a dishtowel over her shoulder and came to Mark from the kitchen. She took his extended hand firmly in her own. "We meet at last. I'm Mary, Amanda's godmother. I live upstairs."

"A pleasure. Amanda speaks highly of you."

She continued to grip his hand. "That's surprising. I never say anything nice about her."

Mark frowned at her stoic expression and brusque words.

She tightened her grip and winked.

"I see where Amanda gets that dry sense of humor."

"I'll be out in the kitchen. The boiled dinner you asked for is about…" she lifted the old watch pinned to her plaid shirt, "…thirty minutes away. You two enjoy a cocktail."

Mark stepped behind the cat, chuckling. Her black head moved steadily, following the pendulum. "She's intrigued. Almost as much as I am." He ran a hand down the corner of the case. "It's a treasure."

"It is that." Amanda walked up beside him, handed him his drink and sipped her wine. The minute hand slipped forward.

Gazing at the clock, Mark said, "I have tickets to a cross-town game at Wrigley next week. You interested?"

Amanda smiled at his profile. "Cubs."

He turned to her, brows knit, chin firm. "Sox. I knew there was going to be an insurmountable issue. This is definitely it."

She turned her back on him and walked toward the kitchen. "I'll convert you."

He continued to examine the clock. "That'll take some doing." He looked down at the cat. "Oprah, we have a serious problem."

Oprah blinked indifferent green eyes and returned her cool gaze to the pendulum.

* * * *

Mark tossed his napkin on the table and puffed his cheeks in satisfaction. "There's one thing certain to win the heart of an Irishman: a boiled dinner prepared by a beautiful woman. This Irishman will be thanking you kindly, Mary."

"You're welcome, at least for the boiled dinner part." She winked. "There's a pot o' blarney in the rest." Mary excused herself after more praise about a wonderful dinner and went back upstairs.

He took a long sip of wine as he and Amanda sauntered to the living room. "Your godmother is a trip. An astute opinion on most everything and an incredible personality."

"Yes, she's wonderful."

"Colorful, to say the least."

Amanda looked up from her wine to Mark's penetrating eyes. "That's an understatement."

He began to move toward her, a thoughtful expression conveying intentions she read accurately.

To her surprise, she found that she both wanted and feared the promise of his gaze. She took a few steps back from him and turned toward the clock. He followed her and she listened to his deep voice.

"Are there any markings on it? A manufacturer, a date?"

She stood in front of the clock, grateful that an awkward moment had passed. Amanda didn't want to encourage him. *I'm not getting involved with him, with anyone.* "The only thing visible on the case is the name Wellington on the back, and a date, 1873."

"You're sure?"

"I suppose I could look harder. I think I'm going to have to see inside to find out much of anything."

The clock began to chime, and they laughed as Oprah jumped at the unexpected sound. Resuming a dignified countenance and with tail erect, the cat stalked from the room.

Amanda made an exaggerated pout. "She sympathizes with the pendulum. It's trapped in there and can't get out."

He raised one brow. "By now I expect she's decided the pendulum is pretty stupid."

"Probably."

Mark's warm brown eyes twinkled back with his smile, and he turned to the clock. "Mind if I move this away from the wall?" Without waiting for a reply, he handed her his empty wine glass. "And pour me a scotch, if you will. Neat." He ran a hand down the side of the case and muttered to himself, "Let's take a look at this big fella."

Amanda returned from the kitchen with his drink

and a fresh glass of wine for herself.

He had slid the clock about two feet from the wall and was crouched behind it, running a thumb along the seams. "You got a flashlight? And a step-ladder?"

"Sure, but it's just one of those kitchen thingies that collapses. Will that do?"

He stood on his toes, stretching his neck to see over the top of the cabinet. "Sure, I just want a look up there. Is the ladder heavy? I'll get it."

"No, just a second."

She returned from the kitchen carrying a white stepstool.

Mark scanned the dark wood from base to tower, paused at the quarter inch black letters, and ran a hand over the word. "This is the name the shop owner referred to, Wellington." He narrowed his eyes and traced the carved word. *What the hell was that?* Mark lifted his hand. *Strange...*

"What?"

Mark rubbed his fingers together. "Nothing, I guess. Just a funny feeling when I touched that name." Turning to face her, he asked, "What's an English name doing in a Belgian clock? It is Belgian, right?"

"It looks like it, but I'm not sure." Touching the dark case, she added, "Continental, anyway. Definitely not English." She wiggled a penlight between two fingers. "Ready for a closer peek?"

He glanced at the light, grinned, and moved toward the door. "I'll be right back. Buzz me in."

Mark returned shortly with a large blue chest and

a police-issue flashlight. "Tools of the trade. Shall we?" He climbed up the small ladder and shone his light around the top of the clock. "The wood is stained the same basic color but not varnished, and there are brass clips securing the decorative portion of the hood, but nothing else I can see." He backed down the ladder. "You must have some keys."

Amanda stepped to a small bowl on the bookcase. "Here."

She sensed more than heard him move up behind her. Mark looked over her shoulder at the selection of keys as he placed a hand on her lower back and she turned her face to his. He smiled at her expression. "Don't look so spooked." He whispered, "I won't bite. Although," his gaze mischievous, "I'll admit that a little nibble might be kind of nice."

Amanda's heart jumped as he leaned down and pressed his warm, firm lips to hers at the same time that she felt him slip the keys from her hand. Mark backed away from her and held both hands up in retreat. "I didn't bite. I told you I wouldn't. It took great strength of will, character and fortitude, but I refrained from inflicting any pain or permanent damage or—"

"Stop it, silly." She stepped back and giggled at his antics.

He studied her for a moment. "For now."

Mark again turned his attention to the clock and unlocked the glass door. He rested his hand against the pendulum rod and the resonant tick stopped. Shining the light up and circling the interior of the trunk, he paused several times, twisting to see. "Did

Ed mention anything about this having been in a fire?"

Startled, she said, "No. I suppose he didn't know. What do you see?"

Mark stood erect and felt along the inside of the trunk, near the clock's hood. He withdrew his hand, and they both looked at black stains on his fingers. He sniffed, rubbed a thumb on the stain. "Well, it definitely was; this is ordinary soot, fire residue." They both looked back at the clock. "Judging by the condition of the exterior, this has been refurbished at some point."

"Somebody's cleaned the interior, but they obviously didn't get all the soot." Amanda stepped toward the open case and looked closely at the forest and animal detail of the cabinet. "There doesn't appear to be any real burn damage, no cracks, no fill, nothing that I can see. Whoever restored this knew what they were doing."

Mark dropped to a crouch at his tool chest and flipped it open, displaying a neat array of tools. She rolled her eyes at the organized chaos. From beneath a mysterious bunch of paraphernalia he pulled out an old-fashioned magnifying glass and held it up to one eye. "We are about to go exploring, acushla. Your fee is another drop o' the craythur, neat. Like the last."

She laughed at his exaggerated brogue. "A cush what?"

Mark grinned. "It means 'dearie'."

Raising her brows, she said, "Okay, Sherlock."

* * * *

Mark began at the bottom inside of the trunk, moving the magnifying glass and his flashlight in tandem, inch by inch. Any minute depression or detail received his attention. As he worked, he paused for an occasional sip of the amber whiskey, pleased to note that the drink was promptly topped off.

"Look." He aimed the beam of light to the very center of the interior rear wall, holding the flashlight at a sharp angle. "Center of the back. You won't even need the magnifying glass."

Space was cramped. As she leaned into the clock, Amanda's forehead was level with Mark's chin and her hair brushed the side of his face. Mark moved aside, and with effort maintained his concentration as he breathed in her delicate scent of jasmine and roses. *Okay, idiot, knees are acting goofy because of the booze...or not. Cut it out. Christ, if she had any idea what I'm thinking.*

High in the back of the case and barely visible, a paper label was glued to the wood. Discolored to the shade of the clock's interior, it bore the faint legend C. KOBLENZ CHICAGO. "That's not possible." Amanda moved back from the clock with a puzzled expression. "There were no clock manufacturers in Chicago in the 18th century."

They repositioned the clock against the wall. Amanda opened the face and reset the time. Mark started the pendulum and locked the bottom door. Together, they stared at the big old clock as he handed her his empty glass and mumbled, "Curiouser and curiouser." He shrugged at the clock and said, "Might have been restor...you know, fixer-upper guys. It was fixer-upped, that's for sure." He looked at her and aimed the lit flashlight at the floor. "Think, my lovely blue-eyed maiden."

Amanda smiled at his words and crooked grin. *He doesn't realize what he just said, or maybe he does. Two sheets to the wind, going on three.*

She took the flashlight from him, turned it off, and steered Mark toward the couch. Amanda pushed her two palms against his chest and he dropped to a seat. She shook her head with a smile. *Appears that Bushmills of his is no drink for sissies.* "I'll be right back. Stay put."

Mark patted the seat next to him. "Sit."

"Yeah, right." Amanda laughed. "Keep 'er steady and stay there for just a second." She went to the kitchen, poured a large cup of black coffee, and returned to see Mark's head tipped to the side, his eyes closed. She watched him for a long moment and then reached for a large brown and beige afghan and draped it over his lap. Amanda turned off the music and all but one dim light, and then glanced back at Mark. She smiled at the whisper of his snore.

Amanda tiptoed from the room. Her tail erect, Oprah followed.

* * * *

Bells. Mark rolled his head toward the sound. *No,*

chimes. The clock. He opened his eyes and peered into the darkness lit only by a dimmed lamp and moonlight through the window behind him. *Amanda's place.* He drifted back to sleep.

There it was again, distant and deep. His eyes followed the sound. A gossamer haze suffused the room with soft radiance. Amanda stood before the clock, her back to him. Her white gown draped to the floor, diaphanous in the surrounding tendrils of a vaporous, billowing veil of shadows. She lifted her hand to the face of the clock.

A ballet of fog danced around them as Mark moved toward her. He drifted through an ethereal mist, and then he was at her side. Her pale face glowed, reflecting the dim light of the room. Pools of tears not fallen sparkled in her blue eyes.

Amanda looked past him and up. He reached out to touch her, and his fingers passed through the ivory skin of her cheek. A breath of deepest longing whispered through him.

Amanda's searching gaze dropped to his.

Tick…tick…tick…tick…tick…

CHAPTER 6

Amanda poured a mug of coffee and carried it to the couch where Mark slept upright, his body slouched to the left, head tilted to the right. She studied him. *That was just a dream. I didn't see him last night. A silly dream.* She leaned forward, wafting the aromatic steam under his nose. Amanda smiled as he began to stir.

She straightened and brought the cup to her waist, holding it in both hands. "Good morning."

He opened his eyes and squinted as he tossed the afghan aside and croaked, "*Maidin mhaith.*"

"I'm gonna assume that's Gaelic." Amanda extended the cup to him. "If not, save your swearing for your cop buddies."

Clearing his throat, he chuckled at the same time. "An Irish 'good morning.' Thanks for the coffee."

"You'll find the bathroom," she raised a hand palm up, toward the hallway, "that-a-way." Amanda twirled a finger toward the kitchen with the other hand. "Then follow your nose to the smell of bacon."

* * * *

Amanda heard the kitchen chair slide and glanced behind her to see Mark take a seat.

"I'm sorry about being an idiot last night." He

63

looked around the small room and ran a hand through his hair. "I didn't mean to…I didn't mean to drink that much. I'd had a long day, and some lovely fairy kept filling my glass. Not an excuse, but—"

"I won't tell anyone if you don't." Amanda glanced at him over her shoulder and gave him a wink. "How do you like your eggs?"

Mark was quiet, and Amanda turned to face him, her eyebrows raised innocently. She met a puzzled frown, his damp hair finger-combed neatly. A day-old beard only enhanced his rugged features.

"Your eggs?"

"Uh, whatever's easiest?"

Amanda smiled and turned back to the stove, fully aware Mark was contemplating his behavior last night. Speaking to a skillet of hash browns she asked, "Well, I like mine over easy, but scrambled, sunny side up? Name it."

"Over easy is great."

She poured a glass of tomato juice, then walked to the table and handed it to him. "Fresh lime in it. Mary's hang-over cure, guaranteed."

"Didn't think I was that transparent." Mark sighed as he reached for the glass. "After meeting Mary last night, I have no doubt that if she guarantees it, this drink will be an elixir of the gods."

She piled hash browns, crisp bacon, raisin toast, and two over-easy jumbo eggs on his plate, one egg and a smidgen of the rest on hers. Amanda ate silently, her mind lost in the confusion of disturbing images from the previous night. She glanced at Mark's coffee and rose to refill it, sitting down again as she placed the carafe on the table. He glanced up from his plate and cleared his throat. She quickly broke her stare from him, looked at her breakfast, and frowned. *Did I see him last night?*

"Breakfast is incredible. You didn't have to do all this. I'm not complaining, mind you. It's great."

Amanda dabbed egg yolk with her toast. "Sure. I mean yeah, thanks. Mark, did you…?"

He waited, fork poised. "You're welcome. Did I what?"

She placed her napkin beside her plate. "I was in the living room last night, and I…" Feeling foolish, Amanda shook her head. "Never mind. It's silly. Would you like anything else? More toast?"

Mark shook his head and glanced at his breakfast. "No, really. What about the living room?"

She studied her plate, without seeing what was on it. "I haven't told anyone this except Mary." Amanda rubbed fingers against her neck, just below her earlobe. "Ever since that clock was delivered, it's been like a magnet to me. I stand in front of it, touch it, listen, even in the middle of the damn night. Sometimes…"

Mark leaned back in his chair and wiped a napkin across his lips. "Sometimes what?"

Amanda rose, and began to clear the table. "Would you like more coffee?" She swished the carafe around in the air. "This is empty."

"If you wouldn't mind. Sometimes what?"

"I know I've seen that crazy clock before. I've

seen it, and I also know that I couldn't have seen it. According to Ed, it's been in the same house on Elm Street for decades, and I'm not decades old." She shrugged. "Well, not enough decades, anyway."

He carried his plate and utensils to the sink. "So, you're telling me you could never have seen it, but you know you have seen it." He leaned back on the counter and crossed his arms. "Did I get that right?"

Amanda stopped bustling around the kitchen, put her hands on her hips, and stared at him. "Do I sound stupid, or what?"

He laughed quietly. "Let's table that for a minute. What is it about the living room that bothers you? The clock?"

Amanda tossed her hands in the air and puttered around the small room, tidying as she did. Her long white silk robe flipped open in time with her steps, glimpses of shapely bare legs distracting Mark. "The living room doesn't bother me. But last night, you were there." She shook her head. "No, that's not what I mean. I know you were there, on the couch, asleep. But when I was looking at the clock I looked at you." Amanda shook her head again. "That's all wrong." She flopped down in her chair and pinched the bridge of her nose.

Mark sat opposite her at the table. "Start at the beginning, step by step. Let's go through the whole scenario, everything. First, you bought the clock, right?"

Tucking dark hair behind her ears, Amanda said, "Yeah."

"Why?"

She frowned at him, uncertain. "I liked it."

"No other reason?"

"Can't think of any. I mean it's nice. But I liked it no more than any other antique." Amanda knit her brows and gazed at him as if searching. "No, that's wrong. The very first time I saw the clock was the day of the accident. When I, when Ed put that towel on my forehead. I remember seeing the pendulum. I was watching the pendulum, listening to the tick." She shrugged. "I must have passed out again, I guess."

"Okay, that's good, you just hurt your head, a concussion. You felt drawn to the clock then, right?"

"Definitely. Drawn. That's the exact word I used when I told Mary. She thought I should go look at it again."

"Next. You made the deal with Ed, right?"

She nodded.

"Anything else? Anything strange?"

"Nothing I can think of until it was delivered." Amanda thought for a moment. "Maybe a little. When you and I were in the shop."

The way Mark was looking at her now told her they were both thinking of her hand under his as the clock chimed. *That expression, his gaze. There is something so familiar.* She was both curious and frightened.

"I remember." Mark tapped fingers on the table. "After it was delivered, anything unusual happen?"

"Since it was delivered, my weird fascination with it has only increased. Every time I look at it, or hear it, and every night, I feel drawn to it, or by it, or something."

"What happens first?" He reached for his coffee. "What makes you look at it?"

"If I'm in bed or in the kitchen, whatever, and hear it, I wind up standing in front of it. I get absorbed by the sound and then can't pull my eyes away from it." *Why do I know him? How?*

"Does the clock frighten you?"

Amanda shook her head. "I don't want to do this anymore. All these questions…"

Mark ran a hand through his hair as he stood and began to pace the small room. "Sorry."

Amanda's heart raced as she stood and faced him. *Dammit, I did see him last night.* "When I was watching the clock last night, I felt you, I felt you touch me, touch my face."

He frowned as he turned to her.

Amanda raised her hand to her face, moving her fingers from cheekbone to jaw. "I felt a physical sensation right here. I'm not sure how to put it, but almost like a breeze. It was very real and I have no doubt it was you."

Mark moved toward her, bafflement in his brown eyes. "I don't understand any of this."

"It's bizarre."

Mark stared at her for a moment, reached out a hand and said, "More than you know. You'd better sit down." He led her to a seat at the table, flipped a chair around and straddled it, sitting close to her. "I'm going to tell you about a very, very crazy dream. At least I thought it was crazy, and I thought it was a dream. Now I'm not so sure." Mark pressed his lips together in thought, returning her gaze. Finally, he said, "Last night, I don't remember if I heard the chimes or what, but something made me look at the clock. And you were there, standing in front of it, dressed just as you are now."

Amanda fingered the locket at her throat.

"You were looking up, past me. I was standing beside you, almost facing you. I reached out and touched your face, exactly where you said." Mark gently brushed her cheek.

Amanda shivered involuntarily and shied away from his touch.

He dropped his hand, his voice husky. "You looked at me, and then behind and above me. All I could hear was the clock ticking." Spreading his hands, he added, "The next thing I remember is you standing there with a cup of coffee."

She started to speak and stopped as he raised his hand.

"I'm not finished." Mark stood and walked to the window, his back to her. "Ever since we were lying on the sidewalk in front of that antique shop, I've had the feeling I know you." He frowned as he turned to her and shook his head. "Not from some goddamned karaoke bar, not like that. Somehow, I've known or met you somewhere. This is not some idiotic come-on to a single girl. It's not a line."

The silence was deafening and lengthy. Finally, Amanda broke it. Her heart pounding, her voice wavering with uncertainty, she whispered, "I think I know you, too. Damned if I know how."

He leaned back on the counter, folded his arms, and studied her for a long moment. His warm brown eyes were puzzled. His jaw flexed, and he walked from the room.

Amanda followed. "Where are you going?"

"Right this minute, nowhere."

He began pulling an array of equipment from his tool chest: plastic bags, rubber gloves, short little tubes with blue rubber caps, sealed cotton swabs, and other more mysterious items.

"What are you going to do?"

He looked up and down the clock. "I need to pull this from the wall and chip a small piece of wood from the back. I won't create a visible scar."

She wasn't too keen on marring a valuable antique, but he appeared determined and she decided not to object. "Okay, I guess."

The polished hardwood floor made moving the clock again simple, and he lay on the floor, head and shoulders hidden from Amanda's view. She flinched as she heard a sharp crack of wood. Mark scrambled to his feet with a small plastic bag.

Sealing the bag, he said, "This is an evidence bag. It'll keep this little chip from other site contamination, like my car."

The clock repositioned, he reached into the little bowl for the door key and continued to explain what he was doing. "I'm going to scrape some of that soot, somewhere I didn't touch it."

"What are you going to do with it?"

"Have forensics tell me whatever they can."

"Like?"

"Like carbon dating the wood that burned, if it was wood." He continued to work. "I'm no expert, but the ash might say something. That chip might give a clue to the clock's general age. I'm also going to take a tiny scraping of varnish; if you don't want to look, go hide and I'll dare you to find where I chip it off. I'm going to take swabs from the back of the pendulum, cables, and movement parts, too. I have no idea what the hell all this might tell us, but it's a place to start." He selected a pair of blue gloves as he added, "We have nothing else to go on."

She was reminded of a surgeon as he pulled on the gloves and meticulously collected his various samples. Mark labeled each vial to indicate where on the clock the sample was from and dropped them all into the plastic bags, carefully sealing each. He snapped off the gloves, turning them inside out as he did, and stuffed them into his pocket. He extended a hand to Amanda and waited.

She looked at Mark's hand and then at his face. She lifted her eyebrows.

"Come on," he said quietly. "Sit with me."

Amanda set her hand in his and he turned to the couch, pulling her down next to him.

"Here's where we are." His eyes moved to the clock.

She felt strangely comfortable with this man holding her hand.

"You saved my life, a few feet from this clock." Turning to her he added, "We're sure we know each other somehow, but we know we've never met, or at

71

least neither of us remembers meeting." Mark nodded toward the clock, but maintained his gaze on her. "We know the clock came from a house on Elm, that it was in a fire. We know you are drawn to it, but we don't have any idea why." He shrugged and turned his attention to Oprah. She had returned to pendulum watching. "I don't see many real mysteries in life. Comes with being a cop, I guess. Seen way too much. But if I expand my thinking a bit and throw everything into a pot, including the strange events of last night, and stir it with a stick, I have a stew that tells me the clock, you, and I are somehow linked. That's all a bit of a stretch, I know."

He released her hand and leaned forward, forearms on knees. The brass pendulum sparkled like fire from a ray of morning sun and they listened to the haunting melody. The chime declared the time to be noon.

Amanda smiled at the errant curl on his brow. Her need to smooth it back into place seemed as natural as breathing. *I want to touch him.* Instead, she reached for the locket on her neck.

"Based on what we know, we have a direction to follow. I'll pull some strings with forensics to get the testing expedited. I'm also going to talk to Ed Morgen. He got the clock at an estate sale, which might be a lead worth pursuing." Mark leaned back and turned to her. "We'll get to the bottom of this."

Amanda looked from Mark to Oprah, still as a statue, except for her tracking of the pendulum's arc.

"There's a big clambake of screaming teenagers flooding Grant Park tonight." He gathered up his flashlight, tool chest, and evidence bags. "Yours truly will be representing Chicago's finest on the back of a horse. If I find out anything, I'll give you a call."

"It's Saturday. What could you find out today?"

"Ed's shop is open until five." He walked to the front door. "I'll stop in and we'll have a chat."

"Mark."

His hand on the doorknob, he stopped and looked over his shoulder at her.

Amanda walked to him and folded her arms. "I'm grateful." She held his gaze. "Thanks."

As his smile spread, laugh lines wrinkled, and his eyes searched her face. Mark leaned down, and Amanda's heart leaped as he barely touched his lips to hers. "I have my reasons." He winked and kissed her again. "Us."

Yesterday

CHAPTER 7

Mark stared at the water, a gust of warm air from the lake tousling his hair. He sat on the stone break wall, his sneakers dangling above Amanda's red flip-flops on the sandy path. This virgin air would soon mingle with the sweet aromas of delicatessens, bakeries and popcorn shops, and the stench of city smog and urine-soaked subway cement. They were in Lincoln Park, surrounded by trees, wildflowers, and a lake like an ocean. The bustling metropolis was out of sight a few blocks behind them, a million miles away.

Amanda enchanted Mark, and not only because she was beautiful. *This is Twilight Zone stuff. Can there be some sort of history between us? Were we lovers once? She saved my life. Was that destiny or simply random chance? And where does that damned clock fit in with all this? Now there's a missing child in the picture. For Christ's sake, we've got the Great Chicago Fire. What the hell does it all mean?* Mark took a deep breath and puffed his cheeks with a long exhale. He reached for Amanda's hand, and she withdrew it immediately.

"Don't, Mark."

At yet another rebuff, Mark slapped both palms against his thighs and slid from the break wall. He stepped in front of Amanda, their eyes almost level. Hands on either side of her hips, he waited.

75

Finally, her eyes met his, with brows knit.

Mark held his temper in check and spoke quietly. "You're going to tell me why not."

Amanda turned from him and crossed her arms.

"I think you'll agree we have a bit in common. Like I reach out and touch you, and you feel a phantom touch from me. And I'm there." He tipped his head to bring her gaze back to his. "We agree we know each other. God only knows how because we've never met before." Mark tipped his head back and sighed at the pillows of clouds overhead, hoping he wasn't pushing her too hard. "We're part of each other's lives, damn it. We both know that. Why shouldn't I reach for you now?"

She looked down. "Because. Because this can't work out."

He moved a hand to her chin. The fear and anxiety in her eyes blew away his anger like a gentle gust from the lake. "You don't know that." Moving his hands to her waist he whispered, "It just might." He shrugged. "I'm sorry, but 'Don't, Mark' doesn't cut it."

She shook her head, unable to look at him. "Get out of my way; I'm getting down."

His voice was calm but firm. "Answer me. Why don't you want me to touch you?" Mark frowned as Amanda covered her face with her hands.

"Because you'll be like everyone else in my screwed up life and die or take off or…" Amanda's voice faded, "…or something." She pushed hands against his chest and glared at him, tears brimming. "Now, back off and let me down."

He clenched his jaw at the stubborn woman before him and tightened his hands on her waist. "You need to trust me, Amanda; I'm not going anywhere."

Her gaze moved across his face and a tear dropped down her cheek.

"I'm not your parents, your brother, or your dead fiancé. I ache for you, for those horrible losses. But I'm not them. I'm here, I'm right now, and I'm not leaving." Mark touched his lips to hers, to her cheek, her chin, and then to her lips again. He murmured Gaelic words. "*Mo mhuirnín.*"

Amanda shivered as she turned from him, a timid rejection he was not willing to accept. She fisted her hands on his chest, but didn't push him away. Not certain this shudder came from her or from deep within himself, Mark drew her to him as he whispered, "It means 'my sweetheart'." He nuzzled her neck and moved his cheek across hers, reveling in her sweet smell and softness. Touching his tongue to her slightly parted lips, he felt her hand move to his shoulder. Mark slid arms around her and pressed his mouth onto hers. Overwhelming warmth rushed through him as she hungrily kissed him back.

Amanda trembled, and with a quick intake of breath said, "No."

Mark stepped back from her, held both of her hands in his, and waited for her to look at him again. "Yes."

"Mark—"

"Your kiss disagrees with your words. So do I, but for the moment, we're going to table this." His gaze traveled down her face and he wiped a tear from her chin. "Only for the moment."

He helped her down from the break wall and they walked down the path at a lazy pace. This time, when Mark reached for her hand, she didn't pull away. "I stopped in Ed Morgen's shop and learned a bit, but I'd like to save all that for when we're back at your place. I think we should include Mary in the discussion."

Amanda wiped the back of her hand across her face and glanced up at him. "Why?"

Ignoring the question, Mark put his arm around her waist as they walked. "Are you familiar with a therapeutic technique called Past Life Therapy? Has Mary ever mentioned it?"

"You mean like regression? Spirit releasement?"

"It would be the same thing. Sounds as if you're familiar with it."

"Well no, no, not really. I know about it, read about it, like a lot of people. I know Mary's had patient sessions pertaining to it, but I never…" They stopped, and she faced him. "You can't think… Isn't that kind of, I don't know, UFOee?"

Mark walked to the edge of the break wall and spoke to a small sailboat tacking into the wind toward Montrose Harbor. "I'm sure having trouble coming up with any plausible explanation for whatever it is between you and me. Maybe we should consider the possibility that we knew each other in some previous existence. I know it sounds bogus, but we're about out of rational explanations. As Sherlock Holmes said, 'When you have eliminated the impossible, whatever remains, however improbable, must be the truth.' And the truth is that we know each other somehow." He turned to face her. "We certainly have an incredible spiritual connection." Amanda frowned and Mark smiled as he reached for her hand. "You can't believe I appear as a ghostly apparition to every girl I meet. I think if we intend on getting to the bottom of all this we haven't any choice but to try exploring our past lives."

He pulled her along in pace with him again. "Mary is a practicing psychiatrist, so this whole concept is nothing new to her. But I'm not going to fool you into thinking it's child's play. It can be dangerous, and needs to be handled by someone who knows what the hell they're doing. From what you say it sounds like she believes in the therapy. Not many professionals do."

Amanda shrugged. "I guess it's worth talking to her."

"How much have you told Mary? I mean, does she know about our *visions* of each other, for lack of a better word?"

Amanda waved a hand. "Like I could ever keep anything from Mary. Yeah, she knows. We talked about it for hours."

* * * *

Back in Amanda's apartment, Mark sat in a kitchen chair and stretched out his long legs, crossing them at the ankles.

Mary and Amanda looked at him with anticipation as he reached for his coffee.

He gazed down at his sneakers, frowned into his coffee, and tapped an index finger on the rim of the cup. "There's a manila folder of geek-speak in my car, if you want detail, but here's a thumbnail. I learned more going through Ed Morgen than I did from CPD forensics. Wood ash contains calcium carbonate as a major component, close to fifty percent. Whatever burned around the clock was wood or paper." Mark ran a hand through his hair and continued, "All this is moot when you hear the whole story."

Amanda and Mary exchanged a glance, wondering where this might lead.

Mary swirled a spoon through her tea as she said, "Mark, dear. Whatever you've learned isn't going to result in a poltergeist bouncing around the clock. Spit it out."

Marked huffed a sardonic chuckle. "I hope not. The age of the wood chip is consistent with what we know; the clock comes from the 18th century. Swabs from the brass show years of machine oil. Under the present varnish are beeswax, whale oil, and more wax. Everything but the varnish is in insignificant traces."

Amanda's knowledge of antiques came forth. "I don't take issue with any of that. We have a clock built in say, 1770. It would have been waxed or oiled. A hundred years later, say 1870, it's refinished with shellac. Shellac caught on in the states in the early 19th century, so that all makes sense. Fifty or sixty years later, 1920, 1930, it gets refinished again with some kind of varnish. What does all this tell us?"

Mary walked to the window over the sink and pinched a dead leaf from a philodendron sitting on the ledge. "Did you learn anything else, Mark? Anything about the ash?"

"Yes, and this is quite a tale." Mark straightened and leaned back in his chair, watching Amanda work the cork out of a wine bottle. "The finish detail just validates the rest; it doesn't tell us anything specific. A woman named Margaret Starks bought the clock around 1870. The clock was refurbished with a new shellac finish. You won't believe this next part: I was told it was restored by a place here in Chicago that rebuilt and repaired valuable items damaged in the Great Chicago Fire of 1871."

Amanda went to a cupboard and withdrew three long-stemmed wine glasses. She walked back to the table. "You're telling me the soot in my clock is from the Chicago Fire? How do you know that?"

"I spent the better part of an hour on the phone with Margaret Starks' great-grandniece, Alice Ormandy. She even has the original bill of sale."

"Ed gave you the name?"

"Yes. Mrs. Ormandy handled the estate sale. There's more to the family lore she wasn't too sure about, though."

Amanda poured the wine and glanced up at Mark. "Like what?"

"The most interesting part, but she's vague, and it probably doesn't have anything to do with the clock.

It seems Margaret Starks acquired the clock around the same time she adopted a child, a girl. Nobody seems to know where this kid wound up. It's a family mystery."

Amanda swapped Mark's empty coffee cup with a glass of wine as he said, "That's all I know."

Mary pointed and walked toward the bathroom. "Right back."

Amanda's face clouded as she walked to the living room. *So now I know this clock was in the Chicago Fire. A child adopted well over a hundred years ago disappeared. What does that mean?* She looked up at the imposing clock. "I wish you could talk."

Mark walked up behind her and put an arm around her waist as he said, "In a way, it can."

Amanda stiffened, but didn't pull away. She spoke to the clock. "That's what you said before, in the antique store. What'd you mean?"

"You and this clock are linked. Listen to it."

She met his eyes and shook her head. "All I hear is tick, tick, tick."

Amanda turned back to the clock as Mark tugged her close and whispered, "Listen."

Tick…tick…tick…

Mark followed her gaze to the clock face. "Listen."

Tick…tick…tick…tick…

Amanda turned to him, with longing, loss, and incredible sadness in her heart. And it had something to do with him. "I hear, I mean I *feel* something."

82

Mary's voice called out from the kitchen. "Dinner's ready, you two."

Amanda headed toward the kitchen and stopped as Mark spoke softly to her back. "I know you do. It's what I felt when I touched your face the other night."

* * * *

Mary sighed at the downcast eyes of her dining companions and poked a fork around her plate. "In our final session, I told him he was an insufferable peckerhead because he thinks the only good screw is some chick named Bambi with humongous boobs."

Both heads popped up, and Mark slid his chair back from the table as he choked back laughter.

Amanda giggled, fighting for breath behind a napkin.

"Must I say something outrageous to get your attention?"

Mark shook his head. "Sorry, but it did work."

"All right, then. Is this none of my business or are you two going to tell me what's up?"

Mark shrugged at Amanda.

Amanda began clearing the table as Mark drummed his fingers on the placemat. He glanced at her back and then to Mary, uncertain how to begin. He decided to just plow ahead.

"Mary, Amanda's told you about these mystical experiences we've been having. Nothing we've found out so far has brought us any closer to an explanation. She says you have some experience in past life therapy." He shrugged. "Frankly, I don't see much choice. I'd like you to try PLT with me."

Amanda spun from the task of loading the dishwasher. "What are you talking about? I'm the one—"

"Hold on." Mary held up both hands, one in the direction of each. "We've jumped light years. Amanda, let me hear a little more."

Mark directed his response to Amanda. "I've had some education in the area and done considerable reading. I know what to expect, and how it works." He shrugged and added, "I told you. PLT can be dangerous, upsetting."

Amanda put her hands on her hips. "Textbook theory doesn't hold much weight when it comes to practical—"

Mary interrupted again. "Mark, how far did you get?"

"Not far enough, just over three years of pre-med at Trinity. I was planning to do my internship there."

"Psychiatry or medicine?"

"Coursework was predominantly psych."

Mary studied him for a moment. "A good five years from practice. Tea, Amanda?"

Amanda broke her stare from Mark, and began making tea for Mary.

"Colleges don't teach this kind of therapy. The beliefs I have are my own, though the theories are not unique."

He slowly set his wine glass on the table. "And those beliefs are?"

Mary lifted a shoulder. "Let's say I'm old enough

84

to be certain I will be young again and that when I screw up, I get a do-over eventually. How deeply are you versed in the subject?"

"I was fortunate enough to have an open-minded instructor who referred me to some authors, both pro and con."

"Like?"

"Cayce, Blavatsky, Kardec, Spanos."

Mary grunted. "Diverse views, aren't they?"

Mark shrugged. "Edgar Cayce, a believer; Nicholas Spanos, a skeptic. I made a conscious attempt to be objective."

"The fact that you request PLT sessions indicates a belief."

"Well, an open mind, anyway." Mark took a toothpick from a porcelain dish and began to pace the small room. "Catholicism tells me reincarnation is bunk, but I fail to see an end-game conflict. The object of any spiritual discipline is oneness with your god, the goal of every religion. Belief in reincarnation in one form or another is ancient, as you know. People who believe in previous lives come from many faiths, and from no faith at all. I've found no reason to stop asking myself: What if?" He turned to Mary, the toothpick resting on his bottom lip. "Will you do it?"

Amanda had been listening to their exchange. She found Mark's enthusiasm for the process odd since she was the one haunted by the clock. "I don't think—"

Mary held up her hand. "Mark, based on what appears to be classic astral projection, I've little doubt you would be a good candidate. You've the intellect, the imagination, if you will, to be susceptible to the process. But I've got a problem."

Mark frowned and lowered himself to his chair. "Go on."

"Astral projection, out of body experience, is not the objective here. Amanda has a deeper sense of something closer to past life experience. If a promise is unfulfilled, a bad decision is made, a vow broken; whatever…in one's life, there are those that believe its effect can carry over to the next life. You've got a connection to Amanda; I've no doubt of that, based on what she's told me. But there's no indication that it's a connection that goes beyond this life."

Mary looked over her glasses at Amanda. "You, however, are a different story." Mary tipped her head toward the clock. "The sound, touch, and simple presence of that clock have permeated your subconscious mind. I've known you since you were born; susceptibility is not a question. The fact that I've known you so intimately for so many years *is* a concern. This would be your regression. I don't want to taint it with my own attitudes or experiences." Mary paused and sipped her tea. "You've managed to convince yourself that disaster in your personal life is inevitable. I think that you're tired of having life happen *to* you instead of making things happen yourself. Some people believe that the soul is doomed to repeat painful acts until it learns by these mistakes. It needs a *tunk* on the head to show it the lessons of karma aren't getting through. When they do, it changes the way you live your life. And when that happens, your karma changes. Maybe it's a touch off-center." Mary shrugged. "But that's what I believe."

Mark smiled as he said, "I've the feeling, Mary, that you enjoy being a touch off center. Cayce had some interesting perspectives, but he also predicted the end of life as we know it, and any idiot who reads the paper can predict Armageddon. What's it going to be…a meteor, a caldera, some knucklehead starting WWIII in Times Square, or the Four Horsemen of the Apocalypse? Take your pick; there are dozens of reasons to hide behind the couch when you watch the news."

The three sat in silence. Mark filled his and Amanda's wine glasses. Mary rhythmically raised and lowered the teabag in her steaming mug.

Amanda sipped her wine and set the glass down. "I want to do this."

Mark met her eyes. "You sure? You might find it a bit unnerving. Frightening, even."

Amanda looked to Mary, and nodded. "Yes. I need to."

Mary took a long sip of tea and set the mug down decisively. "You two go make a CD of St. Michael's chimes. Set it up to run in a continuous loop. I'll bring my laptop down here for session recording."

Mary stepped toward the door. "No time like the present."

Yesterday

CHAPTER 8

Amanda reclined in a lounge chair in front of the old clock. Mary sat upright on the love seat facing her, and Mark's chair across the large living room was out of Amanda's line of sight. It was not Mary's preference that Mark be present at these sessions, but both he and Amanda had insisted. Mary acquiesced on the condition that he observe and not participate.

As Mary instructed, Mark set the chimes of the clock to mute, the microphone on the laptop to record, and the lights on dim. Oprah was in Mary's apartment, upstairs.

Mary looked over her glasses at Amanda, and said, "Some important housekeeping, dear. Listen carefully. First, you are in complete control at all times. Nothing can change that. Nothing. You can stop at any time. Second, you are safe from harm. You won't spontaneously slip into a hypnotic state at some other time, like when you're watching a sunset, or driving a car."

Mary took a pencil from behind her ear and flipped the pages of a black notebook. "If you don't want to experience an event, skip it. It's up to you. Examples are birth and death. Without exception, everything is in your control. Does that sound good to you?"

Amanda nodded.

"I'm going to be an escort, a guide. Listen to my voice and we'll journey down some stairs to a hallway, like a hotel hallway. There are room numbers on the doors. These numbers represent years. Open any door you please, or none at all. And there is another thing. Verbally acknowledge yes or no. Or, raise your right hand to indicate, yes; raise your left to indicate no."

"Okay."

"Good. You need to listen to what I'm saying and answer every question I ask. If you don't know the answer, tell me that. Simply say, 'I don't know.' You will have complete control over what you feel or see or smell, but you must listen to my voice and respond. When I say something to you, you will obey, without question."

"Are you sure I can do that?"

"It's important that you do because I will be your guide and bring you through your journey. Now, become aware of all the sounds around you. This building is pretty quiet, but you may hear the dim sound of an ambulance siren or the slam of a car door. The tick of the clock, a water pipe gurgling, the toot of a horn…these sounds won't disturb you or your journey. Anything usually heard from this room is normal and expected. I want you to narrate everything that you see, hear, and feel as it's happening. As long as I know what's going on, I can help you if you need it. Are you comfortable?"

Amanda nodded. "Yes."

Mark leaned forward, resting forearms on knees, and folded his hands.

"Ready, dear?"

"Yes."

"We're going to do some simple breathing exercises, just like yoga. This is the beginning of relaxation. I want you to watch the clock pendulum. Don't stare or concentrate on it; simply use the steady motion as a tool to relax. When your eyes get heavy, let yourself go, close them, welcome it."

Amanda began to breathe deeply, exhaling and inhaling, following the steady motion of the pendulum and listening to the rhythmic tick.

Mary softened her voice to a gentle monotone and began guiding Amanda to a hypnotic state. "Think of breathing and let the tension leave your body. Relax your brow and your jaw. Feel a peaceful calm move through your neck...your spine...your shoulders...down your arms...your hands. Adjust yourself in the chair, if you need to. Take calming breaths, steady and slow. Allow your mind to clear. Think only of breathing and relaxing. Become completely stress-free, everything about your body is peaceful, gentle warmth. Steady breaths. Your thighs...legs...ankles...your toes are cozy and relaxed."

Amanda's eyelids fluttered and her eyes closed.

"Your body feels soothed and tranquil, melting into a serene peace. You are drifting ... drifting ... drifting further ... stress is pouring from your being. You are floating away to darkness and gentle peace."

The room was still.

Tick...tick...tick...tick...tick

"In the darkness there is a stairway. Do you see it?"

"Yes." Amanda's head leaned back on the chair cushion.

"There is a door at the bottom of the stairs. You know this is a door to beautiful things that you want to see and explore, so you move toward it. There are ten steps. Take one step down, closer to the door. Now, take another step. Three steps, four steps down. You feel more relaxed with each step down. Go down, down deeper toward the door. Each stair takes you lower, deeper, and closer. It is peaceful, tranquil, and you are floating down, floating down the stairs. Five, six, the door is closer. You're not far. Seven, eight. You are drifting down. Nine. Ten."

"You feel yourself surrounded with gentle warmth, comfort. You feel light, free, your spirit relaxed, floating. Thoughts drift into your mind and away. Nothing is important except the lovely warmth around you."

"Behind the door is a hallway, Amanda. Open the door and you'll see an endless hall, welcoming and beckoning you. There are doors on each side of the hall. Do you see the doors?"

"Yes."

"What do you see at the end of the hall?"

"Darkness. Dark blue. Mist."

"Move toward the mist. Do you see anything?"

"Numbers. Numbers on the doors."

"Good. Keep walking down the hall toward the blue mist. Stop at any door; it doesn't matter which one."

"There's a room number, 1990."

"You were six years old in 1990. Would you like to open the door?"

"Yes."

"Open it, reach for the door knob and open it. What do you see?"

Amanda's voice was quiet, but alert. She smiled. "Mom."

"What is she doing?"

Amanda laughed. "She's…she's matching socks on the bed."

"What else is in the room?"

"Curtains, a dresser, a window. This is Mom and Dad's room."

"Describe your mother. What's she wearing?"

Mary waited for several seconds before asking a second time. "What does she look like?"

Amanda was silent, her face relaxed.

Tick…tick…tick…tick…tick

"Are you ready to close this door?"

"Yes."

"Return to the hall and close the door. Take your time. Can you see the stairs?"

"Yes."

"Move to the stairs. I want you to climb the stairs, and with each step, you will feel very comfortable. Your mind will be more alert with each stair."

Only the soft voice and persistent tick permeated the quiet room.

"Up. First step…second…third. With each step

you feel stronger, you feel very good, alert; your arms and legs feel life and energy. Fourth, fifth. You remember everything you've seen and feel great joy and comfort. Sixth step, seventh. You feel more and more energetic, refreshed. Eighth step. You feel your body wanting to stir. Ninth step. Tenth. Open your eyes, Amanda."

Amanda opened her eyes and Mark's features floated into clear focus.

He knelt on one knee beside her chair and laid a hand on her cheek. "How do you feel?"

She touched his chin, surprised at his concern. "I'm fine. Don't be so serious. It was incredibly beautiful." Amanda inhaled deeply and scanned the room. "I feel great." Raising her shoulders and grinning, she added, "Fantastic."

Mary closed her binder and pushed her glasses down her nose. "I'll go make some tea. Would you two like wine, or something?"

"I'll pour drinks for Mark and me."

* * * *

The three sat around the small kitchen table, Amanda drinking white Merlot; Mark, his usual Irish whiskey.

"You were very peaceful," said Mark.

"It was incredible. I saw my mother. She was sitting on her bed with a pile of laundry in front of her. I actually…" Amanda spread her palms on the table. "She smiled at me!"

Mary lowered a teaspoon of sugar into her tea.

94

"Tell me, what is the lesson to be learned from this experience?"

Amanda stared at Mary, then gazed into her wine. "I don't know. Guess I don't think of that type of simple domesticity much."

"I suppose not. I can't picture you matching socks, dear. What you witnessed is one of many reasons for regression therapy. Ever since your mother died, you've dwelt on why and how she died, and not on fonder memories. You likely witnessed her folding laundry as a child, a happy time. Your subconscious is telling you to dig out these good memories. You've lovely memories of Connor and your father, too." Maintaining eye contact with Amanda she added, "And Joe."

Amanda looked back at her wine and raised the glass to her lips.

Mary's voice became stern. "Now, the reason this session was cut short."

"What'd I do?"

"Before the session, I told you to obey the voice of your guide without question."

Mark took a sip of whiskey. "You failed to respond to a direct question." He smiled at Amanda. "Mary was pretty clear about the rules. You were supposed to answer."

"I asked about your mother. I asked twice. You didn't answer. Normally, the first regression session would have you travel further on your journey. Failure to respond to your guide is the reason I directed you back. It's an indication to me that you aren't fully in control of your actions, reactions."

"I don't remember."

"I was trying to get you to describe details. Do you remember what your mother looked like, how she was dressed?"

She stared at the watch pinned on Mary's shirt. "Mom was wearing a red blouse and her hair was up in a French braid. She had my locket on." Amanda frowned. "But there seemed to be a dim white around the edges of the room, like the fog on a bathroom mirror. But only on the edges."

"Did you feel threatened?"

"No. I was curious."

"Your lack of response is no problem this time, dear. It will, however, keep sessions short until you get into the swing of it. With that, your shrink is going to call it a night."

Amanda walked Mary to the door, leaned forward for a peck on the cheek.

"Think about what you have learned, dear. We'll do this again in a few days."

* * * *

Mark studied Amanda's CD collection as he said, "She's a wonder."

Amanda turned at Mark's words; the way he said them told her he was thinking of something else.

Mark made selections and slipped several discs into the stereo. The haunting strains of the Strauss waltz from *der Rosenkavalier* floated through the room.

Amanda walked up to the clock and gazed at the

ivory face. "She sort of pulls stuff out of you. Guess that's a skill that comes with her profession." She turned and said, "I think you'd be good at it, Mark."

He stared into his drink. "Maybe someday."

Amanda turned the lever activating the chimes, and closed the clock door. "You should go back to school."

"Maybe someday."

He had walked up behind her, and Amanda turned at his voice, splashing wine on his shirt. "Damn, I'm sorry!"

Mark took her glass and leaned into her as he set it on the table behind her. He turned his face toward hers as he straightened, nearly touching her lips with his, but hesitating as he raised his eyes to hers. He slid a hand down her arm. "You like to dance?"

Amanda inched back as he held her hand. "I don't know how."

Mark put his other hand on her waist. "Look at me; don't look down."

His toe tapped hers as he winked. "The man's in charge, he leads. I'm going to move toward you as you step back, your foot and mine moving as one. Shift your weight to that foot at the same time that you slide your left foot to the left." His fingers tugged her toward him as he said, "Move toward me when you feel pressure from my hand." He pointed two fingers at her eyes, then to his. "Keep your eyes on mine and you'll instinctively use the correct foot. Don't think; just keep your eyes on mine."

Amanda felt his hand move to the small of her back. Mark smiled as he stepped forward and they began to glide around the room.

"You're a good student."

"I guess." She laughed and looked down.

Mark chuckled and raised her chin with a finger. "Keep looking at me."

They stopped as she met his eyes, feeling her heart skip. His twinkle of laughter changed to a serious gaze, the muscles in his jaw flexed. "You're a lovely woman."

Heat rose to her face at his words and his touch.

He stroked her cheek and whispered, "Very lovely." Mark pressed his lips to hers and Amanda's pulse soared as he pulled her close.

Breathlessly, she extracted herself from his hold and stepped back. *What is it about him? Everything about him is so familiar, his touch, his kiss…how do I know him?* "Mark, I—"

"I'm not going to push you into anything you don't want." He slipped his hands into his pockets.

Mark walked across the room to a chair, picked up his jacket, and laid it over his arm. His car keys dangled from his pinky finger. He moved toward Amanda, his eyes penetrating. "But for some goddamned reason, I know you."

Bristling, Amanda thrust her chin. "I haven't led you on."

Mark's eyes narrowed as he tipped his head. "Led me on?"

"No. No, I haven't." She wavered and reached for the silver locket.

"No Amanda, you haven't led me on." He slowly shook his head. "I simply morph into goddamned smoke and appear at a woman's side like a phantom all the time. It's an everyday thing for me, a source of amusement."

Defensive and uncertain, Amanda pointed to the door. "You should probably go."

Mark stepped toward her. "How in the hell could this be anything other than us knowing each other, and quite well?"

Her heart thrummed at his husky baritone voice and severe expression. "I think you'd better—"

"Did I love you once?" Mark pulled Amanda roughly against him with an expression of fierce resolve. Amanda's pulse pounded as Mark's strong hands held her to him and he kissed her with furious passion. The flaming determination in his gaze belied the tenderness of his voice. "Based on the way I feel now, yes." He kissed her again, a whispered caress of gentle warmth. "Yes, *mo mhuirnín*."

Amanda pushed herself free, struggling to breathe as her heart hammered, but the intense conviction in Mark's eyes silenced her denial. *He can't mean what he says. He just can't!*

Mark walked to the door, opened it, and turned to her. "I've told you I'm not leaving you, and I'm not. I'll wait for you to come to me, for as long as it takes. I've the feeling I've waited before."

Amanda's heart continued to pound as she stared at the closed door. The old clock began the distant song of St. Michael's chimes.

Yesterday

CHAPTER 9

Mary watched Amanda wander around the living room, pensively finger this, straighten that. "You're squirming like a worm on a hook inches from a trout, dear."

Amanda laughed and looked around the room, settling her eyes on Mary. "I am not. Where do you come up with those silly sayings?"

"Twisted mind."

Scooping Oprah into her arms, Amanda plopped onto the sofa, and nuzzled her chin into silky fur.

"He the problem?"

"There is no problem." Amanda met Mary's gaze and added, "You think you're so smart."

"You're an open book."

She glared at the response. Pouring Oprah to the floor as she stood, Amanda walked to the wine rack and waved a bottle of Cabernet. "You?"

"No. But I will have another Earl Grey." They went to the kitchen and Mary pressed. "So. How was it?"

Amanda fumbled with a corkscrew, twisting it into the bottle. "There was no 'it'. He was a perfect gentleman."

The door buzzed as Mary peered over her glasses with a knowing glint. "Too bad."

"Let him in, would you? I'm going to the bathroom for a sec."

Mary walked to the front hall, threw the deadbolt, and swung the door wide.

Mark's eyes scanned over her head as he handed over a bottle of wine, a fifth of Irish whiskey tucked under his arm. "Hi."

Mary leaned her head back and peered up at him through the bottom of her bifocals. "Her claws are retracted, dear. She's in the bathroom."

"Oh." He swallowed.

She closed the door and lightly touched his arm. "Play the chimes on the stereo tonight. Start it low when I indicate, gradually increase the volume, but follow my lead. You'll see when I want you to stop or turn it down. We're going to bring her back further, hopefully."

"You sure it's a good—"

"She'll be fine." Mary waved her hand, dismissing his concerns.

* * * *

Amanda leaned her head back against the bathroom door, arms and ankles crossed, eyes closed. *Why does Mary want him in these sessions now? She didn't before, not at all. I call him one time in two weeks, and you'd think I'd handed him the moon. Why didn't he just get pissed and go away? Maybe I can get rid of the damn clock, send him on his way, put an end to all this. It's nuts. I'm nuts. Maybe we did meet in a karaoke bar...or something. We must have.*

She pinched the bridge of her nose and ran her

102

fingers over the tiny scar on her forehead. Images of that day, and the days since, scattered like the windswept leaves of fall. She splashed cold water on her face, leaned on her hands, rivulets of water dripping from her chin. Tendrils of dark chestnut hair stuck to her pale, damp cheek. *You idiot! Mark's a nice guy, but you treat him like crap. He scares the hell out of you. Why? You want to trust him. Why? You feel sure you know him. How? Think! Tick...tick...shit...tick...tick...tick...shit!*

Knuckles rapped on the door. "Fall in, dear?"

Heaving a sigh, she reached for a hand towel. "No, silly. Be right out."

* * * *

Amanda walked into the kitchen, avoiding eye contact. "Hi, Mark."

"Hi." He sipped coffee, his eyes on Amanda's stoic expression as she poured herself a cup of tea. *Maybe I should have worn riot gear.*

Mary glanced from Amanda to him and then winked. "I'll be in the living room getting the ball rolling."

Mark watched her walk down the hall. "I tried to call."

"Forget it."

He set his mug down, turned Amanda to face him and met her narrowed eyes. He slowly moved toward her, backing her up with each step.

"What are you doing?"

"It seems the best way to get your attention is to

103

position you so you can't escape."

"Well, cut it out."

Her back met the kitchen counter, and he quickly grabbed her by the waist and lifted her to a seat on the counter in front of him.

"Mark! *Dammit!*" She pushed against him and maneuvered to get down.

He put one hand on the counter, fisted the other on his hip, and leaned against her knees. "You might as well quit wiggling because you're not going anywhere."

Amanda shouted over his shoulder. "Mary? I'm ready! You?" She glared at Mark with a so-there sneer. A flush rose to her cheeks, eliciting a half-smile from Mark. "Mary!"

A cheerful voice lilted from the front of the apartment. "Take your time, children, no rush. Be right back. I'm just taking Oprah upstairs."

"You know, you are a stunner when you're pissed, cute as hell. In fact, the pisster off..." He touched an index finger to his lips and mumbled, "Is that a word?" Mark shook his head. "Don't think so."

Amanda struggled against him, trying to move him back. "Let me down, you idiot."

He laughed and slid her back on the countertop. "In a minute."

"You let me down right now, or I'm going to..." She paused.

He crossed his arms and raised both eyebrows. "Sounds intriguing."

Defeated, she slumped back and folded her arms.

"You are a beauty." Mark shook his head at her angry scowl.

His face and posture straightened as he touched his fingers to the counter on each side of her and lowered his eyes. "Listen to me. I'm sorry. I scared the hell out of you the other night when I kissed you." Mark met her gaze. "I haven't slept a wink since." He softened his voice. "I had no right to do that. I was as pissed as you look right now." Mark pursed his lips and sighed deeply. "Which would easily open an oyster at fifty feet. You could chew glass. Spit rivets, bite the ass off a Pontiac, maybe do a three-sixty with your head and puke pea soup, or—"

"Okay!" Amanda fought a smile, shook her head, and held up her hands. "Okay, that's enough. We're good. Let me down."

Mark gently placed hands on each side of her face. "You sure?"

"You clown."

He kissed her nose, lightly touched his lips to hers. "Clown works."

Mark lowered his arms to his sides. He studied her, wondering what was going on behind those eyes. "You gonna let me give you more dancing lessons?"

Amanda smiled as she touched his chin with her fingers. "Yeah, I'd like that."

"You really want to do this regression?"

She nodded.

Mark pulled her close and breathed in her heady scent as he kissed her. "You don't have to,

105

sweetheart."

Amanda met his eyes. "Yeah, I do."

* * * *

Mary glanced at Amanda above her bifocals and scribbled in her binder. "Okay, we're doing the exact same thing we did before. You comfortable?"

"Yep."

"Here we go. Deep breathing, long and relaxing. Watch the pendulum. Don't stare at it, just watch the motion, breathe and relax."

Mary guided her through the process as before. Amanda's face was peaceful, her voice clear. She was responsive and calm.

"All right, dear. Walk slowly toward the blue mist. Don't hurry. Glance at the doors you pass. Open a door, if you wish. The mist is welcoming. You're drawn to it. Move into its lovely color."

Mary looked at Mark and nodded once. The quiet tones of St. Michael's chimes filled the room, the sound distant, soft, and low.

Amanda's head rested on the chair cushion. Mary watched her carefully and signaled Mark to increase the volume of the chimes. Amanda rolled her head to the side and Mary raised a flat palm. The volume was still low, but loud enough.

Amanda drifted into blue mist toward the enveloping warmth of distant bells…

CHAPTER 10

Charleston, South Carolina — 1862

Bats fluttered from louvered slats as the bells tolled nine o'clock. Bonnie pushed sweat-dampened tendrils of dark curls from her eyes and looked up at the towering steeple. The setting sun tinted the white paint orange-red against a deep azure sky. The looming belfry dwarfed the live oaks in the churchyard.

"What are you looking at now, Amanda?"

"A church."

"You know somethin'?"

Bonnie glanced at Jack's profile and stretched to touch her toes on the wide pine boards of the porch floor. The swing creaked.

He tugged at the collar of his white shirt. "When they ring those bells again, this war will be over."

"Papa said it wasn't over yet." Curling the black ribbons of her bonnet around her finger, she studied the tower. "The bells'll ring tomorrow morning 'cause they always do. You're silly."

"Nope."

"They will so."

"You know what they do to church bells like those?"

Bonnie shook her head.

"They melt 'em down."

107

She turned to him, startled. "Who?" Bonnie frowned at the soaring steeple. "How can they do that?"

"I dunno how. The soldiers, they melt 'em down to soup. And make 'em into stuff they need, like cannons and muskets and things. They don't need no church bells."

"You're making this up. They can't do that."

"Your pa says they can. And he's gonna see it don't happen to these."

Stopping the swing, Bonnie looked at Jack, her eyes starting to tear. *There are so many soldiers in town. Maybe what Jack's saying is true.* "Papa'll get in trouble. And they're not gonna hurt our bells anyway."

Jack pushed himself from the swing and walked across the porch, slapping a mosquito on his ear. "Don't start bawlin'. He won't get in no trouble. But the soldiers are gonna take the bells." Jack turned to her and hitched up his britches. "Your pa won't get in no trouble," he said again. He pushed up the canvas brim of his hat and whispered, "Everything's fixed. They're gonna hide 'em about sixty miles north of here, on an abandoned plantation."

"You're gonna get in trouble listening in like that. Magdalene will catch you again, and pinch you 'til you cry. Besides, they can't do that, 'cause the bells are too big."

"Amanda, who is with you?"

"Cousin Jack."

A lumbering dray drawn by two emaciated oxen rattled down Meeting Street. Wooden wheels rolled on broken cobblestone, *rat-a-tat-a-clatter-tat*. Hooves kicked up swirls of orange dust. Jack and Bonnie waved at the driver, Ben. He returned their wave with a broad smile.

"Well, they got it figured out. They're gonna use a big wagon just like that one." Jack added with an excited whisper, "Tonight! And the only way I find somethin' out is when they think I can't hear 'em. Come on."

He grabbed Bonnie's hand and they ran down the porch steps. She stumbled to keep up as they raced across the road into the shelter of thick bushes with red flowers at the side of the church.

"Shhh." Jack pushed her shoulders back against wood siding, excited mischief in his brown eyes.

Bonnie grabbed bouffant wads of skirt and gave him a disapproving glare. "We're supposed to stay on the porch. It's almost dark."

Jack bent at the waist to make their eyes level. With a finger held to his lips, he said, "Shhh." He squinted through the darkness to his left, then right. "We're gonna see if that's the wagon they're fixin' to use."

He pressed his back against the building, looked right, over her head. "Come on."

They sidled along the wall. Bonnie tapped a toe on the flinty red soil beneath the bushes and whispered, "I can't see where we're going. There better not be any worms in here."

"Shhh. Just follow me. All the worms are sleepin'."

Jack stopped at the end of the building and

crouched down. "Look."

Bonnie scrunched her way between him and the building, and followed his eyes to the heavy wagon, now behind the church. She inhaled sharply. "That's my—"

"Bonnie, I know! Shh!" Jack pulled Bonnie back against him, his hand tightly over her mouth.

"Who do you see, Amanda?"

"Papa."

She shook her head to release his hand and whispered, "Let me see, Jack. I'll be quiet."

They scooched back and peeked around the corner of the building, the conversation among the four men muffled.

Bonnie's Pa, John, handed a piece of canvas up to Ben in the wagon, saying, "We need to cover those bells, or we won't get five miles with them." Ben was their Negro foreman. That's what everybody said he was. Bonnie simply thought of him as Ben. He let her watch when he carved little animals out of sticks. Ben was the biggest man she ever saw. She thought of the beautiful plantation party when Magdalene married Ben and jumped over a broom.

John pushed the brim of his hat up with an index finger. "It'll take more than one trip to get them all."

"We gots help." Ben's voice was soft, low. "It'll get done, suh."

Bonnie and Jack turned at the sound of footsteps and made themselves as small as possible. She whispered, "Who are those men?"

"Jumpin'…there's six more of 'em." Jack peered

through the darkness. "Guess that makes sense 'cause there's lots 'a bells." He glanced at Bonnie. "I think they're gonna help your Pa."

John put an elbow up on the side of the big wagon, and scratched a match on the heel of his boot. He puffed on an ivory pipe, embers glowing in the dusk. The sweet, woodsy smell of pipe smoke drifted toward Bonnie and Jack. John shook the match to extinguish it as he said, "You know the big bell weighs in at close to two thousand pounds."

"Michael's less'n dat. Not much, but he ain't no two thousan' pound." Ben raised a hand in greeting to the approaching men.

"Michael?"

Ben sat on the back of the wagon, dangled one foot. "I tells ya 'bout 'em, suh, if'n I kin git a chaw." He pulled the other leg up and rested an arm on a knee.

John chuckled, tossed Ben his leather tobacco pouch, and nodded to the men. "Thanks for coming out. These bells are heavy and I appreciate your being here. Help yourselves to the pouch."

The group of men nodded and shook hands around. Two of the men carried huge wooden pulleys they leaned on the wagon. Two others carried rope as big around as Bonnie's waist. They dropped the rope on the dirt, throwing up swirls of rusty dust.

Ben stuffed a wad of tobacco deep in his cheek and leaned on the wagon rail facing John. He waited until he was certain he had everyone's attention. In a quiet voice, he began the tale of St. Michael's chimes.

"Dem ain't bells. Dey's angels."

"Mmm. You don't say." John blew out a long plume of smoke. He looked down at his scuffed boots and swished talcum-fine red dirt with his toe.

Bonnie and Jack glanced at each other and then back to the shadowed faces. They settled quietly into the bushes, Bonnie snuggled under Jack's arm.

"Where are you, Amanda?"

"Hiding, with Jack."

"Smallest angel we got's a Seraphim." Ben looked around the group and shrugged. "Smallest bell we got's a Seraphim. But dey's de highest, biggest angels dey is. Flies 'round, locked up in a song. Dem bells sings, dey sings like...well, dey sings like angels. And we gots one." He nodded toward the church. "We gots a Cherubim." Ben spit over his shoulder. "Nex' angel is a Cherubim."

John grinned and shook his head. "You're telling me each bell, each one, is an angel?"

"Yup. And the nex' is a Thrones."

"Okay. Far be it from me to argue." John pointed his pipe stem at Ben and laughed. "They sing, too?"

Ben frowned and tipped his head to the side. "S'pose dey do, 'cause dey's angels." His eyes widened. "Dey does more'n jus' singin', though. Cherubims is de Lord's mean 'ol dogs, His guards of paradise. Dey stands at dem gates and checks evvabody out. Now Thrones, dey's kinda, dey's de thinkers. Dey thinks." He spat. "An' sings. We gots one of dem."

Several of the men looked at each other and then

back to Ben. "We gots a Dominion, too. Dey conducts." Ben rolled his eyes at the puzzled faces. "Dem angels all needs one leader, all dat singin', so de Dominion be doin' the conductin'. An' we gots a Virtue angel."

"Hold it." John rubbed his hand over his mouth, his eyes glinting with laughter. "Don't tell me a bunch of angels needs one that specializes in virtue. Where'd you hear all this, anyway?"

"Mah mammy tol' me, an' her mammy tol' her." Ben straightened, puffed out his barrel chest with pride. "Dat's a fact. You kin fine bells in any ol' church. But in St. Michael's Church, dem bells is angels, all eight of 'em, angels."

John knocked the bowl of his pipe on the spoke of a wagon wheel, scattering fireflies of ash. "You'll have to tell us about the rest of the angels later." He glanced at the corner of the church. "You fellas get started. I'll be back directly." He put the pipe in his shirt pocket, hooked his thumbs in embroidered braces, and sauntered toward Bonnie and Jack.

Jack plastered his back against the wall of the church. "Damn."

Bonnie covered her mouth. She looked up at him. "Jack, you said a swear!" She struggled to her feet and took a step toward her father as he dropped to one knee in front of her.

Papa tugged a ribbon on her bonnet, untying the bow, and pulled the bonnet into his hand. He looked up with a half smile and tickled her chin. "What are you doing out here, little one?"

Bonnie looked at Jack and back to her father.

113

"Nothin'."

"Nothing?"

"We, me and Jack. I mean, Jack and I. We were listening about the angel bells."

An ominous bellow emanated from the direction of the house. "Bonnie May Belle Lexington! Jaaacksonn! You two come in heah dis very minute! Bonnie May! Where you at, li'l girl?"

The two children turned to the sound of Magdalene's angry voice.

Bonnie looked back at her father; suddenly struggling to keep her eyes dry, and felt her heart thrum. "Magdalene said to stay on the porch and I, and we…"

Jack sheepishly stepped up behind Bonnie, pulled off his hat, and fingered the brim. "It's my fault, sir. Bonnie came…I made her come here with me."

John pulled Bonnie to him and kissed her cheek. He lifted her in his arms as he stood and whispered in her ear. "It's all right, baby."

"Papa, I'm not a baby!" Bonnie put her arms and legs around him. "I'm too big to be a baby!"

With long, easy strides, John carried her around the church toward the street. "Yep, and you're heavy as a big sack of flour," he teased. "But someday soon Papa won't be able to heft his little girl at all." He rubbed his bristled face into her neck and she fought a giggle. "So for now I will."

John raised his voice. "They're with me, Magdalene." He winked down at Jack as he called out, "Forgot to tell you."

* * * *

Magdalene lifted the black and white silk dress over Bonnie's head. "Bonnie May Belle, dis here dress is yo' Sunday best. Jes' you take a look at it now." She lowered her lean backside onto a wooden chair that protested with a creak. Magdalene shook her head at the dress and puffed out an exasperated sigh. "I'll be scrubbin' out dat dirt fo' a day at leas'."

Bonnie frowned defiantly at the dress and grumbled, "I hate it. I hate these old petticoats. I want my overalls back."

"And what are you doing now, Amanda?"

"I hate the dress."

Magdalene huffed and put her hands on her hips. "Now, Bonnie May Belle, why wouldn't a pretty lil' gal lack you want to be wearin' dis nice dress?"

Bonnie crossed her thin arms. "Because I can't do anything in it. I can't climb over the fence in the back, can't get up Jack's tree. I gotta learn a whole new way to ride on Ben's horse."

Magdalene put a slender hand on each side of Bonnie's face, squishing cheeks together, making her mouth pucker. "But you's a lil' lady, now, Bonnie May. You gots t' do things a li'l different."

Bonnie studied Magdalene's kind brown eyes. "Make Jack wear a dress, too." Her face blossomed to a grin at the idea of Jack in a dress.

"You's a silly li'l gal. I s'pose we might could stuff 'm into one. But it'd likely be like puttin' a mad dog in dat thunder jug. Now, get out o' dem

115

petticoats and put on yo' nightgown."

Bonnie jumped into her canopied bed and Magdalene hovered over her, pulling up the soft woolen coverlets and tucking them around her tiny frame. "Magdalene?"

Magdalene leaned toward the oil lamp. "What, sugah?"

"Are the church bells angels?"

Magdalene's big brown eyes twinkled as she sat down next to her on the featherbed. "Why, dey sho'ly is, li'l gal. Ain't you heard dem angels singin'?"

Bonnie turned and stared up at the gauzy canopy, her brow wrinkled. She looked back at Magdalene. "I guess I have."

"Well den, dere you go." Magdalene pushed herself up and turned off the oil lamp. She walked quietly around the bed and dropped gossamer netting from the canopy.

Bonnie turned on her side, listening to a frog's plaintive song. A cicada buzz soared, softened, and vanished. Crickets chirped. Sleep pulled her eyes closed to a distant *rat-a-tat-a-clatter-tat* of wagon wheels on cobblestone.

* * * *

"Okay, Amanda, you've reached the ninth step, one more."

Amanda stretched and opened her eyes.

"How do you feel?"

Amanda closed her eyes again, covered her face

116

with her hands and pulled them down to her chin. Mark walked toward her from a shadow in the room and she answered, "Great. Like I just had a nap. I feel fine."

"Good." Mary glanced at Mark. "We need to have a post-session discussion as soon as you're ready. I'll be out in the kitchen."

* * * *

Amanda pushed the footrest down on the lounge chair and bent over, rubbing her eyes fully awake. "Did I say anything wrong this time, Mark?"

He chuckled as he reached for her hand. "Not at all, if you think that church bells are really angels in disguise." Mark pulled her up quickly into his arms. "Are you really feeling all right?" He looked down at her startled expression.

"Yeah, I'm good. We should…"

Mark silenced her with a gentle kiss, rubbed his hands on her back as he held her gaze. "Yeah."

Yesterday

CHAPTER 11

Amanda set a rocks glass of whiskey in front of Mark. He flipped through a small notebook, a pen behind his ear. She sat opposite him and sipped her wine.

Mary opened her binder. "Amanda, do you believe you were once a child named Bonnie?"

Amanda didn't expect the question, at least not yet. She was having trouble absorbing the idea herself. Stalling for time, Amanda took another sip, set the glass on the table, and glanced at Mark. He waited for her to speak.

"I think that's true, yes." She looked at Mary and added, "Let me put it this way: That didn't feel like a dream. I felt the way I do when I remember things from my own childhood. If I can have the memories of this Bonnie, then I think I must have lived her life once."

Mark rose from his seat, went across the kitchen and leaned back on the counter. He gazed thoughtfully at the floor.

Looking at her binder Mary asked, "How old is Bonnie?"

"I'm not sure. I'm…Bonnie's very small, so I imagine she's young."

Mark said, "You must be small, your father carried you on his hip."

"What about Jack, dear. Is he taller, older than

119

Bonnie?"

Amanda nodded. "Taller, he's taller." She frowned and added, "But I think he's pretty small, too. Jack looked up at Papa. I mean, Bonnie's father."

"Tell me what you remember about the church." Mary wrote in her binder in rapid, graceful shorthand.

"Why do you do that when you have the session recorded?"

"Helps me think. Besides, these words are like hieroglyphics," she smiled, "mysterious."

Amanda shrugged. "Well, it was tall, I mean, the steeple was tall, and it was white, with those arched louvers, like steeples have. There was a round black clock face, a gold spindly thing at the very top."

Mark's voice was quiet. "Could you draw a picture?"

"Yeah, I think so."

"Good, let's see what you can tell us with a picture." Mary lifted a blank page from her binder and slid it across the table. She tossed her pencil on the table toward Amanda and retrieved another from the binder pocket. "And the church tower, it chimed?"

Amanda bent over the paper and started to draw as she said, "Yeah, sort of, it tolled. The same music as my clock."

Mark stood behind Amanda's chair and watched the detailed image of a pretty church evolve. "You saw all that in one brief glimpse tonight? It looks like you've known that building your whole life." He frowned and looked closely at the picture. "What is that you have falling from the trees?"

Concentrating on the drawing, Amanda said, "There's nothing falling from the trees. Moss is drooping from the limbs."

He looked at Mary. "Trees in the deep South have Spanish moss on the limbs."

"Think. There are many clues in this session. Oxen hauled a wagon that swirled up rusty dust. Soldiers confiscated church bells for cannon and muskets. With only a small bit of information, red dirt and armaments," Mary nodded at the drawing, "and moss hanging from trees…location and era are apparent."

Mark and Amanda shared a glance as Mary stood and walked to the kitchen sink.

He looked back at the picture and muttered, "The Civil War?"

Mary filled her mug with water and placed it in the microwave. "You mentioned a woman named Magdalene. Was Magdalene Bonnie's mother?"

"No, Magdalene was a black woman." She knit her brows and said quietly, "I know one thing for sure. Bonnie loved Magdalene a great deal. I don't know where my mother was, I mean, Bonnie's mother." She shook her head and returned to the drawing of the church.

Mary sat back down with a fresh mug of Earl Grey. "Bonnie being taken care of by a black woman is more evidence of the Civil War." She slowly swirled a spoon through her tea. "My guess is that Bonnie and Jack were children somewhere in the southern states during the Civil War, and Magdalene was a nanny to the children. She could have been a slave, most likely was."

Mary took Amanda through the entire regression, reviewing each statement, each vision. Under her concise, professional questioning, she laid out and examined every possible detail of the session. An hour later, Amanda rubbed her temples and squeezed her eyes closed. "We're done for now, right?"

"I'd say we've pulled everything we can from this session." Mary closed her binder. "Besides, you're looking kind of wrung-out." She took off her glasses and pinched the bridge of her nose. "I think you've pretty well worn out the shrink, too." Mary rose and bent down to Amanda, pointing a slender finger at her own cheek. "Plant one on me, dear."

Amanda laughed and kissed her cheek. "I'll be up to get Oprah in a minute."

Mark raised his glass to her. "Later."

Mary quietly closed the door as she left. Amanda and Mark looked at each other for several seconds. He walked to the table and pulled out a chair next to her, sat down, and rested an arm on the table. "Do you have any idea how many St. Michael's churches there would have been during the Civil War? Don't answer, me either."

"Guess we didn't really learn much."

"Well, I never heard of the angel bells thing. That's a new one on me." He set his drink on the table and linked fingers behind his neck. "Not sure I know how to start researching that. I bet we can find something about the shortages of iron in the South during the Civil War. But the melting down of church bells into artillery? Churches that hid their bells? Wow." Mark shook his head. "Wonder where that's been documented, by the North or the South. There have to be records."

Amanda stifled a yawn. "I think Mary would accuse you of picking fly shit out of pepper." Through his laughter she said, "I never heard of that before, but it makes sense. There wasn't any heavy industry in the South. They would have had to use whatever metal they already had on hand, even church bells. All they had was cotton." Amanda shrugged and added, "Cotton and slaves."

Mark sighed and pulled her up by the hand as he stood. "I'm outta here; it's late." They walked to the door as he said, "Will I get to meet your brother and his wife tomorrow? They still coming to the Grant Park concert?"

"Yep."

He leaned to kiss her, paused as she fought another yawn. Mark smiled and kissed her cheek. "See you then."

* * * *

"Are you shittin' me?" Pete removed his wrap-around sunglasses and stared at Mark.

Mark met Pete's eyes for a moment before turning a watchful gaze back to the peaceful crowd in Grant Park.

"You actually believe in that New Age crap?"

Pete dropped his shades into a saddlebag.

"A few billion people do. Not sure 'crap' is the right word." Boomerang's ears twitched forward in response to a pat on his neck. "The idea's been around as long as the damn human race." Mark lightly tapped stirruped boots and his horse obediently moved forward.

Pete's horse farted a low organ chord. "You tell 'im, Doofus." Pete turned to Mark. "Doofus just confided to me that you're loonier than hell and outta your fuckin' mind."

"All that?" Mark chuckled. "Well, you tell Doofus I appreciate his opinion. Any horse that can carry on a conversation with you is okay in my book."

Each Chicago Mounted Policeman is considered to be the equivalent of ten policemen on foot. They are trained to represent their city to the world, control crowds, and be diplomatic mediators in any situation. Mark and Pete rocked lazily on their horses as they traveled through the park prepared to fulfill these roles, and more.

Chicagoans refer to Grant Park as their front yard. Sailboats, dinner cruises, and occasional tall ships sprinkle the lake. Flowerbeds of colorful summer dahlias, daisies, and geraniums bloom profusely everywhere. Strategically placed statues and stone fountains serve as testament to a collective city pride. Seeming to stand guard over famed Buckingham Fountain, are two bronze warriors, the Spearman and Bowman, astride massive horses.

Even if a quarter of a million people stand shoulder-to-shoulder and listen to a president-elect or a few thousand screaming teenagers gyrate to a rock band, there is rarely disorder in the park. On this day, a staid group of classical music lovers picnicked on wine and cheese as they waited for a Chicago Symphony Orchestra concert. And, typical of mid-summer Chicago, it was blisteringly hot.

Pete grinned at a little girl, about four years old. With eyes as big and round as morning glories, she stared at his horse. Pete leaned back in the saddle to bring Doofus to a stop, and angled the horse toward the towheaded moppet. Her pink cheeks dimpled with busy thumb-sucking as she gazed at the horse, up at Pete, and then back at the horse. Pete reached into his saddlebag, retrieved a red lollipop from his stash, and held it out at arm's length to the child.

Mark smiled at the incongruous Norman Rockwell image as he leaned forward in the saddle to pat Boomerang. *Who would believe a little kid could turn my caustic bastard of a partner into a pussycat?* A woman holding an apple swept up the child and walked toward Pete, whispering to the girl.

Pete brought an index finger to his helmet in an old fashioned tip-of-the-hat to the little girl's mother. In an apologetic tone he said, "Sorry ma'am. The horse can't take the apple, though he'd love it. There's a bit in his mouth right now."

The woman took a step back and said, "Oh, sorry."

"He'll eat it later though, if I don't munch on it

125

first." Pete held down his hand, and the little girl gave him the apple. Pete again extended the lollipop.

The officers laughed as the child nuzzled her face into her mother's neck and the woman stepped back into a large group.

Mark pulled the reins of his horse to a turn. "Did that little girl just tell you to take a hike? I'm afraid you're losing your touch with the ladies, pal."

Pete eyed the lollipop in his gloved hand, shrugged, and stuck it in his mouth. "Which girl? The one with the apple or the one with the pair?"

"It's an apple." Mark looked over his shoulder at the bursting spandex tank top on the woman holding the child. He glanced at Pete's raised eyebrows and said with a roaring laugh, "You putz."

Pete looked around the park and stretched as he stood in his stirrups. "Okay, where they be at, Officer Friendly?"

Mark scanned the crowd and nodded in the direction of a small group. "By the band shell. I've never met Amanda's brother and his family, but that's her, sitting on the blanket."

Pete followed his eyes. "She ever tell ya her brother's name?"

"Tom. His wife is Connie. Tom and Connie Parker. The boys are Ron and Tru, and the little one is Allie, I think."

"What'd ya say we go see if Connie knew me in a previous life?"

Mark inhaled deeply and looked askance at Pete. "Keep your goddamn trap shut, you idiot."

Grinning, Pete looked back at the small group and said his next words with an exaggerated lilt. "I'd be beggin' on me knees for the colleen in the sunhat, me boyo…"

"There's plenty 'a skin in this park, knucklehead. Pick another one."

The men eased the horses through the crowd. Ever wary of disturbance, both repeatedly glanced over the gathering. Faces turned toward them, children and adults alike stared at the horses, smiles widened. The officers paused frequently, obliging curiosity, spreading the good will of the Chicago Police Department.

* * * *

Amanda sat next to Connie on the huge Cubs blanket spread on the lawn. Tom and Mary perched in folding chairs. 'Munchkin,' a moniker hung on Allie by her father, was sound asleep in Mary's lap. The boys hovered over a game of backgammon, iPods plugged in their ears. Mary seemed to be studying the game intently, and Tom's nose was buried in the latest espionage novel.

Connie looked at the two mounted officers and whispered, "Which one of them is yours?"

Amanda reddened. "Neither is 'mine', Connie." She looked into her clear plastic glass of pink lemonade. "The taller one."

Connie feigned a swoon, fanning her hand. "Jeez! He's gorgeous. Tall, dark, an' handsome hunk a' man. He have a brother half as sexy lookin'

127

for me?"

Without raising his eyes from the book, Tom grumbled, "I heard that."

"Quit eavesdropping." Amanda winked at Connie's grin.

Tom closed his book with a sigh and glanced up at the approaching cops. He peered around the crowd, settling his gaze on a group of scantily clad girls. "Okie-doke. It's getting too dark to read. I'll take in my own scenery while you two damsels enjoy yourselves."

Connie playfully touched an ice-cold can of soda to his calf. He jumped and she laughed at his growl. Scrambling to her feet, she evaded his grasp. "Look all you want. Anything else, I'll hurt you." Connie extended a hand to Amanda. "I promise not to flirt with yours."

Amanda stood as the officers approached, the wide brim of her floppy straw sunhat rippling in a breeze off the lake. She adjusted her red tube top and denim shorts and slipped into her camel-colored leather sandals.

* * * *

Mark reined in Boomerang, took off his helmet, and placed it on the baton that hung from his saddle. "Hi, Amanda."

He glanced at Mary, puzzled that she kept looking down at the boys' backgammon board. He was vaguely disappointed when she didn't greet him with the expected tart comment, or look up at his arrival. The boys grinned and stared at the horses.

Amanda swept her hand toward her brother's family. "Mark Callahan, meet the Parker clan. This is Connie, and Tom's my baby brother. Those handsome lady-killers are Truman and Ronald. Mary's got the munchkin, Allie."

Mark smiled at Connie. Tom walked toward him, hand reaching up.

Shaking Tom's hand, Mark said, "Good to meet you, Tom. Amanda lights up when she speaks of you and Connie." He winked at the boys, "And you two."

He twisted in his saddle and said, "This is my partner, Pete Mahoney."

Pete nodded and grinned.

Mark lingered on Amanda's dazzling smile that widened with his own.

He looked again at Mary, and squinted concern. "Mary?" Mark tipped his head and repeated, "Mary?" *She's not watching the game. Something's wrong with her.* He swung from the saddle, reaching Mary's side in two long strides. He shook her shoulder, lifted the baby from her lap, and passed the infant to Connie. "Pete, 11-41, 10-45 Charlie."

Pete spoke into his radio and with practiced moves, began to back picnickers across the lawn away from the immediate area, his horse effortlessly corralling spectators like peaceful sheep. "Folks, an ambulance will be coming through here in about two minutes. I need everyone to move back, make room. Thank you, that's right, step back. An ambulance will be…"

Mark laid two fingers against Mary's neck as he heard a heart-wrenching cry from Amanda.

"Oh, my God, Mary! No!" She stumbled toward him, frantic. "Mary!" She pushed Connie aside and grabbed Mark's sleeve as she fell to her knees. "What is it? What's wrong?"

Mark pushed her hand away and eased Mary from the lawn chair to the blanket. He grasped Amanda's forearm and looked at her sternly, but spoke in a soft voice. "Amanda, go to your brother. Let me help her."

She shook her head, her terrified eyes pleading. "No, I need her. Please!"

Tom pulled Amanda to her feet. He grabbed her shoulders and forced her to look at him. "Amanda, stop! Let the man work!" Tom put his arm around her and they both turned their anxious faces to Mark. Struggling in Tom's grasp, Amanda choked back tears. "What is it? Mark, please don't let her die."

As he watched Mary's rapid, shallow breathing, Mark placed a hand on her forehead, raised her hand, and pinched the nail bed of her middle finger. *She's pale, but she's always pale.* "It's ninety-five out here and she's sitting in the damned sun," he mumbled, ticking off the reasons for Mary's symptoms in his head. He held her wrist gently to check pulse, and couldn't feel a thing. He pressed two fingers again to her neck. *Christ it's weak, fast. She's hot and dry to the touch.* "Connie, do you have any ice? She needs ice packs." *I'm goin' with heat stroke, but damn, the woman is old. Could be dozens of things.*

Connie raced to the cooler, popped it open, and stared into the box. "What do I put it in? Never mind." She quickly whipped a scarf from her waist and dumped ice cubes into it. Then she emptied the cookies from a small plastic bag and filled that bag with ice, too.

Mark yanked the lawn chair over and lifted Mary's legs to it as he spoke calmly. "Has she been drinking water?"

Connie met Tom's eyes, then those of each boy. "I think. Yes, she drank a bottle of water about an hour ago, maybe."

Ron shyly stepped toward them, holding up a half full bottle of water. "Didn't drink much. She gave it to me."

Mark draped the scarf of ice over Mary's torso and held the plastic bag on her forehead. He met Amanda's frightened eyes. *Fuck. If anything happens to this woman. Someone else for her to lose.*

The siren gave loud, short whoops as the ambulance rolled slowly over the grass toward them. Pete held the sea of curious onlookers at a respectful distance, leaving the passage to Mary clear.

Yesterday

CHAPTER 12

Mark stepped through the revolving door of the hospital main entrance as he lifted his navy blue police jacket from his shoulders and shook off the rain. He stepped into the elevator, put his hands in his pockets, and watched the numbers above the elevator door. *God, I hope Mary's okay. Amanda will really lose it if Mary—* The door chimed as it opened, and Mark raised his hands to prevent a collision with Connie Parker.

"Hey, Mark. Sorry."

"Mary?"

Connie laughed and flapped one hand toward him. "Nothing's gonna hurt that old coot, not anytime soon, anyway. Come on, I'll walk you to her room; it's just down the hall. Amanda and Tom are there. I was just on my way down to Starbuck's to get some lattes."

Mark extended his arm and beckoned her into the elevator. "No, let's go down and get the coffee. I'll help carry." He tapped 'L' for lobby. "So Mary's okay?"

"Her electrolytes were low, which is pretty common in old folks, but a little dehydration tipped her over the edge and she passed out. Made her heart act up. They've got her on an IV and she's perking up already."

"If I know anything about Amanda, Mary won't

133

have a chance to pull that again. She'll be on that like stink on… Sorry."

Connie smiled. "You're crazy about Amanda, aren't you?"

Mark stuck his thumbs in his pockets, leaned back on the elevator wall, and studied his shoes.

"Oh, come on, Mark. Anybody'd be blind not to notice. You can't keep your eyes off of her."

He looked up under his brows. "I'm that transparent?"

Connie nodded in assent. "Oh, yes. And you sure are the man of the hour right now. With my boys, the rest of them up there."

Mark smiled and shook his head. "Just doing my job."

"Job or not, you've got a fan club." She gave him a sly smile. "Amanda included."

They stepped out of the elevator and headed toward the coffee shop. As they neared the counter Mark said, "My treat. But you're in charge of the grande-vanilla-raspberry-carmel-on-the-whip-decaf-triple-shot-extra-hot-latte orders."

Connie giggled. "You think somebody would really order that?"

"Not a doubt in the world." He reached into his hip pocket and pulled out a billfold. "Can I ask you something?"

"Shoot." Connie ran a finger down a penciled list of coffee orders. "But I've got a feeling I know what you're going to ask."

"And that would be?"

"Whether or not Amanda has always been so

uptight. The answer is 'no'. She and Tom had a rough childhood. But, and this is according to Tom, they worked their way through it, thanks in large part to Mary."

Mark waited while Connie placed the coffee orders and turned to him, her brows raised.

"Tall black."

She laughed. "Criminy, you are truly a complex fella. That's the same order as Tom's."

The girl put their drinks in a cardboard carrier; Connie nodded toward the condiments bar and walked to it. She glanced at Mark as she poured milk into a cup. "So did I get the question right?"

"Pretty much right on the button."

"Has Amanda told you about Joe?"

"Some, not much. He was her fiancé, and he died in a plane crash in Texas."

Connie snapped the cover on a cup. "Let's sit over there for a minute."

Mark followed her to a table and set down the drinks. They pulled out chairs and sat as she said, "We won't be long."

"I appreciate you talking to me."

"Listen, Mark. I have an ulterior motive. Amanda's a great person, a good kid. I'd just like to see her get it together, and so would Tom. Amanda and Tom went through the same crappy past; they lost several members of their family in a short time at vulnerable ages. Amanda was a little older, so I think that it was tougher on her. The fact that Mary stepped in when she did," she shrugged, "was a life saver."

"Going through one loss like that would be tough for any kid, but both parents and a brother would be devastating, to say the least."

"Exactly. By the time I came along, life had pretty well settled down for them."

"And then Amanda met Joe." Mark slid his chair back and brought an ankle over his knee.

"Yes. Amanda met Joe about two, almost three years ago. There's no doubt his death wiped out years of hard work and therapy and now she's as fragile as a soap bubble hovering over a cactus. She quit her job after that plane wreck. Well, quit or got fired. I've never been sure which one it was. When Joe died, Amanda just turned in on herself. She wouldn't go out, wouldn't eat, drank too much, lost weight, and even took off for Europe." Connie shrugged. "She wound up in Asia, I think, or maybe it was Africa. Anyway, she was gone for at least six months. Just started to get back into some sort of normal life when she ran into you. No drugs, as far as I know, but seeing her grieving was like watching a flower wither. Thanks to Mary, she's making her way back, but slowly."

Mark fiddled with the laces of his sneaker and listened intently.

"Mary tossed out her tenant and made Amanda move into that brownstone several months ago. Found her that cat to keep her company and give her something to care for. She's had dates, a few. But quite frankly, you're the only guy that appears to have the patience to hang in there. Amanda manages to send 'em all skittering, runs them off."

136

"She's not going to run me off, Connie." Mark smiled and reached for his coffee. "Not that she doesn't try like hell."

Connie tapped a polished nail on the table. "Why not?"

Mark looked up. *How do I answer this?* "I can tell that Amanda must be special to you. You're a protective sister-in-law."

Connie shrugged and maintained her steady gaze at Mark.

Mark stood, drummed his fingers on the table, and then ran a hand through his hair. He took a step to the window, jingled the change in his pocket, and scanned the late evening traffic. *I guess it's time to be honest with myself.* Mark spoke to the pedestrians on Huron Street, "I love her." He turned to Connie and shrugged. "I love her."

Connie studied his face. "I think you do." She pushed the tray of coffee toward him. "She can't lose someone again, Mark."

"She won't; not me anyway." He reached for the coffee as she stood. "I'm not going anywhere. The question in her life right now is Mary's health."

They walked to the elevator bank in silence. Connie held the door open as a woman with a walker maneuvered past them. "Mary's old. It's not a case of *if*, but *when* she slips across. Amanda's going to need someone when that time comes. Mary has been her rock. And who the hell knows, that could be tomorrow, it could be years from now. But Amanda's never going to handle loss in her life very well. It's going to take a strong person to keep her

137

grounded. It's going to take compassion, imagination, and probably..." Connie smiled "...a sense of humor to boot. Someone who could corral a Crisco-coated naked kid were the need to arise."

Mark chuckled at the image. "Which one?"

Connie waved a hand. "Tru, little idiot. Smilin' from ear to ear, naked as a newborn jaybird, head to toe in cooking grease." Connie's smile sobered as the elevator opened. "But you know what I mean. Be patient with her. She'll come around."

He nodded.

As they neared Mary's room, they heard laughter. Mark glanced at Connie. "Sounds like we missed a good joke."

She smirked. "Five'll get ya ten, it was Mary's."

"That's a sucker bet." Mark grinned and shook his head.

* * * *

Amanda sat with her legs tucked under her on the end of the bed and followed Mary's glance to the shuffle of footsteps entering the room.

Mark set the tray of coffee on the overbed table and pulled his eyes from Amanda's welcoming smile to Mary's face. "You look a little spunkier than the last time I saw you. Feeling better?"

She looked around the room. "I'm going to pretend the rest of you are not here and whisper into this young man's ear." She wiggled her index finger at Mark, beckoning him to her side.

He lowered his face to her.

"Thank you, dear." She pecked his cheek. "That ice was better than sex."

Mark erupted in laughter as Amanda choked on her latte and spluttered, "Mary!"

Mary rolled her eyes. "I vividly remember."

"Which, ice or sex?" Tom chuckled as he folded his arms.

"Let's just say one's hot, one's not." She waved her hand in a shooing fashion toward the door as she looked from Tom to Connie. "You two get home to those kids. I'm fine. They're letting me out of here in the morning."

Tom and Connie walked to the bed, each bending to give and get a kiss on the cheek. Tom touched Mary's nose with his index finger. "I'll be here at eleven to drive you home."

Mark and Mary chatted about the ambulance and his experiences as a mounted policeman, some colorful stories involving the horses and his partner. Amanda smiled at the curl on his forehead. *He was so calm, knew what he was doing. God, I'm grateful to him. He must think I'm a hysterical dimwit. I wouldn't blame him, but Mary is so wonderful, so important to me.*

He raised his brows and said, "What do you think?"

Mark was waiting for her response. *What did he just say? What do I think about what?* He winked and smiled at the sudden flush to her face.

"Amanda, dear, Mark hasn't eaten. I was asking if you two wouldn't enjoy a late dinner at that Mexican restaurant near home."

"Right. Great idea." Amanda hopped off the bed and scooped her sandals off the floor. She dipped to a knee and fastened a buckle. "So long as it's heavy on the margaritas and light on the nachos, I'm in."

* * * *

Amanda fumbled with the door key, turned to Mark and dropped the keys into his palm. She leaned on the door.

"I think you've had too many margaritas."

Amanda smiled, and tapped her index finger on his chin. "A perceptive and *very* handsome fella." She rested her hand on her locket and shook her head. "Oh be still, my heart."

Mark chuckled and held on to the doorknob to prevent her from tumbling in as she opened the door with the shove of a shoulder. "I'll take that as a compliment."

She weaved toward her room and Mark shook his head with a light laugh. *I gotta go home, I'll just close my eyes for a second, and then get going.* He plopped down into the lounge chair and leaned his head back on the cushion. "You okay in there?"

"Peeeaachhykeeen."

Beginning to doze, Mark scrubbed his hands over his face and dropped them into his lap. Something rocked his knee back and forth. He raised his head and peeked at the sight of a naked ivory leg against his. *I must be dreaming.*

Marks eyes moved up as he scanned the exquisite form and he paused frequently, as did his breathing.

His heart rate, however, rose with his gaze. *Definitely dreaming.*

Amanda smiled down at him and he swallowed as she pulled him upright to the familiar scent of jasmine and roses. Mark studied her face and dropped his gaze to pale, flawless breasts, beckoning all his senses. Her taut nipples were dark. *The shade of her lips, perfect. And God how I've wanted... Shit, I'm drunk. She's drunk. Not this way. Not the first time. I can't touch her. How the hell can I not touch her?*

Mark raised his hand to her waist and she trembled beneath his touch. He closed his eyes, as electric warmth from her silky side ran through him. *Jee-zus. I'm outta my goddamned mind.* Mark's eyes traveled from rose-colored lips to her exquisite eyes, a sapphire-blue sea. *At the moment, drowning in a sapphire sea seems like a pretty damned good way to go. If anybody knew I turned this down... Christ, Callahan. You need to be locked up.*

Mark leaned to his right, pulled the beige and brown afghan from the sofa, and draped it around her shoulders. He allowed his eyes to roam across her pale skin, his dark eyes lingering on nipples that reacted to the caress of the fabric just enough to tease. Mark sighed deeply and took in a vision of the alabaster goddess before him. *On a silver platter, moron. Yours for the taking.*

Mark raised his eyes to hers, clenching his jaw with pressure enough to make his teeth ache. *Not tonight, pal. Not like this.* He shook his head and pulled the afghan around her. "The first time I make

141

love to you, darlin', will not be after we've shared three pitchers of margaritas. Those eyes'll be lookin' at me, not thinking that I'm Robert Redford." *Or some ghost of your past.*

He fell back into the lounge chair and pulled her down onto his lap. She snuggled in and laid her head on his shoulder.

Mark closed his eyes and dropped his head back.

A tequila-laced whisper struggled with enunciation. "bober redf too old, brad p..pitt."

Mark chuckled. "Him, either." Amanda's smooth, pale skin fogged his brain. *My God, she's magnificent.*

Her breath became steady, deep; her warm body melted into him.

Mark raised his head and gazed at her sleeping face. He whispered, "*Mo sonuachar*. My soulmate, you'll be lookin' only at me."

* * * *

Mark rubbed his face, immediately alert. She was gone. Amanda was not in his lap. He sat forward, drawn to the glint of Oprah's green eyes through the rosy light of dawn flooding the room. Amanda stood facing the clock, the afghan wrapped around her. Oprah, sitting like an ebony statue at her feet, gazed at him warily.

Mark stood and paused to look back at his chair, remembering the last time he slept in this room. *I'm not dreaming.* Mark turned to Amanda's soft voice.

"Sorry, I didn't mean to wake you," she said with

a smile.

Mark walked to her, and rested his forearms on her shoulders. "You didn't." He studied her face and smiled back as he lifted a long curl back from her shoulder. "I believe those sparklin' sapphires are lookin' at me."

"They are."

He swept his arms behind her knees and back, kissed her gently as he carried her to her bedroom.

* * * *

Amanda lay on the bed as Mark undressed. Muscles rippled in his arms, across his chest, and through dark curls that narrowed to his groin. Her breath deepened with apprehension and she swallowed hard, anxiety gripping as she met his dark eyes. Mark was powerful. Although he wasn't threatening, his size made Amanda shiver with anticipation. Mark's hungry, purposeful gaze quickened her pulse. Sliding into the bed beside her, he lifted the afghan that covered her.

Amanda's skin tingled as Mark's gaze roamed. He lowered his lips to her breast. Amanda closed her eyes, and her breath hitched as his hot mouth gently teased and tugged. Mark met her eyes and the muscles in his jaw flexed. He whispered, "You are beautiful." Her heart pounded as he moved his hand up her thigh to her side, under her back. He whispered Gaelic words: "*Is breá liom tú*, I love you."

"I love you, Amanda," Mark repeated. The words

were warm and gentle, belying the firmness of his touch. Amanda shuddered at the thrill of his strong arm around her waist and his warm lips on her neck.

Mark tugged her to him, a demanding promise in his mouth on hers.

CHAPTER 13

1862

Bonnie sat on a high wooden stool, resting her chin on her palms, her elbows on the smooth pine table. She swung her legs lazily and studied Magdalene's busy hands making Confederate candles. Magdalene saturated loosely spun cotton thread in a mixture of beeswax and turpentine. She drew the threads through her long brown fingers and then again through the wax. Back and forth, through her fingers, through the wax, until she dangled a long taper candle by extra wick tied into a neat slipknot. Ten candles were already drying on a string tied between pegs on the wall.

"Why do you hang 'em up before you twirl 'em in a circle, Magdalene?"

"Dey is jus' coolin' and dryin' out for a minute, baby."

Taking one of the taper candles from the string on the wall, Magdalene began to twirl the soft wax into a small spiral with a flat bottom, then another spiral on top of that one, and another. Soon she had a ball the size of a goose's egg, and pulled a few inches of the wax above the ball to create the Confederate candle. Bonnie knew Papa used these candles on his hunting trips so he didn't need a candlestick. Magdalene was making more of them

145

than usual, but Bonnie didn't ask why.

"Magdalene?"

"Mmm?"

"When will the angel bells wake us up again?"

"I specs dey hang dem bells back up dah soon's dis war be over, sugar, an' not a minute sooner."

Bonnie looked over Magdalene's shoulder to Jack's frantic wave beckoning her through the window. *His face is red like a cherry.* Bonnie dropped from the stool and stopped at Magdalene's warning voice.

"Li'l girl, don't you go disappearin' now. Ah cain't be lookin' fo' you all de time."

"Yes'm." Bonnie ran to the hall and spotted Jack out on the veranda. She slammed through the door, ran down the steps, and chased after Jack around the side of the big house. He stopped, and Bonnie stumbled into him. His eyes level with the floor of the porch, he held his finger to his lips and peeked through the gap below the bottom rail.

She whispered, "What?"

"Shh. Your Pa's talkin' about the war." Jack pulled Bonnie down beside him. "And it don't sound good." Jack gaped, his eyes wide. "They're talkin' about us all goin' north."

John's ivory pipe wafted billows of white smoke into the deep blue sky. "Not according to *The Charleston Mercury*. If half of what they're telling us is true, Jeff Davis is sipping a julep in the White House right now. I swear, reading this paper will give any sane Southerner nightmares." John folded the newspaper in half and tossed it on the floor by his chair. "Mr. Lincoln's war is coming to South Carolina. Those idiot politicians in Richmond have their petticoats in a knot thinking they're winning the war with news out of Shiloh, but they're not. Some twenty-five thousand men are dead, and near half of them Confederate. The Union navy has blockaded Charleston Harbor and it's only a matter of time before they begin placing heavy guns on the islands. Any fool can see that the fate of this rebellion is sealed." He relit his pipe, puffed pensively for a moment, and said, "The only chance we have is to head north before the Federal forces cut off our escape."

Ben leaned back on the white railing, his arms crossed. "If'n dey does, suh."

"They will." John sighed and rubbed his fingers across his high forehead. "This debacle has been an absurdity since Sumter." He breathed out angry frustration, "And my God, so many men dead. I'm afraid the South is going to lose this war, and *vae victis*...woe to the vanquished."

"I'm not the only one to believe that South Carolina started this." John's voice filled with despair. "They did, the first state to secede. And South Carolinians will pay dearly for this treason, with their lives and with the few resources we have left." He dropped his hand to the armrest of the wicker chair.

A hawk described swooping circles against a darkening sky, sunset turning feathers to gold. Brown wings opened wide and quickly folded as the bird plummeted into a tall clump of palmetto.

Fronds rustled and Bonnie jumped at the plaintive squeak of a small animal. She shivered, sucking in her lower lip as the bird lifted into the dusk, talons holding a limp field mouse. Bonnie turned back to her father's words.

"I wrote of my plans to Patricia's cousin and asked her if I might bring Jack with us to Duncan's in Chicago. I felt he would be safer there than in Virginia. I received a reply today. They agree with my assessment of the situation and would like to join us if we have room in the wagon. Naturally, I will make room for my dear wife's people, even if I have to walk all the way. Their farm in McDowell is no great distance out of our way. Besides, it cannot be denied that there is safety in numbers. I will worry that much the less about the children."

Ben shook his head. "Well, suh. Li'l Bonnie won't have no problem. Magdalene gonna take care o' dat." Ben chewed on a piece of straw and chuckled. "She gonna take care o' Bonnie jes' fine."

Bonnie frowned and turned to Jack. "What's he mean?"

Jack shrugged. "Shh."

"Let's give those horses mange, Ben. We don't want them confiscated by soldiers. If we can make them look bad enough, they're safe."

"Yassuh, dat only take an hour or so."

"You think the wagon is sound enough for this long trip?"

"Yassuh, but ah's been thinkin'. We gonna be needin' supplies, an' dey's all sorts of rascals on de road. Maybe we builds some sorta box, up under de

148

wagon. We gots t' be hidin' dem supplies somehow."

John rubbed his chin. "Not a box, a false bottom." He waved a fly from his face. "Yes, that would work. Can we make it deep enough to hide the children?"

"Ah 'specs not, Marse John." Ben bent over and mimed lifting a trapdoor. "But plenty big enough fo' evvathing dat we don' want nobody to be a'stealin' fum us." He paused to spit a neat stream of tobacco juice over the railing and continued, "We got all dat hardtack an' jerky an' sech-like dat my Magdalene been puttin' up. Put all our powder an' balls in dah, too. Is you gonna be wantin' to bring Miss Patricia's silver?"

"We'll have to bury that in the garden and hope the Yankees don't go looking for potatoes when they come." John eyed the wagon. "Do we have what we need to build this thing?"

Ben fingered the long black whiskers on his chin. "Guess ah use some o' dat wood from de tack room; ain't no use to us no mo'." He turned and looked at the horizon where the sun was balanced like a great red globe. "Ah kin be all done befo' mawnin'. If'n I was to tear up de veranda on de house instead, ah'd be done a lot sooner."

John gazed across the low-lying land of huge cypress and gum trees toward the small family cemetery on a knoll framed by live oaks. Turned blood-red by the dropping sun, gray-green Spanish moss drooped to the ground beneath the stately trees. "Use only the stable walls," he said. "I'm hoping to come back to Magnolia Plantation. Someday I will be back."

John puffed on his pipe as he walked the expanse of the broad veranda. He and Ben continued speaking as they looked to the stable beyond a lush garden of azaleas and camellias. Evening fog drifted over a small field of maize in the distance.

Bonnie peered over the wooden slats of the porch. "I can't hear anymore. Papa's too far away."

"Me, neither. Come on." Jack ducked under the porch and stopped at Bonnie's tug on his leather suspender.

"Wait. They're goin' to the stable."

* * * *

Ben slapped the razor along the long leather strop, ran his thumb over the blade, slapped the strop, and checked the blade again. Satisfied, he walked back to Saffron and nodded to John to hold the horse's bridle steady. The smell of the horses mingled with fresh hay and warm air drifting from the open stable doors. Ben carefully shaved away more patches of the horse's brown coat. The stable floor was covered with tufts of horsehair and straw.

John spoke to Jack. "Okay, boy, rub in more dye. We're about done, so only where Ben just shaved."

Holding Bonnie on her lap, Magdalene wrapped her arms around her. "Ah believes you got dem hosses so ugly, won't nobody come near 'em, fo' fear o' gittin' what dey got."

Bonnie whispered, "Are we going somewhere,

Magdalene?"

Squeezing her tightly, Magdalene said, "Well, we's gonna go fo' a long ride in de country, baby. You like dat, don't you?"

Bonnie nodded.

"More over there, Jack." John pointed at Saffron's leg. "The back of that hock. Good."

Jack wiped a dye-soaked rag down Saffron's front leg, and then stepped back and examined the two horses. "Uncle John, I think Moon's mangier lookin'."

John pointed to Moon's rump. "Make her tail a little rougher, Ben. I think the horses look sufficiently awful now. After we eat, we can start pulling down boards for the wagon box. Make sure we take that razor and strop with us. The horses will need touching up every few days. We'll find plenty of berries on the road to make more dye." John looked at the children and smiled. "You two look a sight. Go get cleaned up for dinner. Ben, Magdalene, I'd be grateful if you'd take dinner with us in the dining room again."

John scratched a wooden match across his heel. The match crackled as he relit his pipe. Short, aromatic whiffs of tobacco smoke swirled through his words. "I'm enjoying your company." John tossed the pouch to Ben as he walked from the stable.

* * * *

The table was set with their best china and

silverware. Crystal goblets gleamed on the snow-white linen tablecloth. Roast goose, potato pudding, boiled beets, and cornbread were Jack's favorite dinner, and the array before them was more than enough for twice their number. John said a brief grace, and as he pulled the long cork from a dusty bottle of wine added, "We might as well have a grand feast tonight. Anything we can't take with us will just go to waste."

Dessert was Idiot's Delight. According to Magdalene, any idiot could make this sauce-covered biscuit, but that didn't matter to Bonnie. She pushed the biscuit to the side of her plate and ate the cinnamon-raisin sauce first. Proud that she didn't drip any of her sauce on the tablecloth, Bonnie next devoured the biscuit. She looked from her father's wink to his dish as she licked her sticky fingers. He replaced her empty plate with his own half-finished dessert as he wiped a napkin across his chin.

"We've a long wagon ride ahead of us to my cousin's home in Chicago. We'll be coming back here, but for now, the South is too dangerous. Jack, your parents are waiting for us at your home in Virginia. They will be coming with us to Chicago."

Bonnie and Jack shared a look of wide-eyed excitement.

Jack nodded, and looked down at his lap. "Yes, sir."

"Bonnie, you'll be happy to hear that you're getting back into your overalls." John laughed. "We can't hide those bright blue eyes of yours, but we can make you look like a little boy. I want you to mind Magdalene. She's going to cut your hair like Jack's. Until we get safely up north, you're going to look and act like a boy." He winked. "Tough job for you, I know."

Bonnie giggled and looked at Jack. "I can't be a boy named Bonnie."

Slipping into the conversation, Magdalene said, "We done worked dat all out. You gonna be called Bobby, 'cause it sound like 'Bonnie.'" Magdalene nodded her head firmly and pushed her chair back. "Bobby an' Jack, two boy-cousins."

* * * *

John pulled the horses' reins and wrapped them around the wagon brake. He climbed down from his seat and raised both hands to lift Bonnie to the grass in front of the ornate iron gate. He took her hand and they walked toward the graves. Ducking under wisps of soft gray moss, he spoke over his shoulder. "The rest of you stay on the wagon. Bonnie and I will only be a moment."

Bonnie looked up at her father.

A gentle breeze lifted his collar. John's somber blue eyes studied the small headstone. "Say goodbye to your mother, Bonnie. It will be a while before we see her again."

He took off his wide-brimmed hat, knelt on one knee, and rested his hand on the stone marker, head bent in prayer.

Bonnie stood next to him and leaned into his chest. He wrapped an arm around her and hugged her close. She smelled Papa's pipe and the wondrous scent of grass and moss. Part of it was something else, though...the smell of Papa. John's eyes roamed the barren rice fields their ancestors had carved out of tidal swamps. Bonnie followed his gaze as he tightened his arm around her, pulling her closer.

His grandfather told him stories about Magnolia Plantation, and Papa had told her some of those stories. Stories about slaves brought from the West Indies and Africa. Slaves who worked this land and other fields like it. They cleared the low-lying swamp, built canals, dikes, and gates that allowed the flooding and draining of fields with high and low tides.

Bonnie knew that Papa was not a slaveholder, even though Grandpa had been. The black people who worked for Papa like Ben and Magdalene were family. They received wages, and raised their own families on the sprawling plantation. Magdalene was the only mother she had ever known. She stared at the gravestone.

Patricia Margaret Lexington
Beloved Wife and Mother
1833 - 1856

John looked at the grand house in the distance.

One of the big rooms hadn't been used since she was born. Papa went in there by himself sometimes. Magdalene said it was Momma's room.

"Bonnie, someday you'll dance in that ballroom,

maybe at your wedding. Remember this house. Remember your ancestors built it from cypress and pine with their own hands."

Tall white paneling in the foyer was made from trees once on the property. Bonnie knew which floorboards squeaked and where the mice lived. She looked up at Papa as he ruffled her short cap of curls.

"Let's go, little one. We have to stop at the church."

* * * *

Bonnie and Jack were in the back of the wagon, concentrating on a game of draughts.

Magdalene mumbled, "Bonnie, yo pappy a man a' many colors."

Ben lifted his gaze from the little wooden squirrel he was carving from a piece of the stable wood. "He be dat, Magdalene. Marse John, he kin do 'bout anythin' he set his mind to, an' dat's a fact."

The children scrambled to the rail of the wagon to see two men standing in front of the big oak door of the church. The men were shaking hands, bidding farewell. Both wore the ankle length black cassocks of the clergy, but one of them was Papa. Bonnie and Jack looked at each other.

"Why is Papa wearing that dress?"

"It's not a dress. That's what a preacher wears. I don't know exactly, but I think he's trying to fool somebody. Guess we'll find out soon enough."

The skirts of the black cassock kicked out with

155

each long stride as John walked back to the wagon. He climbed to the seat and positioned a wide-brimmed black hat on his head. He released the brake and lightly slapped the reins of the horses. Saffron and Moon responded with a gentle lurch of the wagon. The *rat-a-tatter-clatter-tat* of wooden wheels on cobblestone fell in their wake as they headed down the street. John looked over at Ben's wide eyes. "I don't think anyone will bother a wagon with a preacher."

Ben shook his head. "No, suh. No, I don' 'spec' dey will."

John lifted his boot and scratched a match on his heel. "Now, about those angel bells," he puffed. "Where'd we leave off?"

CHAPTER 14

Mark straddled the picnic table bench next to Amanda, snuggling her close so she could lean back on him. They turned to a V of Canada geese moving across the setting sun on the horizon. The air was warm, the sky crystal, not a cloud to be seen. They gazed at the sunset, a giant red ball dropping from view. The sky behind them had already turned a deep cobalt blue. She pointed to the bright star just above the horizon. "I've always meant to look up the name of that star. It's only like that at sunset. Do you know what it is?"

Mark kissed her cheek and whispered in her ear. "It's not a star. That's the planet Venus."

Amanda gazed at the distant light and whispered, "Venus."

He put a notebook on the picnic table in front of them and turned up the gas lantern.

Pointing to the first page, he said, "This list is what you've been able to tell us during your regressions. You're probably in Charleston, South Carolina. The Shiloh battle was in early April, 1862."

Amanda grinned at the list. "Your cop brain is so analytical. And your handwriting isn't bad either."

Mark finished his wine in a long swallow. "I'm not just another pretty face, thank you very much."

She laughed and read through the notes:

157

1. St. Michael's Church
2. The Charleston Mercury
3. The Battle of Shiloh
4. Magnolia Plantation
5. Cousin in Chicago, Duncan (last name?)

Mark sighed, "I'm not sure we've learned anything pertaining to our knowing each other. And there's nothing about that clock."

"But there is." She filled his glass and hers.

He kissed behind her ear, buried his face in her hair, and nuzzled her neck. "What the hell is that? Drives me nuts."

"What?"

"Your perfume."

Amanda smiled and squirmed away. "Eau de Mark right now, but under that is *Joy*."

"I'll buy it for you by the fifty-five gallon drum."

"Sure. About a c-note an ounce."

He pulled her back to him again. "Then we'll just have to live on canned tuna and ramens. You'll never run out of that perfume." He kissed her neck again, his voice a low murmur. "What'd you mean, 'But there is'?"

"Didn't think you were listening."

"I was. Just multi-tasking." He kissed her again.

Amanda laughed and dropped her head back onto his shoulder. "Do men think of anything but sex?"

"Nope. Well, that's not really true. We don't think about it when we change the oil in a car."

Amanda raised her head. Their eyes met.

158

"But even that's marginal; we sometimes use petcock plugs on the oil pan. We start wondering why a screw is called a petcock. Screws, pet cocks." He shrugged. "It's tough being a guy, sometimes."

"A petcock screw." Laughing, Amanda turned to face him and held her hands against his chest. "Mary told me somebody gave her a pet rock back in the seventies. You're not kidding?"

He crossed-his-heart and put his arms around her.

Before he could make any more progress sliding his hands under her blouse, Amanda stood and walked around the picnic table to sit opposite him. She sipped her wine and said, "The angel bells sound just like my clock chimes."

He shrugged. "Bells, chimes."

Amanda stared at him, her mouth opened slightly in a sudden burst of understanding. "St. Michael's!" She stood again and paced back and forth. "Why didn't I think of that?"

Mark struggled to catch up. "What are we talking about?"

"All grandfather clocks chime. Some have more than one kind of chime." Distracted, she mumbled into her wine glass, "Three, usually, but some clocks have only one."

Mark sighed and raised his brows. "So?"

She placed the glass on the table. "There's lots of different kinds of chimes. They can be the Westminster chimes, Whittington, Ave Maria, Oxford, Canterbury, Trinity. There's one called the Beethoven's 9th Symphony chimes, and even one based on an Israeli folk tune." Her blue eyes sparkled with excitement. "There's also St. Michael's chimes."

Mark's gaze dropped to the notes. "St. Michael's Church." He frowned. "But you bought an 18th century clock. The chimes would have been put in the clock a hundred years earlier, in Europe. What's that got to do with a church in the South during the Civil War?" He shook his head. "I'm losing you."

Amanda smiled. "And here I am thinking cops know everything."

He feigned an angry frown, tipped his wine glass toward her in emphasis. "Listen, I wouldn't be so sassy if I were you. You're trapped in the woods with a cop twice your size."

"We know that clock was built in the late 1700s. All the surviving American clocks from that period are made in the Federal style, and this one is obviously European. All that carving and the hunting theme are a dead giveaway to an antiquarian. So the bells in that church must have come first. We have to find a church built in the late 1700's, named St. Michael's, whose bell tower rings that melody. The chimes in my clock are the same as the bells built for that church. I heard them in 1862—Bonnie heard them—and I hear them today. If we can figure out this piece, we'll be closer to solving the puzzle."

Mark pursed his lips. *She makes it sound so simple, but it's not simple at all.* "You think finding the church you saw in your regression is going to tell us how we know each other?"

Amanda sat back down on the picnic table bench

160

and frowned into the deep burgundy of her wine. "I don't know, maybe. We might find out where our paths crossed."

"Hell, we've nothing to lose." Mark took a sip of wine. "Okay, let's say we limit the initial search to Charleston during the Civil War. We can explore the surrounding area if we don't find any clues there. Bad as John said the mails were, it's likely they would only have the local paper, so Charleston's probably our best bet. At least we're not looking for every St. Michael's Church standing on red dirt." He shrugged. "Works for me."

Mark spread a double sleeping bag across the picnic table. "Enough with the clock." He tapped his forehead as he turned off the lamp. "I gotta take this gerbil runnin' in my brain off crack for a few hours. Care to join me on the table? Ground's kinda damp tonight."

Amanda sputtered a laugh. "A gerbil on crack runs your brain?" She stepped up onto the table and looked down at his upturned smile as she undressed. She took off her blouse and Mark's eyes roamed.

He stammered, "I…I'm not so sure the gerbil can concentrate on what it originally planned."

She stepped out of her shorts as she asked, "What would that be?"

He stood and unbuttoned his shirt. "Doesn't matter; this'll do." Mark joined her on the table and brought his lips to within an inch of hers. He whispered, "You're so beautiful."

Amanda leaned into his kiss as she moved her hands to the buckle of his belt, and stopped. She set her hands on his chest. "What'd the gerbil have planned?"

Mark chuckled as he moved his hands down her back. "I forget."

"Come on, what?"

He sighed. "I'll probably shoot myself for saying this, but look up."

Amanda raised her eyes and was silent for several seconds. He kissed her neck as she leaned back and gazed at one of the most magnificent vistas in the night sky, a glorious velvet blanket splashed with stars. The Milky Way arched above them, across the black ink sky of a new moon.

Wonder whispered through her voice. "I think I like this plan. What's that?" She pointed to a glowing spot in the sky.

Mark pulled his gaze from her and followed her pointing finger. "Jupiter."

"How do you know?"

"Cops know everything."

Amanda pushed him away and grinned as she settled on the table, pulling the sleeping bag around her. "I guess they do, smarty pants."

Laughing, he said, "See if you can find that yellow star in these." Mark handed her his binoculars and pointed to another star, brighter than those around it, a tiny sparkle of gold. While she searched, he undressed and lay down beside her, pulling the sleeping bag around them. He took the binoculars and set them aside. "Astronomy lesson can wait." Mark placed his hands on either side of her face and kissed her softly. "Christ, you're breathtaking."

* * * *

Mark sighed contentedly and lightly stroked the curve of her lower back. "This is where we should share a cigarette, right?"

"Since neither of us smokes, what's Plan B?"

Kissing her shoulder, he whispered, "A rematch?"

Amanda rolled to her back and fumbled for the binoculars. "In your dreams, Mr. Wonderful. Now that my eyes are uncrossed, I wanna find that yellow star."

She raised the glasses and scanned the night sky. Mark smiled at a slight intake of breath and knew she was looking at the spellbinding rings of Saturn.

"Mark, it's incredible. I've never seen this before." Amanda lowered the binoculars and gazed at the star. She added, "Except in pictures. It's sort of hard to get your arms around the fact that there is nothing between Saturn and me. How far away is it?"

Amanda looked at the star through his binoculars again, as he said, "Depending on the time of year, between seven hundred fifty million and over a billion miles." A few minutes later, Mark coaxed her away from the sight. There was much more to see.

Using only the points of Cassiopeia, one of the easiest constellations to spot, Mark guided her to the tiny silver mist of the Andromeda Galaxy. They talked about the zodiac, laughed when they learned they had the same sign, Cancer. In a low voice, Mark told her stories of mythology as he showed her how to find several more constellations. He pointed out Mars, star clusters, and nebulas, and at her insistence they viewed Saturn again.

Amanda turned to him. "What do you suppose it all means?"

"What, aliens?"

She laughed. "No, silly. Bonnie, her cousin, what I'm seeing. What do you think of my being a little girl struggling to understand a frightening war? How does that relate to you and me?"

Mark slipped a hand under his head and continued to look at the stars. "Jeez. I don't know. It doesn't relate, as far as I can tell."

"I know." She followed his gaze. "We're obviously missing a big chunk of the story." Amanda sighed at the stars. "Nothing we've learned so far is helping us find out how we could know each other."

"Does it really matter?"

She turned to him.

Mark kissed the tip of her nose. "What if you never find out, sweetheart? You may not, you know."

"Somehow, you know me." Amanda touched his chin. "You knew me before we met. I know you, somehow. Maybe Bonnie knew you, too."

"She's pretty young for you to make that call," Mark kissed her fingers, "based on what you said. But let's assume Bonnie," he nodded to her, "I mean you *as* Bonnie, have someone important in your life. For argument's sake, let's say Bonnie's father, or Ben, or her cousin Jack. If, and it's a huge if, if Mark Callahan and Amanda Parker met during your life as Bonnie, any one of the souls in Bonnie's life could be me. If anything, this whole exercise should convince you that no one ever really dies. One of those souls might have been Connor or Joe. You can even throw Magdalene into the mix. Some people believe that gender is irrelevant to the transfer of souls."

Amanda frowned.

"You don't look convinced. But," he sighed, "your regression sure has me speculating about what might be around the next bend in this river of life…not just ahead of us, but behind us as well. All the complexities that make up a unique being, all that makes you who you are, me who I am, does that simply dissolve into nothing with death? Man's answer to the question is religion, some faith in life after death. The Bible, Quran, Torah, ancient carvings in tombs and caves, these are all explanations created by man for other men to make their case and tout a belief in heaven, hell, God, the Devil, whatever." Mark looked up at the stars and continued, "And all those religious beliefs plant your ass in a state of eternal damnation if you opt for a different but equally credible belief. And there are those that believe you can take your pick of any religion, because all paths lead to the same place. There are those who believe there's no heaven or hell at all, that you create your own with the way you live your life."

"You don't think you'll die someday?"

"Of course, everybody does. Although, a pretty large slice of humanity believes you have lived before and will live again in a different life."

"But people die. People you love die."

"If you believe in reincarnation, people really don't die, honey. You told Mary that you believe you are Bonnie, right?"

"Yeah."

"Do you? Do you really believe that you were Bonnie?"

Amanda met Mark's eyes. "Yes, I do."

He winked, smiled, and tipped his head. "There you go. You are a believer in reincarnation. You were a child named Bonnie during the Civil War. You had a cousin named Jack, a nanny named Magdalene. If you honestly believe that you were once Bonnie, these people are a part of who you are, as much a part of you as the people in Amanda Parker's life today. And if you have walked this earth before, maybe other souls from Bonnie's life walk the earth today, just like you."

Amanda chewed on her lower lip.

"The point I'm making is," Mark kissed her cheek, "what if you never learn how you and I know each other? Does it really matter?"

She nodded. "It matters, it matters a lot."

"Why?" Mark waited as Amanda looked at him, her blue eyes searching his face.

"Sometimes when I look at you, and especially when I don't expect it, someone else looks back at me." Amanda frowned and shook her head. "It's not all the time, but it's like there's someone else deep inside of you and very far away. And then you'll say something, something silly or something profound, again when I don't expect it, and…and it's that someone. I know our lives have touched before. If I could know that it didn't end in tragedy then, I might be able to believe in a tomorrow for us."

He kissed her gently. "Then be patient. I imagine finding out who that 'someone' is might just take a while."

Mark gave her no direction other than to look for three bright stars near the horizon in a fairly straight line, hoping this incredible view would pull her mind from the regression sessions. It didn't take long for her to find Orion's belt. He knew the constellation like the lifeline in his palm. Mark whispered how to find the sword, the Horse Head Nebula. He murmured how to visualize and find the stars that defined the arm, the bow, and how Orion was shooting an arrow across the night sky. Amanda looked at him thoughtfully, her face a reflection of wonder about what she was seeing, and things unsaid, he supposed.

Breaking her stare, Mark turned onto his back, wondering, not for the first time, what was going on behind her enchanting face. He put his hands behind his head, and as he gazed at the constellation, he told her one of the many stories of Orion.

"Apollo is the leader of all the heavens and gods," he began. "So, I won't get into him; but he's important in the mythology. Orion is the hunter, a bow and arrow guy, as you can see up there, and pretty highly thought of by the other gods. All that is incidental to the real story of Orion." Turning to see her reaction, he said, "See, Orion fell head over heels in love with a beautiful goddess named Amanda."

"You're making this up."

"Nope. Well, maybe a little." He smiled and turned back to the sky. "Luscious Amanda and devastatingly handsome Orion were crazy about each other. Pretty easy for them to hook up, since Amanda is the goddess of the hunt. Think about it: It's a no-brainer romance—Orion, the virile hunter and Amanda, the lovely goddess of the hunt. Enter her older brother Apollo, the big kahuna himself. Apollo is none too happy about his little sister's choice in men. He thought Orion was just after her particularly delectable ass."

She elbowed his side as he continued.

"Seriously, gods don't wear any clothes; at least in my mind they don't." Mark shrugged and Amanda laughed.

"Anyway, Apollo tricked Amanda into killing Orion, shooting him with an arrow while she's on a hunting trip by the sea, of all things, while Orion is swimming. She gets him right in the head."

"Orion doesn't shoot the arrow?"

Mark turned and smiled at her wide-eyed interest. "Nope, he gets an arrow shot at him right in the old bean by his lover, the lovely, sexy, and delicious Amanda."

"I'm missing something," she giggled. "How

come he's shooting the arrow up there now?"

Mark leaned up on his elbow and placed an arm across her waist. "Apollo feels so bad about the whole mess that he creates a constellation and names it Orion at the behest of, and removing my creative license with her name, the real goddess of the hunt, Diana."

She studied him for a while and turned her gaze to the glittering image above. Thoughtfully, she said, "Apollo is a peckerhead."

Mark roared with laughter. He rolled on top of her, resting on his forearms. Struck by the starlit luminescence of her face, he kissed her softly. *Whether I loved her before or not, I sure do now.*

Amanda laughed, squirmed, and pointed up at something. "What's that one called?"

Mark quickly put an arm around her waist and pulled her naked body close to his. Her eyes twinkled as she laughed again and tried to twist away. He grinned and tightened his hold. "Settle down. You're like trying to corral a wild colt." Mark chuckled at her teasing, provocative wiggle and smothered her mouth with his own.

Yesterday

CHAPTER 15

McDowell, Virginia — 1862

John Lexington twitched the reins and pulled back on the brake handle. The wagon came to a stop next to a gray barn, its doors and windows the gaping, empty eyes of a skull in the long evening shadows. Moon and Saffron stamped nervously in the long grass. John climbed down from the wagon, swatted dust from his cassock, and called toward the ruined house, "Anthony? Clarissa? Hello! Is anybody here?"

All that remained of Jack's home was a pair of chimneys and part of a wall. The place had been deserted for some time, and weeds had begun to take over the space between the chimneys where a family had once lived. John turned back toward the frightened faces in the wagon. "Jack, I don't know what's happened here, but we can't stay."

At that moment, a bearded scarecrow emerged from the dark doorway of the barn and stood defiantly, a rusty shotgun across his forearm. "You all need to leave, parson. This here is our place now, and they ain't room for anybody else." Two ragamuffin children, barefoot and dressed only in long shirts, peeped around his legs.

John moved between the barn and the wagon and held his arms away from his sides. "We don't mean

171

to stay. I'm looking for the family that lived here, the Wellingtons. Can you tell me where I might find them?"

The man gestured with his gun toward the chimneys. "Can't say you'll like what you see, but I reckon they're still in there somewhere. They was all kinds of sojers through here back in the spring, and I heard tell that Wellington feller tried to keep them from stealin' his property. Dang lot a' good it did 'im. Might a' been Stonewall's brigade, might a' been the Yankees; they was both about equal when it come to stealin'. Anyways, we're here now, so I'll thank you to turn them hosses around and skedaddle." He raised the barrel of his shotgun.

John turned back toward the wagon. He tried to meet Jack's eyes, but the boy's face was buried in the folds of Magdalene's dress, his shoulders silently heaving. "We have to leave now, Jack. We're not safe here. We will all say a prayer together for your mother and father when we stop for the night."

* * * *

Ben's eyes reflected the dim light of lingering flames from the campfire. He whispered, "Dey's somebody out dah. Stay here, Magdalene. Hold on tight to dem chirrens." Ben dropped down from the wagon and disappeared from Bonnie's view.

The sour-sweet scent of animal manure mixed with wet hay and horsehair. Dense smoke from the dying fire burned Bonnie's eyes. She fisted both hands into her eyes and started to cry, chin quivering as Magdalene pulled her into her lap. "Shh, baby girl. Hush." Magdalene whispered, "Jack, you come set here by me." She held out an arm to him. "Come heah, now."

Bonnie whimpered, "I wanna go be with Papa."

"Shh. Papa comin', baby. He jes' gone to see whah we should go. You be still, now."

Jack settled beside Magdalene and leaned back against the wagon slats. Bonnie saw fear in his brown eyes. Smoke and dense fog rolled through the dark forest. Moss-draped oaks muffled the pop of distant gunfire. The acrid scent of gunpowder carried on a gust of damp air. Bonnie shivered at the rumble of a deep and thunderous explosion in the distance and Magdalene's arms tightened around her. Moon whinnied and bucked, the wagon hitched and inched forward. The wagon brake squeaked in protest.

"Well, lookee what we got here." The soldier's words slurred. "Got me a nigger woman and two little white boys."

Bonnie looked up into the sunburned face of a soldier grinning broadly at Magdalene, sandy beard stained with tobacco juice. From the tattered homespun uniform, her eyes went to his mud caked bare feet, and back to his wicked leer. He pushed his butternut cap to the back of his shaggy head. "We are all gonna have us some fun, an' that's a fact."

The man scrambled up into the wagon and to his feet. He grinned down at Bonnie. "You'll be next, lil' fella." He pulled her out of Magdalene's arms and shoved her at Jack.

He yanked Magdalene to her feet and into a clumsy embrace. She struggled as he tugged at her dress and buttons rattled on the wagon floor. The man pushed his whiskered face into her bosom and she yelped.

Jack pulled Bonnie behind him and retreated into a corner in the wagon. The soldier struck Magdalene across the mouth, and her head flew back. She cried out as the man shoved her off the wagon. He wiped the back of his hand over his mouth, looked at it, and grinned widely down at her. "Got me a bitch that bites."

Magdalene struggled to her feet, holding her dress closed. She stepped toward him as he jumped from the wagon. Her face an angry scowl, sweat glistened on her forehead. "Mistuh, you let me back up on dat wagon wid dem chirrens, an' you go on 'bout yo' business."

He belched loudly. "I ain't goin' nowhere 'til I get what I come for."

Bonnie met the man's eyes and he laughed. "Leastways not 'til I'm done with that li'l blue-eyed one." He gave her an ugly grin. The soldier grabbed Magdalene by the arm and she stumbled behind him as he dragged her into the dark woods.

Bonnie's heart thundered. She peeked over the side of the wagon as the man slapped Magdalene again and slammed her head against a tree. Blood dripped from her forehead as she bent at the waist and heaved. He wavered in front of her and fumbled with his britches. The man slapped her again and spun her back to him, pushing her face into the tree. Bonnie watched him raise Magdalene's skirts and lean into her back.

Jack jumped from the wagon and pulled Bonnie behind him. She struggled to keep up as he pulled her to a tall hedge of bushes. They dropped to their knees and he pushed her into the brush. He scrambled into wet dirt, pulled her close, and put his arms around her. His heart pattered against hers. His voice trembling, Jack leaned his head against hers and said softly, "Shh. Don't talk, don't move."

A loud voice filled the air, menacing and frightening, the voice of Bonnie's father.

"Release that woman this instant!" he bellowed.

Bonnie and Jack stood. He pushed branches of the shrub to the side and grasped her hand.

John stepped from behind Saffron, his rifle pointed directly at the man's back. "Now!" he shouted.

The man raised both hands and backed away from Magdalene. Her skirt dropped and she fell to her knees. The soldier turned to John. Showing a grin with broken and yellow teeth, he slowly shook his head. "Well, I'll be. Jes' havin' a little fun here, is all." The man widened his grin. "Preachers don't shoot people."

The soldier started to lower his hands and Bonnie jumped as the loud crack of John's gun shattered the air over the man's head. Jack's hand tightened on hers and he yanked her closer to him.

The man blanched, his eyes wide and face frozen. John smoothly worked the lever, loading a fresh cartridge. "This preacher does." Bonnie's father took a step forward. He growled, "Lift your revolver with your left hand and drop it to the ground."

The man didn't move.

John's voice lowered. "Do it now, or this preacher will send you to hell where you belong."

"Lower the gun, Parson." Another man walked from the darkness. "Lower the gun," he said again, his pistol aimed at John's back. "What's done is done." The man was dressed in the same homespun butternut color, his uniform dirty and smudged, his brown beard flecked with silver. Dried blood caked the side of his torn trousers. A gray slouch hat, decorated with the blue cord of a Confederate officer, covered his brow.

The three men stood their ground.

"I said lower the gun, Padre. Lower it to the ground, nice and slow."

John's eyes darted toward Bonnie's. He gritted his teeth and glared as the soldier smirked and buttoned his britches. John slowly lowered the barrel, and then snapped it back up and fired at the center of the man's forehead. While the first soldier was still falling, John spun and fired blindly into the darkness behind him. A plume of white smoke belched from the muzzle of his rifle. The shot missed its target.

The Confederate officer aimed his own weapon at John, and suddenly his face froze, mouth and eyes opened wide. He collapsed slowly onto his face. Ben placed a foot on his back and with a guttural oath, jerked a long knife from between the man's

176

shoulders.

Screaming, tears streaming down her face, Bonnie ran to Papa. John lifted her in his arms as he stood. "It's all right, little one. It's over." He kissed her cheek and Bonnie wrapped her legs and arms tightly around him as he settled her on his hip. John kissed her forehead and whispered, "It's over, Bonnie. Don't cry. It's over, but we must hurry and leave here. We've no time."

Ben wrapped his arms around Magdalene. "Ah's so sorry, Magdalene. So sorry." He guided Magdalene to the wagon and helped her up. Ben wrapped a blanket around her and crouched beside her.

Magdalene said, "Ah's…ah's all right, Ben. Ah's all right." She mumbled into Ben's chest as he pulled her to him. Bonnie couldn't hear what Magdalene said.

John set Bonnie down on the back of the wagon and boosted Jack to a seat beside her. His eyes moved from her to Jack and back to her. "I need you two to sit close to Ben and Magdalene. Hold on tight to each other and to the wagon rails. We have to go fast and this might be a rough ride for a little while." John kissed Bonnie on the cheek and pulled her to him. He squeezed his arms around her and she inhaled the comforting aroma of pipe tobacco. John stepped back and placed one hand under her chin, and the other hand on Jack's arm. "Are you ready?"

* * * *

Bonnie pulled the musty horse blanket to her nose at the sonorous *hoo-hoo, hoo-hoo* in the distance. "Jack, listen." A far-off pop of gunfire pierced the air, followed by faint laughter. Bonnie started to her feet.

Jack grabbed her ankle and pulled her back down onto the bed of tarpaulins and blankets from the wagon. "That's just one of those soldiers shootin' at shadows again."

Bonnie's chin quivered. "He's shootin' over here."

"No, he's not. Quit bein' a baby." Jack turned toward the gunfire. "Don't you hear those men laughin'? They're just horsin' around."

She burrowed back under the blankets and said, "I'm not a baby. I'm six now. I was talkin' about that old owl, anyway. The colored man that fixed the barn door told me they're haints."

"An owl's just an owl. Besides, Ben told me there's no such thing as haints." Jack rustled around, settled. "Magdalene said to go to sleep."

"Wish we were under the wagon. We always sleep under there." Bonnie sat up and peered at shadows, seeing only dark silhouettes and hearing murmured words. "Who are those people with Papa?"

"You know who they are, the parson from that church we went by, him and his sons."

Bonnie lay back down and pulled the blanket around her. "Are they gonna make Papa better?"

"They're doctorin' your daddy, along with Magdalene and Ben. He'll be better in the morning,

178

you'll see."

"He always says our prayers with us before bedtime."

"Hush, Bonnie. He needs to sleep, and so do we."

The two cousins lay side-by-side, blankets pulled to their chins. One of the horses chuffed quietly and Bonnie gazed at the night sky.

Jack pointed up. "It's like I'm looking in a great big black bowl full of lightning bugs. See the big cup with a long handle on it over there?"

Bonnie followed his finger.

"Ben told me the colored folks call that the Drinking Gourd, and it tells them how to get to freedom. It's how they know they're goin' north, where they don't have to be slaves any more."

"There are lots of stars down there by the river. Do they have names?"

"That's not stars. That's campfires from the Yankee soldiers. Looks like there's as many of them as there are stars."

"I can smell bacon." Bonnie's stomach growled.

"Me, too. Wish we had somethin' besides Magdalene's biscuits and greens." He punched at the roll of canvas he was using as a pillow. "Go to sleep. It could be lots worse. We'll see your daddy's cousin up in Chicago soon."

"I don't think Yankees are like us, Jack. They burned down your house."

He stared at the sky above and a light breeze ruffled his blonde hair. "That's just how soldiers do, I guess. They steal from everybody that's not a soldier too. Maybe it's 'cause they're always

179

hungry." Jack blinked at the stars and a tear ran down the side of his face. "Killing people and burning their houses I don't understand. My ma and pa never done nothin' to them."

"When I'm a Yankee I'm not burning down anybody's house, and nobody can make me." Bonnie sat up again and tipped her head. "I hear music and singin'."

Jack raised his head and looked down the rise toward the riverbank. "The soldiers have a fiddle over there. Somebody's playin' that song from back home."

"Papa doesn't like that song. I hope he doesn't hear it, I hope he's asleep now."

"Ben says the Yankees like 'Dixie' as much as our soldiers do, maybe more." Pulling the blanket snugly around them both, he said, "In the morning maybe your Pa can tell us more about the stars we're looking at."

Lighting her way with a Confederate candle, Magdalene approached them from the wagon. She knelt next to Bonnie and swiftly swept her up into her arms, moaning softly as she cradled her.

"When's Papa coming to say good night? Jack and me want him to tell us about the stars."

"Baby, yo' pappy, he sleepin' now." Magdalene rubbed Bonnie's back. "He love you mo' den anybody can tell, an' he always gon' look out fo' you. He got to go with dat parson now and do God's work."

Bonnie struggled to stand, and Magdalene held her tightly to her breast.

"When's he coming back?" She leaned back and looked into Magdalene's brown eyes and watched a tear drop to her chin. "I wanna go see Papa."

"You cain't see Papa now, li'l girl."

"But…"

"You hush now, baby. Jes' go to sleep." Wiping the back of her hand across her face, Magdalene settled into the blankets, and pulled both children close to her. She whispered, "Yo' Papa be sleepin' with de angels, Bonnie May. Time fo' us all to be sleepin'." Magdalene hugged them fiercely, silent and trembling.

Music from the camp stopped.

Jack took Bonnie's hand.

Crickets, frogs, and stars were all around them.

* * * *

Amanda rolled her head to the side and back, a glimmer of perspiration on her brow, her hand a tightened fist.

"Where are you, Amanda?"

"By the wagon."

"Who is with you?"

"Jack. I don't want to go with him."

Mary looked up from her binder, and asked, "Where does Jack want you to go?"

Amanda cried out, 'No!"

Mark bolted from his seat.

Mary raised a hand in his direction, waving him to sit back down. She maintained a soothing voice. "Remember that you're an observer, Amanda.

181

Nothing can harm you. Where does Jack want you to go?"

* * * *

Columbus, Ohio – 1862

Jack tightened his arm around Bonnie's waist and pulled.

Bonnie gripped the wagon wheel and her heart thundered. A drizzling rain mixed with her tears. "I'm not goin'."

He pushed up the brim of his hat and whispered into her ear. "We gotta go. Your papa said, 'Get on the train.' We gotta go."

Ben pulled Bonnie from the wheel and lifted her into his arms. "Yo' papa, he gone, baby."

She screamed and kicked her legs. "He's not, he's not! Let me go." Her cheeks wet with tears, Bonnie begged, "Please, please wait for Papa."

Bonnie reached for Magdalene's outstretched arms and wrapped herself tightly around her. She laid her head on Magdalene's shoulder and whimpered.

Magdalene patted Bonnie's bottom as she whispered to Ben. "Dat soldier, he lookin' real close at de wagon. You bes' go an' talk to him now."

Ben took a few steps toward the tall Union officer. "Dem hosses ain't got nuthin' wrong wid 'em, suh."

The officer walked around the wagon to the back of Saffron. "Well, they sure look like hell."

182

"We done made 'em look bad, suh. They's good, good as gold, suh."

The soldier scanned the animals and lifted Moon's leg, peering at the horse's hoof. "There ain't no ribs showin'." He dropped Moon's leg and poked a finger into the dried goop on Saffron's rump, brought it to his nose, set his tongue against it, and chuckled. "You used a berry of some kind. Tastes pretty close to Ma's gooseberry pie."

"They be shaved in spots, too. Dat not mange, suh."

The man mumbled, "I hope to kiss a pig it's not mange. I just ate some of it."

The Union officer pushed up the wide brim of his slouch hat, looked at Ben, and grinned. He held out his hand. "You got a deal, boy. Can't give you much, but you got a deal. Horses and wagon."

Ben nodded. "Thankee, suh, thankee."

Ben took Bonnie from Magdalene's arms and carried her to a wooden train platform under a crude, sagging shelter. Rain dripped from the eaves and pattered on the boards below. Ben sat on a cracked bench and stood Bonnie in front of him. He slapped rain from his hat against the bench. "Bonnie, you needs to listen. Ben ain't nevvah lied to you, ain't dat right?"

Bonnie snuffled, breathed heavily, and stared at him through a blur of tears.

Ben pulled a threadbare handkerchief from his overall pocket and began to wipe her face. "You 'member yo pappy done got sick, got sick real fast. You 'member dat?"

183

Bonnie nodded and sniffled. "But, Papa said we were all goin' to go…"

"Yo papa, he with de angels now, Bonnie. You know, dem angels we done talked 'bout? You 'member dem angels? You 'member, I tol' you all 'bout yo papa and dem angels?"

Bonnie nodded. "But…"

He interrupted again and continued to wipe tears and spittle. "Dem angels, dey's all singin' and dancin' with yo' papa now."

Ben smiled, his face lit with rapture, his voice a whisper of wonder. "Bonnie May Belle, dey's all havin' a fine time up dah, flittin' all over, an gigglin' an singin' 'cause yo' papa be dah with 'em. Yo' mama dah too, an' dey's together in Glory. I 'spec' yo mama and papa be singin' and dancin' right along wid dem angels." He shrugged as if the point made was obvious. "Dat what dey's doin' right now."

"But Papa said we should all stay together and that he…"

He held the handkerchief to her nose. "Blow."

She did.

"An' he want us all to get on dis heah train. Dat's what he said we s'pose to do. 'Ben Lexington, you get Bonnie an' Jack on dat train. Get dem on dat train.' Dat's what he tol' me, an' dat's what we gonna do."

Chin quivering, Bonnie's eyes welled with tears as she scanned the Union blue uniforms around the station, desperately searching for the rusty black cassock and wide-brimmed hat of her father. "But,

Ben, Papa has to come. Papa has to come."

Ben whispered into her hair. "He wants us to go, li'l girl. Dat's what yo' papa say, Bonnie May. So dat's what we doin'. Come on, now."

She burrowed her face into the coarse, damp wool of his shirt, and breathed in campfire smoke, tobacco, sweat. Ben wrapped his strong, comforting arms around the ache deep in her chest.

Bonnie turned to the rumble, the tall smokestack a gigantic tulip belching pillows of black smoke into the sky. The earth shook as the big train approached and growled a guttural *chug-a-chug*. A great clatter and a spitting hiss of steam engulfed the platform in billowing white plumes as it slowed to a stop.

* * * *

Bonnie lay still, her legs pulled up on the wicker bench, a rough horse blanket snugged around her as she rested her head on Magdalene's lap. Jack was curled into a ball under the seat, buried under another rough blanket. The *click-clatter-click-clatter-click* of iron wheels on steel rails, the dim glow from a swaying red lantern, and green velvet curtains rocking against smoky, gray windows, all combined to create a lullaby that closed Bonnie's eyes. She listened to Ben's deep, guttural hum of a gospel hymn, timed to the rhythm of the train.

Ben whispered, "I think Bonnie done fell asleep, Magdalene."

"Dat's good."

"Magdalene, we shoulda tol' her when he die.

185

She think her pa…I don' know what she think."

Magdalene rubbed Bonnie's back and Bonnie felt an ache deep inside. "Bonnie knows, Ben. She knows. She jes' don' want to know. Dat lockjaw done took Marse John in a week. They ain't nothin' to do 'bout lockjaw, nothin' to do. We jes' be glad dat church took him and say dey gonna do right by his holy remains." Magdalene gently patted Bonnie's back, and whispered, "Marse John be with de angels of dat church, for dat we can be thankin' the good Lawd."

"I should'a shoed dat Moon myself, Magdalene. I should'a shoed Moon." Ben muttered, "Dat dang horse, Marse John done cut hisself shoein' dat dang Moon, an' now look whah we is."

* * * *

An orange sunrise lit the interior of the car; a bank of tobacco smoke hovered on the ceiling. The ticket master lurched through again, balancing himself by wedging his boot into the iron filigree anchoring each bench to the wooden floor. Ben reached into the breast pocket of his overalls and waved the four tickets stamped last night. The conductor nodded. The only one to get on the train in this car was the slender blonde woman across the aisle.

Ben stared out the window, gazing at forests interrupted by creeks and tiny farms and cabins with gray smoke rising from stone chimneys. The sky brightened with the rising sun, morning dew drifted from green fields in a thin blanket of fog. A massive bull moose grazed in a passing marsh and looked impassively at the train. Water lilies drooped from its antlers like moss from limbs of live oaks in Charleston. Ben wasn't good with numbers, and he struggled to understand the price he had to pay for these tickets, most of the money the officer had given him for Saffron and Moon. It wasn't enough for the four of them to get all the way to Chicago, so they had to get off the train in a town called Cleveland. He didn't know how far Cleveland was from Chicago. Ben gave the ticket agent the money and looked with dismay at the change the man dropped in his hand. He hoped it was enough to buy food for the children when the train got to Cleveland. A gentle voice across the aisle interrupted his thoughts.

"Are those children traveling with you?"

A black hat topped the woman's loose blond curls, anchored with a pearl pin and decorated with a spray of blue feathers. Patent leather toes were visible under a black cloak draped to the floor.

Ben looked at Bonnie, her face smudged with dried tears. "Dis li'l gal's kin all done died, 'cept fo' Mistah Jack heah. He her cousin, an' his kin all got kilt down in Virginny." He nodded to Magdalene, "Mah wife and me, we is takin' care of 'em, bes' we can."

"I see that." She tipped her head to get a better view of Jack. "But they're too thin. They need food." She lifted a colorful carpetbag to her lap. It was decorated with green, black, and red flowers.

187

Bonnie sat erect, scooched close to Magdalene, and pulled the rough blanket up around her until only her eyes peeked through. She watched the woman warily.

Tucking a blonde curl behind her ear, the lady held an apple out to Bonnie. She looked at the fruit, offered with long, delicate fingers. Two weeks after they got in the wagon, hunger had become part of her. Now she could almost taste snowy sweetness, smell sugary-sour juice. Saliva bathed her tongue. Not sure if she should take the apple, Bonnie looked up at Magdalene.

Jack scrambled from under the seat, pulled off his hat, and leaned out to take the fruit. Ben held him back by the arm, but dropped his hand at Magdalene's glare. Jack nodded to the stranger, muttered, "Thank you, ma'am," and tentatively took the apple. He wiggled into the seat beside Bonnie, fumbled around in the blanket for her hand, and whispered, "Eat."

Her wide eyes glued to those of the stranger, Bonnie brought the apple to her mouth and took a tiny bite. Her stomach growled in anticipation of this piece of heaven and she proceeded to munch on the apple like a starving rabbit.

The woman smiled at Bonnie and held out another apple to Jack. "I have one for you, too. What's your name?"

Jack looked at Ben and back at the woman. "Jack Wellington, ma'am."

"And what's your name, little one?"

Bonnie stretched her tongue to catch juicy

dribble on her chin and whispered to Magdalene, "Am I Bobby or Bonnie?"

Magdalene reached for another apple the woman offered. "Ma'am, her name be Bonnie May Belle Lexington. Mah man be Ben, an' ah be Magdalene."

"Well, it's a pleasure to meet you all. My name is Penelope Starks, and I'm on my way to Chicago to live with my sister. I'm a nurse. There is a great need for nurses there, and I'll be working in a hospital near Camp Douglas. Where are you going?"

Ben swallowed a bite of apple. "We is goin' to Cleveland, ma'am. I gots to get dese chirrens to their kin in Chicago, but ah cain't pay fo' dey tickets widdout ah works in Cleveland fo' a month or two first. Engineer done tol' me dey's a lumberyard in Cleveland dat hires freedmen. Magdalene an' me, we ain't no slaves." Reaching for his pocket, he touched the comforting oilcloth wrapping the freedom papers John had prepared for him and Magdalene.

Penelope looked from Bonnie to Jack, as she said, "I'm thoroughly confused. The children have relatives in the city? I thought you said they had no family."

"Well, Bonnie's pa done had a cousin dah, Mistah Duncan Lexington. Marse John give me a letter to give him. Dat was whah we was headed fo' from Charleston."

"You've traveled all the way from Charleston, South Carolina, with these little ones?"

"Yes'm."

189

Penelope looked at the children and then at the adults, one by one. "My goodness. No wonder you all look so worn out. How in the world did you ever get through the lines?"

Magdalene jutted her chin. "We ducked an' dodged an' slep' in churches. Mos' people was nice," she looked at Ben and back to the woman, "some not. We done made it through, but they was plenty o' times we mos' didn't." Her eyes snapped and her nostrils flared. "Dem cannons an' guns was jes' a'roarin' an' a'poppin'." She nodded her head. "Prayin' is what got us through, lots o' prayin' to de good Lawd."

Penelope shook her head. "Well, I certainly don't know many details, but I don't recommend you attempt to go to Illinois."

Bonnie looked at the woman and swallowed. She glanced at Ben. "Papa said to go."

The woman laughed. Bonnie thought her laugh tinkled like bells. "No, darling. I don't mean you. I don't mean Jack."

Magdalene frowned. "What you mean, den?"

Penelope raised her brow and sighed. "Well, I surely don't approve. But it was last February, I think…yes, February when Illinois put a stop to slave migration. Officials convicted former slaves of living in Carthage in violation of the state law. Those poor people were sold, which in itself is against federal law. Illinois has outlawed the immigration of former slaves."

Magdalene furrowed her brow at Ben and looked at Penelope. "But dat 'mancipation paper, dat be de

190

law." Magdalene nodded and added firmly, "We got papers, too."

"You are correct, of course. The Emancipation Proclamation was issued in January, and you are indeed free. I'm sorry to say that the country, north and south, is still in great turmoil, and I fear that this awful war is far from over. We live in perilous times, and justice is not always foremost in men's minds. It will take some time to sort out these inequities."

Bonnie didn't understand all the words, but she liked the lady's voice.

Ben twirled his whiskers around an index finger. "What does you know 'bout Charleston, whah we be comin' from, Ma'am?"

Penelope bent to place the carpetbag on the floor by her feet. "Like I said, Ben, I don't know details. But according to the *Daily Ohio Statesman* in Columbus, Charleston is under siege, with many casualties among the civilian population."

Magdalene looked at Ben. "How we goin' be gettin' dem to Chicago? Bonnie May, she too li'l to go alone."

"I'm not little, Magdalene. Papa said I was big."

"Hush, baby. What we goin' to do?"

"Where are you staying in Cleveland?"

Ben glanced at Magdalene. "We don't rightly know yet, Ma'am."

Reaching into her carpetbag, Penelope pulled out a silver pencil and a piece of paper with roses on the edge. She put the paper on her knee and wrote on it in graceful script, and then handed the paper to Ben.

"This is a Catholic charity in southern Cleveland. Just say you've been directed to them by Penelope Starks of Columbus. They will help you."

Penelope opened her arms to Bonnie. "Would you like to sit with me, sweetheart?"

Bonnie looked up at Magdalene, and then she scrambled off the seat and allowed herself to be lifted to the woman's lap.

"You're such a pretty little thing, and so grown up!"

Bonnie looked again at Magdalene, and said, "Papa says I'm pretty little." She nodded at the lady, and added, "And he says I'm heavy like a sack of flour, too."

Penelope shot the woman a questioning glance and Magdalene returned a tiny shake of her head. "That just means you're very grown up, indeed." She glanced from Ben to Magdalene. "You know, it's only another day's ride on the train to Chicago. Why don't I take the children to their family?"

No! I don't' want to go with her! Bonnie scurried down from the lady's lap and struggled through Jack's legs into Magdalene's warm arms. She squirmed into her lap, wrapped her arms around Magdalene's neck, and whispered frantically, "I want to stay with you. Don't let her take me!"

Bonnie trembled as Magdalene rocked back and forth and rubbed her back. "Shhh, baby."

A distressed frown crossed Penelope's face. "I'm so sorry. I didn't mean to frighten Bonnie. I just thought it was a good idea since I'm going there myself."

"Dat's all right, missus." Magdalene patted Bonnie's back. "We done give our promise to Marse John dat we take dem to Chicago."

"I strongly advise that you and Ben not attempt to go there. That charity in Cleveland will accommodate you all until you can make other arrangements."

Ben stood. "I needs to think." He walked to the end of the car, pulled open the door, and stepped outside.

* * * *

A steam whistle shrieked as the train slowed. The conductor trudged through the car, his voice a monotone. "Cleveland. Ladies comfort available, men to the rear of the station, train leaves in thirty minutes for Toledo."

A cool November breeze blew through the crowded platform. Ben carried Bonnie on his hip and stepped down to a wooden stool set close to the train.

Ben set her down. "You stay close to yo' Cousin Jack fum now on, Bonnie May."

Jack scooped up a handful of dirt and whispered, "Look, the dirt here is black and gray, not red like at home."

Arriving passengers milled on the platform, mingling with hundreds of men in dark blue Union uniforms waiting to board another train. Officers with gold braid on jaunty slouch hats paused and spoke to other men with anxious, darting eyes.

Muskets hung over shoulders and tobacco smoke whisked from mouths. Bonnie heard men mutter 'Lincoln' and 'Shiloh' and 'Antietam', words that Papa had said.

A row of carriages, brass lanterns on the front and gold or red fringe around the top, lined the far edge of the platform. A man in a tall black hat helped a woman wearing a lacy white dress and a girl Bonnie's age into the first carriage. The girl held a doll dressed just as she was, in a yellow bonnet and frilly pinafore. Bonnie folded her arms over the stained and mended dress she'd worn since Charleston.

From the cars at the rear of the train came a low murmur of groans and confused voices. Dozens of soldiers struggled with crutches as they stumbled into the bright sunlight, swathed in filthy bandages. In tattered remnants of uniforms, the men shuffled and shambled to a waiting line of wagons. Faces haggard and drawn, eyes vacant and haunted, bandages smeared black and red on their heads and arms, they carried other wounded men on canvas litters, some missing limbs and some gaunt as skeletons. Women in black and white capes let soldiers lean on them as they tottered along. A dazed man with bloodstained trousers, his arm bound to his side, stood swaying at the bottom of the step. Penelope hurried to help him, bent under his weight as he hopped on one good leg toward a crowded buckboard.

Ben and Magdalene sat on a bench with the children and waited. Magdalene pulled up her straw bag and placed it between her and Bonnie. "Hold dis open, Bonnie May." She searched around in the straw satchel until she found a small, velvet bag tied with a ribbon. Carefully pulling the ribbon free, she poured out two sparkling sapphires and a silver locket on a delicate chain. Magdalene opened the locket, put one blue stone inside and snapped it closed.

Holding the locket and turning to Bonnie, she said, "You hold real still now while I puts dis 'round you."

Bonnie bent her head forward and the clasp clicked. She lifted the heart-shaped locket and the jewel inside glittered through silver filigree.

"Dat locket and dat earbob was yo' Mama's, Bonnie May Belle. You got yo' Mama's blue eyes, and now you got one of yo' Mama's sapphires in dat locket." Magdalene lifted Bonnie's chin and said, "Look at me, Bonnie May Belle. Look at Magdalene."

Bonnie met her moist, dark eyes.

Magdalene leaned close to Bonnie's face, and whispered, "You is to wear dat locket all de time, Bonnie May Belle. You is to think 'bout yo' Mama an' Papa every time you looks at it." She straightened and looked at Jack and back to Bonnie.

Magdalene pulled Jack's overalls toward her and poked the clasp of the other earbob through the rough cotton. "Now, you both gots a earbob. Dey is a pair. You can't be havin' one earbob. Earbobs is a pair, an' dat's what you two is. So dat mean you got to be together. You wear dem earbobs all de time, and you stay together all de time."

Jack looked at the earring firmly anchored in the buttonhole of his overalls. His brows knit and he muttered, "Boys don't wear these earbob things, Magdalene."

She put her rough, warm hand on Jack's cheek. "Now, you listen, Jackson Wellington. Listen to what Magdalene be sayin' to you. Yo' job from dis day on is to take care of yo' cousin Bonnie May." She nodded toward Bonnie. "Bonnie May Belle ain't but a li'l bitty baby girl. You is a big, strong man now, and you needs to watch out fo' yo' cousin. Dis be yo' job now. You keep dat earbob with you so's you always remembers yo' job." Magdalene shook his chin firmly. "You hear me, Jack?" Her voice cracked. "You hear what I is tellin' you to do? Take good care o' Bonnie?"

He looked back at Magdalene and nodded. "Yes, ma'am."

Bonnie studied Jack's face and followed his eyes to Ben and Penelope. Standing by the train, they were talking, but she couldn't hear what was said. Ben nodded. He nodded again and took another piece of paper from Penelope. They walked back toward the bench, still talking in low voices. Bonnie turned to Magdalene, her face hot and her throat tight. She fell into Magdalene's arms, unable to hold back a flood of tears.

Patting Bonnie's bottom, she whispered, "You is to be a good li'l gal, Bonnie May Belle. Dis lady goin' take good care of you 'til you gets to Chicago."

Bonnie whimpered into the musky, warm folds of Magdalene's cotton dress. "Please, please don't make me go with that lady, Magdalene."

She rubbed Bonnie's back, her voice low, soft, and choking through tears of her own. "Bonnie May Belle, you gots to do what yo' Papa said. You goin' be with yo' Cousin Duncan tomorrow." Magdalene pulled Jack to her, squeezed her arms around them, and whispered, "Me and Ben, we come an' see you real soon."

Yesterday

CHAPTER 16

Mark leaned back in his chair in the squad room. He looked at his watch, then up at the wall clock. *Why isn't she calling me back?* He ran his fingers through short, dark hair, leaned forward, and rested his forearms on the desk. A notebook lay open in front of him, and he scanned through his research on St. Michael's Church.

The bells were cast in London in the early 1760s and brought to Charleston in 1764, where they were installed in the belfry of St. Michael's Church. *Amanda's right. They were made specifically for this church.* Rain bounced off the roof of a car outside the smudged window. Mark thought about a tall ship bound for Charleston Harbor, laden with a cargo that included eight massive iron bells. He flipped back pages of his calendar to the date of Amanda's last regression. *Three goddamned days since I saw her, and not a word.* He took a sip of lukewarm coffee and looked back at his notes.

When the British captured Charleston in 1780, they took the bells as spoils of war and brought them back to England. The eight bells were purchased by a South Carolina philanthropist after the Revolutionary War and sent back to St. Michael's in Charleston. In 1823 the bells had developed cracks from use, and the church sent them back to London for recasting.

Prior to the Charleston siege begun in 1862, they were moved from St. Michael's Church to a shed on the grounds of the statehouse in Columbia, South Carolina, some eighty miles away. *That's what Amanda said. Her father helped hide the bells.* He shook his head. *Bonnie's father.*

Badly damaged when their wartime hiding place was burned, the bells went back to the foundry in London again after the fall of Richmond. Mark tapped several keys on his computer, looking for Civil War details about Columbia, South Carolina. Glancing from the computer screen to his notes, he jotted down what he had found: February 17, 1865 - Columbia, South Carolina - surrender. Sherman burned most of the city to the ground. *The bells would have been burned around this time.* Mark tossed his pen on the desk, leaned back over the notes, and his chair squeaked as he continued to scan.

Two years later, in February of 1867, the eight bells went back to St. Michael's. *Christ, the damn things must have weighed tons. Couldn't they cast bells in the States by then? Wait—the foundry in London still had the original molds. Incredible.* The phone on his desk buzzed.

Mark reached for the pen and spoke into the receiver. "Callahan."

He glanced at his watch. "Why not? You're sure she's down there?" He stood, his eyes roaming the squad room before settling on Pete's curious gaze. "Thirty minutes."

"What's up?" Pete followed his partner's actions

200

and stood.

Mark looked out the window at the pouring rain. "Not sure." He swept his cell into a breast pocket, opened the bottom desk drawer where he stored his service automatic, and unbuckled his holster belt. "The ponies are parked for the day. I'm takin' the rest of the day as personal, maybe tomorrow, too." Mark turned the key in the desk lock. "Can you be Boomerang's daddy 'til tomorrow night? His stall's squared away, so he'll only need the usual."

Pete reached for his coffee. "Sure."

"I owe you." Mark logged out of his computer and turned off the monitor. "Cover me for a day."

"You bet, bud. Wanna tell me what's—?"

Mark interrupted, a scowl on his face. "I don't know." He grabbed his jacket and walked around his desk toward the door. "But I'm gonna find out."

* * * *

I love him, that's all it'll take. This life. A previous life. Christ, a life before that. Maybe. Doesn't matter which damned life. Take your pick. Next life? Poof. Whatever life. Why, why does this happen? Amanda leaned her head back and stared at the ceiling. *I can't let Mark into my life. Every time I look at him someone else looks back. I touch him and I'm touching someone else. There is someone else.*

* * * *

201

Windshield wipers slapped quickly, doing little to clear the rushing sluice of rainwater turning Mark's windshield opaque. He shoved the gearshift into park and turned off the engine. Air thick enough to swim in began to fog the interior as he waited for a break in the downpour. Mark peered out the driver's window toward Amanda's place. Mary's apartment was lit like a church on Easter Sunday above it. *Doesn't even look like Amanda's at home.* He frowned at the big drops splattering the surface of puddles on the sidewalk and muttered, "Time to find out what the hell is going on."

Mary's voice crackled, "Hello?"

"It's Mark Callahan."

The gate buzzed, and Mark shook rain from his jacket as he entered the brownstone. He paused at Amanda's apartment and listened.

Not a sound.

He took the stairs two at a time and rapped a knuckle on Mary's door.

She swung it open. "Mark. Come on in."

He scanned the room. Mary's flat was as cluttered with antiques as Amanda's place. He glanced into the spare room and viewed a startling contrast. In Amanda's apartment, this room crammed with what she referred to as more 'treasures'. In Mary's, the same space was the sparsely furnished office of a shrink.

Mark ran his hand through his damp hair. "How do you know she's in there?"

"I hear Oprah stomping around down there."

Mark looked down and shook his head.

"Anything else?" He chuckled at the thought of Oprah 'stomping around'.

"Doors slamming, so she's in there. Come into the kitchen."

Mark followed Mary to the kitchen in the rear of the large apartment.

"Tea? Oh, I forgot that you're a coffee man. I can have some for you in about a second."

"No, don't go to any trouble." Mark moved to the hall, back toward her, and started to pace. "When was the last time you tried her door? Don't you have a key? What's going on? Why'd you want me to come here first?"

"You'll like this. Espresso. Two questions at a time, dear. About an hour ago and the security chain's on." She glanced at him over her shoulder. "For the answers to the other two questions, sit."

Mary's laptop was on the kitchen table. She reached over, pressed a key, and returned to the espresso machine. Amanda's voice filled the room; it was soft and breathy.

Magdalene, don't make me go. I don't want to go.

Mary's voice followed. *You're an observer only, Amanda. You're perfectly safe. What is happening to Bonnie?*

Amanda's voice was more relaxed. *The tall blonde lady is holding my hand. We're walking to the train.*

Mary again. *Where is Jack?*
He's talking to Ben.
What's Ben saying?

203

Mary punched another key on her laptop stopping the playback. She placed the cup of coffee in front of Mark.

His eyes moved from the laptop to Mary. "I remember hearing all this. She went through it with you, right? After the session?"

"No. And this is why I wanted to talk. After you left, after the session was over, she said she was tired and wanted to put the post session discussion off for a day. You know that session analysis is important. It wasn't done. Amanda needs to discuss her journey and what she experienced." Mary raised and lowered a teabag in a cup of steaming water and frowned. "We learned in that last session that Bonnie's father dies. Bonnie is wrenched from more people she cares about, especially Magdalene. Bonnie's young when this happens. Amanda was young when she suffered the traumatic losses in her life, her parents and then her brother. This is my fault. I should have insisted on the post-session discussion."

He sipped his coffee and set the cup down. "Wouldn't Amanda's understanding of her life as Bonnie help her understand her life today? Are we talking about survivor's guilt here? There's no way those losses could've been her fault. She was just a little kid."

"True, but Amanda needs to talk it out—she needs someone to help her understand. Holing up and brooding about Bonnie's loss is a huge mistake. Amanda needs the perspectives of other people in what happened to Bonnie. She needs to talk it through to help her understand that it's not her fault or Bonnie's fault." Mary lowered her cup. "I assumed Amanda's been at her office every day, but I was wrong. When I called the receptionist at Plethora to speak to her yesterday, the woman said Amanda had called in sick the last three days." Mary sighed. "She won't open her door, won't answer the phone. I thought of calling Tom."

"No. I need to talk to her." Mark tossed off the rest of the espresso, grimaced at the bitter taste, and pushed back his chair. "Don't pay attention to the sound of breaking glass. She'll likely throw something at me."

"Nothing too valuable, I hope."

* * * *

Mark banged loudly on Amanda's door with a closed fist. "It's Mark. Open up."

He waited. Nothing.

Rapping his knuckles again, he said, "Amanda, open the door."

Silence.

"Do you want me to pick the lock? You know I can."

Nothing.

As he turned to go back up to Mary's apartment for the key, he heard the deadbolt slide.

The door opened a crack, the chain still attached. A groggy voice mumbled, "Go away."

Mark wedged his foot against the door as Amanda started to push it closed. "Let me in now, or I break the chain. Your call."

Amanda leaned into the door. "Go away, Mark. I want to be left along, alone."

"Stand back or you'll get hurt."

"Wait. Waid-a-goddamn-minute. Shit."

Mark heard a struggle with the chain, another obscenity, and the chain slide free.

She stepped back and wavered unsteadily as Mark pushed open the door. Her hair a tangled mess, gray circles beneath her bloodshot blue eyes spoke of sleepless nights. Pale, pink-splotched cheeks bore traces of dried tears. She was barefoot, wearing a long cotton tee and red sweat pants.

"What the fuck to, do you want?"

Mark clenched his jaw. "Acceptable language, for starters."

Amanda flipped both arms out and slapped her thighs. "Sorry." She turned away and spoke over her shoulder. "Now go away."

Mark grabbed Amanda's arms and pressed her back to the wall, more forcefully than he intended, but he was worried as hell about her, and bordering on anger. "Why aren't you answering your phone? What's going on?"

She squirmed. "'Cause I dint' wanna. Let me go."

He loosened his grip, but didn't release her. His voice softened. "What is it?" *This regression stuff is getting to her. She can't do this anymore.*

"Ya know, iss not a goo' id-, not sush a good idea for you to be around me." Amanda leaned her head back against the wall and looked up at him.

"People around me die, all the good people die." She shook her head and her voice cracked. "Hell, you're a cop, you know everything, right? S' what you said; you're a cop."

Mark searched her face, surprised at her answer. Tears glistened on her cheeks. Worry tightened his chest and he whispered, "What's my being a cop have to do with anything?"

"Lemme go." She looked down and slurred, "Or I'll puke all over your purty blue shirt."

He tightened his grip on her arms, and raised his voice. "For Christ's sake, get a grip on yourself. I need you to tell me what's going on."

She exaggerated her speech. "I'll use your words, officer." Raising her brows, she closed her eyes. "Your call."

Mark raised his hands in surrender and took a step back. *There's no talking to someone this drunk.*

Turning, she steadied herself with one hand against the wall. "Get the hell outta here. I don't want you here." She headed down the hall and into the bathroom.

He followed her and touched the bathroom door as she pushed it closed.

* * * *

Amanda slid her back down the door until she dropped her elbows on her knees, forehead to forearms. *Why did I let him in? I don't want him here.*

The sweet-sour sting of bile burned her throat.

207

She scrambled to the porcelain bowl, raised the lid, and rested her chin on the cool rim.

Poor little Bonnie. Hell, she's me. I'm poor little Bonnie. Stupid clock. Papa, dead. My dad and Bonnie's mother, my mom, dead. Magdalene and Ben, gone. Connor and Joe, dead. Mary? Mark? Mark's gentle eyes gazed at hers though a kaleidoscope of funerals, gravesites...at her, at a laughing, smiling, terrified child. Amanda pinched her eyes closed and tears began to fall. *Not Mark. Not Mark.*

* * * *

Mark surveyed the kitchen. Empty bottles were perched on top of the trash, Merlot, Absolut. Another fifth of vodka, nearly gone, on the counter. A smudged wine glass stood in the sink. The only other thing out was a fresh drink on the counter. He opened the fridge and looked around. The shelves held a full jar of peanut butter, a nearly empty bottle of anchovy-stuffed olives, two eggs in a carton, one lemon yogurt with an expired date stamp, and a package of something loosely wrapped in plastic. Mark pulled out the package, and unable to determine if it was good cheese or bad lunchmeat, tossed it into the trash. He next turned his attention to the freezer. It contained yet another bottle of vodka, this one unopened, and empty ice trays. He took the Chinese restaurant menu from under a happy face magnet on the fridge door and dialed the number on it.

Oprah swirled around his ankles, drawing his eyes to her as he placed his order. He glanced at the cat's bowls. No water, no food. He turned and looked around the kitchen as he spoke into the phone. *Now where the hell does she keep the cat food?*

He finished the call, searched through cupboards until he found the kibble, and filled Oprah's food dish. The dry pellets bounced and rattled in the glass bowl like he was dropping marbles. He rinsed and filled the water dish and dumped Amanda's drink into the sink. Then he walked around looking for the litter box. It was in the back of the laundry room. Mark wrinkled his nose and scowled at the tray. *At least that's not too bad.* After a few more minutes of tending to Oprah's needs, he walked back down the hall and rapped on the bathroom door.

Nothing.

He knocked louder, and raised his voice. "Amanda?"

A muffled response. "Leave me alone."

Mark turned the knob and nudged the door open. Amanda sat on the floor, cheek resting on the rim of the toilet. He sighed and put his hands on his hips. "Get undressed. You need a shower."

"I need to be leg, left alone." She wiped her eyes on her tee shirt. "Go home. Get outta here."

Mark unbuttoned his shirt, pulled it off, and tossed it on the floor behind him. "Fine, you'll take a shower with your clothes on." He took off his watch and set it on the bathroom vanity. Pulling Amanda to her feet with her back to him, he lifted her into the shower.

"What the hell are you doing?" She stumbled as she spun from him.

"This is how we do it at Central Lockup." He turned on cold water full blast over her head and maintained his aim as she stumbled back to escape. She lifted her hands to shelter her face from the onslaught of water. Spitting and choking, Amanda attempted to squirm by him and sputtered a scream. "Let me outta here, you bastard!" Choking on her words, she swung her arms and pushed at the hand holding her against the tile wall in a wad of tee shirt. "Let me go—goddamn you!" Amanda fought the weak battle of the drunken and sleep-deprived. She struggled, blathered incoherent profanity, but soon gave way to furious frustration, followed by tears, and finally shivering.

Mark turned off the water. Her sweat pants, weighted with water and her struggle, sagged below her hips and slid down easily with soaked panties. Mark lifted each of her legs from them and pulled the soaked shirt over her head. Naked, Amanda wrapped her arms around herself, shivered and sobbed. Long dark hair clung to her pale skin.

He swirled a bath sheet around her and pulled her into his chest, rubbing her back for several minutes and working the towel through her hair. Mark sighed as he held her in his arms. *There's nothing I wouldn't do for this woman. Have I loved her longer than I know?* Stepping back and fighting his own ache, he lifted her chin with his finger.

Still sniveling, her eyes red and puffy, Amanda

was regaining control. Her shivering stopped.

He nodded at the bathroom door. "Get into that robe and do whatever else it is you need to do, like rinsing this bender from your breath. It's over." He stepped back. "I'm going to the kitchen to make coffee."

Mark retrieved his watch from the vanity and his shirt from the floor. "Dinner will be here in about fifteen minutes." He straightened, his eyes roaming her face. "I suggest you be ready to eat."

* * * *

Mark scooped wonton, crab Rangoon, fried rice, and chicken with snow peas from the white cartons. He pitched the empty cartons like basketballs into the open trashcan. He tossed soy sauce packets and fortune cookies on the table.

She pushed her damp hair behind an ear, glanced at the food in front of her, at Mark, and looked back at the pile of food. There was twice as much as she could eat on her plate.

"You don't have any lime." Mark slid a glass of tomato juice he'd found in the pantry to her. "But take my word for it, this'll help."

She took a sip of juice, paused, and drank most of the glass. "You can go. You don't have to—"

"You used the same words when you tried to throw me out of your hospital room after saving my life." He speared a piece of chicken and held it out to her. "I chose to ignore you then and I choose to ignore you now. Let's say I'm returning the favor.

211

Eat."

"I don't know what you're talking about."

"Look, if you don't put on the brakes, you're gonna kill yourself. Since that doesn't seem like a good idea, I'm pushing the brakes to the floorboard myself, whether you like it or not."

Amanda pushed her plate away and frowned. "I'm getting another drink."

He slid the plate back. "You haven't put anything but booze in that frame for three days. Time to eat something. I'd have no problem doing a rinse and repeat in that shower all damn night long." Matching her glare with an angry scowl of his own he said, "I'm not kidding."

She pushed back her chair and stood.

Mark followed and began to unbutton his shirt. "Your decision."

Amanda held up both hands, palms toward him, and inched back. "No! I'll eat." She frowned at the mountain of food on her plate and mumbled, "Can I just have some coffee?"

* * * *

Mark cleared the table. He wasn't completely happy with the small amount Amanda had eaten, but at least she had eaten something. He leaned back in his chair, arms folded across his chest, and watched her as she sipped coffee. "You can give me the silent treatment as long as you want, but eventually you're going to talk to me."

She squirmed in her chair and blurted, "You have

no right to come barging in here and—"

"Wrong. You know better. I know better."

Amanda rested elbows on the table, fingers laced under her nose, and stared at the wall above his head. Her eyes began to tear.

"Listen to me." Mark leaned on the table. "You've got the harebrained idea that you're born to lose anyone that ever means anything to you, that daring to love is just crazy, self-destructive bullshit. Have I got that pretty much right?

The narrowing of her eyes was impetus enough for him to continue. "Let's look at some examples of what you call bullshit. You have a godmother that adores you; you have a smart, handsome, talented brother with a nice family. You even have a sister-in-law, who cares a great deal about you. You have a promising career with a bright future in what looks like a fascinating field." Mark sighed. "Amanda, that is not a bullshit life. It is an admirable life." His voice softened considerably and he reached across the table to her, his palms up. "You're also the bravest person I've ever known and I love you more than life itself."

She closed her eyes and swallowed.

"Look, I'm not going to pretend you're through with getting slapped around by life. It's just that it's not *all* shit. Isolating yourself isn't going to protect those you care about, and they love you too much, *I* love you too much, to let you do it. People aren't meant to be alone." He shook his head and stood.

Mark walked around the table and ran a hand through his hair. "There isn't a damned thing in here to eat. I'm going to the store." Lifting Amanda's keys from the rack as he headed down the hall, he stopped halfway and walked back. He raised her chin and scanned her face. "Cuss me out again and you'll find yourself over my knee, as sure as you're born." Kissing her lightly, he added, "Love is also a four letter word."

CHAPTER 17

Amanda rested her head on Mark's chest, listening to the thunder of his heart slow to a steady, gentle beat. She smiled at his deep, contented sigh and circled his navel with an index finger.

"Tickles," he mumbled.

"Sorry." She buried her face into the warm, musky scent of his neck, wrapped an arm and leg around him, and tickled his side.

Mark flipped her to her back. "You still feeling sassy?" He growled and feigned biting her shoulder as he pulled her to him. "You'll be beggin' me to quit before you're an hour older. Maybe two."

"Guess what?"

He stopped struggling with the tangled sheet and raised his head to look at her. "What?"

"The Irish in your voice is thicker after sex." She kissed the stubble on his chin.

With a wink and an exaggerated brogue, he said, "It's about to be gettin' thicker yet, my sweet colleen." He paused again and smiled. "No, I didn't know."

Amanda laughed and squirmed from his arms as Oprah jumped on the bed.

He lifted himself from her, glanced at Oprah, and rolled to his back, his eyes closed. "Saved by the cat."

"Me or you?" Amanda chuckled as she sat up,

215

scratched behind Oprah's ears, evoking a different thunder.

"Wouldn't you like to know?" Mark yawned, rested his hands across his waist, fingers laced. He appeared to doze, the beige sheet low on his hips.

Amanda's eyes traced his form. *Men aren't supposed to be this pretty.* She slowly shook her head and smiled as she studied him. *Mark looks like a damned Greek god that needs to comb his hair.* He was a big man, tall with broad shoulders, arresting enough to turn any woman's head. A square jaw and narrow nose, his weathered face tanned with summer sun. His dark hair was a tangle of soft curls, and as usual one rested on his forehead. Muscles flexed when he moved. Dark hair on his chest narrowed down his hard, flat stomach. Mark had the grace of a panther, as stealthy, and as dangerous. *The big dope has to know how frightening he can be. He's a cop and uses his intimidating looks to his advantage. I've never known this body before; but this person, this arrogant confidence, are as much a part of me as breathing. I've only known the face a few months, but I've known the man forever. And I'm going to find out how.* Mark had just made her soar to heights more wondrous than she could ever have imagined, more tender than anything her soul could dream. Gazing at his naked form brought forth the fluttering wings of a hummingbird in her heart. *It's more than making love with Mark. It's more than feeling his arms around me, more than this magnificent ache and the breathtaking wonder of his body. This incredible electricity between us is too familiar, too much a part of me ... of us. I ... know ... him.*

Eyes still closed, his voice rumbled, "You know, people can tell when somebody is looking at them. I feel the finger of a witch probing the folds of my brain."

"I'll be more careful." She smiled as one bright brown eye peeked at her. "You should work out more, Prince Charming. Yer gettin' flabby."

"It's another workout you want?" He glanced down his chest with a frown, his muscles rippling involuntarily. "Get your lovely derriere over here." He reached for her.

Amanda squealed, wriggled from his grasp, and laughed as he fell back on the bed.

* * * *

The cool water cascaded over her face as she finished lathering her hair. Amanda turned and tipped her head, letting the suds run down her back.

He's an experienced cop who rides a horse for a living. How dangerous is that? He knows what he's doing. She frowned. *What the hell can be more dangerous than being a cop? How can I let myself fall for him? Joe was a damned securities trader, and I lost him. Could I pick anybody more likely to get killed than a cop? Stupid, stupid, stupid. But God, it's amazing how he can make me feel so, like he...* Amanda frowned at the bar of soap in her hands. *Feel like he, like he what?*

She squinted at Mark leaning into the shower, his

217

eyes glinting in mischief.

"You are stunning. Did I really just make love to that gorgeous body?"

Amanda rubbed the soap into a loofah sponge as she watched one of his long legs step into the shower. "Silly, cut it out. Turn around."

He did.

Amanda rubbed the sponge across his shoulders, down his arms, down his back. She smiled at his low growl. *The panther purrs.* Sliding the soapy sponge down his hip, she muttered, "Nice ass."

Mark chuckled and turned to face her. "Thanks."

She glanced up at his grin and squeezed more suds onto a broad chest and shoulders. *What the hell is it about him? I somehow know him so well, but I really don't know him at all. I don't know anything about him.* Suddenly uncomfortable sponging much else, she glanced down his handsome body, chewed her lower lip, and her face warmed.

He laughed quietly. "You are one lovely woman."

Amanda met his eyes.

"And that pretty blush of yours is transparent as hell." He bent to within an inch of her lips and whispered, "I won't bite, promise."

Mark kissed her as he took the loofah from her hand. "My turn." He tossed the sponge over his shoulder, and rubbed the bar of soap in his hands. "I prefer the feel of slippery skin."

She inched back from him and smiled. "You're silly."

"Each to his own, or is it to each his own?" He

scanned her body and shrugged. "I forget."

"I don't think I like taking showers with you." She frowned as he slid strong, soapy hands around her waist and tugged her to him. "The last time you were mean."

He moved his lips across her shoulder. "Far from it, *mo chroí*. I was," he kissed her neck, "persuasive."

She moaned with pleasure at the feel of his strong hands gliding up and down her back. Amanda leaned into him, rested her hands on his biceps and closed her eyes. *Mo chroí, whatever that means. How the hell can a girl who isn't made of stone resist that? God, he feels wonderful.* Her breasts against his chest, their thighs touching, she stood between his long legs and laid her head on his shoulder.

As his hand moved to the back of her neck, Amanda turned her face to the hunger of a kiss that made her heart skip.

He suddenly shook the water from his hair and spun her around, reaching for the faucet. "Too cold."

"I like the water cool." Amanda giggled. "Wuss."

Mark turned up the hot water and eased her against the tile wall. He kissed her long and deep, her breath catching. His strong, soapy hands moved down her back to her hips. "Let's see if you think I'm a 'wuss' in a few minutes."

* * * *

219

Amanda sat at the kitchen table in a canary-yellow fleece robe, hand circling a coffee mug. Mark made breakfast. He flipped a pancake with one hand, turned a sausage link with the other, and whistled *Take Me Out to the Ballgame,* all at the same time. The White Sox game on the kitchen television elicited an occasional tap dance or a fist pump accompanied by a bellowing 'put-it-on-the-board' cheer.

"How did you learn how to do that?"

"Being a life-long Sox fan." Mark glanced at her.

"No. I mean the pancake flippin' thing."

He set a plate in front of her, piled high with more than she could possibly eat. "Making breakfast for my kid sisters."

"Are you and Boomerang related?" She looked at the stack of pancakes and pile of sausage links on his plate. "You have the appetite of a starving horse."

"And you have the appetite of an anorexic parakeet." He looked at his plate, then hers. "Eat."

They watched the game and ate pancakes. At the crack of a bat, Mark shoved both fists into the air, one with a fork, and shouted, "Yes!".

Table cleared, they turned their faces to the game, forearms resting on the table, hands wrapped around warm coffee mugs. "It's been six weeks since that last session." Amanda leaned back and fidgeted with the locket on her neck. "Mary's agreed to do another this evening."

He glanced at her and turned back to the game, "No."

She sipped her coffee, and then held the cup under her chin. "Not your call, officer." Amanda watched his jaw tense and his profile change from a relaxed gaze to determination.

"It damned well is my call. You're not doing another session. Period." He aimed the remote at the television, pushed the mute button, and looked at her.

"I'm fine, and there are good reasons to do this."

He started to speak, paused, and started again. "I don't want you putting yourself through any more regressions. We agreed." He delicately dropped the remote on the table. "How do we know each other? Frankly, my dear, I don't give a damn. And I won't think about it tomorrow. I don't care."

"You got that scrambled. Scarlett decided to think about Rhett tomorrow." Amanda tossed her hair and did a breathy Scarlett O'Hara impression: "After all...tomorrow is another day." She returned his frown. "I do care how we know each other, and I'm going to find out."

Mark stood and leaned on his hands as he bent toward her. "No. You can't handle it. You get all—" searching for the word, he straightened. "You get completely unhinged doing those sessions. I'm not going to allow it. I've spoken, and that's final."

"Final? Quit being so damn bossy. I'm not going to get 'unhinged'. If you don't like it, you don't have to be here at all."

The mischievous glint in his eyes she'd learned to adore vanished. "Sure, and pull your ass out of another goddamned bender." He shook his head. "I

221

don't think so."

Amanda walked around the table, pushed him to a seat and sat on his lap. She dropped her elbows on his shoulders and twirled his dark curls as she smiled at his stern face. "Don't look so grumpy. You'll scare Oprah."

"You are a bone-headed witch."

She kissed his forehead, his nose. "So long as that's with a 'w' and not a 'b', I can deal with it."

"It's a toss up."

Amanda smiled and leaned in for a kiss as he put his hands on her waist and shook her to emphasize his point. "I don't want you to mess with this anymore. How we know each other doesn't matter."

"It does." Amanda struggled from his grasp to her feet. "It matters to me."

"It shouldn't." Mark's voice softened. "I love you for the person you are, not for who you might have been."

"Stop saying that!" Amanda felt her throat tighten, closed her eyes, and took a deep breath. "I didn't mean—" She started down the hall toward the living room, shaking her head. "You simply love the idea of me in your life, Mark. And that's fine, but that's not the same as loving *me*."

Mark followed her and reached for her arm. "That's not true and you know it."

"Don't!" Amanda lifted her arm from his grasp and continued walking to the living room. She felt her heart pound and the heat rise to her face. "You'll just poof out of my life anyway, like all the other people I've ever given a damn about." She flopped on the couch, pulled a throw pillow to her lap and wrapped her arms around it. "Or get hurt."

Amanda drew her knees up protectively as he stormed toward her.

Mark abruptly stopped as her words registered. He ran a hand through his hair and paced back and forth in front of her. "Are you afraid I might get hurt on the job?" He met her eyes and said, "Is that what this is all about?"

"Got it in one." She angrily wiped a tear from her cheek with the back of her hand. "Give that man a kewpie doll."

"Come on." He walked to the sofa and took her hands in his. "Let's go take that walk. We need to talk."

* * * *

Mark dropped his arm from around her waist as Amanda struggled up the stone break wall, refusing his help. She sat and frowned into a breeze from the lake. The light gust from the water at his back was warm. She unbuttoned the top button of her blouse; the silver locket threw a tiny glint of blue on her fair skin.

"I'm not going anywhere." He stood in front of her, nudged her knees apart with his hip, and placed his hands on either side of her. "You can just get that notion out of your head."

"How do you know you're not going anywhere?" She squinted into his eyes. "I'll wake in the night with nothing but memories, memories I struggle to keep, memories that get dimmer every day. Guaranteed. One minute the people I give a damn about are there, the next minute they're not." She shook her head. "You won't be any different."

He cupped her chin, "You need to trust me."

"I do trust you. It's life I don't trust." She shook her head free. "Why should I?"

"I don't know why." Mark lowered his hand and touched his forehead to hers. "I just know that you can, that you should. It was more than mere accident that brought us together." Pulling her into his arms, he whispered into her ear. "I don't know why I know this, honey, but I will always be there for you. And in some strange way I don't understand, I know I always have. There is something between us, something powerful that binds my heart to yours." She trembled in his arms and he leaned back to meet eyes welled with tears. He pressed his hand to her cheek, and whispered, "Don't cry, sweetheart. Shhh. No more tears. I'm not going anywhere." His arms tightened around her. The weeping willow overhead drooped long, swaying branches and narrow, sage-green leaves shimmered against a cornflower sky. He held Amanda against his chest until her trembling stopped.

"As far as loving the idea of you?" Mark stepped back from her, took her hands, and frowned. "You're damned right I do. The idea, and everything else about you. Not to be redundant, I don't give a damn about how we know each other. I do know that I love you enough to wait as long as it takes for you to say the same to me."

Amanda sniffled.

"You will, *mo críona*. I can tell." He bent to kiss her. "That means 'my heart'. Now, if you'll indulge me for a minute, I'm going to tell you a little of what it's like to be a cop."

Mark turned and leaned back on the break wall, stuck his hands in his pockets and gazed at the lake. "And I'm not going to sugar coat it. Being a cop is what I do, who I am. Policemen are killed every year, and many more are injured. So are firemen, so are fishermen, so are bank tellers. You can buy it getting off a train on your way to Plethora. Is being a cop more dangerous than other jobs?" He sighed, and shrugged his shoulders. "I suppose it is." He lifted himself onto the break wall and sat beside her. "In this job, I never know what I'm going to be confronted with in the next few seconds. I may fight for my life minutes after I do CPR on a baby I pull out of a car wreck." Mark watched a flock of ducks glide to the lake surface. "I've been shot at. Fortunately, I've never had to shoot anyone else. But I would, and without hesitation, to save someone's life, or my own."

His gaze swept from Navy Pier across the skyline of the city. "I've learned to stomach smells that would make most people vomit. The dispatcher tells me there's a smell coming from a locked apartment in the middle of a summer heat wave. Nobody's seen the tenant for two weeks. I go check because I have to. I can't say no. I do my job. I had to catch a snake once, been bitten by dogs twice, been kicked square in the balls by an old lady that could've been

225

your granny." He glanced at her, and then his eyes settled on an elderly couple walking a toy poodle. "Trust me: as a career choice, law enforcement isn't for everyone."

Amanda reached for his hand.

That's a first, reaching for me. He lifted her hand to his lips. "I've learned to live with the knowledge that people may want to blow me away just because of the uniform I'm wearing." He felt Amanda's hand tighten on his own and smiled.

Mark jumped from the break wall and helped her down. They continued walking down the lakefront. "Now I'm going to put your mind at ease. All of that is true, all of it. But I don't do that stuff anymore." He wasn't being completely honest, but needed to ease her fears. "One thing you need to understand. The casualty rate of the Chicago Mounted Police is absurdly low."

"What do you mean, absurdly low?"

"Low as in zero, zip, nada. We've never lost one guy, at least not in one hell of a long time. Sure, a hundred years ago, most cops were mounted police and their job was dangerous. Today it's a ceremonial, ambassadors-of-city-pride job. I've told more people Boomerang's name in one day than you could possibly imagine."

He stuck his chin out and made an effort to imitate a Katherine Hepburn voice. "'M-my, o-officer, isn't he b-b-bee-you-tiful?' A tourist. Boomerang, ma'am. 'B-boomerang? W-what an awful n-name for such...' My partner's horse is named Doofus, ma'am."

"You're kidding, right?" Amanda put her hand to her throat, fingered her locket, and laughed.

"Nope. Pete calls his horse 'Doofus'. Not only that, but Pete tells me that the damn thing talks to him." He shrugged. "And it's one hell of an animal. You should see the way Pete can pivot with Doofus. Make Fred and Ginger green with envy."

She shoved his shoulder and laughed, "A horse that talks. Right. Was his father's name Mr. Ed?"

"Since 1999, Chicago's police horses have been named to honor policemen killed in the line of duty. Boomerang and Doofus don't yet have the honor." He glanced at her and added, "Hope they never do."

They walked in silence for a while and Mark reached for her hand. *Please don't bring up the sessions again. Mary might think it's okay, but I sure as hell don't.*

"I really need to do this session tonight. We need answers."

Christ, that didn't take long. He shook his head and looked out at the lake. *I don't want to fight with her.* Tightening his grip on her hand, he led her to a low fence next to the walk and turned her around to face him. He ran a hand through his hair and prepared to make his case.

Instead, Amanda stepped into his arms and her lips met his. Her body melted into him, her kiss deep and lingering. Mark eased back and tipped his head. His gaze roamed Amanda's face and he smiled. "That was a nice surprise." He kissed her nose, and she gasped as he lifted her to the smooth top rail of the fence.

"You idiot." She laughed, and grasped his forearms so as not to fall.

"Your feminine wiles, delightful as they are, aren't changing my mind."

"You arrogant ass." Amanda pushed against his arms, trying to get down. "Let me down from here. There's nothing else I can say to you."

"Then just listen." Mark softened his tone. "Stop wiggling."

She met his eyes with a stubborn glare.

"If you're gonna do these regression sessions, you're gonna follow two simple rules." Mark tightened his grip on her waist. "One, you are not to skip or put off post regression analysis with Mary again, ever. Agreed?"

Amanda's frown deepened, but she nodded.

"Two, I trust Mary completely, but she's old, and may need help. I don't want you regressing without me there. Agreed?"

CHAPTER 18

 our teenage girls strolled past the café window in animated conversation. Returning his gaze to Amanda, Mark pushed his plate back and rested his elbows on the table. "I know you're going to argue this, but hear me out, anyway."

"What are we talking about?"

He brushed his lips with a napkin and signaled the waitress. "Would you like something else, more wine?"

"Cognac and decaf, please. Are you planning to take advantage of me?"

Mark spoke briefly to the waitress. "Not the way you think, honey—well, maybe later. I want to try something different."

"This anticipation is exciting." Amanda tipped her head and smiled. "I can hardly wait."

The table cleared, coffee and brandy served, Mark leaned back in his chair and studied her face. Her hair was pulled back with sparkling barrettes and loose tendrils fell to the sides of her neck. The locket glimmered in the candlelight, matching the sapphire blue of her eyes. "Have I ever told you that you're beautiful?"

"Lemme think." Amanda grinned and cradled her snifter in both hands. "Once or twice."

Eyes holding hers, he sipped his brandy. "The 'something different' has to do with these sessions."

229

Mark reached across the table.

Resting her hand in his, she asked, "Like?"

"I think Mary should regress me the next time."

Withdrawing her hand, she frowned. "I don't think that's a—"

"Before you react, listen to my reasoning. You have to admit these sessions have been rough on you." Mark let out a heavy sigh. "Look, I just had to scrape you off the floor. You lost it completely, and you know it."

"You're the one who suggested this regression thing." Amanda stared into her drink. "And it's working."

"Yeah, it's working. But you need to watch someone else go through the process. You need to see what I see. It'll help you understand my reluctance to let you continue."

"I've got to keep going." Amanda sipped brandy and met his eyes. "There's something there, I know there is." She set her glass down and tapped fingers on the table. "You've wanted to do this all along. The reason Mary's doing it with me is she doesn't think you have the kind of past life issues I do."

"This isn't just my idea." The check arrived, and without looking at the bill Mark handed it back to the waitress with a credit card. "I've already talked this over with Mary, and she agrees."

* * * *

Mary's monotone guided Mark down the stairs. He reached the bottom step and moved into the broad hallway. Numbers on gray doors floated by, 1983, 1979... A vaporous blue haze roiled gently around him, rose above his head, and began to thin. Mary's words were distant, echoing. "You're between lives now. When you've passed through the mist, you'll be in another life."

1948...1936, he continued down the long corridor. Again, the blue haze. 1921... 1919, and another haze. 1910... 1894... 1873. Mark stopped. *The year on the clock.*

He turned the doorknob and stepped into a large, high-ceilinged room lit with gaslights on the walls. Men leaned on a long workbench littered with wood shavings and gleaming tools.

A tall dark-haired man, bearded and balding, spoke, "The master clockmaker will be here at four." He walked around the tall case of a soot-blackened clock. "From what I can see, he'll only be dealing with smoke damage. That shouldn't take him long." He rubbed an oiled rag over the carving of a squirrel's face, lightening it with each pass of the cloth. "What a beauty. You fellows are in for a rare treat."

That's the same clock. Amanda's clock.

Blue mist rose around him.

Another doorway appeared at his left. He stepped across the threshold to 1871.

* * * *

His hands rested on the white railing of a front porch. A man stood next to him, holding a wooden keg on his hip. His left sleeve was pinned to his shoulder. A stiff breeze swept wood smoke toward them, prickling his nose. The bottom of a looming cloud glowed shades of orange and gray. An enormous explosion sent burning debris arcing in all directions. Seconds later, the earth beneath the porch shuddered and the air filled with rolling thunder.

"Mother of God, that's the gas works." The man's eyes narrowed at the approaching firestorm. Flames shot from the roofs of houses and small buildings, victims of the falling timber. A chimney dropped from view. "We've no time to waste. Grab another keg from the kitchen. It's likely we'll have to boil lake water, but we'll be grateful to have these."

Mark entered the house and the gas lamps on either side of the front door flared, flooding the foyer with white light.

The hallway shimmered. He rested his palm on a door marked 1922 and frowned. *Is this part of the same life? Only a handful of doors here...what's that mean?* He reached for the doorknob.

* * * *

Yellow ringlets of flypaper dotted with black specks hung from thumbtacks pushed into the ceiling. A dim lightbulb dangled over the bed, trailing a knotted string. A hot, moist breeze from an open window lifted threadbare curtains and caused the string to sway. In the yard outside, a dog barked. On the pillow beside him lay a worn teddy bear, stuffing peeping from where its eye should be. House slippers slapped on the wooden floor.

"There, baby. Mama's here." She smiled wearily. Uncomprehending, Mark raised his eyes to the woman leaning over him. Loose blonde curls clung to her tear-streaked cheeks. His face was burning, breath coming in gulping gasps, and the rag she pressed to his forehead felt damp and cool.

The floorboards creaked under a heavy step. A man moved behind Mama and wrapped his arms around her. He whispered, "Honey, Calvin is gone."

She closed her eyes, leaned her head back against his shoulder. "Calvin. Dear God."

"Mrs. Gunderson is still in the other room." The man wiped a red bandana across his brow. "She thinks Sissy might make it, but there's not much hope for Joey."

Joey? Is he talking about me?

Mama crushed the rag to her mouth, tears leaking from tightly closed eyes.

The soft glow from the bulb above him bloomed...bloomed and flooded the room with pure white light.

Dense blue fog swirled gently around him. Doors were dimly visible, but the numbers were wrong. 1732... 1751... 1764. Mark started to move to his left, then stopped, uncertain. *I think—I think I died. But that was 1922. How the hell did I wind up here?* He turned the knob.

* * * *

A low coal fire cast fitful red gleams on the face of a youngish woman. Tendrils of thin red hair escaped from beneath an embroidered mob cap. Though she could not be thirty, few teeth showed through the slightly parted lips. Her elbows rested on a scrubbed oaken table between them, its surface carved with mottos and initials of patrons long dead.

Throat parched from a long day in the sweltering foundry, he peered into his pewter tankard, hoping in vain to find one last sip of flat ale within. "Sally, we poured the last of them bells today, the big one. Old Jerry says when we breaks it out of the mold come Monday week, me and the lads can splice the mainbrace." He eyed her gin and water wistfully. "In honor of the occasion, like."

"What, them bells for the Colonies?" Sally laid her hand over her glass.

"Aye, for a great big church in Carolina, says Jerry. What I wouldn't give to hear them ring."

"Father thinks we should take the bounty and go to the Carolinas before the little one is born, Henry." She patted her belly beneath the coarse muslin apron. "He says England is no place to raise a family nowadays. Mayhap we'll hear them bells ourselves."

"There's plenty of work there for an honest man, Sally." Henry looked into his wife's eyes. "It's now or never."

"Mark?"

"Yes?"

"It's time to come back. Are you ready?"

* * * *

He opened his eyes as Mary pulled the drapes. Twilight over the lake cast lavender shadows on the wall where the clock stood. "I've got a lot of questions."

Amanda rose from the sofa. "I'll bet. Do you feel okay? Can I get you anything?"

"I'm fine." He reached for her hand, pressed it to his cheek. "Like you, I feel like I just woke from a nap. I'll have a glass of wine if you'll join me."

"Black tea for me, straight up." Mary picked up her pad and flipped to a blank page. "Shall we head for the kitchen and get to work?"

Mark leaned forward in the lounge chair and pushed himself to his feet. "I wasn't in the rooms long enough to learn much." He frowned as he shook his head and held up an index finger. "One instance has me completely baffled."

Mary nodded. "The child? I imagine so."

"And why did I jump all over the damned place? There didn't seem to be any logical order to the room numbers."

Amanda paused at the wine rack, her hand poised over a bottle as the clock began to chime. *Angel bells. What are you trying to tell me? Are the bells from my church the ones in Mark's regression? Does that tell me anything about me? About the future? About us?*

Mark stopped and peered closely at the case of the clock for a moment, then spoke to Mary's back as they continued down the hall. "Did I die?"

"Sounds like you did, dear." She went to the sink and filled a mug with water. "Let me make some hot tea, and we'll talk about that. A bit traumatic?"

"Well, yes and no." Mark sat at the table. "It was traumatic as hell for a few minutes. I couldn't breathe and my skin was on fire, hot. I was a sick little kid, a kid named Joey. Then everything got bright and I was back in the hallway."

"You said 'Mama'. Do you remember?"

"Yeah, and there was a man, my father, I think." Mark tapped his finger on the stem of his wine glass. "Why did I have this experience? It has nothing to do with Amanda and me."

"The hallway you walked through is not the same as Amanda's. You were looking at your own soul's journey, and this was one of your lives. So it has a great deal to do with you. You have a strong relationship with your mother and siblings. We can assume that it was the same with this earlier family, if only because your passing caused them so much pain. You died young, but the soul in that little body is no different from the one that looks through your eyes today." His expression was quizzical until she added, "Your subconscious mind guided you to that door." Mary lifted a shoulder, dismissing the behavior as normal. "You're curious by nature, as evidenced by your comments. You wanted to find out what was behind that particular door. I see nothing mysterious."

"What about the years jumping around? Late 1870s followed by 1922, then sometime in the 1760s? Why not 1922 first?"

236

Mary set her teaspoon on the placemat. "Time is linear, relative, circular, objective—who knows?" Not waiting for an answer, she continued, "Beliefs about time are all over the board, pick one. Carl Sagan defined time as 'profoundly resistant to a simple definition.' That's the best observation, as far as I'm concerned, because it says we don't really know squat. Clifford Pickover and Albert Einstein believed time travel was theoretically possible, but outside of the laws of physics as we know them today. Others believe it is in fact possible, but only in one direction, either past or future. The ideas are as old as Methuselah, and it all comes down to speculation. We can skip the theory for now and talk about what we actually know, the experiences you described to us during your regression. Let's go to the 1870s and your visions of that time."

Mark reached across the table and took Amanda's hand. "Here's one thing I know for certain: the clock in your living room is the same one I saw in that workshop. I watched a man wipe soot off a squirrel's face, and it's absolutely the same carving I was just looking at." Mark released her hand and turned to Mary. "In the other room, in the 1700s, I'm pretty sure those bells were cast for St. Michael's Church. We talked about the Carolinas."

Mary wrote in her notebook. Without looking up she said, "Mm-hmm. The time frame falls in line with your Internet research of the church."

Amanda refilled his wine glass and eyed him intently. "Could you have been my cousin, Jack?"

Mark folded his hands around his wine glass, studying the dark red liquid as if it held the answer.

CHAPTER 19

Chicago — 1862

Bonnie woke from a restless sleep to the warmth of Penelope's cape wrapped around her and the comforting weight of Penelope's hand on her back. She lay still and stared at the cameo brooch centered in the high collar of the woman's brown dress. Surrounded by a thin band of golden swirls, the brooch depicted the profile of a girl with a head of curls. Bonnie felt her own curls and listened to the hypnotic rhythm of the train. She began to descend into sleep again as she heard Jack's voice.

"Are there sharks in there?"

Bonnie scurried to her knees and placed both hands on the window.

"No, sweetheart." Penelope glanced out at the water and back at Jack. "That's not an ocean; it's a lake, Lake Michigan. And it's not salty like the ocean where sharks live."

"It sure looks like an ocean." Jack's brown eyes darted across the window. "Looks like the sea at home. Bet there are big fish in there."

"I imagine there are, because fishing is important in Chicago, especially now. The city is shipping fish and all kinds of supplies like grain and meat to the army. When this train pulls into Central Station, you'll see what I mean. You'll see big storage silos

239

and granaries on the lakefront by the tracks." Penelope rubbed Bonnie's back. "You'll see lots of tracks and buildings right next to the water."

Jack put a finger on the window. "Is that a fort out there?"

"Way out there, on the water?"

Jack's eyes remained on the round brick building on the lake as he nodded.

"My sister Margaret's letter said to look for that; she called it Chicago's new water intake crib. I've never seen it before."

Nose to the window glass, Bonnie asked, "Can I see the babies?" That was the most she had said in hours, hardly a word since her tearful questions about where they were going. Why couldn't Magdalene and Ben come with them? Are there angel bells in Chicago? Could she go back home? What happened to Moon and Saffron? And where is Papa now? She had clung to Jack through the night, shrinking away from Penelope's outstretched arms. Eventually, she had succumbed to sleep and leaned into Jack's shoulder.

"No honey, it's a different kind of crib." Penelope patted her back. "Just imagine, Jack. That little building is supposed to be loaded with bricks at the base, sunk deep into the lake bottom. From what Margaret said, two groups of men are working around the clock to dig a tunnel out to it. The intake crib has something to do with city water and sewage."

"I don't see a tunnel." Jack craned his neck.

"Of course you don't. The men are working very

240

deep, below the water."

Jack threw a sidelong glance at Penelope. Bonnie was sure he didn't believe they could build tunnels under the water.

Penelope looked at the lake and placed a hand on Bonnie's waist to steady her. "I must say, it smells better than the last time I was here."

Bonnie looked back at Penelope, uncertainty in her voice. "Did it stink worse before?"

Penelope bent to whisper in Bonnie's ear. "Do you need a water closet, dear?"

Bonnie shook her head and whispered back, "Not yet."

"To answer your question, I do believe it did smell worse before. They've apparently made some progress with the water quality. We'll learn more this evening. The station will be a flurry of soldiers and dockworkers. I think it's best we wait for the horde to thin before we leave our seats."

Bonnie looked out the window. Muddy brown water changed to deep blue at the horizon. "Jack", she whispered. "I don't wanna go on the water. I wanna stay on the train." She moved to the opposite seat and sat close to him. Bonnie gripped Jack's hand and frowned.

"No need to be afraid." Penelope reached out and cupped Bonnie's chin. "Look out the other side of the train. It's not all water, little one."

Bonnie looked into kind, bluebonnet eyes and her chest tightened. "That's what Papa calls me."

"Is that what I should call you? Little one?"

She shook her head. "Call me Bobby. Magdalene

241

calls me Bobby."

"Look out there." Penelope brushed a finger on Bonnie's cheek and smiled.

Bonnie leaned around Jack and followed Penelope's glance to the opposite side of the train. She was right. Black smoke whirled by the window from the front of the train as it lurched and sputtered to a slower pace. Bonnie stretched to see the buildings and houses in the distance. Some were small; others soared to unimaginable heights, four windows tall. Train cars lined the tracks as they neared the station. The doors on some were open and men passed big bags of grain and wooden crates to other men inside the cars. One of the tall granaries stood next to two stone silos, and four horse-drawn wagonloads of burlap bags thundered by the train window. A clutter of small buildings and men in coveralls passed. Everything around Bonnie darkened and her heart skipped. Gas torch lamps crept by the window, throwing dim light through the car as it inched into the cavernous station building lit by morning daylight from tall narrow windows.

* * * *

Bonnie and Jack gazed at the new wood block paving that covered the streets around the Michigan and Illinois Central Railroad tracks. Penelope complained that some streets still used simple wooden planks.

The wind blew sharp and cold from the lake as

242

they boarded a black buggy Penelope called a cab, a cabriolet. The two-wheeled horse-drawn carriage accommodated the three of them. The driver wore a top hat and slid Penelope's carpetbag and trunk into a bin under his angled seat, high above and behind them.

With the snap of a leather whip, the horse stepped out briskly and the carriage lurched, rocking on its springs. Bonnie's eyes widened and she gaped at the bustling people and the other buggies around them. She held Jack's hand so tightly that her wrist ached, but she wasn't about to let go. The cab passed tall buildings and horse-drawn passenger wagons that Penelope called "streetcars". Men bent against the wind as they held onto top hats, their long coats whipping and flapping about their legs. Two boys unloaded boxes of tomatoes and apples from a wagon in front of a store. The cab passed more shops selling tobacco, leather goods, and clothing. Sour odors of fish and meat markets wrinkled Bonnie's nose. Fireplace smoke billowed from the chimneys of the small wood frame houses and bent to the wind from the lake. Traffic swirled around hotels that touched the sky. Bonnie silently mouthed the names on the gilded signs: Fortuna, Richmond House, Washington Hotel. Jack gawked at all the activity in and around the river. A ship with towering masts lay moored to a long dock, its sails lashed to the yards as sailors worked in the rigging. Fishing boats unloaded nets of large fish onto the dock, crowded with men in baggy overalls and tall rubber boots.

Bonnie whispered to Jack, "What are those fishes?"

"Look like trout, but lots bigger than the ones I caught with your pa." He looked at Bonnie and back at the dock as he shrugged. "I never seen trout that big, but maybe they grow bigger 'cause there's so much water for them to swim in."

Two policemen on horses stopped the cab at the end of Michigan Avenue. One of the policemen tipped his hat and smiled at Bonnie as he waved them through a wooden gate by the Rush Street bridge master. Bonnie started to ask Jack about the piles of coal by the dock as they crossed the Chicago River, but the creaking timber below the wagon's wheels stifled her words. She looked at her cousin and his hand tightened on hers.

Once past the river, the big city congestion of homes, businesses, and buildings thinned considerably. The buggy bounced through rutted dirt roads and hooves clopped on wood when they turned to another street, and clattered on cobblestones at the next. Stately trees lined most of the streets. Bonnie wondered why the big trees didn't have the pretty moss hanging from the limbs like the trees had at home. Small houses were interspersed among barns and livestock pens with pigs and more houses and small shops. The cab turned left into a long driveway across the narrow street from a church with a steeple as tall as St. Michael's; ahead was a forest. The long dirt road curved to the right around a circular path. They came to a stop at the steps of a large three-story house, with a row of gabled windows, a sharply pitched roof, and a broad front porch.

"Jack! There's a swing on the porch, just like my house!"

* * * *

Bonnie stood behind Penelope and peeked around her skirt at the woman who stood in the door. She was small and nearly the same age as Penelope. Her dark hair was parted in the center and a tightly wound bun sat on the crown of her head. She wore a long purple dress and a starched white apron.

"Don't you realize there is a war on, Penelope Starks?"

"Dreadful, isn't it?" Penelope unfastened her hat and swept it off her head, fluffed her blonde curls, and reached both arms behind her to place them on Bonnie's and Jack's shoulders. "These lovely victims of that tragedy will be with us for a short time until we can locate their family."

The woman looked sharply at Bonnie and shook her head. "Refugees? Well, I suppose…there *is* a war on, isn't there? Your foundlings must be hungry. The dear Lord knows, they do look a sight. Who are their people?" Like dawn breaking, her face changed from frightening to welcoming. She opened her arms to Penelope. "But first things first. Give your big sister a proper hello."

The women laughed and hugged and chatted about their parents in Columbus, the war, the changes in Chicago since Penelope's last visit. Bonnie's eyes roamed the foyer and she and Jack stepped further into the house, following Penelope. They moved to a room lined with books. Jack's lips parted as he walked to a shelf and tipped his head to read the leather spines. A tall wooden ladder leaned against a track that circled the room. Jack went to a chessboard centered between two plush chairs in front of a lit fireplace and studied the current game.

"Margaret, I'd like you to meet Miss Bonnie May Belle Lexington, and the handsome young gentleman is Master Jackson Wellington." Lowering her voice, she added, "I've a long tale to tell you."

Jack frowned. "What's a foundling?"

"Something you're not. Margaret is being a silly." Penelope set her carpetbag next to a large desk, cluttered with more books. "I think you both need to get cleaned up, and maybe a short nap would be in order before we have something to eat."

Jack thrust his chin at Penelope. "I can take care of myself."

Bonnie met his eyes.

Jack scratched his chin and looked at the floor. He mumbled, "Bonnie might need some help to…maybe you can help Bonnie."

Penelope nodded and her curls bounced. "It would be my pleasure. You take the spare room at the back of the house. Margaret will show you. I think you'll find everything you might need."

Margaret stepped to Jack and gently lifted his chin. "Independent young fella, huh?" She smiled. "Good at chess?"

Jack maintained a steady gaze, but stepped back. He glanced at the board and back to her. "Four moves, check-mate."

"Don't tell me." Margaret went to the board, studied it and muttered, "Well, fiddle that."

Bonnie looked at Jack. At his nod, she bit her lower lip and looked up at Penelope, taking her hand.

Penelope and Bonnie started up the curving stairway as Margaret said, "Sister, I think I've found myself a talented chess companion. I'll add some water to that stew and make a nice, rich soup for the four of us."

* * * *

"You don't do that right." Bonnie stood in the shallow copper basin in the middle of the bedroom floor. She squeezed her eyes closed as Penelope wiped her cheek with a soapy rag.

Penelope sat back on her heels, adjusted the towel on her shoulder, and blew a blonde curl from her forehead. Resting wet hands on her knees, she laughed. "And tell me, Miss Bobby, how do you suggest I do it?"

Bonnie took the rag, squeezed out the water, scrubbed her chin with vigor, scooped up fresh water and rinsed. She looked at Penelope.

"Perfect." Penelope turned her around and scrubbed her back and shoulders. "But, you forgot your neck, ears, back, hair, and those little piggies."

Bonnie felt the warm water from the ewer run

down her back and whimpered as soap ran into her eyes. Her lip quivered as she fought tears. "I wanna go. C-can I go find Jack now?"

"He's downstairs with Margaret, remember? Tip your head back, sweetheart. We're almost done. We'll get you all dried and dusted down, and you can go find him."

Bonnie lifted her arms as a fluffy towel was wrapped around her. She felt fingers tickle her sides through the towel and fought unplanned giggles. Penelope sat her on a bed and laid out a flannel nightgown.

"We'll cut off an inch or two of this and it will be perfect for you until we go shopping and do some sewing."

Bonnie watched as Penelope cut the nightgown. She wasn't sure how much an inch was, but she thought it must be big because Penelope cut the nightgown in half.

* * * *

Bonnie scrambled to the end of the big bed and looked over the footboard at Jack. He was stretched out on a thick mat on the oak floor, buried in a colorful quilt. She was glad Penelope had let him stay in the room with her. Peering around at shadows, Bonnie turned quickly at the motion of a long gossamer curtain. She looked down at Jack and whispered his name.

He didn't move. Shivering, Bonnie inched back to the center of the bed and wrapped the soft comforter around her. *He'd just call me a baby. Jack always calls me a baby when I get scared.* Light from the moon created more mysterious shadows as the small candle sputtered and died. Bonnie started at the crackle of a dying ember in the black iron woodstove. Ominous darkness grew from each corner; the tap of a branch on the window and the creak of wood in the old house made the warm room seem to live and breathe. A horse neighed in the distance, and Bonnie snapped her eyes to the window. She peered into a corner by the door. *Was there a table over there? I don't remember. Is that a candle?*

Moonlight filtering through the trees out the window cast dark silhouettes on the floor. Bonnie's chin quivered at the gently swaying monsters reaching toward her. A black shadow slithered from the open door toward the bed; her heart thundered and tears sprang to her eyes. Breathing through her mouth, Bonnie shuddered and stared into darkness. Her voice caught as she weakly stammered, "J-Jack?"

Bonnie gasped as an ebony kitten scrambled up the lace coverlet and settled in a patch of moonlight in front of her. It curled a long fluffy tail around its paws and blinked at her with sparkling green eyes.

Yesterday

CHAPTER 20

"No! I won't go on the wagon! I won't!" Bonnie woke to sunlight streaming through the tall window onto her coverlet. Her cheeks were streaked with tears, dark curls plastered to her damp forehead. Margaret and Penelope sat on either side of the bed, brows furrowed with concern. Bonnie's heart thrummed with fear as she wriggled to the headboard and looked frantically around the sunlit room. Penelope took her in her arms, and only held her tighter when she struggled to escape. As the women sought to comfort her, tremors wracked Bonnie's small body, and she wailed and screeched blubbering gasps into Penelope's uncertain embrace. Hot tears poured down her flushed cheeks as she panted, sobbed, and shrieked for Papa, Magdalene, and Jack.

Jack sprinted into the room and skidded to a stop. "Leave her alone!" He glanced at Bonnie and glowered at the two women.

The two sisters exchanged startled glances. Margaret extended her hands, palms up. "It's not us that've frightened her so, Jack. She'll barely let us near her. Your young cousin is in miff-nettle hysterics from a nightmare about—" she hesitated, looked at Bonnie, "—what? Something about a wagon?"

Bonnie watched Jack hurry toward her and scowl

251

at the wet stain on the bed. His brown eyes met hers and his cheeks reddened as she scrambled to him. Jack eased Bonnie back onto the bed, his eyes and face stern as he whispered, "Stop, stop your bawlin'. I'm right here." The heaving sobs quieted to a whimper, her lip aquiver like an aspen leaf as he turned to Margaret. "She didn't mean to wet the bed, ma'am. I'll take care of it."

Penelope faced him as she sat on the edge of the bed and wrapped her arm around Bonnie. "I think not, Jack. And no one is angry." She leaned her cheek against Bonnie's and wiped tears as she cooed, "Hush now, everything is all right. You're both safe here with Margaret and me."

She lifted the sapphire earring fastened around a button on Jack's overalls and murmured to Bonnie. "Magdalene told me about this, and the one in your locket."

With a gasping shudder, Bonnie reached for her locket and nodded.

"We'll look for a nice fob or something for you to wear with your stone, Jack." Penelope squeezed his arm. "Something very manly and grown up." She reached up and placed a hand against his cheek. "You're a wonderful protector for Bonnie, a good and loyal friend. No one is going to hurt her and she's not in trouble. Why don't you go downstairs with Margaret and help her with breakfast? Let me take care of Bonnie. We'll be right down."

Bonnie sniffled as she looked at him. Jack returned his steady gaze to Penelope, nodded, and left the room with Margaret, pausing with his hand

252

on the walnut doorjamb to glance back at Bonnie.

* * * *

Penelope eased a dollop of blueberry jam from a dainty silver spoon to a soda biscuit. She handed it to Jack as she asked, "How old are you?"

"Ten, eleven next summer, ma'am."

She wiped an embroidered napkin across her lips. "You're very tall for your age. I would have guessed you were at least twelve." She turned to Bonnie. "And you?"

Bonnie looked at Jack and held up one hand, all her fingers spread wide.

Margaret chuckled and slapped hands to her thighs. "Five? You're an old lady!"

"She had a birthday while we were on the wagon." Jack hovered a spoon over a bowl of oatmeal. "She's six."

Bonnie nodded, her mouth full of biscuit. She swallowed. "Magdalene said I used to be a handful, and that I bees more than a handful, now."

Penelope and Margaret exchanged glances as Penelope covered her mouth and put her elbow on the table. "I'll be looking for your family and hopefully we'll get lucky right away, but remember, this is wartime. It may take months to find them. You can still enroll in school this year, Jack, as it's only November." Although the law didn't mandate school, Penelope's voice brooked little discussion.

Jack looked from Bonnie to Penelope and swallowed. "Yes, ma'am, but where? They have schools here like in Charleston?"

Bonnie knew that Jack liked school. He told her once. She looked from Margaret to Penelope and said, "I wanna go to school with Jack."

"You will, but not until you start full time. You'll go to the same school." Penelope sipped green tea, her pinkie finger extended to balance the delicate teacup.

Bonnie reached for her juice, holding out her pinkie finger. She couldn't make her own pinkie stay out like that and hold the glass at the same time.

Jack set down his glass of milk. "Don't girls stay home with tutors here, ma'am?"

Margaret stood and began to clear the table. "Sometimes, but usually not. You'll like our public schools. Alice Barnard is the principal of Dearborn School, and a good friend of mine. We'll go see her next week."

The black kitten sat patiently, its glowing green eyes focused on Bonnie, waiting for another crumb to fall. With biscuit-filled chipmunk cheeks, she asked, "How come you call her Electra? That's a funny name."

"Don't talk with your mouth full, dear. Electra's the name of our mayor's wife." Margaret shrugged at the kitten. "She looks about as mean and ugly as this cat."

Bonnie put a hand over her mouth to keep a piece of biscuit from escaping with her giggle. "Electra's not mean and ugly."

Penelope pushed back her chair. "With that, I think we'd better get going on our shopping trip. A

254

good friend will be here for supper at five o'clock. If we have time, we'll ride by Dearborn School."

* * * *

Bonnie and Jack walked behind Penelope in a dressmaking and millenary shop as she selected fabric for dresses and shirts. She held bolts of material to their faces, nodding to show her acceptance of some and frowning as she rejected others. A tailor measured Jack for school clothes. They stopped in a shoe store and Penelope bought them new shoes. Bonnie held Jack's hand, and they followed Penelope into a shop that sold hats, gloves, perfumes, and miscellaneous extras. The wood floor creaked with their steps as the warm smells of new leather, lilies of the valley, and old books permeated the air. Penelope scrutinized a pink bonnet and shook her head. She selected royal blue velvet and tied the wide dark ribbon at Bonnie's cheek, stepped back, and nodded. "I like this one because it makes those bright blue eyes twinkle. Do you like blue?"

Bonnie's face scrunched up as if she was swallowing castor oil. "I like my overalls."

"I'm glad you like your overalls," Penelope laughed. "You'll need them to help me in the garden."

Jack wandered off to study the contents of a shelf behind the long wooden counter as Penelope talked to the merchant. Bonnie went to Jack's side, followed his gaze, and gasped at a doll on top of two books. Her eyes widened. "Papa brought me one just like her when he went to Columbia," she whispered to Jack.

The doll was a tiny four inches tall with a china head, black painted curls, blue floral cotton gown hemmed in lace, a black ribbon around the waist, and a matching bonnet. *Papa said it looked like me.* Bonnie stared at the doll.

He turned to Bonnie and then looked down at the floor. "I know. We don't have any money right now." He turned his attention to a black wooden locomotive and examined it carefully, turning the wheels with his fingers. "We can't buy it today, but I'll get a job and we'll come back. Come on." He set the train car back on the counter, put a hand on Bonnie's shoulder and they turned to see Penelope standing behind them.

Penelope spoke to the shopkeeper. "Can you show me that little doll up there?" She winked at Jack, "And oh, that black train engine—no, the big one above it—yes, that one." Penelope looked the toys over critically and handed the train to Jack. She studied the doll, lifting the skirt to examine the frilly petticoats, and glanced at Bonnie as she did so.

The shopkeeper's wiry white eyebrows met as he scratched his beard. "Thirty cents, ma'am. Three years ago, I would have had a dollar for them. War time I don't get many toy buyers, and I'm glad to have one of my best customers back."

"Wouldn't you like to have this, Bonnie? It looks just like you." Penelope pursed her lips at the doll and held it out to her. Bonnie watched Jack spin the train's wheels on the counter and thought about what he had said about getting a job. She sucked in her lower lip at the doll and whispered, "No thank you, ma'am."

"We have some chores around the house that you can help me do." Penelope handed Bonnie the doll. "You and Jack can pay me back." She ran the back of her fingers down Bonnie's cheek. "We have one more stop, Jack. The shop around the corner at State and Lake Streets has a nice selection of men's jewelry."

* * * *

The big dining room table, covered with a white lace-trimmed linen tablecloth, was set for five, an eight-taper candelabra in the center. Bonnie put the engraved silverware around each plate the way Margaret had shown her, running from sideboard to table for each piece. She watched Penelope position each high-backed chair exactly right. Bonnie frowned, and asked, "Do I have to wear a dress every day?"

"Don't run with silverware in your hands, Bonnie. You're a girl. Girls wear dresses."

"I didn't have to before." She flipped the ribbon taming her curls and scowled.

Jack rested his hands on the back of a dining room chair, and said, "Yes, you did, Bonnie, most of the time."

Heads turned at the sound of the doorknocker.

Bonnie and Jack followed Penelope to the foyer, lit with two iron gas lamps hanging on either side of the door. Gleaming round brass plates behind the flames reflected glimmering light and framed the doorway in a dim glow. Bonnie balled her hands into fists and stamped her foot at Jack. "My name is Bobby!"

He pulled loose the white ribbon in her hair, and scrambled to the other side of Penelope as she swung the door wide.

She smiled at the visitor and backed up as her arm extended an invitation to enter. "Hello, Chester!" Penelope leaned into him for a kiss on the cheek.

Bonnie stared up at the tall man: a gray top hat over chin-length blond hair with trim mutton chop sideburns, gold rimmed spectacles resting on his long, narrow nose. As he bowed to Penelope, he handed her a bouquet of winter straw flowers. "I stopped breathing when you went to Columbus, and will start breathing again today."

Penelope tapped her index finger to the deep dimple in his chin and smiled. "You foolish rogue."

Chester removed his gray topcoat with its long fur collar and longer white scarf. He handed them and his hat to Penelope. Bonnie stared at the left sleeve of his jacket, folded and neatly pinned just above the elbow. *He got hurt, like those men by the train.* Chester extended an open palm to her. "I heard all about those sapphire-blue eyes. You're right, Penelope. They are dazzling!"

Bonnie looked at Penelope, and receiving a nod, placed her own hand in Chester's palm and dropped a curtsy. He lowered his head and brushed his lips on her fingers. Bonnie snapped her hand back with a giggle. He straightened and placed his fist on a hip. "A princess, indeed. You and I have much to discuss, Jack." Chester extended his hand. "I understand you play chess."

Jack shook hands as he glanced at Penelope. "Yes, sir."

* * * *

Bonnie and Jack crouched in the darkness of the long staircase. He squeezed her shoulder and whispered in her ear. "You better go back to bed."

"No!" Bonnie wrenched free from his grasp. "I don't wanna go—I wanna hear what they're saying."

Penelope leaned forward and placed a delicate crystal glass on the table in front of her. "I met them on the train, Chester. The poor little things were exhausted, filthy, and starving. The couple who entrusted me with them in Cleveland were darkies." She tossed her hand. "You know what that means. Coming to Illinois could have been deadly for them."

Chester nodded and tamped tobacco as he spoke around the pipe stem in his teeth. "Your advice to them was sound." Holding the unlit pipe in his hand, he added, "The authorities would have taken the children immediately, I believe. What would have happened to them then?" He shook his head and mumbled the answer to his question. "Chicago Orphan Asylum, probably."

259

"My word." Margaret's hands slowed down as she wound a ball of yarn. "I hadn't thought of that, but you're right, of course."

"Bonnie had a horrible time of it, leaving those people, I mean. It was just the four of them, the black couple and two little white children. I was curious, and asked who the children belonged to." Penelope shook her head, and added, "The conversation simply blossomed, and here we are." Penelope leaned her head back on the lace chair doily. "It was a stressful train ride, until Bonnie quit fighting sleep." She raised her head. "Jack was quite stoic, thank goodness."

Chester leaned back in his chair and crossed his ankles. "What was this couple able to tell you about the children?"

"Ben, the Negro man, said that Bonnie's father was named John Lexington, and that he was a plantation owner in Charleston. Jack is her cousin, and lived in Virginia. The five of them drove all the way from South Carolina in an open wagon. They planned to join up with Jack's parents, only to discover that the Wellington farm had been burned to the ground. Apparently, John died of tetanus somewhere along the way." She shuddered. "Bonnie's father cut his hand while shoeing a horse, poor man. God himself would fear the horrors those little ones endured on that journey." Penelope handed Chester a wrinkled letter. "Ben gave me this. It is addressed to Duncan Lexington from Bonnie's father."

Jack stood and reached for Bonnie's hand.

"Come on, we should go back to bed."

She turned to him, forcing a whisper into her voice, "No!"

He sighed and lowered himself to the stair just below her.

Bonnie peered into the dark parlor, her eyes glistening. "I wanna hear what they say about Papa."

Chester perused the letter. "I'm afraid looking for this relation of theirs is not likely to be successful. If he was not yet married, as you say, he's likely conscripted and there are over two hundred thousand men from Illinois under arms in this war. Looking for only one of those men is going to be a challenge, if not near impossible. I'll get to work on it tomorrow to see if we can find him." He lifted his empty sleeve and smiled. "My old commander owes me a favor. Perhaps Duncan was able to pay the bounty. You say this would be her father's cousin?"

Penelope nodded and said, "From what I understand from those darkies, Duncan Lexington is the only remaining living relative to the children."

Jack wrapped his hand around a banister post. "Your pa's cousin's in the Union army, maybe. That's what they think."

"Is he?"

Jack shrugged, "Dunno. Shh."

"...perfect for apprentice in my factory. A little young, but he's got the gumption, I believe."

Margaret pulled another hank of yarn to her lap. "I've the feeling he'd be enthused. He's an ambitious youngster. Quite the competitor in chess,

I might add."

Penelope moved to sit next to Margaret and held her hands out for the skein while Margaret wound the yarn. "I might have more luck with Mercy Hospital. They have listings that may help with information about someone in particular. But I don't hold out hope. If he's conscripted, as you believe, he could be anywhere. I'll have a better idea once I get to the hospital."

The woody aroma of tobacco smoke wafted to the stairway and Bonnie looked at Jack. "That smells just like Papa's pipe!"

"Yeah, it does. Shh."

"You may never find him, Penelope. What will you do then?"

"Chester, it's not something I care to think about at the moment. Those children are safe, warm, fed. For now, we'll just have to be content with that and take it day by day."

"In the meantime, bring Jack by my shop and I'll show him around. Who knows? I'm in need of a new apprentice. This young Master Wellington may find a career in fine furniture."

CHAPTER 21

"**Y**ou revealed quite a bit during this regression, Amanda." Mary pulled a pen from behind her ear, scooted her chair to the table, and looked at her watch. "Let's get started discussing what you've learned."

Mark set his coffee in front of him, lacing his fingers around the cup. "What interests me most is the name 'Wellington'. In my regression I saw your clock, covered with soot. Wonder if one of those boys was Jack."

Amanda traced a tiny rose on the placemat with her index finger. *Wellington. Was Mark once Jack Wellington? 18th century clock, fire residue, soot from 1871? The war doesn't end until 1865, so...*

"Hey, Sputnik, think out loud." He laid a hand over hers.

She slid her fingers through his as she frowned. "I'm spacey sometimes, but not *that* spacey."

Mark pursed lips and nodded.

"Am not."

From the darkened living room, kitchen lights reflected off the mellow brass of the pendulum. "My cousin, I mean, Bonnie's cousin, whatever, he..." She squeezed Mark's hand and shook her head. "Jack's last name was Wellington. That's the name in the back of the clock, and he was going to be apprenticed to Chester in his furniture factory. We

263

know this. Since the Chicago fire was in 1871, I guess he'd have been about sixteen, so you're right. He might be the Wellington in the clock. There's so much I don't know yet."

Mark stared at the ceiling as he spoke. "We know Bonnie and Jack left Charleston and crossed half the continent in the early 1860's. I'm guessing 1862 because of the information I found about the church bells. Our fire doesn't happen until six years after the war ends." He shook his head and looked at Amanda. "Margaret Starks bought it before the fire, remember, in 1870?"

Amanda sipped her coffee and said, "We're on the same page."

"During the regression session," Mary dropped a sugar cube into her tea, "did you see the clock in the house?"

Amanda shook her head with a sigh. "Nope."

Stirring her tea, Mary looked up. "You answered quickly. Are you sure? Walk through the rooms in your mind."

Amanda turned to a flash of lightning outside the kitchen window. *A thousand one, a thousand two, a thousand three, a thous...*An angry rumble faded to rolling murmur. She stood. "Bonnie is so little. I shouldn't see it, the timing isn't right, from what we know. I think I'd remember." She retrieved the coffee carafe on the counter. "I see the silly things that a child sees. The train seats are cane, the pillows on her bed have stripes, and the floors are dark wood with colorful rag rugs everywhere. Margaret and Penelope wear shoes you fasten with a hook, there's tatted lace on the backs and arms of chairs, and tiny bubbles in windowpanes. The sun made a rainbow on the floor from the chimney of a lamp." Amanda filled Mark's coffee as she said, "There's more, like a chifferobe in Bonnie's room. They have a black cat named Electra. A street of parquet-like blocks. I remember touching them. How helpful is all that stuff?"

Mark leaned back in his chair. "There's a wood block alley off State Street, one of two left in the city. Even though none of this seems to have much to do with a connection between you and me, your memories of those images are enviable. I seemed to be mired in flashes, snatches of time, not long enough in any one place to absorb anything. What's a chifferobe?"

Amanda waved a hand in the air as she sat and placed the carafe on the table. "It's a tall dresser, sort of an armoire. You usually hang clothing on one side of the cabinet, and sometimes it has a mirror. Chifferobes are typical Civil War era furniture, like those huge wardrobe cabinets that became popular in the early 20th century. Houses didn't have closets, as we know them until long after that. But there's no clock, I don't think."

Mary swirled a shorthand note and flipped to a new page. "We're going to explore a bit of why you feel blue and a little edgy."

"I don't feel edgy."

Mark scratched his sideburn, but said nothing as he reached for his coffee.

Mary laid her pencil on the binder and sipped her

tea. "Tell me what you remember of Bonnie's nightmare. It was obviously traumatic, but you were not clear about why Bonnie was upset."

"Yes, I remember." Amanda rose and dumped her coffee in the sink. "Drink, Mark?" She walked down the hall toward the wine rack.

He called out, "I'm easy."

Carrying Mark's whiskey and a bottle of wine for herself and Mary, Amanda paused at the towering clock as it began its distant chime. Lightning filled the room as she muttered at the face, "You started this."

Oprah, on pendulum duty, ignored her words and a growl of thunder.

Amanda set the bottles on the kitchen table and went to the window. She struggled with opening it as she said, "Damn thing is stuck again. I love the smell of rain."

"Let me get it." Mark rose and moved behind her.

She stepped aside and rested a hand on his lower back as he lifted the window. Damp earth, wet grass and a hint of rotting leaves carried in the night breeze. He slipped his arm around her as she took a deep breath and said, "Sweet air! Thanks."

Mark studied her face. His warm brown eyes reflected concern, and laugh lines deepened. "You're doin' great," he whispered. He leaned in for a kiss, but hesitated at Mary's words.

"I'd tell you two to get a room, but it seems you have one down the hall and would likely leave me to amusing Oprah, or vice versa."

Amanda's cheeks warmed at Mark's chuckle. Not sure if he laughed at her or at Mary's silliness, Amanda backed away and went to the cupboard, retrieving wine and rocks glasses. "Yes, Bonnie was upset. The first image to hit me was her father pointing a gun and yelling at me... at *her* to stay in the wagon."

Mark turned at Amanda's words with a clenched jaw and lowered himself to the chair.

"It was dark; there was the deafening roar of a big gun of some kind and...and an image of Papa, Bonnie's father, snapping a long whip over his head. Magdalene's face...she looked terrified. This wagon took off fast, and Magdalene held me down with a blanket or something. I think it was Magdalene. I've never been..." Amanda stared at the top of the wine bottle. "Bonnie was petrified." She twisted the corkscrew. "Bonnie woke up...*I* woke up, and then Jack looked angry. He wasn't mean, no. He just..." she eased the cork from the bottle. "Jack wasn't mean."

Mark stood and walked to the window, viewing a lightning show on the lake. "You were just a little kid. It's no wonder she had nightmares."

"You have it as screwed up in your head as I do. 'You were a kid' and 'she had a nightmare'. We're one and the same."

Mark turned and ran a hand through his hair. Chagrined he said, "Sorry, you're right."

Mary scribbled in the binder as she spoke. "You experienced an escape, I'd guess. Given it was the Civil War; the 'big gun' must've been a cannon. So

267

you were in close proximity to a Civil War battle or skirmish. As you point out, you viewed this scene through a child's eyes. You and Jack, your father, Ben, and Magdalene — all of you escaped unharmed."

Mark asked, "Do you remember the name of the town where you boarded the train? This battle would have been south of there, I think."

"Sorry. I was just a kid, remember?"

He shrugged.

Amanda took a swallow of wine. "I looked at a blue jewel on Jack's button. It made me feel better, but I don't know why." She reached for the locket on her neck and frowned.

Mark set down his drink. "What?"

"There was something important about the jewel on Jack's button, but I can't remember what."

Mary walked to the sink, rinsed the mugs, and placed them in the dishwasher. "Tell me more about Chester."

"Everything Chester said was way over my head. I didn't understand much of it at all. Bonnie is...*I'm* just a child during all this."

"Think, dear. You said Chester wanted Jack to work for him?"

"Yes, that's really about all I understood." She sipped her wine. "And, oh. He smoked a pipe and Jack was urging me to go back up stairs."

"You were afraid of him?"

"Chester? No, not at all." Amanda looked at and rubbed the back of her hand. "He's Penelope's beau, I think. Isn't that what they said back then, *beau*?

268

He kissed my hand."

Mark raised his brows. "A gallant gentleman of 19th century traditions."

"Yeah, kinda came across that way. Wore a gray top hat, too." She looked at him with a sly smile. "I'll buy you a black one. It'd be sexy on you."

Mary swirled a few shorthand hieroglyphics and closed the binder. "I'll take that as a polite invitation to leave you paramours to your prurience while I go upstairs and enjoy a few moments of passionate solitude and relish an afterglow cigarette."

Mark spit some scotch, coughed, and bent at the waist with a bellow of laughter. Amanda rose with a combined snort-snicker and wrapped her arm around Mary's waist. They leaned into each other as they walked down the hall. "You are a treasure," Amanda said and kissed Mary's cheek.

Mary opened the door and turned as she removed her glasses. "That young man has the patience of Job with you, Amanda. Be good to him."

She froze as Mary's sparkling gray eyes bored into her own, waiting for a reply. Amanda nodded.

* * * *

Mark stood at the sink, his back to Amanda as she walked down the hall toward the kitchen. Sleeves rolled up his forearms, he twirled her wine glass under the tap.

"Maybe I'll get you a gold top hat." Amanda stepped behind him and put her arms around his waist as he wiped the glass with a dishtowel.

Mark chuckled and swirled his rocks glass under the hot water. "Black." He looked over his shoulder at her upturned smile and added, "more Lincolnesque." He tossed the dishtowel on the counter and turned to her.

"That play we went to, *A Chorus Line*, they all wore gold ones."

He wrapped his arms around her and she leaned into him, sighing up at his dark eyes. Mark kissed her brow. "Tired?"

Amanda tipped her head to the side and smiled. "What do you have in mind?"

"Oh, I'm easy," he shrugged, "content just lookin' at that smile of yours." Mark looked over her head out the window. "It's late and it's raining." He grinned, returning his mischievous gaze to her. "We could go to bed and I'll work on that pretty smile."

Amanda stepped back from his attempt to kiss her and slid her hands down his forearms. "Let's go for a walk in that rain."

He followed her down the hall. "People only walk in the rain in sappy romance novels."

"Not true. People walk in the rain for all sorts of reasons."

Mark mumbled as they went out the door. "Can't imagine a *good* reason."

They walked hip-to-hip, his arm around her shoulder. "Still can't think of a good reason to be out in the rain when you don't have to be," he grumbled.

"Okay, start counting the reasons. One, it's great

for your skin." She smiled up at him. "The humidity. It's great for your skin."

Wiping a drop of water from his brow, he said, "Okay. Two?"

Amanda snapped her umbrella open and rested it on her shoulder between them. "Rain smells wonderful."

"Smells better in the open country, but I'll give you that one. Three."

"You don't need to smear on that goopy sunscreen before a walk in the rain."

Mark laughed. "Four."

"Look around." She swept her arm out in front of her. "It's so peaceful. There are no crowds."

"Because most people are smart enough to come in out of the damned rain." Mark took the umbrella from her, held it over them, and pulled her close to his side as they walked. "Five."

"Flowers. When you walk by a rose trellis or a lilac bush in the rain, the aroma is heavenly."

"Never noticed."

She nodded. "Because you don't walk in the rain."

"True. What are we on…six?"

"Memories. You'll have memories of a night you walked in the rain for no good reason."

Mark looked down at Amanda and returned her smile. "Seven."

"If it's daylight and the sun peeks through the clouds, you might see a rainbow."

He shook his head and his smile widened. "Eight."

271

"Eight. No one can tell if the drops on your cheeks are rain or tears."

Mark abruptly stopped and stepped in front of Amanda. He lifted her face to his. "I will always be able to tell, *ghrá*." He kissed her cheek and whispered, "When I kiss your tears, they taste sweeter than rain."

Amanda smiled at him and returned his kiss.

Muffled and distorted by the patter of rain, a distant *rat-a-tat-a-clatter-tat* carried toward Amanda and her heart skipped. *Wagon wheels.* She peered into the suddenly ominous darkness and drizzling rain around them. *Horse hooves.* Her eyes wide, Amanda looked at Mark. "What's that?"

"Easy, sweetheart. It's nothing." Mark pulled her into step with him. "Just one of those horse-drawn tourist carriages."

* * * *

Pete and Mark swept from the backs of their horses. The men sprinted toward the open door of a laundry on Water Street. They were the closest officers to the scene. This one was theirs.

The dispatcher said there were shots fired in the bank down the street, a teller dead on the scene. Suspects had been seen entering this small dry cleaning plant seconds ago. A marked squad car squealed to an angled stop. Mark ordered the two cops to move civilian traffic away from the storefront and cover the rear exit.

He flattened his shoulders against the cool brick

272

wall and a trickle of sweat slid down the small of his back. He breathed deeply to steady and slow his heart rate, pointed his automatic skyward, and nodded to Pete.

Pete held up three fingers, two.

The pistol gripped in both hands, Mark pivoted with lightning speed through the door. He crouched and aimed low, arms rigid, Pete high. *Christ, racks everywhere, the bastards could be behind any of 'em!*

A catwalk surrounded the two-story interior, with a circular track full of more dry cleaning. Drapes, clothes, white identification tags and plastic wrap, rippled from the breeze of a rotating fan.

Pete rolled to his right on the concrete floor.

Mark spotted the wide blue eyes of a dishwater-blonde girl crouched behind a waist high counter. He held a finger to his lips and belly-crawled to her side. "Are you hurt?"

She shivered a "No".

"Anyone else in here?"

She whispered, "Everybody's at lunch. Oh God! Sue, she works here, too. She'll be coming through the back door any second."

"No matter what happens, don't move."

Pete tapped fingers on his chest, pointed to open cement stairs in a corner leading to the catwalk, and moved toward them with the stealth of a lynx. His hazel eyes wide and steely, his gun panned the racks as he crept up the stairs.

Blistering heat poured from dryer vents along the floor. Sweat ran into Mark's eyes. He swiped his hand across his forehead and inhaled an acrid mixture of cleaning fluid, steam, and bleach. He peeked over the counter and glanced up at Pete as a loud report shattered the window behind him. In a commanding voice, Mark barked, "Police! This place is surrounded. You don't want to do this." *They aren't surrounded yet, but SWAT will be here in seconds...tear gas, flash-bangs, the works.*

A whoosh of air from an opening door was followed by a woman's scream. Muffled cries and sounds of a struggle gave Mark the time to sprint between two racks and half the distance to the rear.

He was huge, over six-five. The terrified woman's button-eyes glistened and blinked wildly at Mark. *Gotta be Sue.* The man's tattooed arm crushed her against his chest, her feet dangling several inches above the floor. The silver revolver he held to her temple was cocked and his hand trembled.

Christ, he's just a damn kid.

Dirty blonde hair, jeans, and work boots caked with dried mud...Baltimore Orioles cap perched on his head. There was white lettering on his black sweatshirt, partly hidden from view by the frightened girl.

Mark's eyes darted through empty aisles between racks of dry cleaning, and up to the catwalk. *There's two of 'em. Where the hell's the other guy?* He stepped into clear view, pistol aimed at the kid's nose, arms rigid, knees slightly bent. "Drop the gun. Let her go."

The woman's mouth grimaced wide with fear,

tears welling a silent plea to Mark.

"You drop yours, motherfucker...I'll blow this bitch's ass away, I fuckin' swear it!" Sweat ran from his pasty, pockmarked face and his wild eyes flashed.

Distract.

"No, you won't. Hey, I used to play ball for Baltimore. Triple A."

Negotiate.

"I'm Mark. What's your name?"

The man's eyes darted around the plant.

Buy time.

"Used to play first base."

The kid tightened his arm around the girl, evoking a whimper as he snapped his gun toward Mark.

Blood pounded in Mark's temples as he looked into the barrel of a .38. *Hollow points. Mother of Mercy.* Sweat slickened the grip of his Glock. *Steady. Hold 'er steady.*

"Back the fuck off, pig. I'm goin' out this door."

He pulls the trigger, that's it. I'm done.

Edging to his right to give Pete a better shot, Mark maintained his cool gaze. "Won't work. You got an alley full of cops out there. Drop the gun, let her go, and this is over." *Where's the other guy?*

The man licked his lips and seethed, "Back off, fucker, or the bitch is dead!"

Keep him talking.

"You know I can't do that. I'd get my ass chewed, right?"

The woman squinted her eyes closed, tears ran

down her cheeks; a pool of urine formed beneath her dangling feet. Her chin jiggled as Mark calmly said, "Where's your buddy?"

The kid's hand was shaky and he twitched the gun back toward the redhead's temple.

The instant the barrel moved away from Mark and toward her, a double bang slapped echoes through the plant walls and the kid was punched backward, a burst of red spraying the wall, two neat holes in his forehead.

The woman screamed as she dropped from the kid's grip and the revolver clattered to the concrete.

Mark dove to protect her body with his own from the ensuing gunfire. As they fell, he flinched at a sting on the side of his neck and clapped his hand under his ear. Thick, warm blood pulsed between his fingers, and the shoulder of her shirt darkened as if he'd tipped over a can of bright red paint. She struggled under his weight.

Shouts erupted through the doorways and gunfire roared through the air. In the sudden silence that followed, spent cartridges tinkled to the cement floor. The bitter odor of oily smoke mingled with the coppery scent of blood and the stench of the kid's voided bowels.

Pete…hope they got the other guy.

* * * *

Amanda felt the vibration of the phone and discretely glanced at the display as she said, "It will bring at least three hundred thousand in private auction, Alex. I suggest you leave the original frame."

Mark knows better than to call me at work.

She let the call go to voice mail and slipped the phone back into the pocket of her black slacks. The dark blues of the oil painting evoked images of the grandfather clock. She momentarily envisioned the moon dial.

Alex Bennington made a note on a clipboard and dropped it to his side. "You don't think the painting might bring more if we went with an antique gold finish?"

Amanda studied the painting. "No, I don't think so. The frame is original, even if it's not what's popular today. Let's leave it; I don't feel comfortable messing with original artwork."

Grace knocked and opened the door. "Sorry to disturb you, Amanda. There's a call for you from Northwestern Hospital. Shall I take a message?"

Oh my God, something's wrong with Mary. "No, put it through to my desk. Excuse me, Alex." Amanda walked quickly down the hall. She leaned over the desk, punched the flashing key, and lifted the receiver to her ear. "Amanda Parker."

"Hello, this is the emergency room at Northwestern Hospital calling for Officer Pete Mahoney. He wants you to come to the hospital right away. There's a squad car waiting outside Plethora to drive you."

"Pete wants me to come? What's this about? Is it my godmother? Mary Axelrod, is she…?"

"No, but Officer Mahoney wants you here right

277

away."

Amanda scanned the room as she walked around the desk, stretching the curled cord of the phone. The words made no sense. *Not Mark.* Her heart accelerated with dread at the memory of a similar call from Texas Airlines almost a year ago. "What happened? Is it Officer Callahan? Is he all right?"

"The police car should have arrived at your office by now. Please, Miss Parker, quickly."

CHAPTER 22

Mark could barely hear the whining of the siren from inside the ambulance, but he had no trouble hearing the paramedic's voice. "Keep your eyes on me, Mark. Don't go to sleep. You're doing fine. Don't close your eyes." She stood over the stretcher, her face inches from his, and pushed both hands against his neck, hard. "You're doing great, Mark."

Mark looked into bright green eyes. *Sure I am, if you'd quit trying to strangle me.*

The medic kept glancing at Mark's neck, increasing pressure as she leaned into him. "Keep your eyes on mine, Mark." The ambulance jerked to a stop and the doors opened. Bright overhead lights made him wince as the wheels clattered onto cement and they jostled to a smooth roll. The medic leaned into him, continuing her mantra in a low voice. "C'mon, stay with me, Mark. Just stay with me."

Peppermint gum. Tired as hell.

Another paramedic ticked off Mark's vitals, weight, height, and age. A different voice growled in urgency, "Keep the pressure on; don't let up. You cramp, give a yell."

That blue pajama guy's sure excited.

A lock of the medic's brown hair fell to her forehead as she nodded. She smiled at him as fluorescent lights created halos around her that flashed and faded. "You're doing great, Mark." The automatic doors swished open, followed by a cold blast from the air conditioning. The pungency of antiseptics prickled his nose.

Yep, I'm good.

The pressure on his neck changed. Another set of hands. "Okay, I got him."

Mark couldn't tell who was speaking. It seemed like dozens of voices spoke at one time. He registered the exchange of blood-soaked gauze for fresh, white gauze. A man's firm hand forced Mark's head to the side, pressure on his neck increased.

I'm fine. I'm doing great. I'm gonna be fine.

More blue pajamas scurried around him, jostling the stretcher, passing IV bags from one silver pole to another.

"One, two."

On three, they slid him from the collapsible ambulance stretcher to the ER's as controlled chaos enveloped the cramped room. More people in blue pajamas hovered over him in a swarm, shouting orders in medical jargon.

A woman's face leaned into his, and she rested her hand on his shoulder. "Don't go drowsing off. Stay awake. Keep your eyes on mine, Mark."

Yeah, yeah, she said that, too. I'm lookin'...I'm lookin'.

Another voice battled with the buzz in his ears. "Gunshot right carotid, he's lost maybe two units. BP's eighty systolic, HR's one-twenty, breathing on his own. We need a stat CBC, chem 8, and a PT/INR. Crossmatch for eight units of O Pos. Tell the OR we'll be there in two."

Settle down you guys. I'm fine. She said so.

Voices peppered the air with orders, numbers, more vital signs.

Right, no allergies. Just like it says on the ID.

The pajamas scrambled through a tangle of hoses attached to beeping machines. Fat bags of fluids dangled over Mark's head. He watched a young man hang a dark maroon bag on a pole.

Why'd he do that? Oh yeah, that red paint, that was blood. Mine. Shit. Man, am I tired. He closed his eyes.

"His veins are flat…I can't thread the line."

Yeah, well. Give 'er another try. Wake me up when you're done.

"Let me. Get his legs up."

"Pressure…hold on, I've got it. 60 over palp, falling…."

You're all talking at once. Stop. Sleep. That paramedic lady is gone, good. I can sleep.

"Mark, come on." A man's loud voice. "Stay with me. They got you this far. Stay awake."

Mark opened his eyes to a slit.

You betcha. No prob. God, so tired.

A blurry face wearing a mask appeared upside down over Mark's head. The mask poofed with an angry voice, "Keep the pressure on. Let's get him tubed quick!"

Ah, shit. I'm outta here.

Mark looked down at the chaos from above. *This is better. Whoa. This is ... not ... good.*

He floated down from the ceiling as a man

pressed more round stickers to his chest. The top half of the ER table was red with blood, dripping to the floor.

They cut my uniform; I gotta pay for that damned thing. They're makin' a hell of a mess with their footprints.

He scanned the monitors to a machine that squealed like a teakettle, green lines jumped like dancing fleas.

That oughta get their attention.

A nurse screwed a baby blue football onto a tube and began to squeeze.

Hey, she's the one who made coffee last week.

"He's in v-tach!"

"Charging, 200 joules."

A doctor fisted one paddle to Mark's chest and the other to his side.

"Clear!"

This isn't good. I don't think this is good.

"Shocking now."

"He's still in v-tach!"

"Charging, 360. Clear!"

"Shocking now."

Shit. I've had about enough of this goddamned excitement. They'll figure it out. Wonder what's going on out there?

Mark drifted to the nurses' station. Three pajamas jogged past him into his treatment room, snapping on baby-blue gloves as they ran.

Here comes the cavalry, guys. They'll fix everything.

Mark drifted through a door and into the hospital

ER waiting area to a sea of CPD uniforms. Four more policemen slammed through the door.

Hey, look at that. Haven't seen you clowns in a while. You bunch of idiots, what the hell's the rush?

Pete rhythmically tapped his head on the wall behind his chair, his eyes closed. The front of Pete's uniform and the full length of one sleeve were covered in blood.

You're a mess, bud. She said I was fine. Hey, here comes the boss.

Lieutenant Gordon elbowed his way through blue uniforms and anxious faces. He took the empty seat next to Pete. "What've you heard?"

Pete bent forward and rested his forearms on his knees. There was dried blood on the back of his hands. "It doesn't look good, boss. They don't hold much…it's not good. The bastard got him in the carotid. I tried to…" Pete's voice thickened as he straightened. "He took one for the girl. It woulda nailed her."

Didn't plan it. Just kinda worked out that way.

"That's what I heard, too." Gordon's eyes roamed the room as he pushed his hat back with one finger and the two men sat in silence. Finally, Gordon said, "I gotta get up there and donate blood. Callahan's family here yet?"

My family?

Pete leaned back in his chair; his eyes focused on the quiver in his hands. "On their way, even the girlfriend. She's on her way," he nodded to the reception desk, "according to them." He tipped his head back against the wall again.

283

Amanda? Coming here?

Pete's voice trembled. "I…better if she doesn't get here in time. She's had one fucked up history. Mark was just breaking through a boatload of baggage with that chick. She shit-sure doesn't need to watch him die." He shook his head. Pete's Adam's apple bounced and his face wrinkled in anguish, his freckles deepened in color. He resumed tapping his head against the wall and choked, "Fuck, fuck, fuck."

Die? What the hell are you talking about, moron? I'm not going to die!

Mark snapped back through closed doors and watched CPR compressions continue smoothly as two pajamas switched position.

You guys got that under control?

"Come on, Mark!"

"Charging. Clear!"

* * * *

Mary tucked a pillow behind Amanda's back and snugged a blanket over her lap. She leaned in for a kiss. "See you tomorrow. Get some rest, dear."

"Thanks." The door hinge squeaked as Amanda sighed. *Finally. Finally some time alone.*

Amanda pulled the pillow from behind her, rested her head back, and closed her eyes. Snapshots whirled as glass shards in a kaleidoscope. Gleaming dark wood coffin with dull silver hardware. Roses, a heavy scent. Red. Loving Brother, a gold sash. Organ music. A priest. Beloved Son. Somber faces.

284

Lilies. Wrinkled white tissues. Whispers.

Shaking her head, Amanda scattered the images from her mind like a frightened flock of sparrows. *Thank God it's not going to happen this time. Not this time.*

She kicked down the footrest, moved to the side of the bed, and lowered the chrome safety rail. She lifted Mark's hand, careful not to disturb the tangle of tubing, and rested it on her lap as she faced him and looked up at the monitors. Green arrows jumped up in lines of even regularity, numbers blinked, IVs dripped mysterious fluids in sync with the quiet cycles of breathy machines.

Amanda reached over and lifted a dark curl from his forehead and whispered, "I love you, Mark."

He stirred with her touch, but didn't wake.

He's dozing. They said he would for several hours. Why didn't I tell him I loved him before? I do love him. Waiting…hours of waiting. Pacing, knowing he would die. Of course he would die…the people I love die.

Amanda's tears welled again with thoughts of the two men in her life that she loved, Joe and Mark. She had loved Joe, too. But not like this, not with such conviction. Amanda rested her hand on Mark's chest and gently twirled his chest hairs in her fingers.

I know this man. I know the amazing person inside, the essence of him. I also know…know…he was not always Mark Patrick Callahan, but a soul from my past. Were we lovers? Amanda touched the locket. *I've let him into my heart…but I think he was*

285

already there. Is it true that souls return to be with other souls for eternity? Amanda watched his face for a long time, the breathing steady and deep. Mark's eyelids flickered with sleep, his features relaxed and peaceful.

A wave of exhaustion swept over Amanda. The sleeping pill Mary had pushed on her was taking hold. Mark wasn't restless at all, but deeply asleep. Deciding to lie down for a few minutes, Amanda walked over to the small sofa on the other side of the room, stretched out, and draped a hospital blanket over her legs. *How do I know him?* Amanda looked back at Mark. *A bigger question is how long have I known him.*

A library book in her tote caught her eye. Amanda opened it to Chapter One and smoothed the page. *Cassiopeia is a constellation in the northern sky. It is one of forty-eight constellations listed by the second century Greek astronomer Ptolemy, one of eighty-eight constellations defined today.*

The camping trip to Indiana. The big crooked W he'd pointed to that night. The tiny silver mist of the Andromeda Galaxy.

Cassiopeia was the queen and consort of King Cepheus in Ethiopia. Their daughter, Andromeda, was...

Amanda closed her eyes and rested her palm on a drawing of the Big Dipper...

CHAPTER 23

Chicago — 1871

Daniel Collins laughed easily and oozed charm. He leaned toward a pretty girl standing next to him who was sipping pink punch. "I'll show you tonight when it gets dark," he said. "It's always in the same place, night or day. Use only two stars of the Big Dipper and you'll find Polaris, the North Star. In a few seconds, you will know how to navigate the world. The big chair, close to Polaris, is Cassiopeia. With me for your astronomy teacher, you'll know dozens of constellations in no time. The night sky is a particular specialty of mine."

The crowd peppered the handsome young man with questions.

Collar-length dark hair and long trim sideburns framed his classical features, brown eyes sparkling with playful mischief. His comments on the night sky captivated the group and he moved to a discussion of Andromeda, a galaxy he said was visible to the naked eye. A bevy of young girls vied for his attention.

"Turned into quite the handsome devil, wouldn't you say?" Margaret slipped an arm around Bonnie's waist, leaned in and kissed her cheek. "Hardly the gawky rapscallion Jack brought home all those years ago."

Bonnie tipped her head and maintained a critical gaze. "He thinks so, obviously." *Arrogant as can be...wonder if there's anything the man doesn't know.*

"Your next birthday, you'll be fifteen, about time for your pretty head to be turned."

Bonnie smiled as Margaret scurried to the kitchen. *Certainly not by that pompous ass.*

Jack walked up behind Bonnie, his words drawing her attention. "You should get to know him better. You know he's worked for Koblenz Furniture longer than I have, and he's studying to be a doctor besides."

Bonnie pushed past Jack to a floral arrangement of white roses and adjusted some fern fronds and white ribbons to her liking. "Not in this life. The man is a boor, always has been."

He laughed at her back. "I can think of no one better suited to taming your saucy tongue. You look lovely by the way, cousin. You're as beautiful as the bride."

She blushed as she met his smile with a smile of her own. "Your words, charming as usual, are nonsense. The bride is in hiding for a few more minutes and you haven't even seen her." Bonnie took Jack's arm at the silvery tinkle of a bell.

Margaret called out, "Everyone, please take your places for the ceremony."

Bonnie brushed a hand down her pale blue satin skirt, admiring her profile in the pier glass next to the stairs. The fashionable bouffant bustle draped to a small train, her first grown-up dress. Long chestnut curls cascaded down her left shoulder, a crown of white tea roses woven through her hair, and the silver locket nestled in the hollow of her pale throat. She looked up at Jack. "Are you ready to be a best man?"

"As ready as you are to be a maid of honor." Jack leaned in and kissed her proffered cheek.

"I shall be taking my leave to assist the bride."

Slipping her reticule over her wrist and moving through the crowd, she glanced at Daniel Collins to find him staring at her. Turning to face him, she met his appraising gaze with a steady glare of her own. He won this silent contest of wills with a smile. Flustered by his boldness, Bonnie's face warmed as she pulled her eyes from his, gathered her skirts, and hurried up the curving stairs to Penelope's room.

* * * *

The house had been turned into a fairyland. White roses hung in garlands across the large front hall. White tapers in silver candelabras and a gaslit crystal chandelier shimmered, suffusing the rooms with a golden glow. The curved mahogany banister rail was decorated with tiny white tea roses and white ribbons. Expectant guests filled the room.

A chamber orchestra of clarinet, cello, violin, and piano welcomed the women down the stairs with the opening strains of Mendelssohn's *Wedding March.* Preceded by a flower girl dropping petals from a basket, Penelope seemed to float down the stairs. Her dress of white satin with its long lace sleeves was adorned with hundreds of hand-sewn pearls. Penelope's father met her at the bottom of the stairs, his arm extended.

She lifted the small bouquet of lilies of the valley from Penelope's hands. Bonnie smiled at the blatant adoration on Chester's face as he grinned at his bride and whispered, "You look lovely."

Penelope returned his smile through a tulle veil held with a tiara that was her "something old," having been used in her grandmother's wedding in England.

Bonnie stepped back to her place and listened to the preacher's sermon and the couple reciting their vows. *Anything Jack and I have needed, and more, always. The parents we lost. What would have happened to Jack and me if not for these two wonderful souls? Penelope and Chester have loved Jack and me as our parents, and they've loved each other, too. And Margaret, a tolerant and gentle woman who has taught Jack and me that family doesn't necessarily mean blood ties.*

Jack stepped forward with the ring.

Chester lifted Penelope's veil, bent to her lips for the kiss, and the room erupted in whistles and applause.

Bonnie handed Penelope her bouquet, returned the bride's tearful hug and stepped back, stumbling into Daniel Collins' arms. He steadied her, grasping her waist from behind as he whispered in her ear. "You are my wife in a fortnight, if you catch that bouquet. No man will steal your heart from me."

Penelope and Chester were surrounded with

raucous laughter and the boisterous cheers of well-wishers. Men eagerly leaned in from all sides to kiss the bride. Bonnie turned to Daniel, her face flushed with anger. She looked up at a playful grin and confident eyes. "Mr. Collins, that is the freshest, the most disgraceful and arrogant thing anyone has ever said to me. You've the manners of a..."

He raised a finger to his lips. "Shh." Slipping his hands into his pockets he raised his brow. "You'll draw attention to yourself, my dear. Today the sun shines only for Penelope."

Disarmed by his words and mocking smile, Bonnie frowned. Her name was shouted among the squeals of single young women gathered in a crescent in front of Penelope. Bonnie walked to the center of the girls and glared at Daniel Collins as he stood with folded arms. He tipped his head and examined her from satin-clad toes to dark curls. Her face burned as she stepped back from his stare, allowing the bouquet to be caught by other anxious hands. She turned and joined the giggling girls around her, stealing a discreet glance over her shoulder. Daniel Collins' audacious roar of laughter was infuriating enough without the addition of his cocky wink.

Her flustered reaction unnerved her, but Bonnie did her best to exude enthusiasm and nod to the other girls at the appropriate times. Her mind whirled. *I've known that man since he was a boy. He never looked at me the way he just did. Who does he think he is?*

The gathering settled into a casual reception and

291

Penelope glowed with the happiness of a beautiful bride, sharing champagne toasts. Her cheeks shone with tears as Jack made his best man's toast: "To the best parents in the world, to Penelope and Chester."

* * * *

Jack only stepped on Bonnie's toes once as they danced and appeared grateful for a tap on his shoulder. He bowed to her and stepped back as she turned to Daniel Collins' smiling eyes. Daniel pulled Bonnie toward him and spun her into a waltz.

She pushed her hands against his forearms, attempting a smooth extrication from what was sure to be an uncomfortable encounter.

Daniel moved toward her again, and swirled Bonnie back into step with him as he whispered, "Better not, darling. You'll cause wildly embarrassing gossip among the hordes of biddies in this room."

She glanced around, and yes, they were being watched. She whispered between the clenched teeth of a forced smile, "You are the most arrogant young man I've ever had the misfortune to know, Mr. Collins."

He smiled down at her, a disobedient curl on his forehead. With the confident moves of experience, Daniel whirled Bonnie around and around through graceful steps leading toward the open porch. "A practiced art, don't you agree? Being an arrogant young man, I mean."

Bonnie returned Daniel's smile with one of her

own, as dazzling as she could muster. "One dance, you ostentatious fool. You will then take your leave."

He softened his tone. "I don't think so."

Uncertain how to reply, she said, "Penelope's friends are not 'biddies'."

He tugged her waist toward him as he waltzed her to the porch and then suddenly stopped, holding her in his arms and chuckling softly. "Oh, yes they are, as in cackling hens." His eyes held hers, his laughter friendly and contagious.

Bonnie giggled at the thought of 'cackling hens' and glanced around. "They are, aren't they?"

Daniel lifted her chin and she met his disarming, penetrating gaze. He whispered, "Those are the most breathtaking eyes I've ever seen."

She stepped back. "You really are a silly fool."

With a grin, he pulled a pipe and leather pouch from his pocket. Tamping the bowl of the pipe in his pouch, he sauntered across the porch. "Let's discuss the details of our nuptials."

Bonnie followed him, suddenly feeling as though her heart was skipping rope. "Our...our what?"

Daniel turned and leaned his tall frame against the porch railing. He scratched a wooden match on the heel of his shoe. His dark bourbon eyes reflected a sparkle of flame. He underscored his stunning words through the blue tendrils of fragrant tobacco wafting toward her. "I wasn't joking, Bonnie. I'm going to marry you. It's been my plan for years, you know. Not until you grow up, of course. You're what, soon to be seventeen?"

She sputtered, "Fifteen. You are also a presumptuous idiot. I would sooner marry a..." Bonnie thrust her chin. "I'd sooner marry the great-great-granduncle of one of those old biddies."

He laughed warmly through whiffs of smoke. Daniel's handsome face quickened her pulse. "I think you'll agree that two years is a very respectable period of engagement, Miss Lexington. We'll have a lovely wedding, just like this one." He puffed on and then nodded at his pipe. "Most certainly we'll be having babies before you're twenty."

"You..." Bonnie shook her head and felt her heart thrum as his eyes traveled again from her toes to the curls around the tea roses in her hair. "Babies? You are more than simply arrogant, Daniel Collins. You're mad."

He chuckled. "Hardly." Daniel pushed himself from the railing and moved toward her. "You are the woman I claim as my own and will love for eternity. Shall I ask Jack for your hand now, or must I win your heart first?"

At a complete loss, Bonnie stepped back. *The man is beyond any semblance of reason.* "That's absurd." Bonnie's hand went to the locket on her throat. "We've known of each other since we were children, Mr. Collins. But we don't know each other at all."

His laugh lines wrinkled with his smile. He stepped close to her and held her eyes with his own. Daniel whispered, "Oh, but we do, Bonnie May Belle Lexington. We know each other very well, indeed." He touched the back of his knuckles to her cheek. "And winning your heart will be a delight."

Bonnie inched back from him toward the parlor door.

Daniel's dark brown eyes held hers through his confident and mocking smile. He tipped his head toward her with an elaborately polite nod, and winked.

Bonnie turned and stormed into the house to his laughter at her back. *Brazen, arrogant ass! I'd rather die an old maid!*

* * * *

Bonnie tossed her bonnet and cape on the chair in her office and took down a clean apron from behind the door. Tying it on as she hurried into the front of the store, she looked around appreciatively. The store belonged to Chester, but as soon as she graduated from high school it would be all hers. In the meantime, she was to run the shop and stock the merchandise; he would help her manage finances and clerks. Chester Koblenz Furniture would be tastefully displayed with her antiques. She would also continue her schooling with tutors in the evenings.

Bonnie had arrived early that day to take delivery of an old grandfather clock from England. Her description of the piece had intrigued Margaret, and she was coming by with Chester and Penelope to see it.

The deliverymen were extremely helpful

removing the crate and packing materials. They even mounted the decorative portion of the hood and swept up the excelsior from the floor. Bonnie wound the cable drive, set the time, and pulled the lever that turned on the chimes. She locked the beveled glass door and opened her inventory ledger on the counter. As she was finishing the entry, the clock began its resonant chimes. Bonnie raised her eyes to the solemn ivory face. Hypnotized by the sound, she moved slowly toward the melodious song of St. Michael's Church and whispered, "Angel bells…Ben's angel bells."

Penelope's lilting voice mingled with the tinkle of a bell over her head as she called, "So sorry we're late!"

Bonnie turned from the clock to Penelope, Margaret, and Chester. The women chattered gaily as they exchanged hugs.

"I'm so glad you came, Aunt Margaret." Bonnie glanced at the clock. "It's finally here."

Chester's footsteps creaked on the polished maple floor as he circled the sparkling store and said simply, "Impressive, impressive."

Bonnie smiled as Chester's eyes roamed across the assortment of antiques from all over the world. Crystal chandeliers hung from the ceiling, Irish and English bone china artfully arranged on shelves and counters alongside Limoges porcelain and Japanese lacquerware. Elegant Persian rugs hung on the walls, lending an exotic air.

"How enchanting everything looks." Penelope lifted the ruby glass prism of a lampshade. "Chester, this would be a lovely addition to the dining room. You know, on that little table by the sideboard?" She walked to a coral-colored porcelain basin with a matching ewer. "And for the guest room, isn't this pretty?"

"Nothing in here is as impressive as this." Margaret stood in front of the imposing clock. The mahogany case gleamed, the steady tick subtle but authoritative. "This is absolutely exquisite, Bonnie. You've no idea how long I've wanted one of these."

"I knew it was exactly what you wanted when I saw it in the dealer's catalogue. I doubt you'll ever see another one like it." Looking up at the clock's filigreed face, Bonnie continued, "I wish I knew more about its history. I only know that it's likely exhausted after the long voyage from Europe, and of course this shellac finish is fairly recent. Let me set the hands ahead so you can hear the chimes. The sound is lovely, the angel bells of Charleston. Its warmth resonates through the store. I so hope you want it."

"I'm afraid she does." Chester chuckled as Margaret scrutinized the case.

The old clock came to life with the distant and quiet song of St. Michael's chimes followed by a commanding gong.

Margaret mumbled, "Angel bells. Yes. Oh yes, I believe I do want it."

* * * *

Chicago — October 8, 1871

9:00pm

The light of the full moon pierced the darkness, creating patches of light in the front hall. The gas lamps were turned down to a gentle glow. Faint voices and the tinkle of dishes emanated from the kitchen at the back of the house.

Tick...tick...tick...tick...

Electra settled in front of the clock, her fluffy tail circling her paws. The arc of the pendulum held the glitter of her green eyes.

Tick...tick...tick...

Bonnie tiptoed up to Electra and smiled down at her. The cat's black head moved steadily back and forth, following the pendulum intently. Bonnie frowned at the flicker of light on the lace curtains.

What on earth is that orange glow?

CHAPTER 24

Mark worked saliva into his mouth, flexing his jaw. Where he was and why he was there came back to him through a drug-induced fog. *Dry cleaning plant ... girl ... tattooed arm. Red paint ... white blouse. First time I ever saw Pete scared. Must've thought I was....* His eyes snapped open. He could see a clock on the wall next to the window, blinds drawn. He turned his head on the pillow to read the time, and tape tugged at his skin, from his left shoulder all the way up to his ear. Reaching up, he felt a thick gauze bandage on his neck.

Settle, let the brain clear. He closed his eyes again. *Wake up.* He swallowed, raised his head and surveyed his surroundings. *Amanda. I've got to see her.*

Mark struggled with the tubing around him. *I've got to get out of here.* With the nurse call button out of sight, he dropped his head back and closed his eyes again. *Dammit. I've got to get out of this place. Amanda must be scared out of her mind.*

He scanned over his head at hanging fluids and monitors. Ticking machines dropped tubes that disappeared under his sheet to places he wasn't sure of, and IVs spidered from black-and-blue bruises on his hands as well as in the crook of his arm. Mark concentrated on the dimly lit ceiling.

A phone. I can call her.

He looked around. *Where is the damn thing? It's supposed to be right here, somewhere.* He flopped back again and blinked. *I think they got the other guy. Yeah, yeah, they did. Hope I didn't hurt that girl.*

An IV pump bleated a high-pitched demanding beep.

Fire drill. Wonder how long I'll have to put up with this crap. The call-the-nurse thing. Where is it?

He sighed and closed his eyes. *I was better off wherever the hell I was. I saw Pete sitting next to Gordon in the ER. How the hell can that be?* Mark looked at the ceiling. *Doctors working like crazy on a guy on a stretcher.* Mark's pulse quickened as memories flooded back. *Shit, that was me that damn near died!* He touched the gauze on his neck. *Almost got a peek at what's around the next bend, smart-ass. The invincible Mark Callahan.* Closing his eyes again, he clenched his jaw. *Was that astral projection again? Like what happened at Amanda's place?*

A shuffle of footsteps was followed with a rustle of motion as someone turned off the sound from the machine and began to tinker with it.

Mark's low voice growled. "Morning, if that's what it is."

Silence.

The woman laid her hand on his arm and reached over his head to flip a call button and turn on a light. "Hey, handsome! How are you feeling, a little groggy?"

He felt the bed vibrate as she pushed the control

raising him to a sitting position. Amanda was sound asleep on a small sofa across the room, curled under a hospital blanket, a book under her arm. His heart skipped a beat as relief flooded through every fiber.

Feeling vulnerable, and not sure he wanted Amanda to see him so helpless, Mark said, "Pull that curtain around the bed, would you mind?"

"That girl hasn't left your side since you got up here, officer. She's exhausted. Her godmother finally talked her into a sleeping pill. She's not going to wake up for a while."

He mumbled, "Come on, gimme a break. At least keep the decibels down so she doesn't."

The woman laughed. "You bet, Officer Callahan. But she's not stirring anytime soon." She walked around the bed pulling the curtain. "Give me a sec to call the doctor. Your girlfriend's going to be out for a while. And you're not getting up just yet yourself."

"The hell I'm not." He fisted the bedding around him and flexed his legs, his buttocks, his back. *The hell I'm not. I'm stiff, but I'm up.*

* * * *

This is a new experience: Some cute little nurse I don't know, standing there and watching while I piss and brush my teeth. She thinks I might fall on my ass, and by some act of God she's gonna catch me. Yeah, right. No shower 'til tomorrow. News flash. I'm outta here tomorrow.

The nurse had disconnected all but one of his IVs

301

and opened the blinds. *Daylight. But what day? Thought I was back in that hallway for a minute there.* Mark glanced at Amanda, still fast asleep. Her occasional twitches might have been stored-up tension, or she could be dreaming. He paused on one of his bathroom runs to slide the book from under her arm and pull the blanket over her shoulder. *Mary must have given her a nice stiff Mickey Finn.* He frowned at the book's cover and flipped through a few pages. *A Walk Through Stars.* Bending to kiss Amanda's forehead, he found himself grasping the back of the sofa to steady himself.

Mark grumbled as he shuffled back to bed. The doctor's lecture filled his mind. When the carotid artery is compromised, death within minutes is guaranteed if there is sufficient blood loss. Recovery, when the artery is properly repaired, is also nearly instantaneous. But he'd lost a ton of blood, and between the surgical incision and the exit wound, he was still going to be laid up for a couple of weeks. Mark was an athlete, physically and mentally strong, but the rules were defined for a reason. Bending over to kiss Amanda's forehead made the room spin. He'd been warned.

Don't bend over, Mark. No shower, Mark. Crap. But I can still shave. Using the overbed table mirror, he lathered up, and removed what looked like a week's growth of dark stubble. When he finished, Mark wiped his face and earlobes, careful not to disturb the gauze pad on the side of his neck. Not much pain, but Nurse Betty said it was a pretty big incision. The woman's name was actually 'Betty'. It fit. She looked like the actress in that movie, *Nurse Betty*.

Replacing Mark's toiletry gear and soiled towels with freshly brewed coffee and a pitcher of ice water, she gave him an exaggerated wink and jutted her chin at his neck. "It's going to leave a gorgeous scar to enhance your already foxy looks."

Flirty and cute. Cops have it good in the hospital. He smiled and sipped coffee. *God this coffee sucks. Musta just cleaned out all the drain traps in the kitchen.* "Thanks for this. How long has she been out?"

Nurse Betty glanced at Amanda. "Ages. She went down at least a couple of hours before you decided to return to the land of the living. Shall I wake…"

"No, no. Let her sleep. You said she was exhausted."

"The lady has been with you every second. You're a lucky fella. Course, she's had all of us dancing to her tune. Wanted you treated like a visiting dignitary. Threatened to call the mayor's office if we didn't hover over you like you were the king of Siam. You bein' a cop, a genuine hero and all…" Laughing and shaking her head, the nurse looped a TV-bed-call button gizmo around the safety rail. "The kitchen will be sending a liquid diet up here for you and a regular diet tray for your friend in a couple of hours. Take a nap; you're gonna wear yourself out. Give a jingle if you need anything."

"No damned jello and apple juice. Bring me

something real to eat."

Nurse Betty smiled and her fist went to her hip. "Great big macho cop. If the doctor says it's okay, you're on. Might as well settle in for a while, tough guy. You ain't leavin' here 'til the doctor says so."

Mark frowned, waved a hand at her and mumbled, "Out."

Amanda's dark hair draped over her neck, and the locket she wore glittered with each breath. *Something blue inside it sparkles. She's always wearing that thing. Wonder why?* Mark leaned his head back and watched her sleep. *She said "I love you, Mark," didn't she? Or did I dream that?*

Amanda stirred, rubbed the fingers of each hand on her forehead, and yawned. She swung her legs to the floor.

She looks good. God, does she look good. It wasn't a dream.

"I love you, too."

Amanda turned to him, her eyes wide. "Mark?" She sprang to her feet and rushed to his bed, tears welling before she pressed his head to the pillow with her kiss. She shuddered, pulled back from him, and her sapphire blue eyes scanned his face. "Mark! I was...I thought...you shaved..." She kissed him again as he moved her back with his mouth on hers.

"Careful, you'll pull out this damn garden hose and Nurse Ratched will kick my sorry ass."

Amanda looked down at the tubing. "Oh...oh, sorry." Her chin quivered and her brow furrowed as she pressed her lips together, fighting tears.

"I'm okay, honey. Just a nick."

Her voice cracked and she shook her head. "You scared me so much. I thought you...I thought you were going to...." A freshet of tears burst forth. Amanda leaned into him, resting her forehead on his shoulder, her body wracked with sobs. She raised her head and kissed him gently, everywhere, wiped her tears from his face, her voice breaking. "My God, Mark, I love you so."

He rubbed her back, closed his eyes and whispered, "I know baby, I know. No more tears." He pulled her to him. "I'm just fine, honey." A tear broke from the corner of his eye as he tightened his grip. He smiled as he thought of her words to him: "*I could walk a barbed wire fence with a wildcat under each arm.*"

* * * *

His first visitor was Pete Mahoney. Mark didn't know it, but Amanda wouldn't let anyone in his room except his mother, his sisters, and Mary until he was up and around. She did allow his lieutenant a brief visit. Mark had the feeling that Amanda had read him the riot act about him not returning to work right away.

Pete's relief to see Mark in one piece was so palpable that Mark felt sorry for the guy. "Pete, that shit can happen to any of us. You know that. You did everything you could. Quit beatin' yourself up."

Pete paced the room and ran a hand through his russet hair. "Christ, I'm glad you're okay. Scared the livin' crap..." He glanced at Amanda and meekly added, "Sorry. You're okay, right?"

Mark chuckled. "I've no doubt it was scarier from where you were sitting. I've been enjoying being pampered by pretty nurses." Mark glanced at Amanda and grinned. "Got one here you might like, bud. Name's Betty." He laughed at Pete's raised eyebrows. "No shit, Nurse Betty."

Pete grinned. "Yeah?"

"Don't ever change, pal. I'll be outta here by noon tomorrow."

"I don't think so," Amanda uncrossed the ankles she had rested on his bed and stood. "He's 'outta here' when his doctor says he's 'outta here', not before." She rubbed Mark's leg. "I'm going to run down to the coffee shop so you two clowns can exchange Nurse Betty's vitals. Tall blacks for both of you?"

"Just for Mark. I gotta get back on Doofus 'fore I get chewed out."

Mark smiled at her back as she left the room. "Pushy little shit, isn't she?"

Pete grinned. "*Pushy's* puttin' it mildly; a tigress with scary fangs protecting her young is more accurate, pal. Sounds like you got somebody runnin' your life. Not all bad, sometimes. She good?"

Mark directed his gaze out the window, a slight frown on his face. "I think we might have a few words on what I do for a living, but yeah. She's good, real good."

"Hey, you're gonna love this." Pete paused with his hand on the door. "Remember that guy we nailed, the one with all the tattoos?"

Mark nodded, the mental image made him wince momentarily.

"We couldn't see his sweatshirt with the girl in front of him, right? Looked at it afterward, and it said 'Have You Hugged a Cop Today?' Made me feel kinda bad."

The second visitor was the pastor of Mark's church. A man equal to his own six-two but more slender, Father John had dark hair with prematurely salt-and-pepper sideburns. Mark always wondered how a man with his looks found such comfort in the collar of the Catholic Church.

Mark extended his hand as the priest approached his bed. "No last rites today. Sorry, padre."

"Blew my program, huh?" Father John shook his head and laughed. "You character. I can tell you're feelin' pretty good. You've been in my prayers. Your mother arranged a novena for you."

"Thanks, John. And there's no surprise in that one. You guys at St. Michael's have put permanent dents in that poor old woman's knees. You should also feel guilty for her contributing enough to pay the church mortgage."

"It's substantial, but not that substantial. Wouldn't hurt for you to bend your knees once in a while. You on for a foursome first of the month?"

"Set the tee time and I'm in." Mark turned to the door as Amanda entered the room carrying a tray of coffee cups.

* * * *

307

She froze as her eyes met those of a priest wearing a long black cassock. *Wagon wheels on cobblestone. The earthy scent of pipe tobacco. Horsehair, biscuits, raisins. The snap of a leather whip. Gunfire. The terrified screams of a child, of Bonnie, of her.*

The tray crashed to the floor.

Mark leaned forward on the bed. "You okay, honey?"

The priest scrambled from his seat. "No harm done. Let me help."

Amanda quickly grabbed a handful of towels from the nightstand and tossed them on the floor. Blushing furiously, she began pushing them around with her foot to sop up the mess. "Sorry, just clumsy, I guess."

CHAPTER 25

Mark's brow furrowed as he flipped through pages of the newspaper. Amanda wondered what he was thinking. It was obvious he wasn't reading, or else the headlines were typical "who-cares" blather. Mark's mother and sisters were grateful that Amanda had insisted that he stay with her during his recovery. They knew he'd sneak out of his own place to get back to work, that he'd take orders from her that he'd ignore from them.

Amanda found that working on the article for *Plethora Magazine* was a refreshing change from watching the steady green lines of monitors and silent drips from IV machines. She had concentrated on nothing but Mark when he was in the hospital. Now she made serious progress with the article and it was nearly half finished.

"Dinner's almost ready. Wine with your steak, Mark?"

"Coffee."

Amanda glanced at him. *Definitely more than coffee brewing here.*

Freshly ground Colombian beans and the aroma of Mary's apple pie mingled with Mark's musky aftershave as Amanda kissed his cheek and took her seat at the small table beside him. Mark stared at his plate, steak knife in hand.

"You need anything?"

309

"No, nothing. This looks good."

They ate in silence interrupted only by the tinkle of silverware, soft jazz from the stereo, and the distant tick...tick...tick...

Mark sipped his coffee. "Is your office giving you a hard time about being away so long? I mean, shouldn't you be getting back to work?"

"Nope. Working from home is no big deal, as long as I meet my deadlines. I can connect remotely and handle my email. Why do you ask?"

Mark tossed his napkin on the table and resumed flipping through his paper, from page one. He looked down at Oprah. She sniffed kibble, blinked green eyes at him, and settled at the dish. He shrugged at the cat. "No reason."

Amanda began clearing the table. "You can just put it out of your head."

"You into mind-reading now?"

"You're not going to be an arrogant ass and get back on that horse. You're not Superman. You almost died."

She leaned over him to retrieve the silverware and he pulled her onto his lap. "A practiced art, don't you agree? Being an arrogant ass, I mean."

He leaned into her for a kiss and she pushed his shoulders back. "What did you just say?" *I've heard that before. 'A practiced art'. But where?* She gave Mark a peck and rose to continue clearing the table.

"I'm going back to work next week."

"No. No, you're not. You just got out of the hospital. The doctor said to take at least a month off."

"No way it's going to take a whole month, Sputnik."

"Yes it is, Mark." Amanda spun on him and drew in a breath. "The department has no issue with your taking full medical leave. Pete has no issue with it, either." She tossed her arms. "Boomerang has no issue. I have no issue. You're taking the time you need off. No debate."

"I've put up with your hovering mother-hen routine long enough." He walked up behind her as she closed a cupboard door and turned to face him. He moved his hands to her waist.

Amanda wiggled from his grasp and pushed him away. "You're not trapping me on that stupid counter again to make a macho point." She backed away.

"On to me, huh?" He walked toward her with a grin.

"You need some mother-henning right now. You were shot, for God's sake."

Mark held her eyes as he moved toward her. "I can think of no one I'd rather have taking care of me."

"You're changing the subject. You said you'd take time off to rest and think about leaving the police force to go back to medical school."

"You're right, that's exactly what I said. I've rested and I've thought."

"Dammit, Mark." Amanda frowned and crossed her arms. "You could at least give it more than four days."

He placed his hands on her shoulders, and leaned

in for a long kiss. "You, Miss Parker, are not in charge." He moved his hands down her arms. And in one swift move, she was over his shoulder. Amanda spluttered his name as she exhaled.

"That sounded like 'Fart''. You okay up there?"

"You damned idiot! Put me down."

"The doctor said, 'Take it easy.' So, I'm taking it easy. He also said, 'She's bossy. Nail her ass to a mattress for a few hours.' I'm just following doctor's orders. Quit squirmin', you're gonna fall."

Mark rested a hand on her bottom as he made his way down the hall and she laughed and struggled to break free.

She pushed on his shoulder and sighed. *Like moving a goddamned oak tree.* "Let me go. Sometimes you're such a big... Your doctor? He wouldn't say that."

"Forgot. It was Pete."

"You fool." Amanda laughed again. "He didn't say that either."

Mark bent at the waist and she flopped back to the bed.

She rested on her elbows and took in his broad shoulders as he pulled a tee up over his head. The sun had darkened his muscular forearms. His warm brown eyes sparkled with mischief, enough to turn a woman's knees to jelly. He needed a haircut and more than the usual single stray curl fell to his forehead. *Say something to me in Gaelic you big dope, and I'm all gooey.*

He pulled the tooled leather belt from his jeans as he toed the back of a sneaker. "Git nekked, woman, 'er I'll be gittin ya nekked."

"Sounds like an outtake from *The Quiet Man.* Is that the best Gaelic John Wayne you can do? And now who's being bossy?"

* * * *

Mark lowered himself to her, his heart thundering against hers. He dropped his head to her shoulder and smiled at breathy words whispered in his ear.

"It's amazing, Mark. You're amazing."

He lifted himself up and looked into her blue eyes. Mark frowned with alarm at a tear dropping down the side of her face. "What's wrong, honey? Did I hurt you?"

Amanda shook her head, both hands against his chest. "No, no. It's nothing. You're just amazing, that's all. It's so…"

Mark waited as she struggled for words and touched his chin lightly. He kissed her fingers.

"I know what it is."

"You do?"

"Yep. I know we've done this before, many, many times. We have made love before in a different life."

Mark kissed her, lovingly, deeply. He whispered, "You and me." He kissed her again and said, "And from that perspective, I agree completely, it is absolutely amazing. But me, amazing?" He chuckled. "I hope so."

He admired Amanda's shapely back as she walked to the bathroom. He shook his head in

313

wonder as she moved with the grace of a ballerina. *She is beautiful.* In a few minutes, she climbed back into bed and snuggled up beside him.

He pushed himself up on his elbow, pulled her soft nakedness close to his, and met her eyes. "I love you."

She stretched to reach his lips.

Sweet. Soft.

They needed to have this discussion, but he didn't want to lose her and he didn't want to argue. He smiled back. *One minute, I think she'll crumble like a straw flower, the next she's a bearcat.* "I like being a cop."

"But..."

"Wait. Hear me out. I know this has been a nightmare. You've no idea how hard it is for me to think that I'm contributing to the crap you've gone through." He rolled to his back and pulled her close. The breeze from the ceiling fan cooled his chest.

Amanda ran a smooth leg down his and rested her head on his shoulder.

"When my father died, because it was in the line, the FOP—that's the Fraternal Order of Police—they took care of everything, couldn't do enough. Paid off the house for Ma, put a nest egg together for her. I'd just started med school at the time. The FOP was great, willing to pay for school. But I had a sister graduating from high school. I chose to help put her through college and play the man-of-the-house role I found myself thrust into. That sister is wrapping up her internship next year and the other is in her second year. The Chicago-way wheels greased me through the academy." He stroked her hip. "You know the rest. Life happens; weeks become months and months become years. Being a doctor is something I don't even think about any more. I'm a cop. It's what I do, and it's who I am."

Amanda sighed.

He rose to his elbow again and rolled her to her back. "That girl in the dry cleaners, she was so scared she pissed down her leg. I saved her life. You've no idea what an incredible high it is to save someone's life." Mark dropped his head to her shoulder. "I can't believe I said that to you, of all people."

"Forget it."

"I wasn't thinking."

She shrugged. "Not to worry; I'll get even."

Mark laughed. "There's a scary thought." His gaze was drawn to the locket resting in the hollow of her neck. He lifted it on its delicate chain and kissed her there.

"Is this the locket your mother was wearing? I noticed it the day I met you."

Amanda ducked her chin to look at the silver heart in his fingers. "She gave it to me before she died. Her mother gave it to her. The story in our family is that whoever has the locket is protected by our ancestors as long as they don't take it off. Something like that. I only wear it because it was my mother's. Well, that and I think it's pretty."

"What's inside? Looks like something blue."

"A sapphire stone. You're looking at the main reason I know I was Bonnie Lexington. It's the one given to her by Magdalene. I'm certain of it."

* * * *

Fog off the lake was damp and cool. Mark's jog slowed to let Amanda keep pace. They stopped.

Amanda bent at the waist, her hands on her knees. She gulped in foggy air as her heart stopped pounding and she panted. "You're trying to kill me."

Jogging in place he said, "You're the one who wants to trail me like a puppy."

She walked to the break-wall and deciding she didn't have the strength to scramble up, turned and leaned back on the cool stone. She wiped the perspiration from her forehead, wondering if allowing him to run like a maniac was considered taking it easy.

He began doing push-ups against the wall. "The plan is to drive you crazy enough to want me out of your hair so I can get back to work."

"Think of a new plan. The current one isn't working."

Mark stood upright, his hands low on his hips. "I'm going to be bored out of my mind soon." He scanned her from head to toe with a smile. "That is, unless I continue to follow doctor's orders at least once an hour."

"Pfft. Macho man." She tipped her head. "Hey, I need to visit a couple of museums for this Plethora article. Why don't you come with me?"

"Where to?"

"Would you believe Charleston?"

* * * *

The next morning, they were at a cruising altitude of 60,000 feet. Mark leaned forward and angled his paperback into the seat pocket. He tipped his head to read the title of the article Amanda was reading. *While You're in Charleston.* "Guess we have time to do whatever you want, since we don't have a schedule to meet."

"Says here there's a city cemetery with Confederate graves, a recommended tourist attraction. It's called Magnolia Cemetery. Wonder if Magnolia Plantation still exists?"

Yesterday

CHAPTER 26

Charleston, South Carolina

Hands in pockets, Mark stared at the harbor from the window of their room at Mills House Hotel. A distant cruise liner conjured images of exotic ports, rainy days at sea, sunburns, and made-in-Taiwan souvenirs. Amanda was at the College of Charleston, a half-mile away.

Situated downtown, the hotel was close to some historical areas of Charleston, many within walking distance. Mark suspected they'd be strolling the King Street Antique District, so he decided to skip that for the moment. He crammed his cell phone and a room key-card into his pocket and set off.

Wandering down Meeting Street, he paused at tourist-trap window displays and on impulse, decided to do what cops do best, investigate. He looked around and blew a piercing whistle through his teeth, halting a cab.

"Magnolia Cemetery."

The cab driver looked in his rear view mirror. "Don't reckon you're from around heah, are you?"

Mark smiled at the Southern drawl. "Nope. Yankee tourist."

"You sure you want a cab to take you one block, sir?"

"It's downtown?"

"Depends on which one you was wantin'. We got two. The hysterical landmark up the street, or the big one with all them Confederate monuments."

Mark laughed. "Hysterical landmark?"

The guy shrugged. "Your pleasure, sir. They both called Magnolia Cemetery."

Which one?

Mark handed a five-dollar bill across the seat. "Point me to the 'hysterical' one. I'll walk."

He headed down the sidewalk toward a stand of ancient live oaks bearded with Spanish moss.

* * * *

Amanda slid her fingers over the keys of her laptop, pausing at the dancing bzzz on the table as her cell phone rang. She glanced at the tiny screen, and saw a text from Mark.

'eat?'

She texted back.

'nt yt'

She clicked the cursor at the end of a line of text as she turned the page of an old leather-bound ledger.

Another ring, bzzz.

Amanda frowned at the phone. The clock told her it was almost five.

When she texted 'nt yt', she meant she didn't want to eat yet; not that she hadn't eaten yet. *The art of texting; will I ever get it right?*

She grinned at the cryptic readout: "suk hd eat tl", an address, and "hr".

The tourist guide from the airplane had prepared her for this bit of local color. "Suck the Head and Eat the Tail" is a Southern expression for enjoying a plate of mudbugs, more commonly known as crawfish or crawdads. Amanda would not indulge, but she knew Mark would. She wrinkled her nose at the thought. *I don't want to eat little red fishy bugs. They're bound to have salads, though.*

Sighing, she looked at the readout again, drawn to another bzzz; ready to punch him for bugging her. An hour was about what she needed to finish gathering notes for the article.

'cmpny'

Company? Who does the social butterfly know in Charleston? We having dinner with a hotel maid?

Deciding not to pursue it, Amanda punched back a text.

'k'

* * * *

Mark kept an eye on the restaurant dining room entrance as he listened to Maggie Salinger. In the carefully modulated tones of an educated Southern woman, she was explaining her interest in genealogy while they waited for Amanda to arrive.

"There's scarcely a single person of African descent who doesn't wonder about his antecedents, Mister Callahan. We have the advantage, if you could call it that, of being descended from ancestors who were valuable property, so the records are often more complete than they would be for the typical

321

Southern white of that period. As I told you earlier, it was an entry in an 1870 census document that brought me to Charleston in the first place."

Miss Salinger taught English and drama in a Columbia high school. Disarmingly beautiful, she was tall and slender, her flawless skin a warm cinnamon, her hair in a neat French twist. The soft-spoken woman was probably about forty and the single mother of two toy poodles, one white and one black. She had named the white poodle Doctor King and the black one Princess Di. Not certain how to react to this information, Mark maintained a stoic expression. She winked as he sipped his drink, and they both burst out laughing.

Miss Salinger reached for her watermelon crush, a local favorite made with dark rum and Grand Marnier. Amanda would like it, he suspected.

He looked past Maggie as Amanda entered the restaurant.

"No question of who just walked in. Your face is lit up like God's own daybreak."

Mark chuckled at the remark as he stood and pulled out a chair. "This is Miss Maggie Salinger, Amanda." A waiter arrived at the table. "Miss Salinger is having a watermelon crush. It comes highly recommended."

Amanda glanced from Mark to the woman. "Sure, sounds great. It's nice to meet you, Miss Salinger." She raised a quizzical eyebrow to Mark.

"Oh, call me Maggie. It really is a pleasure." She extended her hand to Amanda. "In the few hours I've spent with your charming companion, it has been made abundantly clear that you have completely stolen his heart."

Amanda smiled at Mark and shook the woman's hand. "Oh, he's as sweet as a Georgia peach."

Maggie smiled demurely. "I'm sure you meant a South Carolina peach. They're ever so much sweeter."

Mark's face reddened. "Okay, you two, that will be enough."

The women laughed and Mark cleared his throat. "Maggie and I met at a cemetery not far from here this morning. She's doing research into the genealogy of her ancestors, and found some of her people there." Mark reached for Amanda's hand. "Hon, she didn't just find her own ancestors there. I think you're about to be a bit surprised. 'Maggie' is short for 'Magdalena.' It's not a coincidence."

Magdalena's almond eyes moved from Mark to Amanda as she said, "Don't look so startled, sweetheart. I've been looking for my great-great-grandparents, and I believe I've found them. My ancestors were slaves on Magnolia Plantation."

Amanda's throat constricted. She whispered, "Their names. What were their names?"

Miss Salinger looked at Mark over her drink. With his slight nod, she looked at Amanda, and said, "Magdalena and Benjamin Lexington."

Oh, my god. Amanda stared at the woman. She whispered, "Magdalene...her name was Magdalene." *Bonnie's father didn't think of Magdalene or Ben as slaves. They were treated as family, but were they really free? Bonnie was so*

323

young and thought of Magdalene as her mother. Being raised by a black nanny fit into the big picture of the South at the time, as did the surname "Lexington". Slaves often took the name of their master or his plantation as their own back then.

The waiter placed fresh drinks on the table, interrupting Amanda's thoughts. Amanda spoke into her drink. "They weren't always treated as slaves."

Maggie sipped her drink. "I'm anxious to hear what you know, of course. In the last few hours, Mark's told me about your past life sessions. I think you'll be able to tell me far more than I can hope to tell you. And don't worry; contrary to the conservative inclinations of the South, I'm very much a believer in reincarnation. Sadly, I was probably not the high priestess of Rome, but the barefoot wife of some sodbuster in Coffeeville, Kansas."

Amanda thought Magdalena Salinger looked more like a Roman high priestess than a barefoot housewife. "I missed something." She leaned forward in her chair. "You're saying Magdalene is buried in that cemetery? That can't be. She can't be there. We were on a train going to Chicago." Amanda frowned and shook her head. "Ben and Magdalene went north. They took me and Jack to Cleveland."

Mark squeezed her hand. "You don't know how old Magdalene was in the early days of the war, nor what she did after the war. She and Ben obviously made their way back to Charleston because they are buried here."

Maggie gestured with her drink. "I can help with that. Magdalene was forty years old in the 1870 census, and Ben was forty-six. His occupation was listed as Carpenter. They had three children."

Mark rested a hand on Amanda's knee under the table. "This entire area is on land that was once Magnolia Plantation. The little cemetery contains grave markers you need to see."

Yesterday

CHAPTER 27

Maggie and Amanda exchanged cell numbers, and shared a long hug with promises to keep in touch. Then Amanda and Mark headed off to Magnolia Cemetery, a short block away.

A modern bronze scroll identified the space as being the original Magnolia Plantation cemetery plot and described the history of the property. A knee-high wrought iron fence and a well-maintained flowerbed of azaleas circled a park setting of ancient headstones. The carving on some of the stones was completely illegible. Smooth indentations alone hinted at a time long past, richly elegant and tragic.

She reached for his hand as they walked slowly among the markers, pausing at several. The largest stone marked the resting place of the original plantation owner, John Alexander Lexington, Sr., and his wife. Separated from the family plot by a small space were the graves of several people thought to be plantation slaves, among them Magdalene and Ben. A tall vase of white calla lilies stood by their simple marker. Mark used his cell phone to take several photos.

In the deep shade of an oak bough draped with gray moss, Amanda's gaze fell on a pair of marble headstones. Her skin prickled with a powerful sense of déjà vu as she walked around them to read the inscriptions, knowing what she would see there.

327

Patricia Margaret Lexington
Beloved Wife and Mother
1833 – 1856

John Alexander Lexington, Jr.
At Peace in the Lord
1825 – 1862

Amanda whispered, "He's not in that grave."

"You said he was buried somewhere near where Bonnie got on that train south of Columbus, Ohio." Mark stepped up beside her. "If I understood you, the people who took his body for burial thought he was a preacher." He glanced at the lilies on Magdalene and Ben's grave. "I suppose they must have put that up when they came back here after the war."

He pressed a palm against his brow. "God, that's why you were upset by Father John at the hospital. I'm sorry, honey. I should have put that together. The cassock is the last image Bonnie, *you*, had of your father."

"I've seen priests my whole life, but his black cassock sent my head spinning." Amanda rubbed the locket between her fingers. "I was Bonnie again, cowering in the bottom of a wagon, shrinking in terror from the roar of a cannon and the crack of John Lexington's whip."

She walked over to Magdalene's gravestone, knelt, and leaned back on her heels. The stone was rough and cool to the touch, and she traced the shadowed letters with the tips of her fingers. Ben's name was there, but barely. "Bonnie loved them so, because they were so kind to her, so…" Her voice cracked as she added, "I was Bonnie, so I guess that means I loved them."

She shivered, even though the air was warm.

Mark slipped a hand under Amanda's arm and brought her to her feet. She buried her face in his neck, inhaling his familiar musky scent as he wrapped his arms around her. He eased her chin up and she looked into his warm brown eyes. Mark wiped tears with both his thumbs. In his gentle baritone, he said, "Don't grieve, darling. You were here once as Bonnie. You're here today as Amanda. Isn't that so?"

She nodded and held his gaze. "Am I really so special?" She tipped her head toward the gravestones. "Do you suppose any of the *other* people of yesterday might be wandering around today, just like me? And why wouldn't someone in my here-and-now life move on to explore the Andromeda Galaxy tomorrow? Like Joe, Connor, or my mother?" She laid her head on his shoulder, resting her hands on his biceps. The lush grass was thick and dark green. Broken rays of sun danced over headstones through the live oaks overhead.

He tightened his arms around her. "It's only yesterday, sweetheart. There are wonders awaiting you in tomorrow's unknowns, maybe exploring those pretty rings of Saturn you love." He kissed her and Amanda looked into his dark eyes, as he softly said, "Your life is with me today." Mark turned to

329

John Lexington's grave and Amanda followed his gaze. He whispered, "And yesterday."

* * * *

Mark leaned back against a stone pillar in the store, arms and ankles crossed as he watched Amanda browse. As he'd predicted, they were roaming the King Street Antique District and she had wandered into yet another shop. He waited patiently as she ambled through the store, fingered a lace doily, and examined a silver knick-knack box. He smiled as she peered at the bottom of the box, decided that it didn't pass muster, and placed it back on the shelf with a frown. So far, she'd made few selections. "We need to get moving."

Without glancing up from a pair of earrings in a display case, Amanda asked, "What's the rush?"

"Sunset."

She flapped her hand dismissively, again without looking up, "I have the protection of a mean-ass Chicago cop after dark. Not to worry."

"I have something for you to see before the sun sets." He looked at his watch. "We have about twelve minutes."

Amanda walked to him with a smile and took his arm. "Okay, I'm done shopping."

He looked down with a side-glance at her upturned face. "I only rolled my eyes once."

"You're a prince."

"Thanks. I think."

They sauntered down the street, the sky turning a

dark blue in the east, rose-gold to the west. At the corner of Meeting Street Mark stepped in front of her as he said, "Okay, close your eyes. Don't peek."

Amanda tipped her head. "What are you up to?"

"Just close your eyes. No cheating."

She closed her eyes and shrugged. "You're silly."

He placed a hand on her back and one on her arm. "Okay, small steps and don't peek."

"This better be good." She followed his lead. "I feel like an idiot. We're on a street crowded with people."

"Don't open your eyes yet. There's a park bench behind you. Sit."

Amanda eased back to a seat and laughed. "Now?"

"Yes."

The steeple of St. Michael's Church towered before her, white paint stained bright red-orange with rays of the setting sun. Live oaks draped long strands of pale green moss swaying in a light breeze, tendrils of silk tinted coral by the sun. An ornate finial at the very top of the steeple glistened a rosy gold. Below the galleried cupola the minute hand of the black clock face, with the stoicism of centuries, inched to nine o'clock.

Birds fluttered from louvered arches as angel bells began to sing.

They sat and listened to St. Michael's chimes and a toll of nine o'clock. The steeple turned brilliant white as floodlights brightened.

Mark stood and took her hand. "Come on. I have something else for you to see."

331

A historical marker near the white pillars of the church recalled much of Mark's research regarding the church bells and a history of the church itself since 1751. A lighthouse, a navigation aid for Charleston harbor, a lookout tower during the Revolutionary War, the church had witnessed much of the history of the young United States. Brass letters ended with a list of the bells: Nineteen hundred pound Michael, Gabriel, Raphael, Virtues, Dominion, Thrones, Cherubim, and down to the smallest angel, five hundred pound Seraphim. All the bells were originally cast in 1764 at a foundry in London, repaired several times, hidden in a shed from the Confederacy during the Civil War, and finally returned to their belfry in 1868.

* * * *

Mark gazed out the small window of the airplane. A towering thunderhead with an anvil top glowed pink and then darkened to deep rose from the sun dropping to the horizon. He stretched his long legs in the aisle. Amanda's head rested on his shoulder as she slept. Patchwork farms, water towers appearing as golf tees, fall-colored trees as sugar-popped cereal, all moved by at a creeping pace that belied the speed of the plane.

CHAPTER 28

Chicago

Firefly sparks raced up the flue as the gray bark of an ash log curled, smoked, flashed into brief flame. Low flares of blue and white pulsed from the bed of embers below the iron grate. Amanda knelt on the hearth and stared into the fire, the brass poker in her hand forgotten. Tiny jets of steam made odd hisses and moans as her thoughts drifted. Distant ticking measured the passage of minutes, hours, lives. A pocket of sap exploded with a sharp pop and a bright flash, bringing her back to the candlelit living room, the scent of wood smoke. She rose from her knees in a fluid motion and replaced the filigreed screen.

Mark wrapped both arms around her from behind and leaned his cheek against her temple. In silence, they watched the red and yellow flames dance. "Don't stay up too late, hon," he whispered.

"I'm a couple of paragraphs away from a pretty good article here. I'll come to bed as soon as I wrap this up."

He squeezed his arms around her and kissed her cheek. "See you in the morning."

Amanda curled up on the couch and opened her laptop. She glanced at the book Mark had been reading. *The Great Chicago Fire: The Death &*

Birth of a City. Oprah broke from pendulum duty and sprang lightly to the sofa. She nosed under Amanda's hand for attention, purred thanks for a scratch behind the ears, then returned to her vigil.

Amanda leaned her head back on the cushion and gazed into the fire. Her mind wandered to her own past, other pasts. To Bonnie and Jack, to Daniel and Mark. To questions without answers, striving without purpose, lives without meaning. *No. Everything that happens has a purpose. Every life means something.* A burning log collapsed into the embers in a shower of sparks.

Tick...tick...tick...tick...tick...

* * * *

October 8, 1871

Bonnie stepped to the window, drawn to a dim glow of red-orange on the lace curtains. *What on earth can that be? The sun set hours ago.* She separated the curtains and turned at Chester's voice.

"Fire on the far southwest side of the city. We spotted it from our room, so we'd better keep an eye out for a while." He lit the oil lamp on the sideboard and carried it toward her.

She smiled at him. Chester was clad in a long nightshirt and house slippers, his balding head wreathed with an unruly thatch of blond hair.

"It's bone dry out there." He set the lamp on the table and pushed his round spectacles up his nose. "There hasn't been more than an inch or two of rain since June."

Penelope came down the stairs carrying a silver chamber stick; her flannel dressing gown draped her rounded belly. She handed Chester a long robe. "We'll be able to see better from the front porch."

A strong wind from the south carried the faint smell of wood smoke toward the house on Pine Street. Chester leaned on the white rail and peered at the orange radiance in the distance. "There have been over a dozen small fires in the last week. Four blocks burned downtown, and just yesterday we had three or four more fires. Those firemen must be exhausted." He squinted into the wind and added, "That looks to be right by the dairy farm. Close to it, anyway."

Bonnie tugged the shawl tightly around her nightdress.

Jack went to stand next to Chester. "Bateham's Lumber Mill is just north of there, I think. That's what, a mile from the gas works?"

"Less. Six, eight blocks, maybe."

"Well, one thing is certain," Bonnie said, "the idea of having only a hundred and fifty firemen for a city of this size is absurd."

They stared at the glowing sky in the distance.

The clatter of hooves on cobblestones announced the arrival of a black buggy jouncing to a halt in front of the porch. All heads turned as Daniel Collins swirled the reins around the brake lever and sprang to the ground.

"Daniel!" Jack strode to the top of the porch stairs, a hand extended. "Which way have you

335

come? Is this part of town in any danger?"

Daniel jogged up the steps and tossed his deerskin coat over the porch railing. "I was on my way home from a party on Astor Street. Seems like there's always something burning around here lately. I wouldn't be too concerned." He nodded at faces on the porch and settled a smile on Bonnie as he shook Jack's hand.

That arrogant smirk. Bonnie met Daniel's dark eyes and frowned. The tanned, patrician face brought forth a flutter in her that was unexpected and unnerving. Bonnie huddled further into her shawl and gazed at the dense gray haze blurring the far horizon.

Chester put his arm around Penelope and guided her toward the front door. "Don't need you getting chilled."

Jack held the door open for them. "All we can do is keep an eye out for a while, see what happens."

Bonnie had begun to follow the rest of the group into the house when Daniel blocked her path. She started to speak, but stopped as his brow rose. The door clicked shut, leaving the two of them alone on the porch.

Dropping her gaze, she raised a hand to the locket on her neck and tipped her head politely. "Excuse me, Mr. Collins. I wish to pass."

Daniel stepped toward her and she moved back. "Miss Lexington, I've waited patiently for months now, resigning myself to a life of virtuous solitude."

Bonnie's pulse jumped as his brown eyes met hers. She wished she'd put a cloak over her flannel nightdress instead of a shawl.

He spread his arms and smiled. "Now you appear before me as the vision of an angel." Daniel placed his hands on her waist as he said, "And I think it's about time you started paying attention to what I have to say."

Bonnie gasped as he gently lifted her to the porch railing, and she grasped his forearms so as not to fall. "You fool. Get out of my way or I'll scream."

"It seems the only way to get your attention is to position you in such a manner that you can't escape." He slowly shook his head. "Look at you. My God, you are lovely."

"Let me down. I've nothing to say to you."

Daniel softened his tone, drawing her eyes to his. "Then you will listen. You might as well stop wiggling, as you're not going anywhere." His face serious, he asked, "Do you believe in love at first sight?"

Bonnie thrust her chin defiantly. "No."

"Neither do I." Daniel chuckled. "The first time I saw you, you were six years old. It wasn't until you so politely called me an 'arrogant young man' that I fell hopelessly in love." He lowered his eyes to her mouth and his voice to a murmur. "With you, Bonnie."

He kissed her gently. When he eased back, she studied his face. Daniel's laugh lines deepened with a smile. Dark hair and long sideburns framed a proud nose and generous mouth. He leaned in and pressed his warm lips firmly to hers again. In the unseasonably warm October air, Bonnie shivered as his strong arms moved around her. His shoulder muscles flexed beneath her hands as he opened his mouth and returned her curious touch of tongue to lip.

Breathless, Bonnie pushed him away and struggled from the railing to her feet. Her chest heaving and mind spinning, she sputtered, "That…that was not the behavior of a gentleman." She walked toward the door and stopped at his words.

"Nor that of a lady."

His pompously confident smile enraged her. Furious, Bonnie turned and slapped him with every ounce of strength she had.

Hand to cheek, he grinned. "Delightful as it was."

Her face burned. "You arrogant ass."

"Exactly!" He roared a laugh and stepped back, bending at the waist. "You indeed have my heart, Bonnie. You own it completely, for eternity, in this life, the last, and the next." Laughter ran through his words. "I adore you. I've always adored you."

Bonnie shook her head in frustration. Anger turned to exasperation. "You silly idiot."

Daniel straightened, his smile warm. "Tragic as it is for a few, wood smoke smells good, doesn't it? A warm Christmas fireplace." He moved toward her and lifted her hands with both of his and kissed her fingers. "Never fear me, Bonnie. I will lay down my life for you." Dropping her hands to his waist, he squeezed them tight, leaned in, and kissed her lips again.

Her heart skipped at his words and her mind whirled at her sudden fascination with a man she'd known since he was a boy. The gentle touch of his lips intoxicated her and sent warm, unfamiliar flutters through her.

He lifted her hand and slipped a sparkling diamond ring on her finger. It was a dream from afar as he whispered, "You are mine, Bonnie, for all time."

Bonnie gasped with an effort to steady her breathing. She stepped back and raised her hand to eye level. Her eyes widened. "Daniel Collins! I've no intention of…"

"Nonsense. Your intentions are quite clear, my love." Daniel pulled her into his arms. His lips nearly touching hers, he murmured, "Clear, indeed." His firm kiss sent fog through her mind and her knees weakened.

She steadied herself against the railing, his kiss and his words whirling in her mind. *This is insane. He is trying to addle my wits, and I'm letting him!* Holding her hand at arm's length, she examined his ring. Its stone sparkled gold and orange on the darkened porch. She glanced from the ring to him, but his eyes were no longer on her.

"Look."

Bonnie followed his gaze to a gust from the south. A spiraling tower of fire arced to the horizon followed in moments by the distant boom of an explosion. Gold porcupine arrows burst and faded like a fireworks display on the ground.

Daniel walked to the railing and frowned, his

339

brown hair whipped back. "This is getting worse," he muttered. Billowing acrid smoke spilled toward them, the horizon bright yellow-gold, a distant hammer of hooves and the distinctive ring of alarm bells carried on the wind.

She stepped to his side and pushed away the ivy obstructing her view. Strong wind from the direction of the inferno lifted her hair. The fire had tripled in size since she last looked. The windows of a distant church steeple reddened. Flames curled around the belfry and a whirlwind of fire spun above and around it. She gasped as the tower tipped precariously and slowly dropped from sight. A ball of flame burst from the ground and spewed sparks high above the glowing roof of the church. A swirl of flame fingered through the sky. She looked up at tiny gray snowflakes whisking through the air. Backing away from the porch railing, fear prickled the hair on her arms. She whispered, "My God..."

Daniel held the front door open for her. "You and the other women had better get dressed. That's not slowing down and it's headed this way."

CHAPTER 29

Chester, Jack, and Daniel were gathered in the parlor. As the men spoke, Bonnie descended the stairs tying the ribbons on her blue bonnet into a bow at her neck. Margaret and Penelope returned to the kitchen to retrieve a bag of fresh pears from the pantry and a basket of apples from the cellar.

Chester turned a silver key in the door of the tall oak gun case. He distributed a selection of handguns and rifles to Daniel and Jack. The men sorted through boxes of ammunition.

Loading a Colt's pistol, Jack said, "We need to move fast. Penelope can't make a trip to the Koblenz factory and another north. She's too..." he struggled for the words, "Penelope is in a very fragile state."

"Agreed." Chester looked at Daniel. "We'll not be leaving the women to fend for themselves. You stay with them. Jack and I will retrieve the contents of the safe from the factory and join you. Head toward Lincoln Park and take the Lake Shore Trail as far as you can. With the drought, it's not as swampy as usual, but there may be patches of soft sand. The closer to the lake you can get, the farther you are from the fire and the cinders this wind is carrying. We'll meet you there. You'll take my wagon; it's enclosed, so it will contain most of the supplies and will be more comfortable for

341

Penelope."

Bonnie lifted a carpetbag to the table, her heart beginning to race. *I don't want to be in a wagon. I can't be in a wagon.* "I'll go with you and Jack, Chester."

Chester held her arm, his eyes stern. "No, Bonnie."

Her heart skipped at his uncharacteristic glare.

"A dangerous situation is developing. In a few hours that fire has covered the entire southwest horizon. Chicago is a tinderbox, complete with seventy-five miles of tarred wood streets, and that wind is carrying the fire this way. In no time at all we can expect to see thousands of people trying to escape the fire, and panic does not make men rational." He stepped to the table and continued to speak as he filled a knapsack with boxes of cartridges, a knife, a small axe, and other tools. "I'll not be putting you women in danger."

A finger of panic crept up her spine. "Do you really need those guns?"

Daniel cinched the buckle of a holstered weapon around his waist, eyeing her with concern. "The buggy and wagon are loaded with enough supplies for us to function for several days. There are others who will not have had such foresight. We must be prepared to protect what we have and ourselves. Maybe it won't be necessary and the fire won't get this far, but the weapons are better with us than stolen."

Jack took her hand. Bonnie's eyes welled as she stepped into his arms and looked up at his worried eyes. "I want to go with you, Jack."

"You must look after Penelope and Margaret. They'll need you." He kissed her forehead. "Go with Daniel, Bonnie." Jack leaned back and gently wiped the back of his fingers across a tear on her cheek. "Do this for me; Daniel will take care of you. You're to do as he says."

Throat tight, Bonnie glanced at Daniel, his eyes on her but his face unreadable. She wanted to argue, to beg and plead. More tears threatened to spill. She clutched the locket at her throat. "Come back to me, Jack. You must."

"You can be assured of that, cousin." He kissed her cheek. "I imagine we'll be no more than two hours behind you." He smiled and wiggled her chin. "I think it's time you found Electra and stuffed her into that carpetbag. I wouldn't miss that sight for the world, fire or no fire."

* * * *

Daniel hefted a large canvas bag to his shoulder and his eyes met hers. "You must change your bonnet to one like Margaret's and Penelope's. They're waiting in the wagon. Hurry."

"Don't be a fool. I like this bonnet."

He started to turn and stopped at the defiance of her words, lowering the bag to the floor. Placing his hands on his hips, Daniel clenched his jaw and sighed. He glanced at the grandfather clock and returned his eyes to Bonnie's. "A wide brim will protect your face from ash and cinders." He gestured at her hat. "Pretty as it is, that hat will not."

She narrowed her eyes. "I'll be fine."

Daniel stepped close and lifted her face to his. He brushed her lips with his own, and whispered, "You will change the bonnet, Bonnie. The only question is whether or not it involves a spanking." He winked. "Your decision?"

Her heart thundered and her face warmed as she stepped back. She yanked the ribbons from her chin and went to the cloakroom. Fuming, Bonnie fumbled through a shelf until she found a black broad brimmed hat, which she plopped on her head. She turned and glared at him.

Daniel smiled, nodded politely, and extended an arm to the door.

She grabbed the carpetbag by its leather handles and stormed past him.

Electra cried pitifully.

* * * *

The wagon trundled north on Pine Street and turned east toward the lake. The sky to the south glowed orange and the snow of ash blew in horizontal gusts. Showers of glowing sparks fell like hail all around them. Bonnie sat in the seat next to Daniel and held the wide brim of her hat low over her face, grateful for his insistence that she wear it. A powerful blast of smoky air closed her eyes and she turned her face into his shoulder.

Daniel put his arm around Bonnie and pulled her close. "We're turning north again in a few blocks.

The wind will be behind us." Moving forward at an agonizingly slow pace, a woman carrying an infant walked next to them. Bonnie met his eyes as he squeezed his arm around her. His voice barely audible he said, "If we help everyone we pass, we too will soon be walking. Think of Penelope."

Bonnie jumped at a distant thunderous blast and the shout of a man to "Leave the goddamned painting!" The wagon jostled through furniture in the street. A bizarre clutter of satchels, suitcases, furniture, and a broken wooden box of toys littered their path, all deemed valuable enough to take from homes but then discarded as too cumbersome to carry.

"Get in the back."

"I'm going to stay here."

Daniel slipped the hammer thong, freeing the revolver. His eyes darted around them and he flashed an angry glare. "At any other time, Bonnie, stubbornness is a part of you I find most charming, but tonight I need you to do as I ask." Daniel met her eyes and his face softened. He pressed his cheek against hers, his voice a whisper. "I know you're frightened, Bonnie, but listen to me. I've got to move the wagon through this crowd, and there might be trouble. The front is not safe. It's no place for you."

I don't want to get in the back. "Please, Daniel." *I don't want to be in the wagon.* "I don't want to."

"Everything will be all right." He reached for her hand. "I need you to keep the other women calm and tell them to hold on to something." Daniel squeezed her hand, as he said, "Go, Bonnie." He glanced over her shoulder and then met her eyes. "Go and get in the back."

A loud boom shook the ground and a surge of terror swept over her. Daniel shouted "Hiya!" to the team of horses and loudly snapped his whip.

She stumbled as the wagon lurched forward and catapulted her into the back. She slammed her shoulder into an oak barrel of drinking water as she dropped to the floor. Bonnie grimaced at a brief stab of pain and a complete loss of dignity. She shook her head at Margaret's offer to help her to a seat. With skirts and cloak atangle, she decided the safest place to be was the wagon floor. As she looked around the wagon, her heart thumped with dread. *Keep calm.* Her voice shaking, she shouted over the clamoring noise of the wagon and the people in the horde around them, "Daniel said to hold on to something. We're not to be afraid."

Margaret grinned as she said, "I guess you forgot to hold on."

Bonnie looked at Penelope with alarm. A thin glaze of perspiration shimmered on her pale face. "Are you all right, Aunt Penelope?"

Penelope clenched her hand into a fist around a white handkerchief. "I must say, this is far from a gentle ride in the country." She rested a hand on her swollen belly, and gripped the wooden side rail of the wagon as she looked around, her blue eyes wide. "I...I'm going to be fine. I hope we don't have to travel far."

Bonnie inched toward Penelope and laid her hand

on her knee. "I think we're nearly there."

The three women shrieked in unison as the wagon tipped precariously.

Bonnie scrambled back to Penelope, helping her to the wooden bench. "There, you didn't fall. You're fine. Hold tightly to the rail."

Penelope nodded, a sudden grimace on her face. "Oh, dear." She held out a hand to Bonnie and Margaret, "No, it's nothing. Nothing, I'm sure."

Bonnie sat on the floor of the wagon, hugging her knees to her chest with her back against Penelope's legs. She jerked her head up as her body lurched violently. Silhouetted against the orange sky, Daniel had a kerchief tied across his nose and mouth against the hot ash that filled the air, his hat pulled down to his eyes. A dark figure leapt to the seat next to him and stood over him brandishing a heavy cudgel. Bonnie sat frozen in terror. The man struck Daniel's shoulder and tried to grab the reins with his free hand. Struggling to control the horses, Daniel hunched forward, unable to defend himself. The man raised his stick again. "I'm taking this wagon! Get down now or I'll scatter your brains!"

Bonnie acted without thinking. Bolting to her feet, she seized an axe from the heap of supplies under the seat in front of her. She swung the axe at the man's head, catching him above the ear with the flat of the blade. He fell away from Daniel, dropping back into the crowd.

"I didn't know you had that in you, Bonnie! Now get back there and hold on!"

Bonnie stood behind him, swaying with the

movement of the careening wagon. She dropped the axe as her knees buckled and she fell back into the wagon. At a snap of the whip, and another bellow, the wagon jumped and lurched again and again. She wedged herself between two bouncing cartons of fruit, closed her eyes and whispered, "Please stop soon."

Distant explosions roared. The brutal bruising of a different wagon, the angry snap of a different leather whip, and another flight for her life whirled in Bonnie's mind. Her heart pounded. A distant gas line thundered the explosion of a cannon, and bursting windows popped like musket fire. Each assault jumped through Bonnie's spine as she slammed and bounced on the wagon floor. Fists clenched, her nails dug into her palms. Hidden from the other women by the wide brim of her hat, Bonnie's face was flushed and her heart raced with the thundering hooves of horses. Moon. Saffron. Battered and terrified, she pinched her eyes closed as tears ran to her chin. She pressed her hands to her ears. Her body trembled. Panic engulfed her and she stopped fighting screams.

Hands tugged at her arms and someone wanted her to listen, to hear. *No! No, I'll not hear. I'll not listen!* A firm, steady voice commanded her to be calm, but she could not stop screaming. Bonnie flailed and swung her arms, pushing and fighting strong hands lifting her from the wagon floor. She struggled and cried and called for Papa. *A man, a soldier, dust, gunfire, blood, darkness, smoke. No! No!!*

Whispers. "Shh, Bonnie. It's over."

She couldn't move, couldn't breathe, she cried and whimpered and struggled against the strong arms wrapped around her. Someone whispered, murmured. Bonnie strained to hear the words, to focus.

"Stop, Bonnie. Don't cry. It's over."

Daniel.

"No more. Stop, shh. No more tears." Daniel pressed his hand to her cheek. "Take a deep breath, Bonnie. It's over. You're safe." Daniel held her on his lap in a field of tall grass.

Her panicked gasps subsided, each slower than the last.

His face smudged with soot and a spot of dried blood on his chin, Daniel's dark eyes reflected his exhausted relief. He slowly shook his head. "You probably saved all of us back there. That fellow had the jump on me, and from the look in his eyes he would have stopped at nothing to take our wagon." As Margaret approached them from the wagon he whispered, "You're my Joan of Arc."

Bonnie wiped her cheeks with a trembling hand and looked up at Margaret. "Is Aunt Penelope all right?"

"Not to worry, dear. Penelope says she's fine, but she's very pale. Let's go show her you're fit as a fiddle." Margaret extended a hand.

"Electra?"

Bonnie tried to stand and stumbled back into Daniel's arms, her strength shattered.

"Sit with Daniel for a while and collect yourself.

349

Electra is fine. Affronted, dignity ruffled. But she's settling down."

Daniel held her, his sheltering arms strong and warm. A blustering wind blew from the southwest. The dark expanse of Lake Michigan shimmered with whitecaps and gold coins danced on the surface.

Daniel lifted her chin and she looked into his eyes. He gently stroked her cheek. "No one will ever hurt you again, Bonnie. I promise." He lowered his lips to hers, his firm mouth strong and gentle. Daniel looked over her shoulder, sadness and worry in his eyes as his arms tightened around her.

She turned and followed his gaze. The city in the distance burned. Indistinct figures, shadowy ghosts, moved through swirls of smoke. Bonnie reached under her cloak and touched the silver locket. Her eyes blurred with tears.

Jack.

CHAPTER 30

Sunrise Monday morning revealed the south end of the city smoldering, while flames towered further north. The fire had jumped the Chicago River overnight. From the vantage point of Lincoln Park, the entire city burned, engulfed in swirling flames and black smoke bent by relentless wind. Bonnie tugged her cloak around her and scanned tired faces. Most people huddled in small groups; quiet murmurs sprinkled through the crowd. Cemetery headstones served as a macabre means of separating families into clusters. The initial panic of escape had given way to exhaustion and many people slept where they had fallen. Other men and women walked through the crowd seeking loved ones, peering from bloodshot eyes. Some were directed to tearful reunions, handshakes and hugs. Most, disappointed, simply moved on with dazed expressions. A woman nearby suddenly wailed and fell to her knees, rocking back and forth as her man stood helplessly, his arms limp at his sides.

Bonnie turned to watch Daniel administer aid to a small boy with an injured arm. Kneeling in front of the child, he created a makeshift sling from the sleeve of his shirt and the boy nodded shyly to a question she couldn't hear. The little boy stepped into Daniel's arms for a hug and smiled.

She scanned the distance again, the wind lifting

the wide brim of her hat. *Jack said he and Chester would be two hours behind us. Those two hours are now twelve hours. They're alive. Jack is alive. Maybe one of them is hurt. They just had to stop for a while. Maybe it's the buggy. Maybe it's the horse or a buggy wheel.*

Daniel walked toward her, hunching around the flame of his match as he lit his pipe. Still handsome despite a two-day growth of whiskers and a sleepless night, his face smiled down at hers. "That mask of soot does nothing to diminish your beauty. I must say, though, the vision of you and your axe fails to live up to the classical image of the damsel in distress." His dark curls, caught by the wind, danced about his head.

"Do you think Jack and Chester are all right, Daniel?"

Daniel turned to the flaming city, puffs from his pipe swirling in the air. "I've known Chester for years." Putting an arm around her waist he added, "And your cousin since we were both boys. They are strong and determined men. Yes, I do think they will be fine." He turned to her. "Jack is blessed with your strength of spirit."

Margaret called from the wagon, "Daniel!"

Tightening the strings of a white apron around her waist as Bonnie and Daniel walked toward her, Margaret said, "You are going to put your medical education to work, Daniel. We are about to have a baby."

His eyes widened. "Margaret, I'm just a student. This...I...I've never even watched a baby being born!"

Bonnie rested her hand on his arm. "Neither have I, Daniel, but we're about to." *I can help him. Rags, I need to tear up that shirt, it's ruined, and that old skirt.*

"But I can't do this." Daniel shook his head. "We must find a doctor."

"Daniel Collins." Bonnie faced him, her eyes narrow. "You have made it very clear that you consider yourself an expert on women. This is not the time to change your tune, so just tell me how I can help you. Penelope needs us."

The muscles of Daniel's jaw flexed and he nodded. "We need to fill that pail with lake water and boil it."

* * * *

Hours upon hours passed as Bonnie and Margaret took turns holding Penelope's hand. Penelope's grip was so tight in the last hour that Bonnie's hand ached, yet still the baby refused to emerge.

Bonnie wiped perspiration from Penelope's face, and her heart skipped at Penelope's anguished scream. "You must push, Aunt Penny."

Penelope cried, tears falling. "I can't. I am pushing!" Her body quivered as she arched her back with another spasm of pain. She bit her lip and blood trickled down her chin. She moaned and closed her eyes.

"Margaret, move behind Penelope." Daniel wiped his brow on his sleeve. "Lift her shoulders and let her lean against you." He sat on a box between her legs, placed one of his hands on her ankle, and lifted her skirt. "You need to keep trying, Penelope. I know it's hard, but you'll soon be holding a beautiful baby."

Daniel tipped his head to see if the birth of Penelope's baby had started. His face blanched. Meeting Bonnie's eyes, he whispered harshly, "The baby is breech."

"I don't know what that means. What do you want me to do?"

Daniel inched the wooden box he sat on closer to Penelope. "It means I'm not looking at the crown of a baby's head, but at a tiny foot." Moving the petticoat to bare her legs, Daniel placed his hand under Penelope's skirt to rest it on her swollen stomach. "I have to...I have to turn it. I have to move the baby back and turn it."

Penelope cried out and begged for Chester.

Margaret cooed in Penelope's ear. Bonnie couldn't hear what she said, but Penelope squeezed her eyes shut and leaned her head back on Margaret's shoulder. Tears streamed down Penelope's pale face.

Daniel leaned over her belly and closed his eyes. The skirt moved and Bonnie knew he was feeling for the baby's position. With a gentle voice, he said, "Listen to me, Penelope. Chester is coming, and you will hand him his baby soon. Don't push, wait. I must turn your baby if it is to live. This will be quick, and it will hurt."

Panting and fighting for breath, she met his eyes

and nodded. Daniel leaned across Penelope, almost on top of her. He closed his eyes tightly and dropped his head as he pushed. She cried out, digging her nails into Bonnie's hand. Penelope's prolonged groan bloomed to a deafening scream.

Within minutes, a healthy bellow pierced the air, muffled by laughter and quiet cheers from the small crowd surrounding the wagon. Rose Bonnie May Starks Koblenz angrily entered the world on the night Chicago burned, on the night that Penelope Starks Koblenz died.

* * * *

Margaret's heart-wrenching cries pierced the air as she rocked Penelope's body in her arms for close to an hour. Her near hysteria helped Bonnie fight through her own grief as she helped Daniel to gently lay Penelope on the bench in the back of the wagon. She knelt beside the body and rested her cheek on Penelope's hand.

After a long while, Bonnie whispered, "Daniel, what will I say to Chester?" She choked through her tears and a hard lump in her throat. She shook her head and murmured, "What can I possibly say to Chester?"

Daniel eased Bonnie back from the body and draped a brown and beige afghan over Penelope, covering her face, as he said, "You will tell Chester the truth, Bonnie. You will tell Chester that Penelope's last words were of him."

This was a nightmare and she would eventually

wake from it. They found a wet nurse among the crowd. Margaret sipped tea laced with a strong dose of laudanum and she soon nodded off to sleep.

Daniel left the wagon. Bonnie didn't know where he went. Like her, he'd been awake for hours, near collapsing with exhaustion. He probably fell asleep beneath her under the wagon, or tried to.

The roof of the wagon quietly pattered with raindrops.

The tightly swaddled infant stared at Bonnie with Penelope's pale blue eyes. She wiped a drop of water from the baby's tiny chin and looked up to see where the wagon was leaking. Her throat tightened; the water was her tear.

Bonnie held Rose to her bosom and wept softly as it rained.

* * * *

Holding Electra in her arms, Bonnie waited on the porch. Daniel insisted on walking through the house before they entered. Most of the trees were burned, but Daniel said that in a fire of this speed sometimes the damage was superficial. He said the trees might again show life in the spring. It was fall. With some of the old trees Bonnie couldn't tell if the leaves were burned away or they had simply fallen.

Finally, Daniel nodded her inside as he secured the pistol in his holster. "It appears safe enough, but not a pleasant sight, I'm afraid."

"I wish you'd take off that gun. You're scaring

Electra."

"This city is teeming with vagabonds, sweetheart. General Sherman is dispatching a thousand troops to patrol the city. I can assure you, Electra is no more unnerved looking at it than I am wearing it. Until I'm comfortable with what I see, this revolver will remain on my hip." He bent to her lips and smiled. "And you will not be out of my sight."

With his arm around her waist, they weaved through the rubbish of the parlor. The main portion of the house was intact, in spite of severe smoke damage and the inevitable vandalism. It didn't appear that people had taken anything beyond what they could steal from the pantry and kitchen. The southwest roof of the house had collapsed over the library, but the rest of the first floor was only blackened with smoke.

"The bedroom windows and doors were closed, and those rooms are quite livable. The water closet is damaged from the roof collapse, so chamber pots need used regardless. I'll go check the kitchen pump."

Daniel took Bonnie in his arms. "It's a god-awful mess, darling, and there is much work to do. At least you're not homeless, though. According to the *Tribune*, over one third of the people in the city are without shelter." He kissed her forehead.

She turned to the grandfather clock, the mahogany case ebony black with soot. Electra curled her tail around herself and gazed at the still pendulum. Deer etchings, encrusted with grime, stared back at Bonnie, the blues and greens of the oil painting in the moon dial obliterated, the gold filigree invisible. The clock's glass face had cracked from the fire's heat. The old clock would no longer sing like the angel bells of St. Michael's Church.

"There's no point to any of this, Daniel. Everyone. Everyone I've loved all my life." Tears pooling in her eyes, she pointed at the blackened clock. "Everything I've cared about is gone." She buried her face in his chest and shook her head. "Papa, a mother I never knew, Ben, Magdalene, and now Aunt Penelope. Even people like Jack's parents and Duncan." Bonnie choked, "If that's all I have to look forward to, I don't want to go on."

He lifted her chin and wiped tears from her cheeks. "You can and you will. Never underestimate your strength and the power of your love, sweetheart. I was a boy of twelve when I first heard of you from my best friend."

Bonnie looked at him quizzically.

He smiled, stroking her cheek, and whispered, "Jack."

"What did he say?"

"He told me stories of your courage, stories that filled my heart. I loved you long before we met." Taking the handkerchief from her sleeve and dabbing her cheeks, he continued, "And then I saw a little girl swinging on the porch of this house, years ago. Jack and I were helping Penelope plant roses, remember?"

Bonnie nodded. "You kept looking at me."

"Chester also told me about the tragedies you both endured, your fierce determination to not let life beat you down. You're a strong woman, Bonnie Lexington. I've seen it with my own eyes. I saw your bravery there in the wagon, your resourcefulness during the birth of a child. You witnessed the death of someone dear to you." He tightened his arms around her. "Yet you keep going and inspire others to carry on. That strength of character is deep in your soul. You will prevail no matter what life throws your way." Daniel kissed her gently. "This is the wonder, the magic of you that I love. I love you with all that I am, and for all time."

Bonnie put her arms around his neck and kissed him back. The diamond on her finger glittered. "I love you, too." She slid her hands under the collar of his waistcoat, leaned back, and studied his face. "What happened to Jack and Chester? I mean, what do you think happened to them?"

Daniel looked over Bonnie's head, and back at her. His face lit with a warm smile, and his brown eyes glinted mischief she didn't understand. He leaned in and kissed her lips. "I'm going out to the wagon to get Margaret and Rose." He winked. "In the meantime, you spend a minute talking to that handsome mug behind you."

Bonnie frowned. She turned around to see the most bedraggled, filthy, but beautiful sight she could imagine: Jack. He stood at the door, leaning on a broken lath strip, his trouser leg torn and bloodied.

Blinded with tears and repeating Jack's name over and over, Bonnie stumbled toward him. She glanced behind him at the carriage lane, looking for

Chester. "Jack, you're hurt!" She pulled his arm across her shoulder and helped him to a soot-covered chair.

"No, Bonnie. No." He muttered wearily, "Well, a bit."

She stepped to the threshold and looked around the empty porch. Bonnie closed the door and turned to Jack, meeting his eyes. Kneeling before him, she placed a hand on his knee. "Where is Chester?"

Jack's hand trembled as he reached for hers. His face reddened and his eyes welled.

Bonnie's heart began to race and she whispered, "Oh my God, no..."

* * * *

Amanda's knees buckled when she bolted from the sofa. She dropped to the hardwood floor, tears welling as she gasped, frantic and unable to breathe. Cold sweat stood out in beads on her cheeks and forehead.

Chester too!

A brilliant flash of lightning filled the room, followed instantly by an ear-splitting crash of thunder. Amanda screamed and her eyes darted around the room in terror. The storm raged and the rumble became the roaring of artillery, the explosions of a city in flames. The drumming of rain against the windows was the galloping of panicked hooves on a dirt road, on echoing wooden streets; it was the racing heart of a frightened little girl and a shattered woman.

The rain moved out over the lake, carrying the uproar of the summer storm with it, receding into the distance. Amanda's gasping breaths, the pounding in her heart slowed, and she looked around at the dark shadows on the walls of the living room. The embers in the fireplace still glowed softly under ashes in the grate. She rose cautiously to her feet and leaned against the tall clock.

Tick…tick…tick…tick…

The song of St. Michael's chimes filled the air and the mahogany case reverberated beneath her hands. Amanda lurched back from the clock as if the dark wood burned.

She trembled, panting for breath. "No! How can you sing now? Your angel bells died in the fire! I saw you standing there, dead and still!" Her eyes roamed from the clock's pendulum to its gleaming ivory face. Amanda groaned with dread. *Wood and brass and ivory and bells come back to life, but people die and they're gone forever! The people I love die! They all die!*

Amanda struggled for air and sobbed as she staggered back and collapsed on the sofa, her chest heaving. Chester's kind eyes, his warmth now only an empty ache. *Papa, Joe, Magdalene, Connor, Ben.* She buried her face in her hands and sobbed, willing thoughts to stop. *Mom, Daddy. Penelope. When will my love finally kill Mary? Kill Mark?*

So many already…how many more? My God, I can't do this. I can't do this to Mark.

361

Yesterday

CHAPTER 31

Mark stretched, yawned, and opened his eyes to Oprah's. Cat and man blinked at each other and his early morning voice croaked, "Woulda swore you were a better lookin' chick last night."

He stumbled into the bathroom, into his sweats, and into the kitchen. Pouring coffee, he called out, "You ready for a run?" He sipped and grimaced. *Cold coffee?*

Silence.

"The plan is to make you beg me to quit runnin' and then beg me to quit bouncin' your noggin on the headboard, all within an hour. Let's get going."

Silence.

He walked down the hall to the living room, scratching the top of his head. *She probably fell asleep on the couch.* He shouted into the air, "Wake up, Sputnik."

Cell on the table, laptop on the sofa. His book lay on the coffee table, opened to a large photograph of the Chicago Firc monument in Graceland Cemetery. He walked through the apartment, searching. *She's not here.*

Mark took the stairs two at a time to Mary's apartment. He banged his knuckles on the door until he heard her mumbled voice.

"Hold your horses. There's an old lady fumblin' around in here."

363

He spoke as the door opened. "Amanda here?"

Mary's hair, in a long gray braid, was fluffed by sleep. She cinched the tie of a robe around her waist and looked up at him over her glasses. "Of course not. She lives downstairs. Thought you knew."

"She's not there. I thought maybe she came up for coffee or something."

The park.

Mark flew down the stairs. Over his shoulder he said, "Sorry, she probably thought I'd catch up with her. Later." He slammed through the door, the gate, and sprinted toward Lincoln Park. *Something's wrong.*

Mark scouted their usual paths at a fast jog. A light breeze from the lake and a timid drizzle kept him cool. He sprinted past the chess pavilion, North Avenue Beach, Lincoln Park Zoo, the break wall. Out of breath, Mark paused. He bent at the waist, hands on knees, and closed his eyes. *Think. Where would she go?* He tipped his head back, eyes drawn to a waft of fog above the trees, obscuring the skyline. *Looks like...Christ, it looks like the city's burning.* His mind flashed back to the open book on the coffee table in Amanda's apartment. *Graceland?*

He resumed his jog under Lake Shore Drive, dodged through traffic and pedestrians west on Irving Park Road to the entrance of Graceland Cemetery. Mark slowed and scanned the grounds. The rain came at a faster clip. There were few people in the cemetery. A service was being conducted in the distance, a cluster of black umbrellas and two limousines with a dozen or so vehicles parked in a neat row.

Mark thought about the last regression session. *An orange glow on curtains. Chicago fire soot in the clock.* He trotted through the monolith markers of famous Chicagoans: Mies van der Rohe, Pullman, Palmer, Pinkerton, Louis Sullivan, Marshall Field, Kimball, and Daniel Burnham on his lonely isle. He stopped at a small green sign with an arrow.

THE GREAT CHICAGO FIRE

He followed the sign for a few hundred yards looking for the monument and spotted her.

Amanda sat on the grass, resting her forearms on her knees. She was soaking wet and as still as the statues around her. Her pale skin glistened like the rain-drenched marble wall before her. Mark watched her for several seconds and finally asked, "Who?"

Amanda's thoughts were interrupted by his voice behind her. She pointed to the upper left corner of the marker: *Penelope and Chester Koblenz.* Her voice was soft and barely audible, as she said. "They're wrong. Penelope died giving birth in a wagon as the city burned. Chester died the same night. Thugs killed him for his buggy."

"You regressed? By yourself?"

Amanda scrambled to her feet and stepped back from his grasp. "I didn't try to. It just happened." She turned away and spoke to the tree branch above her head. "Maybe I did try. It doesn't matter." She shook her head and faced him.

"You know that can be dangerous. Mary told

you…"

"Stop, Mark. Stop." She took a step in his direction. "I'm not a child."

"Why didn't you wake me?"

"Stop! You're smothering me!" Amanda held her hands up and lowered her head. "This isn't working." *Run him off. He's got to go away. I'm not going to love him. He'll die. I'm not going to love him or anyone.*

Her heart ached for him as his brow furrowed, his eyes searching hers in confusion. She covered her face with both hands. Rain had straightened her soft curls and they clung to her face and her wet blouse. His arms wrapped around her, but she struggled out of his grasp. "We're done, Mark! I need to be alone. You need more than I can be. This isn't a life meant for me, for you."

He opened his arms. "Honey, whatever it is that you experienced doesn't have anything to do with you and me today."

"I'm not your 'honey', dammit. And you're right." Amanda inched back. "What I experienced doesn't have a goddamned thing to do with you. Nothing. We don't know each other. We never met before. That's all stupid, coincidental crap."

Mark's fists clenched, and then relaxed. "What the hell are you talking about? You know better."

She backed away from him and laughed. "Know better?" She started to jog away. "Yes, you're damned right I know better."

Mark overtook Amanda and turned her around to face him, the brilliant flash of her eyes a startling blue in the gray of the storm and the headstones around them. "What's going on?"

She struggled against him. "You just don't get it. I want you out of my life. I want you to go away."

He held her shoulders until she looked at him. "I told you months ago that I wasn't going anywhere. I don't know what this is about, but you can't just throw me out of your life without telling me why."

Lightning cracked through the air, followed by an immediate roll of thunder. Mark slid his hands around her back, pressing himself to her, looking down at sapphire eyes reflecting fear and searching his own. "I know I love you, darling. I love *you*. Not who you were, but who you are." Mark touched his lips to hers. He moved his hand to the nape of her neck and pressed his mouth firmly to hers.

Amanda turned her face from his, and gasped for breath as he murmured, "Don't, sweetheart. Don't push me away."

She struggled from his arms, her chest heaving as she stepped back. "No. This isn't me. I'm not the person you think I am. You need to leave me alone." Amanda's voice, barely above a whisper, implored, "Please, Mark. Please. Go."

It wasn't rain now, but tears. Tears that begged him to leave her alone, begged him to go.

The sky burst open with silent lightning and then a roar of thunder. Fat drops slammed the walkway. Mark held up both hands as he stepped back. Her blue eyes held his until he turned, walked away, and didn't look back.

He moved from a walk to a jog to a muscle-punishing run, soaked sneakers slapping through puddles. Mark stopped and leaned back on the cool bricks of an apartment house. He dropped chin to chest, grinding his teeth as he breathed deeply and closed his eyes. *She's convinced that loving someone again is a disaster in the making.* Shaking rain from his hair, he resumed his pounding pace until he reached the gate of the brownstone. He leaned on the wrought iron filigree of the gate to catch his breath. Rain streamed down his angry face as he vaulted the gate and jogged up the stairs. *Dammit! Dammit to hell!*

Mark slammed the door of the apartment closed, causing Oprah to jump in angry protest. Her back arched and she peered at him.

He stormed through the apartment, tossing his things into his duffle bag. He unplugged his cell charger and dumped in the second shelf of the medicine cabinet—toothbrush, razor, and the painkillers he never took. He walked to the door, pulling the key from his pocket. Mark set the key on the table, his eyes drawn to Oprah. Her back to the pendulum, she blinked her green eyes at him.

His cell phone sang *Go, Cubs, Go.* Amanda had reprogrammed the ringer and he couldn't figure out how to change it back. He looked at the tiny screen. *Ed Morgen?* Mark took a deep breath, closed his eyes, and spoke into the phone. "Callahan." Glancing at the old clock face he said into the phone, "Sure. Gimme an hour."

He frowned at the cat and at the key on the table. The muscles in his jaw flexed as Mark reached for the key, tossed it in his hand, and slipped it back into his pocket. "Later, Oprah."

Yesterday

CHAPTER 32

Amanda stood in a puddle at the door to Mary's flat shivering, her drenched hair and clothes plastered to her skin. She lifted the knocker and tapped twice.

Mary pulled it open with a flourish, then her welcoming smile changed to surprise and concern. "Get in here and towel off before you catch your death."

Within a few minutes, Amanda sat at the kitchen table huddled in a brown woolen robe, hair gathered in a turban made from a striped bath towel. She blew steam from her mug of black coffee and waited for the warmth to seep into her.

"First things first." Mary set a teapot on the table and pulled out a chair. "Are you all right?" She filled her cup, placing a cozy shaped like a cat over the pot.

Amanda muttered into her coffee, "I think I'm losing my mind."

"I doubt it, dear. Tell me what's wrong."

"Last night I regressed to being Bonnie again. I swear I wasn't trying to...at least, I think I wasn't. It just happened."

"Does Mark know about this?"

Amanda's chin quivered and she met Mary's eyes. "I just kicked him to the curb." Hot tears spilled down her cheeks. "My love for him is

371

nothing but a death sentence. He barely survived that shooting, Mary. He deserves better."

Thunder rolled in the distance and Amanda pulled a tissue from the box Mary held out.

"You have a connection to that young man that goes beyond this life, Amanda. You both see this clock during your regressions. The entire objective in continuing this process has been to analyze your past and how it relates to your future. Just because you slipped into an episode doesn't mean you're finished. You're still searching. Don't you think 'kicking him to the curb' is a little premature?"

"What I saw scared the hell out of me. This cycle of pain and loss isn't anything new. It happened to me as Bonnie, the same thing." She wiped her eyes and added, "As soon I make a deep connection with someone, they die. I'm not going to let that happen to Mark because of me."

"Think about what you're saying, dear." Mary mused for a moment, toying with the reading glasses that hung around her neck on a silver chain. "Do you really believe that your love, or Bonnie's love, could be the cause of someone's death? I would say, in my own humble opinion, that love is a giver of life." She stood abruptly and vanished into her office, returning with a legal pad and her laptop. "We need to get this down while it's still fresh in your mind. Start at the beginning." She placed the glasses on her nose and pressed a button on the keyboard to record.

"I don't know how it started. Mark had gone to bed, and I was working on my computer in the living room. I had a fire going, and I think I sort of dozed off while I was looking at it."

"Amanda, this is important. What were you thinking about just before that?"

"I guess I was thinking about them. You know, Bonnie, Jack, Penelope…all those people from that time. I was remembering something you always used to say about everything having a meaning, how nothing is accidental."

"So you're trying to make some sense out of all this. That's good. You've gone from being a spectator to taking an active part in the drama that's been playing out in both lives, your own and Bonnie's. I think it's too early for you to conclude that either of you is going to end up surrounded by ashes."

"Ashes! Mary, that's exactly what happened." Amanda pressed the wrinkled tissue to her eyes and choked, "Penelope, poor Chester."

"Don't forget, I missed this particular time-shift. Tell me about it."

Heaving a sigh, and reaching for a fresh tissue she said, "I was looking into the fireplace, and my mind sort of wandered. The next thing I knew, I was Bonnie, and the whole city was burning."

Thinking out loud, Mary mumbled, "That must be the Chicago Fire of 1871. Mark's forensics of the soot—"

"I think Daniel proposed to me."

"Has it occurred to you that Mark may very well have been Daniel?"

"I don't know." Amanda stared out the window

373

behind Mary. "I also remember Bonnie didn't like Daniel...I think." She shook her head. "He could also have been Jack, or neither one."

Mary rested her hand on Amanda's. "Go on, dear. Try to tell me everything you remember."

Touching the locket and then reaching for her coffee, Amanda said, "We all had to run to get away from the flames. The sky was all lit up, and there was noise everywhere. I had to get in a wagon, and I didn't want to. All I could think about was Papa and Magdalene and the war. I was crying, and Daniel made me do it, to escape with Margaret and Penelope. We wound up somewhere—I think it was a park, but there were headstones, a cemetery. We watched the fire." Amanda squeezed her eyes shut and began to sob, setting her coffee cup down with trembling hands. "Penelope was pregnant, and she had her baby there in the wagon."

Mary rose and stood behind Amanda's chair, rubbing her shoulders and speaking in a soothing voice. "You made it through okay, and a baby was born. Why are you crying?"

"Mary, Penelope died in childbirth, right there in that wagon. I...I was holding her hand. And poor Chester. Chester was killed trying to get through the crowds to be with her." Amanda covered her face with her hands. "I wish...I wish Bonnie had died instead."

"This is no place to stop. You're not at the end of Bonnie's story, but you've already decided it ends in pain and loss. Those are part of everyone's lives, my own included." Mary tightened her hands on

Amanda's shoulders. "I want you to let me take you back again."

"No. No, I can't do that anymore."

"No life is free of tragedy, dear. But you're unable to go forward in your own life because you're sure you know what's going to happen, because of what's happened to Bonnie. No life is completely devoid of happiness either. You need to find out what happened to Bonnie in later years."

"I don't know." Amanda stood, rubbed her temples, and retied the long robe. "I'm not sure I want to go through that again."

"I'll be with you every second, dear." Mary took Amanda in her arms. "I think this is something you need to do." She stood back, holding Amanda's shoulders. "Let's get you downstairs and dressed in something comfortable. I know you'll be glad we did this."

* * * *

Soft candlelight bathed the room in a flickering glow, casting overlapping shadows on the walls and ceiling. To the slow, rhythmic movement of the burnished pendulum ... tick ... tick ... tick ... tick ... Amanda closed her eyes.

She was standing in the long hallway again. Mary's voice came from far away. "Are you there yet?"

"I see the mist."

"Good. Go through it now, dear. Walk past the doors and read me the numbers."

"1871." Amanda's brow furrowed. "I don't want this one."

"Turn around. You don't want to go back that far. We're looking for a door to a later year, to a happier time in Bonnie's life. Find one with a higher number, closer to 1880."

"1873...1875...1878..." *This one.* "I want to look in here."

"You know best, dear. Go ahead. I'm right here."

She turned the knob.

* * * *

Bonnie reclined on a chaise of flowered chintz in the front parlor of Margaret's house on Pine Street. A blue baby blanket in a fan and feather stitch, half-finished, lay draped over her rounded belly. "I still wish you could have found some way to stay in medical school, Jack. It's not as if we're doing so badly here. Margaret is more than willing to help with the finances. Her father left her and" she paused, bit her lip, and continued, "Penelope with a handsome living."

"I'm only twenty-six, dear. Plenty of fellows don't even start medical school until they're thirty. Koblenz Furniture is Chester and Penelope's legacy to little Rose, and I owe them everything. We both do. While you keep the home fires burning for Rosie, I'm looking out for her inheritance the best way I know how. Besides, a girl could do worse than a master cabinetmaker for a husband, don't you think?"

"So much of adult life seems to be about obligations to others." Bonnie sighed and continued knitting. "Do you ever think about the old days, before we had any responsibilities? We were like a prince and princess on Magnolia Plantation, weren't we?"

Jack leaned forward in his chair. "That seems like another life now." He lifted the corner of Bonnie's knitting and grinned. "What makes you so sure this one's going to be a boy? Do you already have a pink blanket put away somewhere?"

"Margaret says she'll lay me any odds that I won't have two girls in a row. She says the girls need a baby brother to keep them busy and learn how to boss a man around."

Jack laughed and shook his head. "Poor little fellow. I'd say they already have the men in this house under their thumbs as it is. Speaking of Daniel, why don't I ever see him these days?"

"He sleeps at the hospital more than at home now that he's a resident." Bonnie smiled. "Maybe staying at Koblenz wasn't such a bad idea, after all."

The door to the hallway slid open with a crash. Rose and Penny ran breathlessly into the parlor. Rose skidded to a halt in the center of the room, and Penny collided with her legs before she could stop. Rose curtsied daintily and held out a bunch of bright yellow dandelions tied up with a piece of grass. "Aunt Bonnie, may we please go in the spring house next door and see the frog? Penny doesn't believe me that there's a frog in there, but I can hear him from my window at night. Uncle Daniel says he

377

used to be a frog until a princess kissed him."

Margaret appeared in the doorway, drying her hands on an apron. "You girls get upstairs this minute and change into clean pinafores. How Minnie is going to get those grass stains out is more than I care to imagine." She bustled off toward the kitchen in the back of the house and her voice faded as she herded Rose and Penny ahead of her. "Honestly, you two are more like wild Indians than young ladies."

At that moment the clock in the hallway began its quiet chime. Bonnie cocked an ear toward the sound and said, "I never hear those angel bells without thinking of Ben. Don't you wish we could see him and Magdalene again?"

Jack waited until the tolling had finished before he spoke. "I miss them every day. I suppose they stayed in Cleveland."

"Penelope tried to get in touch with them, but that charity lost track of them before the war was over."

"I'm glad Daniel and I were able to get Margaret's clock fixed up, though."

"Poor old clock." Bonnie slipped a thread counter between the bone needles, quickly wrapping the blue yarn around her finger. The needles clicked as she spoke. "I was so proud to show it to her when it first came to the shop. You two are magicians. It looks better now than the day she bought it, but I don't think we'll ever get the smell of the fire out of it."

"There's not a house in Chicago that doesn't

smell the same, if it's more than seven years old."
Jack struck a match with his thumbnail, lighting a
cheroot as he spoke. He puffed busily until his face
was surrounded with blue smoke. "The only good
part is that the ladies can no longer complain if we
smoke in the parlor."

"I suppose that's true, but would you mind
opening a window, dear? My delicate condition, you
know…" She fluttered her eyelids dramatically and
then became serious. "Jack, in all these years, we've
never talked about your family in Virginia. I was so
little then, and so much was happening so quickly—
Papa dying, losing Ben and Magdalene, coming to
Chicago. Everything about that wagon trip was like
a bad dream, and I think I just tried to forget it all.
You were older, though, and it was your parents. It
must have been very hard for you."

"Would it surprise you to know that I handled it
the same way you did?" Jack blew a smoke ring and
watched the gray circle drift lazily toward the
ceiling. Finally he continued, "Grief was a luxury
none of us could afford when the whole world
seemed to be in flames. There's not a day goes by
that I don't think of them, the same way you
remember your papa." He sighed, settled back in his
chair, and crossed his ankles. "Losing people you
love is part of life. We lost Penelope and Chester,
but think of the joy that Rose has given us to take
their place. Think of little Penny and Master Blue-
Blanket. Have you decided on a name for him?"

Bonnie looked down at the knitting in her lap. "I
wondered how you would feel about 'Daniel'."

As she spoke, the blue of the blanket blurred and became a swirl of mist in the dark hallway.

Amanda stood at the door for a moment and turned toward the stairs. *That's the first one I'm glad I opened.*

* * * *

The clock ticked quietly. Amanda blinked and rubbed her eyes with both palms. Rising to her feet, she raised her arms over her head and stretched.

Mary leaned back. "My eyesight must be going. I would've sworn you were smiling back there."

Amanda looked around the room, gathering her thoughts. "That was different. No fires, no deaths, just a peaceful scene at home with Jack." She turned to Mary. "There was a child, my child." Shaking her head, she added, "Bonnie's child. And Penelope's little girl, Rose."

Mary stood and placed her arm around Amanda's waist as they walked down the hall toward the kitchen. "Sounds lovely. Remember what I said, dear? About karma and how paying attention to its lessons can change the way you live your life?"

Amanda leaned in for a kiss on the cheek and nodded.

"The thing to take away from this regression is that a story's beginning doesn't necessarily predict its end. Your attitude toward the past, present, and future helps to determine what turnings your life will take. It's going to unfold in its own way, and you can count on this: what you expect will usually happen. If you resign yourself to a life of tragedy, you can expect tragedy."

Amanda stood at the sink filling mugs from the tap. "That makes me feel a little less helpless." She set the cups on the glass carousel in the microwave. "I was happy...Bonnie was happy, knitting a baby blanket." She reached for some teabags as she said, "Chamomile okay with you?"

"Earl Grey, if you don't mind. Chamomile's for sleeping. I need my wits about me."

Yesterday

CHAPTER 33

Mark walked into Ed Morgen's shop wearing jeans and a White Sox tee shirt and cap. The tiny brass bell tinkled over the door.

Ed didn't recognize him right away, but his eyes soon widened with his smile. "Officer Mark! No uniform, you're not working?"

"Nope. Got some time off for good behavior. How you been?"

Ed nodded with each word. "Good, good, very good." He wrinkled his brow as he looked at Mark's neck. "I see you on the news again. You got hurt pretty bad, huh?"

Mark wanted to be friendly, but wasn't in the mood. His hand went to the narrow bandage on his neck. "Nah, it's nothing. I'm great, Ed. What's this about a diary?"

Ed hesitated a second, held up an index finger as if remembering why Mark was in the shop. "The lady where I bought that clock, Mrs. Ormandy?"

Mark nodded. "Alice."

"Coffee?" Ed turned and headed to the back of the shop.

Mark started to shake his head, refusing the offer. He sighed and resigned himself to the process. "Yeah, coffee sounds great." He followed Ed to the back of the shop and leaned back on a file cabinet. He pushed up the brim of his cap and crossed his arms. "So, you were saying?"

Ed looked up from the coffee pot, appearing lost.

Mark lowered his head and patiently said, "About Alice Ormandy?"

"Ja, Alice Ormandy." Ed nodded and pulled two mugs from a cabinet. "She stopped in yesterday, with a journal." Ed shrugged. "She found it in a trunk of old books in the attic of that house. You should take it." He glanced up at Mark. "Take it for Miss Amanda. You talked to Mrs. Ormandy. You remember, don't you?"

Mark pulled at his earlobe, the aroma of coffee enticing. "Yeah, I talked to her several months ago. So she's got a diary about the clock?"

"Not so much about the clock, but about the lady who *bought* the clock. Mrs. Ormandy wants that book back. A girl named Rose wrote it. This Rose is Alice Ormandy's great-great..." Ed struggled for the right relation, and settled on, "something. I don't remember." He poured two fresh mugs, looked up at Mark, and handed him a steaming cup. "You remember, Alice Ormandy said a woman named Margaret Starks bought the clock."

Mark frowned and mumbled into his mug, "Yeah, I remember."

Ed waved his hand in a circle as he spoke, "There are more people in the diary, she doesn't know all of the names." He sipped his coffee, and said, "Quite a bit about a woman named Bonnie."

Mark's heart skipped. "Bonnie?"

* * * *

Mark entered his apartment as he snapped his cell phone closed. For some reason Mary had not seemed surprised when he told her of Amanda's unintended regression. Maybe it was intentional. Regardless, she needed to talk it through and she wouldn't talk to him.

He opened a bottle of Guinness and took a long pull of the stout as he headed toward his bedroom. He pushed up the light switch with the lip of the bottle and set the journal on his bed.

Settling his back against the headboard, he opened the dull maroon leather binder. The musk of aged linen, the smoky tang of old leather; a century drifted from the diary in an instant. The pages were stiff and yellow, the script graceful and fluid, the copperplate letters almost calligraphy. He saw perfect swirls in even rows, the alignment of letters and words flawless. Mark began to read.

Dear diary,

Today is October 10, 1883. My name is Rose Koblenz. I was born in Chicago. Today is my twelfth birthday. Aunt Bonnie said it was time I started a diary. I don't have anything important to tell a diary. She said to pick out days in my life that were fond memories and tell the diary about them. A fond memory is the day I was flower girl and played a very important role in a wedding. It was the day Aunt Bonnie married Uncle Daniel. I was very little, but I remember. It was a wonderful day.

Mark gazed out his window at windows across the courtyard garden. *Why in the hell would Bonnie Lexington get married to a man she despised? Well, Amanda sure despises me at the moment.* He reached for his Guinness and continued to read.

It was St. Valentine's Day when they got married. I think that is a romantic day for a wedding.

* * * *

February 14, 1876

Bonnie twirled around in front of the mirror, and said, "What do you think, my little Rose?"

Rose giggled. "I think you are a princess, like me."

Bonnie's lips formed a circle and her eyes widened at the sound of St. Michael's chimes. "It's time!" She knelt down and swept Rose into her arms. "Are you ready? Everyone will think you are such a beautiful princess." Bonnie held her at arms' length. "And you are!"

"Uncle Daniel will think you're a princess, too. He tells me stories about them, so he knows all about princesses."

Bonnie stood and laughed. "Much of that extensive knowledge is a dim memory, I hope."

Margaret pushed open the door, holding a basket. "Rose, here are your flowers. When the music starts, you walk in front of your Aunt Bonnie and scatter the flowers around like we practiced."

Rose leaned over to study the contents of the basket. "Petals, Aunt Margaret. Not flowers."

"I stand corrected," Margaret chuckled. "Let's go."

* * * *

Mark sipped pensively, calculating dates and Bonnie's age. *There was no way to know Daniel's age, but he was probably four or five years older than Bonnie. According to Amanda, Bonnie was about sixteen when she witnessed the Chicago fire in October of 1871. She married Daniel five years later, which would have put her in her early twenties.* Mark shrugged at the words in the journal.

I stood in front of Uncle Daniel and Uncle Jack. Uncle Jack gave Aunt Bonnie away that day. I listened for the words "Who gives this woman to be this man's wife", because it was my signal. I stepped in front of Uncle Jack and he placed his gold watch fob with the blue sapphire in my hand and said, "I do. The care of this woman is now passed to Daniel Collins." I handed the gem to Uncle Daniel. He winked at me as he took the fob from my palm. Uncle Daniel whispered, "Thank you, Rose. I will take good care of her." My role was done. I stepped back and stood next to Aunt Margaret. I didn't understand much of what was said during the rest of the vows. Before the wedding kiss, Uncle Daniel said something to Aunt

Bonnie that I didn't understand. I think I do now, though. Uncle Daniel said: You are mine for all time, Bonnie. And then they kissed. Everybody smiled and laughed when it was all over.

Mark gazed at the plaster wall at the foot of his bed, then at the rosewood box on the dresser. He reached for the Guinness and drained the last few swallows. *Coincidence and more stout.* Fetching a fresh bottle, he dropped back onto the bed and carefully turned to the next page.

It wasn't until years later that Aunt Bonnie told me the story of the sapphire and how it once belonged to her mother. She told me about Magdalene and the day Magdalene put it into her locket and pinned the other sapphire on Uncle Jack's shirt. Uncle Daniel has carried the watch fob with the pretty stone, always, ever since Uncle Jack gave it to him on the wedding day. Aunt Bonnie wears hers, always. It is a very romantic story. I hope to one day have a man love me the way Uncle Daniel loves my Aunt Bonnie. She says some day her locket will be mine, and I should give it to my first daughter to keep the story alive for always.

Mark stood and began to pace, running his hands through his dark curls. *This can't be.* He stopped pacing and stared at the jewelry box on his dresser. *There is no way in hell that can be the same sapphire. No way in hell.* He lifted his grandfather's

388

pocket watch from the box and unfastened the fob from the heavy chain. It was fashioned of knotted gold wire, about the size of a robin's egg. Through openings in the ornate mesh a blue gem glinted in the light from the nightstand. He pressed his thumbnail into a shallow depression on the side, and the fob opened on its hinge, spilling the stone out on the bedspread. Mark picked it up between his fingers, held it up to the window, and contemplated the perfect blue sapphire. *Amanda's eyes are just that shade of blue.* He went to his small kitchen, pulled a bottle of Bushmills from the cupboard, poured two fingers into a coffee mug, and downed it in a long swallow. *What's with the damned clock?*

Returning to the bedroom, he sat on the bed and carefully turned the pages of the diary. *According to Alice Ormandy, the clock was repaired after the fire. Amanda had said that Jack Wellington and Daniel Collins both worked at Koblenz Furniture Company. Jack repaired the clock. Amanda said Chester wanted to hire Jack Wellington as an apprentice. That means the two younger men in my regression were Jack and...*the sapphire winked in his palm...*am I really Daniel?* Mark scanned the pages, but everything else was schoolgirl crushes, holidays with turkeys, and cutting down a Christmas tree. He stopped at the words

Moving Day

Mark slowly stood as he read. He was right; it was all there. Elm Street, clock repair…

Aunt Margaret says this poor old house has never been the same since the fire. She bought a beautiful new home on Elm Street for all of us to live in. I am to have my own room in the cupola, with a window facing south for Electra to sit in. Uncle Jack and Uncle Daniel and some boys from the Koblenz factory moved Aunt Margaret's big old clock from the old house yesterday. Aunt Bonnie loves the sound of the chimes. She calls them "angel bells".

He slowly shook his head at the words about Rose leaving for finishing school the day after they moved, some school in the east. *Hell, Rose never disappeared at all. Doesn't say anything in here about any adoption, either.* He stared over the diary at the floor. *Wonder if Bonnie and Daniel adopted Rose.*

Mark began to pace again. He walked to the window, shoved his hands in his pockets, and watched water drip from an air conditioner across the courtyard. *I need more, dammit. I need more.* He reached for the phone and touched the speed dial number for his sister.

Sitting on a kitchen chair, he rubbed the sapphire between thumb and forefinger. "Yeah, sis, I'm good. No, nothing's wrong." He shook his head and closed his eyes as he said, "No, it doesn't hurt. No, it never did hurt too much." He stood and slowly walked around the perimeter of his small kitchen. "Listen, aren't you the one Ma gave that old family Bible to?"

It took her a while and a magnifying glass, but his sister found the name, smudged with an old stain she said looked like tomato soup or maybe red wine. In parentheses, after the name "Daniel Alexander Collins", was the name "Bonnie May Belle Lexington".

Mark smiled at her next words. "Appears the two of them were a pair of bunnies. Daniel and Bonnie had lots of descendents."

"Sis, wait. Before you hang up, look through that list of descendents. Any of them named 'Rose'?"

Mark closed the phone and stared at the glistening blue gem in his palm. His lips formed a silent whistle and he murmured, "I'll be damned."

It was just after ten at night. He reached for his phone, hesitated for a moment, and grinned as he dialed another number. *I know just the place.*

Mark heard Pete Mahoney's voice. "Yo. Wussup?"

* * * *

Amanda sat in the back seat of Tom's Volvo and stared out the window at the dark expanse of Lake Michigan as they sped south on Lake Shore Drive. Tom and Connie chattered like teenagers in the front seat, but Amanda was not following the conversation. The lights of Navy Pier shimmered on the placid surface of the water, blinking out one by one as the restaurants and arcades closed for the night. The outer rim of the Ferris wheel was still illuminated, though the ride had shut down hours earlier. She smirked privately. *Guess you don't ever turn off a landmark.* As she watched, the rest of the wheel lit up. She leaned forward over the console between her brother and his wife. "It's late. How did you manage to get them to do this?"

Tom's eyes glanced at her in the rear view mirror. "I told you. My office made the reservation, a sales award thing." He laughed with boyish giddiness and glanced at Connie. "We have the whole damned Ferris wheel to ourselves, go figure. I have no idea how the hell they pulled it off."

Connie jumped over his words, "Gosh, what a clear night to do this. We should be able to see for miles."

Tom parked in front of the entrance to Navy Pier, no other traffic in sight except a couple of patrol cars. The gate opened and Amanda followed Tom and Connie down the pier. The tall wheel sparkled against the black sky, white lights spiraling from hub to rim and back, throwing shadows across their faces. An attendant smiled. "Mr. & Mrs. Parker?"

Tom held out his hand to the man. "You got 'em!"

Shaking Tom's hand, the man nodded toward the open gondola. "Step aboard, sir; she's all yours. Enjoy the ride."

Tom, Connie, and Amanda stepped into the brightly lit car. Amanda looked around as she walked to a railing, the pier quiet and deserted. The gondola doors closed, the interior light dimmed, and the car lifted smoothly. Amanda took a deep breath and sighed. "Time to start oohing and aahing at the sights, you two."

When she didn't get a response, Amanda glanced over her shoulder and started. She turned to face Mark Callahan. They were alone in the car. Flushing, Amanda looked around. "I should have known. Where are Tom and Connie?"

His smile widened, eyes sparkling with mischief. "This car was full. They had to take the next one." Leaning an elbow on the railing, he watched Amanda, scanning her from head to toe. Mark met her eyes and winked. "You might as well relax and enjoy the view. You can't escape. Besides, I'm an arrogant ass." He nodded at the lights of the city coming into view. "Ooh and aah for a while, compliments of Chicago's finest."

Amanda glanced toward the city and back to him. "You've had your fun. Now put this thing down."

He pushed away from the railing and moved toward her. Amanda stepped back as he said, "I can't. The Ferris wheel only goes in one direction. Sort of like life, sweetheart. It goes 'round and 'round in one direction." Mark's warm brown eyes held hers as he said, "Some of us are lucky enough to remember each trip around."

Amanda pulled her eyes from his to the leather-bound book in his hands.

Mark held it out to her. "Sit and read the two marked pages."

"It's too dark in here to read."

He walked to the side of the gondola and held up an index finger. The car shuddered to a stop and the interior again glowed. "Stubbornness is part of your charm, so I'll ask again. Sit and read the two marked pages."

Her eyes widened. "How'd you stop this thing?"

He started to respond when she shook her head and held up a hand.

"Never mind." She took the book from his hand and sat.

Mark scanned the skyline as he waited. The brilliant glitter of the city was crystalline on this cloudless night. He tried to imagine Chicago in 1870, 1880. A skyscraper back then was only a few stories tall and electricity didn't light the city until the 1890s. There would have been only a scattering of dim gas streetlamps. Candles flickering in the tiny windows of the low houses would barely be seen across a river. Today, glass towers sparkle as they reach for the sky, visible to astronauts orbiting the earth.

Amanda whispered, "Rose's diary? Where did you get this?"

He spoke over his shoulder. "Ed Morgen. It's a long story. I'll tell you about it sometime. For now, just read the pages I marked."

The gondola was quiet, a gentle breeze from the lake swaying it as a mother rocks a cradle. Amanda finished reading, closed the book, and ran her hand lightly across the faded cover. She mumbled, "I must be a descendent of Rose. Bonnie gave her my locket." Mark turned to her as she said, "Bonnie loved Daniel. I didn't think she did. She thought he was an arrogant ass."

"Daniel." Mark chuckled. "Gotta love that guy."

She started to speak as he stepped to the railing and made a circle in the air with his index finger. The gondola dimmed again, and the car moved.

"Like I said," Amanda stood," you've had your fun. And yes, you are definitely an arrogant ass. I already told you this isn't going to work. Let me off."

Mark smiled and said, "Sorry, the Ferris wheel will run until I say so. Sit back down and think for a while about what you've just read. Take your time, Sputnik."

Her eyes narrowed and she sat. *What is he trying to tell me?*

Mark glanced at her neck. "Take the stone out of your locket."

Amanda frowned and held her hand to her throat, covering the silver heart. "Why? I told you, it's the sapphire Magdalene gave me, I mean, gave to Bonnie..." She shook her head. "Magdalene gave it to me."

The errant curl on his forehead stirred with a gust from the lake. "So you said. I remember. She gave the other sapphire to Jack." He tipped his head and smiled. "Lucky bastard."

"Jack?"

Mark shrugged. "Him, too, I suppose. But no, I'm thinking of someone else in your life."

She thought about the words he had spoken to her at the Magnolia Cemetery in Charleston: *Tomorrow, today, yesterday.* She thought of words he'd said when they went camping: *People never*

395

really die. His eyes were teasing.

"Honey, I'm thinking of the guy that shows up in your life with the sapphire that reunites a pair of earrings. *He* is one lucky bastard."

He knows something. Amanda stared at him. The pages of the journal fluttered in a puff of air. *Jack gave his sapphire to Daniel when Daniel married Bonnie.* Her mind reeled. *What am I saying? Daniel?* Echoes of her words filled her mind: *Are other people of yesterday wandering around today?*

Amanda slipped her nail under the clasp of the locket. She held the sapphire out to him, her hand trembling.

Mark dropped his own stone into her palm and closed her fingers around the two jewels. He pulled Amanda to her feet and into his arms. His eyes twinkled in the glitter of the Ferris wheel lights. "These are a matched pair, just as we are." Mark leaned into her and her heart soared with his kiss, the gentle, loving warmth of his mouth on hers, his sheltering arms around her.

Amanda opened her hand and trembled as she held the two sapphires. She could not tell them apart and the jewels blurred through her tears. "Are you my Daniel?"

He lifted her chin, glanced at the sparking gems, and wiped a tear from her cheek.

Amanda looked up at eyes that loved only her, had always loved her.

He winked and whispered, "What goes around, sweetheart." Mark lowered his lips to hers.

AUTHOR'S NOTES

Yesterday is a work of fiction, but not entirely. Much of the story is based on historical fact. Here are some of my sources.

St. Michael's Chimes

The origin of St. Michael's Chimes is the chiming clavier, or keyboard, located one floor above the ringer's room and one floor below the bells of St. Michael's Church, built in Charleston, South Carolina in 1751. At that time, Charleston was an English colony. The clavier is no longer used; the bells chime electronically today.

St. Michael's Church

When the American Civil War began, the government of the Confederate States of America confiscated large bells and recast many as cannons and other artillery needs. This recycling was necessary because iron and brass weren't available in the South. The bells of St. Michael's escaped this fate because the local citizenry hid them before they could be seized. The bells cracked when the shed in which they were stored burned in the taking of Columbia, South Carolina during Sherman's March to the Sea. At war's end, the Vestry reclaimed the metal and had the bells recast in London at the original foundry. Bells one through five are named for the order of the angels. Bells six, seven and eight are named for archangels.

For more information, visit *stmichaelschurch.net* to view a chart which identifies each bell, 1943lb Michael through 509lb Seraphim. The bells are listed by weight, note played, and name. The chart also identifies the year the individual bells were cast, and the years they were recast.

The Confederate Candle

Courtesy of an authentic 19th century cookbook, here's the recipe for the Confederate Candle that appears in Chapter 13 of *Yesterday*. I don't recommend that you try this at home, though!

"Melt together a pound of beeswax and a quarter of a pound of rosin of turpentine, fresh from the tree. Prepare a wick 30 or 40 yards long, made up of three threads of loosely spun cotton, saturate this well with the mixture, and draw it through your fingers, to press all closely together, and to keep the size even. Repeat the process until the candle attains the size of a large straw or quill, then wrap around a bottle, or into a ball with a flat bottom. Six inches of this candle elevated above the rest will burn for fifteen or twenty minutes, and give a very pretty light, and forty yards have sufficed a small family a summer for all the usual purposes of the bedchamber." *Confederate Receipt Book: A Compilation of Over One Hundred Receipts ... Introduction by E. Merton Coulter © 1960 by The University of Georgia Press*

Chicago Wood Block Streets

The Gold Coast Wooden Alley runs east and west between State Street and Astor Street, in the landmark Astor Street District of Chicago's Gold Coast area. It is directly behind the Archbishop's Residence at 1555 North State Parkway. This alley serves as a reminder of the days when the streets of Chicago were paved with wood blocks and covered with tar, which led to the fact that "streets were burning" during The Great Chicago Fire of 1871.

The alley is one of two remaining wood block alleys in the city; the other is in the 2100 block of North Hudson Avenue. The Gold Coast Wooden Alley has been restored.

Cabs - Streetcars

Our modern word "cab" is a shortened form of *taxicab*. The word originated with the French "cabriolet," a light two-wheeled vehicle drawn by a single horse. The cab referenced in *Yesterday* is the "hansom cab," patented in 1834 by Joseph Hansom. *scottisharchitects.org.uk*

Public transportation began in Chicago in the mid

19th century. The first streetcars were horse-drawn and entered into service on April 25, 1859. The first line ran on State Street between Randolph and 12th Streets. The original streetcars were 12 feet long, held 18 passengers, and were drawn by four horses. *chicagobus.org*

Idiot's Delight

As described in *Yesterday,* this dessert was fed to the Confederate soldiers in great quantities. Made with a biscuit covered in a cinnamon-raisin sauce, it is nutritious, filling, and easy to prepare. The dessert got its name, in fact, from its ease of preparation. As they said back then, "Any idiot can make it." There are many recipes on the Internet. Here's one you may want to try:

Filling:
1 cup brown sugar
1 cup raisins
1 T butter
1 t vanilla
4 cups water

Batter:
7 T butter
1/2 cup white sugar
2 t baking powder
1/2 cup milk
1 cup flour

To make the filling, bring the first five ingredients to a simmer, stirring frequently so the sauce doesn't burn or stick. To make the batter, combine the next five ingredients in a large bowl and stir briskly to form a biscuit batter. It may be a little lumpy. Drop the batter by spoonfuls into an 8" x 8" greased baking dish. Pour the filling over the top. Bake in 350°F until golden brown.

Mrs. O'Leary's Cow

The causes of the massive blaze, which destroyed much of Chicago in October 1871, were perilous conditions: a long drought during a very hot summer, and the fact that the city had been built almost entirely of wood.

Within a few days of the fire, a *Chicago Republic* reporter named Michael Ahern wrote an article including the rumor about Mrs. O'Leary's cow kicking over a kerosene lantern, igniting hay in the barn and starting the fire. The story took hold. In 1893, Ahern admitted that he created this fiction for colorful copy. Nonetheless, the story persists today.

Although no one disputes that a fire started in Mrs. O'Leary's barn at 9:00pm on October 8, 1871, whether or not the cow started the blaze is a 140-year-old debate. *chicagohistory.org*

Lincoln Park - Cemetery Park

In 1860, Cemetery Park, the precursor of today's Lincoln Park, was established by the city. Five years later, on June 12, 1865, the park was renamed to honor the recently assassinated President Abraham Lincoln. Burials ceased in 1866, except for pauper graves. At the time of The Great Chicago Fire, many of the gravesites and tombstones of the city cemetery were still in the park, although they were in the process of being moved to Rosehill and Graceland Cemeteries, just west and north of the park.

Thousands of Chicagoans escaped the ravages of the fire by taking refuge in the park and at the lakefront. They spent several days and nights among tombstones and unmarked pauper graves, many Civil War casualties from Camp Douglas, initially a Union Army training center, ultimately a prisoner of war camp four miles south of downtown Chicago.

One mausoleum remains, built on-site in 1858 as the final resting place of the Ira Couch family. Too monolithic to move, the tomb stands in the south end of Lincoln Park today, as it stood on October 8, 1871. The Couch mausoleum is thought to be the oldest structure left standing in The Great Chicago Fire zone. *hiddentruths.northwestern.edu*

Daniel Burnham 1846 - 1912

Daniel Burnham, the world-renowned architect, became known for his dictum, "Make no little plans." And indeed, he practiced what he preached. He was chief of construction for Chicago's 1893 World's Fair, the Columbian Exposition, which included the first giant wheel created by George Ferris. Burnham's Chicago Plan of 1909 is a primary reason that Chicago's lakefront has been preserved for the enjoyment and recreational use of its citizens and tourists. Most of the lakefront of Chicago is free and open to the public. There is no fee at any of the public parks, beaches, bike trails or footpaths, including free admission to beautiful Lincoln Park Zoo. So it seems fitting that Daniel Burnham's final resting place is on a pleasant, wooded island in the Graceland Cemetery Lake. *gracelandcemetery.org*

The Lincoln Park Chess Pavilion

Mentioned only in passing in *Yesterday*, this pavilion exists. Located near North Avenue Beach and constructed in 1957, the founder of the Hammond Organ Company donated the pavilion to the city. It is home to a thriving and diverse chess community and is quite beautiful. *chicago-neighborhoods.com*

Chicago Police Horses

In 1999, the CPD began honoring fallen officers by naming police horses after them. This writer chose fictitious names for the horses in *Yesterday* so as not to disrespect the ultimate sacrifice made by the brave officers of the Chicago Police Department. *chicagotribune.com*

Boomerang

As stated in *Yesterday*, Boomerang is, in fact, the name of a famous Irish horse. *cowboyway.com*

* * * *

Please visit *samyann.com* for author information and details about upcoming works.

Made in the USA
Lexington, KY
03 May 2013